TO TURN THE

In the battle for the Caveness ... war in human history, the fate of billions rested in the hands of a few. *Admiral Josiah Gilbert's* Polar Fleet had halted the forces of his old enemy *Frye Charltos* at the Matthews System, but at a terrible price. To break the power of the U.C.S. war machine, Gilbert defied his superiors in a desperate high-stakes gamble.

Ayne Wallen, the traitorous scientist who held the key to an ultimate weapon, became a pawn in a greater game. But his treachery brought together two lovers separated by war, the smuggler *"Lucky" Teeman* and his beloved *Marsha Yednoshpfa*, and confronted them with an agonizing choice.

Torn between her loyalty to her father and her love for a man suspected of treason, *Captain Mica Gilbert* found herself drawn to correspondent *Henley Stanmorton*, who was forced to choose between his committment to victory— and to truth. And, near the Satterfield systems, *Admiral Pajandcan* and *Admiral Dawson* launched a daring campaign on two fronts to turn the tide of war.

Praise for *Midway Between*, the first volume of THE DOUBLE-SPIRAL WAR:

"Tackling with ease a story that most writers only dream about, Norwood has managed to bring humanity and understanding to a vast array of sentient alien intellects, while at the same time showing us the horror and futility that is war. There are no good guys and bad guys in *Midway Between;* there is only the struggle to survive, only the anguished cries of souls caught in something beyond their control."

—Mike McQuay
author of *Jitterbug* and *Pure Blood*

POLAR FLEET

Warren Norwood

BANTAM BOOKS
TORONTO • NEW YORK • LONDON • SYDNEY • AUCKLAND

POLAR FLEET

A Bantam Book / June 1985

ISBN 0-553-24877-4

Published simultaneously in the United States and Canada

Bantam Books are published by Bantam Books, Inc. Its trademark, consisting of the words "Bantam Books" and the portrayal of a rooster, is Registered in U.S. Patent and Trademark Office and in other countries. Marca Registrada. Bantam Books, Inc., 666 Fifth Avenue, New York, New York 10103.

PRINTED IN THE UNITED STATES OF AMERICA

O   0 9 8 7 6 5 4 3 2 1

To
Gigi Sherrell, friend and teacher,
who saw it through the roughest of times,
and
Ernie Pyle and Samuel Eliot Morison,
historians of a different war.

STYLIZED VIEW OF CAVENESS GALAXY FROM
THE SOUTHERN POLAR PERSPECTIVE

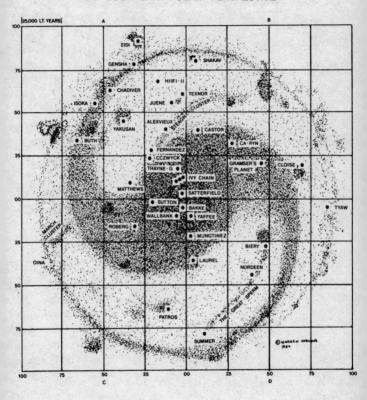

United Central Systems

Auxillary Forces	Specialists	Planetary Forces	Space Forces
(12)			Admiral
(11) Marshall		Meister	Vice-Admiral
(10) Commander		Force Meister	Commander
(9) Vice-Marshall		Brig Meister	Vice-Commander
(8) Group Leader		Force Leader	Group Leader
(7) Attack Leader		Brig Leader	Sub-Group Leader
(6) Actual		Warden	Captain
(5) 2nd Actual		Volk Leader	Vice-Captain
(4) 3rd Actual	Chief	1st Volk	Lieutenant
(3) Miker	Petty Chief	2nd Volk	1st Lieutenant
(2) Timino	Enseeoh	Cell Leader	2nd Lieutenant
(1) Leo	Connor	Celler	3rd Lieutenant

Non-Officer

(17) Ax		Barman	Coord
(16) Attack Coord		Ringer	Range Coord
(15) 2nd Ax		Keyman	Boater
(14) Gunner		Locker	Boater 2nd
(13) Piper		Bunker	Boater 3rd
(12) Flager		2nd Bunker	Crewer
			(12 grades)
(11) Niner		3rd Bunker	
(nine grades)			
(10)		Ace (6 grades)	
		Yarder (4 grades)	

Sondak

Planetary Forces	Flight Service (Corps)	Warrants/ Specialists	Space Forces
(12) Commander- General	Pro-Avitor (never used)		Admiral
(11) General	Avitor		Fleet Admiral
(10) Post-General	Avitor Once		Post-Admiral
(9) Quarter-General	Avitor Duce		Quarter-Admiral
(8) Brigadier	Flight Leader		Commander
(7) Colonel	Co-Flight Leader		Post-Commander
(6) Captain	Pilot	Chief Warrant Officer-4	Captain
(5) Post-Captain	Fleet Pilot	CWO-3	Fleet Captain
(4) Co-Captain	Ship Pilot	CWO-2	Ship Captain
(3) Lieutenant	Rank Pilot	CWO-1	Quarter-Captain
(2) Post-Lieutenant	Co-Pilot	Warrant Officer	Lieutenant
(1) Co-Lieutenant	Nav-Pilot	Ante-Warrant	Fleet Lieutenant

Non-Officer

(15) Sergeant	Fleet Tech		High Tech
(14) Post-Sergeant	Fleet Gunner		Tech
(13) Gun Sergeant	Flight Tech		Tech Help
(12) Tech Sergeant	Flight Gunner		Tech's Mate
(11) Co-Sergeant	Ship Tech		Gun Tech
(10) Squader/Brevet Sergeant	Ship Gunner		Watch Leader
(9) Co-Squader	Rank Tech		Watch Help
(8) Trooper (8 grades)	Rank Gunner		Watch Mate (3 grades)
(7)	Gunner/Tech (7 grades)		Spacer (5 grades)

Chronology

Ninety-two years after the signing of the treaty that officially ended the Unification Wars, Earth sent forth the first two generation ships to seek new homes for mankind in the stars.

The *Bohr* and the *Heisenberg* together carried a total of three thousand seven hundred eighty-three pioneers and crew members. Each ship was powered by ten linked Hugh drives that eventually pushed them to a speed of one-point-four times the speed of light relative to Earth. At that speed their Benjamin drives took over and they crossed Einstein's Curve where relative speed could no longer be measured.

Two hundred forty-one ship years later the descendants of those first pioneers celebrated the thirtieth anniversary of their landing on the planet they named Biery after the woman who led their forebearers from Earth. Much to their surprise and fear, that celebration was interrupted by the landing of an alien ship containing a race called the Oinaise. To everyone's relief—including the Oinaise's—the contact was peaceful.

Nine years later the Kobler calendar was established and set the date of the first landing as New Year 2500. The following chronology gives a brief listing of major events dated according to that calendar.

2530—First contact with the Oinaise.

2575—First pioneers arrive on Nordeen, the most Earth-like of any planet ever discovered in the galaxy.

2599—Approximate date the last generation ship left Earth, carrying fourteen thousand new-human pioneers, genetically altered people known as *homo communis*, whose major difference from *homo sapiens* was a greatly extended longevity.

2648—The anti-intellectualist riots.

2657—Beginning of the early expansionist movement seeking other planets and star systems suitable for human settlement.

2664—Last known message from Earth indicating war, famine, and increasing chaos.

2681—A group of Nordeen's brightest people call themselves *homo electus* and leave aboard the *Mensch* in search of what they hope will be a better home for the intellectually elite.

2723—The Gouldrive tested and proven. Marks the beginning of the Great Expansionist Movement, the settling of many independent systems, and the establishment of true interstellar trade. The phrase, "a planet for every clan," became popular at this time. During the whole movement scientific research and technological progress were extremely limited.

2774—News reaches Nordeen from the so-called *homo electus's* first contact with the alien Verfen, a reclusive race inhabiting a cluster of star systems near galaxy's center.

2784—First contact with the crab-like, methane-breathing Castorians.

2846—Discovery of Cloise.

2862—Foundation of Sondak, a loose federation of fifty-eight sparsely inhabited planetary systems. *Homo electus* demanded and received recognition as a separate human race as the price of joining the federation.

2893—Foundation of the United Central Systems, twenty-seven planetary systems inhabited mostly by *homo communis*. The establishment of the U.C.S. marked the end of the Great Expansionist Movement.

3021—The first galactic war between Sondak and the U.C.S.

3024—The U.C.S., unable to match Sondak's capacity for producing the tools of war, sued for peace. After extended negotiations during which the fighting continued, The U.C.S. promised to pay heavy economic reparations to Sondak and the independent systems, and also agreed not to produce new war materials for one hundred years. Neither promise was kept.

3029—Seemingly spontaneous civil disorder broke out on several planets populated mostly by the fair-skinned, racially distinct, politically fractious pikeans. Although called by some the Pikean Civil War, the dissidents had neither the numbers nor the equipment to fight a true war, and consequently were forced to leave their home planets. Many of them chose to go to systems controlled by the U.C.S. where they quickly aligned themselves with the political factions that supported a new war with Sondak.

3033—The Cczwyck Skirmish occurred when U.C.S. Admiral Nance made an officially unauthorized attempt to take control of that independent system just as a Sondak border squadron was making a courtesy visit. There was no serious fighting, but the political repercussions caused the U.C.S. to accelerate its secret rearmament program; caused Sondak to increase its economic pressures on the U.C.S. and also on the independent systems that refused to join the confederation; and caused Cczwyck to become more isolationist.

3034-3042—Sporadic raids on U.C.S. chartered freighters by unknown agents were blamed on Sondak despite fierce diplomatic denials and a total lack of evidence.

3038—Long-range plans began in the U.C.S. for a new war against Sondak.

3046—The so-called "Double-Spiral War" began with raids on ten isolated Sondak systems and several independent systems. During the year the U.C.S. captured the independent systems of Fernandez, Cczwyck, the water planets of Thayne-G, the three systems in the Ivy Chain, and Ca-Ryn. The aliens of Oina and Cloise found themselves drawn unwillingly toward participation in the war.

Matthews system, strategically located midway between Sondak and the U.C.S., was the target of an attack and invasion planned and directed by U.C.S. Commander Frye Charltos. The attack failed due to the planning of Sondak Admiral Josiah Gilbert, with the help of Admirals Pajandcan and Dawson, and a great deal of luck. The system was saved, but with a great loss of ships and personnel on both sides. Matthews system's principal planet, Reckynop, was rendered a watery ruin by U.C.S. neutronic missiles that exploded over its poles and melted its icecaps. However, the battle for Matthews system was considered a victory for Sondak.

3047—The year opens with the launching of a new U.C.S. weapon which marks a change in their tactics.

POLAR FLEET

1

"Release ship," Captain Ruto Ishiwa ordered calmly.

Giant magnetic mooring clamps slowly opened with gentle thrusting movements. The hunk, *Misbarrett*—the first operational Wu-class subspace hunter-killer in the U.C.S. Fleet—drifted free in space beside its tender at fifty thousand kilometers per hour. Named the *Misbarrett* by U.C.S. Fleet Command, the ship was immediately called *Olmiss* by the crew, believing as they did that every ship had to have an ekename to make it safe.

"Separation complete," Lieutenant Bon reported.

"Course zero-zero-three-hundred by seven-eight-two-hundred." Ishiwa gave the heading from memory. The deck hummed slightly under his feet as the engines powered up.

"Attention," he said through the ship's loudspeaker, "this is Captain Ishiwa. You will be pleased to know that this is not a training mission. *Olmis* is going to hunt Sondak ships."

Cheers broke out among the crew, and Ishiwa allowed himself a smile. He had trained the crew for five hard months without respite before reporting to Bridgeforce that they were fully prepared to undertake their mission. Within weeks there would be a fleet of twenty Wu-class ships operating in Sondak space. Within months there would be two hundred. But their *Olmis* would be the first. "Good luck and good hunting to us all," he said before turning off the loudspeaker.

It was a great honor for him and the crew, and a great responsibility. As the first of the long-range hunter-killers, it was incumbent upon *Olmis* to prove the value of the new design, by striking a series of lethal blows for the U.C.S.

Earlier hunks, with a few exceptions, had experienced only minimal success. The ships themselves had been poorly designed, and their weapons and equipment had been inadequate. But one of the early hunks that had done well in spite of its handicaps had been the *Pavion*, commanded by, then Lieutenant, Ishiwa. Now he was expected to do great things with the same basic crew and a Wu-class ship. Such expectations would require the greatest effort from all hands aboard, including Lieutenant Bon, their kyosei political officer.

"Proceed to subspace speed, Lieutenant, then report with Chief Kleber to my cabin for the reading of the orders."

"Aye-aye, sir."

Ishiwa had nothing against Lieutenant Bon except the fact that he was kyosei. The lieutenant had proven an above-average hunk pilot during their training missions, but Ishiwa still had to remind himself that the man was worthy of his position. The problem was that Ishiwa had never been comfortable around the kyosei and their political fanaticism.

The kyosei were protectionists who argued that the war must be fought on limited terms—terms that would bind the hands of any aggressive commander. Was that why Bon had been assigned to his ship? He had heard of such appointments for similar reasons before. As he slid down to the work deck he reminded himself that he had no choice but to accept things as they were.

But Ruto Ishiwa had never been comfortable accepting things as they were. Such complacency was for less ambitious men. He had always prided himself on seeking challenges, and on challenging the status quo. That was why *Pavion* had succeeded where others had failed. Ishiwa had refused to accept the limitations of the old hunks. He had pushed *Pavion* close when long-range attacks failed and repeatedly taken risks that neither his commanders nor the enemy had expected him to.

With great anticipation he broke the seal on his orders and pulled the shiny grey disk from its envelope. As he inserted the disk into the slot under his viewscreen, he knew what to expect. Supreme Admiral Tuuneo had honored him with a personal viewscreen briefing before they left Yakusan, yet even that briefing had not prepared him for the sweeping nature of the Operating Orders that appeared on his screen.

Misbarrett was directed to act as an independent command and interdict any and all shipping along routes to and from Sondak's polar systems.

It was an even greater honor than Ishiwa would dared to have dreamed. Bridgeforce trusted him to act alone in the heart of some of Sondak's most important shipping lanes.

Such an opportunity to achieve greatness came to few men, and Ruto Ishiwa accepted it with a proud heart. He would impress upon Lieutenant Bon and Chief Kleber the necessity of exceeding Bridgeforce's highest expectations. Together they would lead *Misbarrett* to glory against Sondak.

* * *

Civilians on a hundred planets were celebrating Sondak's victory over the Ukes in the battle for Matthews system. The military people weren't celebrating anything. They knew that despite the victory, the immediate odds were still against them. That much was obvious to Henley Stanmorton as he sat outside Fleet Admiral Gilbert's office.

Henley was impatient with the waiting. He would rather have been on Sutton with the planetary troops, or in the crew's quarters of a launchship, or anywhere with the men and women who were doing the actual fighting. There was a war going on out in the galaxy and he wanted to report it as it happened.

Henley allowed himself a small grin and wondered what was really bothering him. Interviewing a fleet officer was not an assignment he would have chosen, because most officers at the top of the echelons didn't interest him at all. But there were scores of Tellers who would have paid thousands of credits to be in his boots at this moment. Everyone was interested in Admiral Josiah Gilbert, the hero of Matthews. Henley should have been pleased with this assignment. Instead he felt annoyed.

However, the scene around him lessened his annoyance. With a reporter's curious eyes and ears Henley observed the soldiers and spacers moving quickly and seriously through the halls. There was a tension in their actions and conversation that infected the air with an old, familiar feeling. He could sense the deep concern that filled this headquarters and his reporter's mind responded by trying to catch snatches of conversation.

Henley always thought of himself as a reporter even though the term was archaic and rarely used. He never thought of himself as a Teller like most of the members of the Efcorps he knew, because he never fully understood what a Teller really was.

Tellers claimed to "tell" what was happening when they covered a news story. Worse, as far as he was concerned, they truly believed that they actually did understand what was happening. Henley never claimed such understanding and could not begin to. He only reported what he saw, and heard, and felt, and left it for others to try to "tell" what that meant.

"—almost certainly the polar systems, even if the Joint Chiefs refuse to admit it," a passing officer said to one of her colleagues.

"But, Jas, there just aren't enough ships to do that and defend the home planets, too. I'm afraid we're going to lose those systems like we lost . . ."

The rest of the captain's response faded away from Henley's straining ears as he watched the trio of spacers move down the hall. They hardly looked old enough to be officers.

"I said, are you Mr. Stanmorton?" a new voice asked.

Henley looked around quickly and saw another captain standing in front of him with a slight smile on her face. "Yes, ma'am," he said as he rose to his feet, "I'm Stanmorton."

"Admiral Gilbert will see you now."

Before he could respond, she turned and led him through the doorway to the admiral's anteroom. He wondered if he had read her name tag correctly. "Pardon me, Captain, but—"

"Yes, Mr. Stanmorton?" she asked as she turned to face him.

"Uh, forgive me, Captain, but you wouldn't be Captain Mica Gilbert, would you? The Admiral's daughter?"

Captain Mica Gilbert appraised this Efcorps Teller with cool disdain. He wasn't bad looking for an older man, and there was something ingratiating about his manner, but she had no use for him or any other member of the Efcorps. "Yes, I am," she said flatly. "But you mustn't keep the admiral waiting."

"No, certainly not." Henley had been around far too long not to catch her dislike of him—or the Efcorps—it didn't matter which. "May I talk to you—I mean after I talk to the admiral?" he asked suddenly. "It wouldn't take very long." He knew she had been present at the Matthews battle and he hoped she would tell him about her part in it.

"You'll have to ask the admiral," she said as she opened the door to the inner office.

Her tone told him she had no desire to talk to him, but that only made him more determined to try. "Of course. Thank you."

"Admiral, this is Mr. Stanmorton, from the Efcorps," Mica added with a wicked grin. "He wants to talk to me after he has interviewed you."

"Give him ten minutes," Admiral Gilbert said, barely looking up from his desk. "And sit down, Mr. Morton."

Mica's grin started to fade, but came back again when the teller said, "It's Stanmorton, sir." Ten minutes with him might be an interesting diversion, she thought as she closed the door.

Henley sat comfortably waiting for the admiral to finish the notation he was making on the small stack of papers in the middle of a very full desk. He sensed that Gilbert's involvement with the paperwork was not a ploy to put him in his place.

"Now, Mr. Stanmorton," Gilbert said finally as he pushed the papers aside and leaned across the desk, "what can I do for you?" He was surprised that the teller looked as old as Gilbert felt.

"Well, sir, I'm not exactly sure," Henley said slowly. The admiral looked tired and strained, and Henley regretted imposing himself on the man. "Efcorps sent me here to interview you about the Matthews battle." He paused for a moment then decided to go ahead. "But in all honesty, sir, I'd rather be interviewing the pipe jockeys and spacers who fought it, or out with the troops on Sutton."

Gilbert stared at the teller for a moment then surprised them both with a short, crackling laugh. "I think I know who you are, Mr. Stanmorton."

"I beg your pardon, sir?" The admiral's claim following the laugh threw his thoughts off balance.

"You were in uniform in the last war, weren't you?"

"Yes, sir."

"What unit?"

"Ninth Fleet Marines, sir. Spent most of my tour attached to the Four-Twenty-Fifth Planetary Corps," Henley said without hesitation. After all these years the quick military response still hadn't left him.

"Doing what?"

"I was a Combat Teller, sir."

"I thought so. Wrote for the *Flag Report*, didn't you?"

"Yes, sir." Suddenly Henley understood where this was leading, and a slight knot of apprehension tightened in his stomach. He had angered more than one officer with his stories and reports back then. They hadn't appreciated his honest recounting of the problems the troops faced. Was Gilbert one of those he had angered?

"Wrote good stories, too, as I remember them. Damned good stories. I especially remember a series you did about the LeHew invasion where you went in with the first assault team. Made me feel like I was there." Gilbert leaned back with a smile.

The knot softened in Henley's stomach. "Why, thank you, sir. I never suspected you might remember—"

"Look, Stanmorton," Gilbert said with a wave of his hand at his cluttered desk, "I really do not have time to give you much of an interview right now, but if you will come to my quarters tomorrow evening, say twenty-hundred hours, we can discuss the Matthews battle—and anything else that's on your mind—at a little more leisure."

Henley was surprised by the admiral's invitation, and flattered that Gilbert had remembered the LeHew series. He always thought of that series as some of his best writing of the war. "Of course, sir, I would be delighted to come."

"Good. I'll make sure that Mica is there, too, although getting her to tell you anything will be your problem. Now get out of here and let me get back to work."

"Yes, sir. And thank you, sir," Henley said. He resisted a strange urge to salute and left the office quickly and quietly, flushed with a kind of pride he hadn't felt in years.

"Ran you off, did he?"

Henley was startled to see Captain Mica Gilbert standing in front of him. "Certainly did," he said with a smile to counter her smug look. "Told me I'd have to talk to him in his quarters tomorrow at dinner." The change on Captain Gilbert's face amused him and added to his good feelings.

"He what? You can't be serious." Mica was shocked that her father would do such a thing.

"Oh, but I am serious, Captain. I am. Seems your father is an old fan of my writing. See you tomorrow." Henley gave her a mock salute with a feeling of satisfaction and left her standing in the middle of the anteroom staring after him.

With a quick shake of her head and a shrug of her shoulders Mica dismissed Stanmorton and his absurd comments. The grim new reports from Sutton had to be analyzed and added to her father's briefing book. Admiral Stonefield expected an update on the fleet repairs. And Commander Rochmon wanted her for still another debriefing session. There was too much work demanding her attention to worry about some crazy old Teller from the Efcorps.

2

Commander Frye Charltos almost smiled as he left the meeting. Bridgeforce's final judgment against him had been amazingly mild. They would place in his record a sealed document reprimanding him for his loss at the battle for Matthews system. There would be no public reprimand, and no loss of command. In fact, they had laid most of the blame for the defeat on poor intelligence, and consequently enlarged his area of command responsibility. If the U.C.S. won the war, the letter of reprimand would be destroyed. If they lost—well, if they lost, the reprimands would come from the enemy.

Frye wished Marsha could let him off as easily. Since the battle she had barely spoken to him outside of the line of duty. Despite the fact that as his AOCO she was forced to speak to him many times each day, she never said more than was necessary. Her condemnation of him was as clear as though she had engraved it permanently on her face.

Even before the meeting with Bridgeforce his mind had been churning with ideas and problems surrounding the next major offensive against Sondak. But now as he and Marsha walked back to his offices, he felt the need to try once more to break through to her. "Bridgeforce seems to have disagreed with your assessment, Marsha."

"In what way, sir?" She knew what he meant, but she wasn't about to make it easier for him.

"You heard them. They commended me for saving as many lives as humanly possible." The look on her face told him he had said the wrong thing again. Why couldn't he find the key to her?

"Bridgeforce said what it had to. You're the best space strategist they have. But you and I know the truth about those people you deserted."

"Dammit, Marsha, what kind of truth do you believe in? I told you then, and I'll repeat it for you now. We didn't desert them. We did what we had to do to save our forces from further destruction. Anything else would have been—"

"I'd rather not talk about it, sir."

"I wish your mother could hear you!" As soon as he said that a brief, dark wave of emptiness swept through the place in his heart that had once been filled by Vinita.

"You leave Mother out of this." Suddenly Marsha was angry and finally, finally she was ready to confront him. "You want to talk about what happened? You want to talk about us? All right, let's talk about us. But let's wait until we're back in your office so I won't embarrass you in front of anyone."

"As you wish, AOCO." Frye took her anger as a good sign. Maybe this was the breakthrough he had been waiting for.

Marsha let him take the lead through the crowded halls, and let her anger simmer. Only now was she beginning to understand how much anger she held for him—anger at him for separating her from Lucky, anger at him for deserting so many people in Matthews, and most surprising of all, anger at him because her mother was dead.

No matter how rationally she understood that his act had been merciful—no matter how rationally she understood that her mother would otherwise have died a horrible, lingering death—Marsha still could not accept the fact that he had given her mother the poison that had killed her.

Then as Marsha followed him into his office, her mind revealed a fleeting glimpse of what lay behind all of her feelings. If he had ever been able to love her she might have felt differently. But he could not or would not give her what she needed most from him. He would not give of himself. She closed the door carefully behind them and walked to the window with her arms folded across her breasts.

"Shall I start, or do you want to?" he asked.

"You're the commander," she said bitterly.

Frye hesitated. "No, not here, not now. I'm your father and you're my daughter, and it is time we cleared the air between us. No rank. Not this time."

The emotions surging through her threatened her self-control, but she held them down. "All right, then, daughter to father." She turned to face him, took a deep breath, and tightened her arms around her chest. "Let's start at the beginning and move rapidly forward in that neat, concise way you like so much."

Frye refused to respond to her sarcasm. Regardless of what she said, he meant to hear her out.

"In the beginning you ignored me—or, more accurately, you ignored my need for a father who cared about me. Then you ran me off. Then you ignored my communications. Then you . . . then you killed Mother."

Her voice was breaking, but she had to go on. "Then you told me you didn't—couldn't love me. And then, then, you abandoned all those people! And you wonder why there is tension between us? Do you really?" Suddenly the tears filled her eyes and Marsha turned away from him.

There was nothing Frye could say, and he knew it—not because he had no defense against her accusations, but because he knew she wouldn't listen. He should have been angered by her stupidity and childishness, but instead of anger he felt only a cold distance from her.

"Well?" she asked as she spun around. "Aren't you going to tell me how wrong I am and how righteous and noble you are?"

"No, Marsha, I'm not."

She couldn't believe it. There she was laying it all out for him and he was just sitting there as stoically as though she had told him night was falling. "Why? Are you afraid of it? Are you afraid to talk about how you feel?"

"Of course not. Don't be stupid." As quickly as he said that he shut his mouth. She had struck a nerve. Anger broke through the cold. But he had no intention of telling her how he felt—not yet.

"Then tell me," she said after a long pause. "Tell me how you feel—about me, about Mother, about all those spacers you left out there. What's the matter, you bastard, don't you feel anything for any of us?" The tears ran down her cheeks in little streams of quiet desperation.

"That's enough!" Frye was again startled by how quickly she could rouse his ire no matter how fiercely he guarded against it.

"Why? You putting your rank back on, Daddy?" Now she wanted him to see her tears, and maybe, just maybe understand how much his actions hurt her.

"I'm your father," he said sternly. "You have no right to talk to me that way."

"And I'm the daughter you never wanted, so I can talk to you any way I damn well please."

Frye stared at her in wonder, as though she were a stranger who was accosting him. How could such a woman be his own flesh and blood? How could she be Vinita's daughter? Suddenly the final bit of understanding came through to him and he realized what he had been blind to all along. He had been looking for Vinita's traits in Marsha and failed to see his own.

"Yes, you can," he said, pacing his words with as much discipline as he could muster. "You can say anything you want. And so can I. Do you want to hear what I have to say?"

"No. I'm just here for the weather."

"Then put on your storm gear, daughter-of-mine, because you're going to need it."

Marsha wiped the last of the tears from her face and wondered what he meant. There was a look in his eyes she wasn't sure she had ever seen before—a look that reinforced his words.

"Might as well make yourself comfortable," he said. "This is going to take a while." He wasn't sure where he was going to begin, but somewhere in the course of what followed he planned to convince her of what he felt.

He might not be able to love her in the way she wanted to be loved—might not be able to show her the affection she thought she deserved. But somehow, some way, he had to convince her that he needed her by his side solely because she was his daughter.

"You are a great deal like me," he said quietly.

Marsha was shocked. She couldn't be—not like him. "I am not," she protested.

"Ah, but you are, Marsha. You are. Think about it for a minute. You might have acted differently than I did at Matthews, but our motives were the same—to save as many people as possible. And you are just as selfish as I am, too."

Marsha felt angry tears welling in the corners of her eyes, but she knew the anger was at herself, not him. Was he right? Was she selfish? Had she picked up as much of his personality as she had of her mother's?

Frye wanted to let her think this through with as little pressure as possible. "I'll get us something to drink."

As he moved across the office to the small alcove that served as pantry and kitchen, he thought he understood how much she was like him. If he could convince her of that, the two of them just might work out their differences and learn to appreciate one another. For him that would be sufficient. He dared not guess what it might mean to her.

Marsha fought the tears as she listened to him fixing their drinks, and didn't know if she was angry or sad. To be like him meant to be someone she didn't understand, and the fear of losing what little understanding she had gained of herself caused all of her defenses to rise up inside. No matter what he said, she would never believe that she and her father were really alike. No, not at all.

* * *

In the central prison in Esqueleada on the polar planet Sutton, Sondak General Fortuno Mari sat naked, dirty, and cold on a bare metal bunk. One arm hung useless at his side, broken and swollen with infection. The commander of the Polar Defense Force wrapped his good arm around his shivering body and wept.

His pikean guard laughed. "What's the matter, Fortuno? Do you want me to comfort your body and let you beat me like you used to?" Giselda asked. "Is that it? Do you miss beating me? Is that why you weep like a child?"

Mari heard her through a dim, painful ringing in his ears, another of the legacies from the repeated beatings he had received at the hands of his U.C.S. captors. He wanted to stop crying, wanted to shut out her taunting voice, wanted to escape the endless pain, but his body was no longer under his control. Only his mind fought back.

The U.C.S. invasion forces had beaten his planetary troops and destroyed or vanquished what few POLFLEET and Flight Corps ships he had under his command. A third of his troops had died in space. Many more had died in the chaos on the ground. Half the pikean troops had revolted and joined the Ukes or simply fled the fighting. There had been no time to establish an adequate defense. Consequently, the Ukes had quickly reduced most of Sutton's population centers to isolated masses of frightened humanity even well before he had been captured.

But landing on a planet was relatively easy compared to conquering it. That was a totally different matter. Mari knew there had to be hundreds, maybe thousands of groups still fiercely resisting the Ukes, still following his order of no surrender. Sometimes he could even hear Sutton's antique artillery firing in the distance, its hollow, booming sound the only thing that gave him hope.

As long as there was continued fighting, Sutton retained a slim chance of beating the Ukes, and he still had a chance to be freed from these endless rounds of torture and interrogation. Because of that, he also knew that whatever the Ukes chose to do to his body, his mind would resist until the end. They had gotten no information out of him, and they would get none so long as he was alive to resist. He would follow his own standing order: no surrender.

"What?" she asked. "No answer from the great general? Perhaps you would like some encouragement."

Before he could answer Giselda stuck a nozzle through the grating and sprayed him with a burst of cold water. That brutal shock was followed immediately by a searing wave of pain that spread from his broken arm.

Mari clutched the bare metal frame of his cot with his good hand. Tides of blackness threatened to overwhelm him. Only his hatred of her and the Ukes kept him from falling to the floor unconscious.

"More, Fortuno? Would you like more?"

A second blast of water knocked him against the wall. His

head bounced off the smooth stone. As he slid slowly down the slippery surface a faint warmth spread with the pain in the back of his head. The sound of his own moaning deepened Mari's understanding of how much a man could hate.

Forcing himself upright, he tried to focus on Giselda, tried to concentrate his hatred in his eyes and let her know she could never defeat him. But no matter how hard he fought to burn her with a stare, his rheumy eyes failed him. Warm tears mixed with the frigid water running down his face and he let his eyes close.

Why? he wondered as fatigue and despair dragged him toward oblivion. Why don't they just kill me?

A third blast of water jolted the answer loose in his mind. Have to escape . . . or kill myself. Know too much. Escape. Kill myself. Escape . . . no surrender . . . escape.

The thought of escape mixed with hundreds of blurred images in his mind—images of troops and battle, of enemies and friends, frail images that refused to hold still in the fading dimness of his mind. Yet deep in the recesses of this thoughts he knew that escape or death were his only alternatives. And the image of death caught and held, an image of horror that slowly wrapped him in its blackness.

Fortuno Mari did not feel the fourth blast of cold water, nor the fifth, nor the sixth. He did not know that gentler efforts were made to revive him. For the first time since his capture seven weeks before he had found a temporary refuge where no one could harm him.

3

"We are here, Proctor," a ringing voice called from the back of the crowd.

"We are here," the crowd responded in ritual chorus.

Leri Gish Geril barely acknowledged the greeting as she slithered through the packed Grotto of Conjunction. She sensed their awe, for never before had she allowed so many of her people into her presence at once. Never before had there been such a gathering of Cloise's best. Somehow that fact lightened her burden and lessened her resentment that the Grotto of Conjunction was the only place large enough for such a meeting to occur.

"Leri, Leri, Leri," they whispered as she moved down the narrow aisle they made for her. "Leri, Leri, Leri."

Waiting on the side of the low dais were the larger soulless Oinaise and his human ambassador, both in their protective suits, their alien presence almost a desecration of this holy ground. Yet even as she moved toward them she knew their presence was necessary—perhaps even vital to the survival of Cloise and all she held dear.

Lucky Teeman watched her approach the dais with a shiver of fear. She was more than the appointed ruler of this alien hell. The rest of the salamanders obviously regarded her with utter respect, almost as though she were some kind of religious figure. Yet to Lucky she was a creature whose long, snake-like body evoked mythic shadows of evil in his mind. Bands of red, yellow, and black scales covered everything but her pink, wrinkled arms and the grotesque nipple behind her pointed head.

Red and yellow, dragon fellow. That curious refrain had popped into his mind the first time he saw her. He didn't know where it came from, and now he couldn't get rid of it. Being alone with her had been bad enough. Seeing the respect she received from the hundreds of her kind in front of him made his stomach twist and churn with irrational fear.

Lucky glanced at Morning Song as the crowd whispered her name in a haunting chant, but he could read no expression through the Oinaise's faceplate. He only hoped Delightful Childe's son would carry most of the burden in this meeting. He wanted it to be over.

Leri pulled her body into a coil beside the aliens and reared higher above them than was polite. She knew the human—like all the humans she had met—feared her physical presence, as well he should. In a fraction of a second she could generate oxygen, mix it with the methane in her gills, spark it with her teeth, and incinerate him in a lovely fireball. She had done it before easily enough.

But now as she lowered herself to a more acceptable level, she set that pleasant possibility aside. It was time for serious business, perhaps the most serious business ever to face a ruling proctor.

"We are here, Proctor," the voice said again.

Leri knew it was Ranas, her loyal mate and assistant who led the chant, and knew that Weecs, the lover she had banished him for, was in the crowd as well. Deliberately she avoided looking for either of them.

"Welcome, be welcomed," Leri said finally. She could smell the heavy scent of tension in the grotto. "Be at peace, my companions, for in peace there is wisdom."

"And truth is born of wisdom," they responded.

Lucky listened as the salamanders went through a seemingly endless series of ritual exchanges. Some of them made no sense at all, but he knew he was getting a literal gentongue translation from the small unit on his belt, and used the time to calm himself. The words became rhythms that massaged his mind and helped relax his taut muscles. He let his thoughts drift.

"—a human representing the Oinaise, who brings us an offer and a request. Will you hear him?"

With a start Lucky realized she was talking about him.

"Yes, yes, yes," the crowd chanted.

It was a long moment before Lucky understood that he was expected to respond. "I am honored to be here," he said finally, the quaver in his voice barely perceptible, "and doubly honored to accompany Morning Song, whose father has sent us to greet you." Some kind of amplifier boomed his words through the grotto and back at him.

"I, too, am honored," Morning Song said. "Let it be known that Captain Teeman speaks for me, my father, and all of Oina."

That's a lie, Lucky thought. But it was a lie he knew he would have to live with, because Morning Song obviously wasn't going to carry his weight. Well, he thought, no sense in wasting any more time.

"Our galaxy is cursed with troubled times," he said quietly, hoping to reduce the amplification. He couldn't tell if it worked or not, so he decided to ignore the feedback. "As Proctor Leri has said, we have come with an offer for Cloise, and a request. The offer is simple. Oina will pay twenty percent more than the current rate paid Cloise by Sondak for all the methane you are willing to let us export."

A chorus of unintelligible comments forced him to pause until the audience quieted. Lucky had no idea if they were pleased or angered, but judging from Leri's response in private, he thought the offer would please them.

"The request," he continued, "is not so simple. Oina respectfully requests that Cloise join with it and all other neutral races in a mutual protection pact against Sondak and the United Central Systems."

Red and yellow, dragon fellow. This time Lucky could guess what their noisy reaction meant. The crowd writhed angrily like a mass of giant snakes. They seemed to be surging forward as though they were about to attack the dais. It took all Lucky's will to keep from turning and running, but he held fast.

Finally Leri rose up from her coils and silence suddenly filled the grotto. "Such a request," she said simply as she looked out over her people, "angers and frightens you, as it does me. But it must be considered. The humans fight to annihilate one another. What will keep them from annihilating us?" Leri prayed to the Elett that the assembled directors were listening with their minds and not their hearts.

"But *he* is human," Ranas said, pointing a long arm at Lucky.

"He represents Oina," Morning Song said quickly.

"He represents death," another voice said.

Red and yellow, dragon fellow. Lucky shivered uncontrollably as arguments broke out among the shifting snakes. It was time to get out of there and let the Proctor handle this by herself. "Directors of Cloise," he shouted, "forgive us for angering you."

The noise slowly subsided as heads turned again toward the dais. Lucky took that as a good sign. "Let us withdraw and return to our ship to await your decision. Proctor Leri has the details of our request. She can answer your questions."

"Protocol," Morning Song's voice whispered in his ear on the suit channel. "It would be wrong to withdraw."

"I don't think so," Lucky whispered back. Again his voice boomed through the grotto. He cursed silently at himself for forgetting to turn off his suit speaker.

"What do you not think, human?" Leri asked in the following silence as she rose up again.

"I, uh, I was telling Morning Song that I didn't think it would be wrong for us to withdraw, Proctor." His instincts all screamed for him to flee.

"You are only partially correct, human. Go now. I am tired of your quivering frame. Morning Song shall stay."

Lucky left without hesitation and shakily made his way through the tunnels back to the surface and *Graycloud's* shuttle to wait for Morning Song.

Behind him tens of arguments filled the grotto. Morning Song stood patiently waiting for Proctor Leri to quiet them again. Leri relaxed into her coil and waited for her people to exhaust themselves. There was no hurry, no need to rush the proceedings. An answer would come in due time, the answer she had already decided upon.

As much as Cloise's directors needed to argue and debate the problem to prove their worth to one another, they needed someone who would make the final decision. That someone was always the proctor. As much as her people felt themselves free to choose, in the end they always relied on the ultimate authority to make their choices for them. And whether she liked it or not, she was their ultimate authority figure.

When Lucky reached the shuttle he was angry, and frightened, and annoyed, but as he took off his suit exhaustion pushed his other emotions aside. "The war, the damn war," he cursed. "Why in tensheiss did the damn Ukes start it anyway?" He secured his suit and moved up to sit in the pilot's couch.

For a brief instant a vision of Marsha flickered in front of him. Then it was gone, leaving him with only the pain that was the legacy of their relationship. The war had claimed her, the war and her damned Uke father. No matter what Lucky wanted to believe, he doubted if he would ever see her again.

Red and yellow, dragon fellow, echoed through his head, and he hoped Morning Song would be all right.

* * *

"It is not necessary, Captain," Lieutenant Bon said.

"Perhaps not, Lieutenant, but it is my custom to keep my crews fully informed of their mission."

"In my opinion, sir, that is an unwise custom."

Ishiwa frowned. "In your opinion, Lieutenant? Or in the opinion of the kyosei leadership?"

Bon spoke without hesitation. "Both, sir. If something were to happen to us and crew members were captured and questioned, they could give the enemy vital information."

"Such ideas are defeatist, Lieutenant Bon. I do not intend for anything to happen to us. Neither do I intend to keep my crew ignorant because of some misplaced notion of the kyosei that the common spacers are incapable of trust."

"Sir! I strenuously object. I meant no such disrespect for our crew."

"No? Your party does, Lieutenant. I have read *The Leadership of Man* by your vaunted Ilizabet. Its elitism offended me, as did every other kyosei tract I read. Ideas like that have no place in the military."

When Bon responded, his voice was cold and emotionless. "I would remind you, Captain, that we kyosei control the government. Comments such as yours could have an unpleasant effect on your military career."

"Is that a threat, Lieutenant?" Anger simmered inside him as he stared at his junior. How dare a subordinate threaten him with political retribution for his opinions?

"No, sir. I mean no threat," Bon said. "I only seek to present you with the facts concerning your status as—"

"Then if it is not a threat, I will remind you of something. It was one of your kyosei, the ever popular Marshall Judoff," he added sarcastically, "who deserted the confederation and imperiled our valiant attacks on Matthews and Sutton."

"She was well within her rights to withdraw reserve—"

"I don't give a corpse in space what rights she was within, Lieutenant," Ishiwa said, keeping his anger firmly under control. "As far as I am concerned, she cost us thousands of lives and should be considered a traitor!"

"Sir, I don't think—"

"And I don't care what you think about this matter." Ishiwa wanted to lash out at Bon. Only his training held him in check. "The subject is closed between us. Is that understood?"

Bon stared at him for a long moment, then dropped his eyes. "Understood, Captain. My apologies for angering you."

"Accepted on one condition, Lieutenant."

Bon looked surprised. "Sir?"

"You must read the orders to the crew. If you will do that, I will forget that we ever had this conversation."

"You ask a great deal, Captain Ishiwa."

"I ask only obedience and loyalty, Lieutenant Bon."

"Of course, sir," Bon said without hesitation. Then he paused as though searching for what to say next. "I will read the orders," he said finally, "and I, too, will forget that we had this conversation."

"Excellent, Lieutenant." Ishiwa reached over his head and pulled the commander's microphone from its niche in the bulkhead. "You may do it from here."

It gave Ruto Ishiwa great pleasure to hear Bon read the orders to the crew. Their morale was of utmost importance to him, and knowing what they were assigned to do was one of the best ways of keeping their morale high. Obedience was also important to him. Bon had the potential to be a good hunk commander, but until he got his priorities in the proper military order, he would have to be watched constantly.

"Then let us proceed to destroy the lifeblood of Sondak for the glory of the United Central Systems," Bon concluded. With a faint smile he handed the microphone back to Ishiwa.

"Well done, Lieutenant," Ishiwa said before turning off the microphone.

The compliment echoed over the small speaker in the companionway outside his cabin and Bon looked startled.

"I wanted the crew to know I approved," Ishiwa said. "They should know of my respect for you." 'Praise softens all blows,' his father had said. Ishiwa hoped it would work on Bon.

4

"Will we be receiving additional ships, Admiral?"

"Negative, Major Nickerson—at least no additional fighting ships, not for a while. The Joint Military Command will be reinforcing our supply lines, and of course, we have picked up

several Flight Corps wings from Roberg." Pajandcan could tell
by their expressions and the quiet whisperings that none of her
officers were much pleased with her answer. But then, neither
was she.

"What about dirtside?"

"There are two legions of newly activated Planetary Reservists landing now on Satterfield, and two-and-a-half legions are
on their way to Bakke. Yaffee and Wallbank will also be
receiving additional legions as soon as they are available.

"As most of you know, we have already set up preliminary
defense zones around Satterfield and Bakke, similar to the
ones we used to defend Matthews system. Quarter Admiral
Dawson has prepared a general description of those zones
which each of you will find in your briefing book."

"Begging your pardon, Admiral," a commander in the back
of the room said, "but is this the same Dawson who coordinated the last wargames?"

"The same," Pajandcan said with a smile. "The same
Dawson who put you through your paces in the last two full-
fleet exercises. The same Dawson who was defense coordinator for the Gyle Coalition during the Salimar Rebellion.
And now, Acting Quarter Admiral Dawson, most recently the
defense coordinator for Matthews system." There were several
low whistles of appreciation. Pajandcan wished that Dawson
could have been there to hear them, but he was already out at
Satterfield getting ready for the Ukes. "Anything else you want
to know about Admiral Dawson?"

When no one responded, she said, "Very well. Now for the
hardest news of all. Our forces on Sutton have apparently put
up far more resistance than the Ukes expected, and slowed
what we think was their plan of advance. However, the Joint
Chiefs have determined that Satterfield and Bakke are both
equal targets of opportunity for the Ukes as soon as they
subdue Sutton. Consequently, their strategy calls for us to
divide the defense elements of Polar Fleet equally between
those two systems."

"Damn!" a single voice said above the low groans of the rest
of the officers.

"I'll second that," Pajandcan responded, "and double it."
She wanted these officers to know she felt the burden of their
mission as much as they did. It was going to take all of them

giving their absolute best to carry out the orders the Joint Chiefs had given POLFLEET.

"What about Wallbank and Yaffee?" an aging quarter-admiral asked, rising to his feet. "Aren't they just as vulnerable?"

"Not according to our intelligence reports, Admiral, uh, Dimitri, isn't it?" When he nodded, she continued, "Cryptography thinks Wallbank and Yaffee will only be secondary targets in the Uke plan after they have secured a main line of approach across the galactic pole."

"Well, I think Cryptography's wrong, Admiral. Damned wrong. And I think we're taking an awful chance concentrating our defense in two systems. We're stretched too thin as it is."

"Hold your comments on that until the commanders meeting, Admiral. In fact, what I would like to do at this time is to give you all a few hours to study your briefing books with your staffs. Then I will meet with all senior commanders in the Operations Room to hear your comments and suggestions."

Pajandcan paused and carefully surveyed the assembled officers. Already she had a fairly good idea which ones were going to give her trouble, but she wanted to be as fair to them as possible. "I will need all your help and assistance in developing a plan to carry out our orders," she said slowly. "Consequently, I need your criticism as well as your advice. That will be all for now."

As she left the room Pajandcan felt sure she was going to hear more criticism than advice at the commanders meeting, but that was to be expected. What she would have to do was channel that criticism into constructive uses. She had to make her officers understand that as little as they might like the terms under which they had to achieve that mission, Polar Fleet could and would carry it out to the best of its ability.

Three hours later, despite her mental preparations, she was surprised by the vehemence of the objections and arguments she had heard from her subordinates. How had Josiah Gilbert controlled them? she wondered. What had he done to make them willingly follow his lead?

The same thing he did when I followed his lead, she thought. He used ruthless logic combined with his incredible force of personality. For a brief instant she doubted if she could do as well. Then she dismissed that doubt. She had no choice.

"All right," she said, calmly interrupting the heated discussion. "Perhaps we should approach our problems from a new direction. How many of you want to be transferred to other commands?" The stunned looks she saw on their faces confirmed that she had used the right approach.

Finally Admiral Dimitri spoke in a voice that seemed barely under control. "You don't seem to understand, Admiral Pajandcan. None of us want to leave POLFLEET. No matter what they say about us on Nordeen, we know we're the best fleet in the whole damn Service."

"Why?" Pajandcan asked.

"Because we do a bigger job with fewer ships and men than any of the other fleets, that's why. And we do it better."

"Exactly."

Someone chuckled and suddenly Dimitri laughed. "Your point, Admiral. Now you're going to tell us that we have to live up to our reputation."

"Doesn't sound like I have to, Dimitri. Under Josiah Gilbert's leadership POLFLEET made its mark as a fleet with a 'can do' attitude." Pajandcan smiled. "Now you get the chance to prove yourselves."

"You can't stop the Ukes just with attitude," Commander McQuay said.

Pajandcan looked the sour-faced commander straight in the eyes. "Correct me if I'm wrong, but I believe your grandmother would have disagreed with you."

Dimitri laughed again. "Old Battleaxe McQuay—toughest woman this service has ever seen. Better think on that again, Gwendy."

"What do you know about my grandmother?" McQuay asked, her face turning red.

"My first launchship command was the *McQuay*, named after your grandmother," Dimitri said quietly. "I probably know more about her than you do. For instance, did you know that she once stopped a mutiny on the cruiser *Siros* when she was just a lieutenant? And that was after she had been stabbed twice and left for dead."

McQuay looked startled. "My parents never told me that."

"Well, maybe they never knew. But the service knew. It's all in her records."

"She was also the first commander of Polar Fleet," Pajandcan added. "In fact, this fleet was her idea." She paused only for a second. "So maybe we ought to keep her in mind as we start to work on our plans. And you, Commander McQuay, can give us a summary of her career at our next meeting."

"Yes, ma'am," McQuay said with downcast eyes.

Pajandcan felt better about this meeting already, and even better about Admiral Dimitri. She suspected he would be a key figure in the coming plans. "But as interesting as all that is to us, there is still much we have to discuss."

"Admiral? I'd like to say one more thing."

"Yes, Dimitri?"

"If our main objectives have to be the defense of Bakke and Satterfield—and I know we can't argue with that—then I think our secondary objective should be offensive. All this talk about Admiral McQuay made me remember something she said once. 'Attack from your knees,' she said, 'so they can't be sure that you're down.' If we could harass the Ukes while we're putting those defenses together, we might be able to catch them off-guard and delay their attack."

"Harass them with what?" Quarter-Admiral Nackiniv asked.

"Anything, Heydron. Anything we can."

Pajandcan liked the idea, but— "That's a dangerous suggestion, Dimitri, and one the Joint Chiefs probably won't approve. However, I see no reason why we can't include it as a possibility in our operations plan. Certainly the Ukes don't expect us to take the offensive, despite what happened to them at Matthews. Anyone else want to comment on that?"

By the time the meeting ended four hours later, they had all commented on that and just about every other possibility. Pajandcan divided them into operational groups and demanded the first outlines of their plans in thirty hours. They wouldn't get much sleep, but then neither would she.

Yet she left the meeting feeling good about what had happened. If anyone could accomplish the mission the Joint Chiefs had set for them, these officers were the ones. They might be opinionated and outspoken, but they were also pragmatic realists who let her know they would use every resource available to them. Gilbert might just have been right when he told her she couldn't ask for a better command.

Now if Mari's troops could continue to delay the Ukes on Sutton, that would give POLFLEET the time they needed to

complete their plans. Then they would find out if they
deserved their reputation.

* * *

Ayne Wallen stood before the Uke officials with his head
bowed. The woman was Judoff, the same one who had
bargained with Xindella to bring him to this place. She was
even uglier in person than she was on the vidscreen. The fat
man with her was obviously a foot-kissing assistant, but Ayne
did not want either of them to be angry at him. They might
withdraw his ration of gorlet, and Xindella had gone to great
pains to teach Ayne exactly how addicted he was to that sweet
Oinaise candy.

"I asked you a question," Marshall Judoff said.

"Be you pleased," Ayne said softly, "is difficult to answer
with precision."

"You'd spacing well better answer with—"

"Easy, Kuskuvyet," Judoff said. "Our friend is obviously
upset. Perhaps he can explain why."

Ayne hesitated for a moment, then decided he had nothing
further to lose. He was already a traitor as far as Sondak was
concerned, and the only thing protecting him was what he
knew. "Is difficult to explain concept if you be not familiar with
writings of Guntteray. Has to do with spacetime theory and
physics of subatomic dilations."

"I don't want the physics of it," Judoff said curtly. "Right now
I only need to know what the effects are."

"No," Ayne said, looking up at her finally. "What effects
could be. Could be greatest weapon ever invented. Could
be—"

"You mean there is no such weapon?"

Ayne heard the anger in her voice and lowered his eyes
again. When he answered, his voice trembled. "Drautzlab be
working on such, but—"

"Can you build this weapon?"

"With proper facilities and assistance, yes," Ayne said finally.
He had no idea if he actually could build the weapon or not.
Drautzlab's Ultimate Weapon was still only a set of equations
in his head.

"What will it do?"

"Destroy stars," he said simply.

Judoff laughed. "You're insane!"

"Not insane. Have the secret here," Ayne said looking at her again and tapping his head. "Can be done." Her eyes had a look of the madness she accused him of, and he looked away. Cold fear spread through his bones.

"Well, we paid for you," Judoff said finally, "so we might as well find out if you're telling the truth. You will go with Commander Kuskuvyet. But let me tell you something, scientist. You'd better be telling the truth. If you can't build this fantasy weapon, you will pay for your failure every moment for the rest of your miserable life. Do you understand that?"

"Yes," Ayne said softly. "Understand." Doubts joined the flood of fear in his mind. Suppose they wouldn't give him the proper equipment? Or sufficient help? Or suppose he couldn't do it? Suppose the Ultimate Weapon was a fantasy? What would happen to him then?

The man, Kuskuvyet, grabbed Ayne by the arm, and anger pushed back the fear and doubt. "Will show you," he said suddenly. "And Sondak, too. Will blow them all to dust." The last thing he heard as Kuskuvyet dragged him from the room was Judoff's laughter, a laughter that pierced his soul.

5

Explosions rocked the prison walls. General Mari howled with pain as he was thrown from his bunk. A thick cloud of hot dust swept through the grate into his cell. As he struggled to his knees he realized that his broken arm was strapped to his side in a rigid cast over his coarse brown coveralls.

What had happened? What was going on? How long had he been unconscious?

From the distance came the sounds of shouting voices and the staccato blasts of small-arms fire. Suddenly Mari understood what it meant. His troops were attacking the prison!

He crawled to the grate and pulled himself to his feet,

choking on the dust. "I'm here," he tried to shout, but all that came out was a croaking whisper.

Moments later a pikean sergeant, his fair-skinned face blackened with camouflage paint, appeared through the dust. "Get back and down, sir," the sergeant said.

Mari had barely moved away from the grate when the sergeant fired several automatic bursts from his rifle. Splinters of shattered metal richocheted off the slick stones. With a loud crash the grate fell back against the cell wall.

"I'm Sergeant Edwards, sir. General Porras sent us."

"Porras is still alive?" Mari asked as Edwards helped him to his feet. Only then did he see more troopers in the hall.

"Alive and kickin' Ukes. Sit down, sir," Edwards said, pulling off his pack.

Mari obeyed without thinking and Sergeant Edwards pulled a pair of allsize emergency boots out of his pack and slipped them over Mari's feet. Seconds later he had the bindings comfortably tight. "That ought to hold you, sir. Now for your weapon."

Edwards thrust a twelve millimeter combat pistol into Mari's hand, then fastened an ammunition belt around his waist. Mari was startled by the weakness in his arm. The pistol only weighed nine kilograms, but it felt like fifty. "Don't think I can shoot very well left-handed," he said.

"Then let's hope you don't have to. Now listen carefully, sir. We're going right down this hall approximately eighty meters. My squad is holding the breach there. The company is holding the compound wall. Once we're through the breach, keep bearing left. Got that?"

"Got it." Mari felt a surge of adrenal energy that fought against the weakness of his body. "I'm ready."

"Then let's go."

Sergeant Edwards led the way with Mari following him and three troopers behind them. Automatic weapons chattered louder and louder as they moved quickly toward the light-filled breach in the wall. "First team coming through," Edwards called.

Even through the firing and shouted commands Mari could hear that message repeated, passed on to the men outside. Just as they reached the breach several explosions rocked the outside compound.

"That's our cover," Edwards said. "Move out!"

Suddenly they were moving through the breach in the wall. Hands grabbed Mari and pulled him over the rubble. Bullets whined and spat over his head. It was either dawn or dusk, he couldn't tell which. The dim air was full of smoke and dust.

Pain lanced through his body at a hundred points as Mari followed Sergeant Edwards in a low, running crouch. When Edwards fired to the right, so did Mari. He couldn't see what he was shooting at, so he just pointed in the general direction enemy fire seemed to be coming from and squeezed the trigger repeatedly. Each recoil of the pistol harshly jerked his arm, and Mari remembered how much he had hated training with the twelve millimeter hand-cannon.

As they reached a second wall, new hands grabbed him and suddenly he was being jerked from man to man. He clung to his pistol. His head swirled. Explosions roared behind them.

"Jump, sir!" a voice commanded.

Mari barely understood what he was doing when he saw the opening to the tunnel and jumped in. A mutilated body lay directly in front of him, smelling of feces and death. The stench struck him like a wall and his knees buckled. Someone grabbed him under the arms and dragged him thirty meters back from the opening. Seconds later the hole filled with troops.

Gasping for breath, Mari checked his pistol. It was almost empty. "Trooper," he said to the soldier closest to him, "reload this for me."

The soldier looked startled, but quickly took the pistol and loaded a new magazine. "Have to move back now, sir," he said as he returned the pistol to Mari. "We're gonna blow the entrance to the tunnel so the Ukes can't follow us."

With the soldier's help Mari got to his feet, then moved in a low crouch behind him through the darkness. The glowlamp on the trooper's utility belt cast a faint light on the damp walls of the tunnel, and Mari had to strain his eyes to keep from tripping or running into him. Every time he raised his head too high he bumped it against the hard dirt roof.

Less than a minute after they started, a faint series of thumping explosions shook the tunnel behind them, but the trooper never hesitated. Mari stumbled along behind him, his breaths coming in long, jagged gasps. His broken arm throbbed with miserable pain. His legs screamed in protest against the low crouching movement.

"Keep moving, troop," a voice behind him said when Mari slowed to stick the pistol in his belt. "We've got to get the general out of here."

Mari would have laughed if he could have. Whoever was behind him obviously didn't realize who he was following. But Mari clenched his teeth, and quickened his pace as instructed.

Each mechanical step was a lesson in pain. Each ragged breath was an insufficient claim for oxygen. Time became meaningless. Only movement was important. Keep moving, keep moving, his mind commanded. Somehow his body obeyed.

The trooper in front of him stopped without warning and Mari ran into him.

"Easy, sir," the trooper said. "We're almost there."

"Where?" Mari gasped.

"Exit," the trooper said simply. "You can stand up now."

Mari tried, but his muscles screamed in protest. His knees gave way and he collapsed onto the damp floor. Moments later two troopers grabbed him and pulled him up.

"Just a few more steps, sir. Can you make it?"

"Yes," Mari said hoarsely. Amazingly his body again complied with his commands. Ten more steps and they were out of the tunnel. Twenty steps beyond the exit a skimmer sat in the twilight, its engine whining in readiness. Before he knew it he was aboard the open skimmer with six or seven troopers. Then the skimmer lifted and headed out into the growing darkness.

Clinging to the seat brace with his good hand, Mari finally realized with amazement the extent of what had happened. He had been rescued, by Porras's pikean troops—those same troops Mari had despised so much. Now there he was riding with them as they chatted happily about what they had just done. Three of their number had been killed, and seven more wounded, but they had accomplished their mission.

As the skimmer bounced gently through the dark over the rough bottoms of dry gullies and across low, rocky hills, Mari wondered how the driver could see where they were going. The man seemed to have a sixth sense about the terrain. For the first time in Mari's life he regretted how he had always treated the pikeans before—even Giselda. They might not be the smartest human ethnic group, but the courage of these pikeans at least, was undeniable.

Suddenly the skimmer slowed to an abrupt stop beside a rocky embankment. Mari could hear running water close by, and overhead the stars of galaxy center shone like a bright cloud through the thin haze of Sutton's atmosphere. He shivered with cold, then shuddered with pain.

"General Mari?" a figure called from the darkness.

It was General Porras. Mari recognized his voice. "Here," he said as he climbed slowly from the skimmer.

"Bless the stars! How are you, General?"

"Battered, sore, and damned grateful, Porras." Mari stuck out his left hand. "Those are fine troops you command."

"Only the best, sir." Porras accepted Mari's awkward handshake, then immediately said, "You're freezing, sir. Let's get you inside."

Mari followed Porras up a wide path, then through three heavy blackout curtains into a large, low-ceilinged cavern crammed full of equipment and supplies. In an alcove off to one side he could see a bank of manned radios, its operators all busy. At the far end of the cavern troopers were loading crates into several old freight skimmers. "Incredible! How did you manage to save all this?"

Porras laughed as he led Mari to a small area walled off by boxes. "Some of it was already here. We started transferring supplies, equipment, and ammunition to hidden depots right after the Ukes hit Roberg. Figured the Ukes would get to us sooner or later, so we decided to be ready for them."

"Excellent planning, Porras. I'm frankly amazed." Mari sat on one of the bunks in the cubicle, and almost immediately a trooper appeared with a mess box full of steaming food.

"As soon as you've eaten and rested, sir, I'd like for the medics to check you over."

"Yes. Of course," Mari said around a mouthful of savory meat. "But right now I'd like a report on our status."

"I can give you the details after you've rested, sir, but you might as well know that we're in pretty grim shape. We have roughly one hundred eighty thousand troops of one sort or another operating on the planet, most in units of five hundred or less. About half of those are really civilian guerrillas and

various militia units, including a local artillery battalion you
might have heard pounding in your neighborhood."

"Good sounds," Mari said. He swallowed a chewy lump of
sweetbread and added, "Gave me hope. Numbers sound much
better than I expected."

"The trouble is, sir, not only do the Ukes outnumber us
about six-to-one, but we're having a terrible time supplying
our units. We probably have enough ammunition to hold out
for a long time, but getting it to where it's needed, well, that's
something else. We're using everything from captured Uke
heavy transport skimmers to civilian lorries and even pack
animals. But we're restricted to night movement in most
areas, and short of transport everywhere."

Mari set the half-empty food box on the floor and tried to
concentrate on what Porras was saying. His whole body ached
and his stomach churned against the unaccustomed richness of
the food, but he couldn't rest until—

"However," Porras continued, "our immediate concern is to
abandon this headquarters tonight. After our raids on Esqueleada, there will be Ukes crawling all over the countryside
as soon as it's light. We need to be well gone by then. Better
get some sleep while you can, sir. I'll wake you when we're
ready to leave."

With a sigh Mari lay back on the bunk. "Thanks, Porras. And
thank your men. We can talk about the rest of . . ." Mari
knew there was something else he was supposed to say, but he
was just too tired. His eyes closed. A jumbled procession of
images crowded his mind, images of fighting and death.
Floating above those images was an eerie cloud of peace. His
mouth twitched in a smile as he fell quickly to sleep.

* * *

After receiving Admiral Gilbert's message delaying their
dinner meeting, Henley Stanmorton called on every military
source he had searching for a story. Much to his surprise, when
he called the Cryptography headquarters an aide consulted
with Commander Rochmon and then invited him for an
interview.

The following morning Henley was ushered into Rochmon's
office five minutes ahead of schedule. "Good morning, sir. It
was good of you to see me on such short notice."

Rochmon smiled. "It's part of my new job, Mr. Stanmorton, or hadn't you heard?"

"No, sir. I just arrived from Biery ten days ago."

"Well, what can I do for you?"

"I'm not sure, sir. I've been hearing a lot of rumors since I hit Nordeen, and I'm hoping you might verify some of them— or at least clear out the bad ones for me."

"Shoot," Rochmon said with a smile.

Henley knew that time was precious, so he pulled out his list without hesitation. "Do the Ukes have a new design subspace hunter-killer?"

"No comment." Rochmon's smile faded, but he liked the straightforward question.

"Has Sutton surrendered?"

"On the contrary. Forces there are fighting more fiercely than ever."

"Are some selected polar systems being given lower priority for reinforcement and supply?"

"Negative. Make that absolutely negative," Rochmon lied.

Henley marked his list and smiled. "This isn't going to take long, is it?"

"Negative," Rochmon said, returning his smile. "I don't have the time."

"All right, Commander, is it true that Admiral Pajandcan has taken command of Polar Fleet?"

"That is classified information," Rochmon said slowly, "but I can tell you that she is with POLFLEET."

"Will she be given that command?"

"No comment."

"Is it true that some of the fleets are going to be combined under one command?"

"That's one I haven't heard," Rochmon said with a laugh. "Better ask the Joint Chiefs about that."

Henley sighed. "I tried, but couldn't get past their staff, much less get an answer." He wondered if he should ask the last question on his list, then decided he had nothing to lose.

"One more thing, sir. There are a variety of rumors surrounding your headquarters, but most of them even I can dismiss. However, there is a persistent rumor that can't be dismissed. People are saying that one of your civilian cryptographers has been relieved of duty and is under suspicion of being a spy for the Ukes."

Rochmon knew that rumor had been circulating, but was not about to give it credence. "No comment," he said quietly.

"None, sir? If it's not true, wouldn't it help to deny it?"

"No comment," Rochmon repeated. He believed that Bock was innocent, and when his belief was proven correct, he didn't want anything smirching her record. "I think your time is up."

Henley rose immediately. "Thank you, sir. I appreciate your help." The look of concern on Rochmon's face as he shook his hand told Henley the spy rumor was probably true.

6

The quiet pinging of *Misbarrett*'s bridgecaller woke Captain Ishiwa instantly. It only took him a few seconds to pull on his jumpsuit and less than a minute to leave his cabin and climb to the command deck. "What is it, Bon?"

"Multiple Sondak navigation signals, sir. Headed in our direction. Estimated crossing time, approximately two hours. Estimated firing window, fourteen minutes at minimum speed."

Ishiwa smiled. "Excellent, Lieutenant. This is sooner than I expected. All crew to battle stations. Slow to minimum subspace speed and prepare to attack. Adjust course for greatest possible firing angle."

"Aye-aye, sir."

As the crew fitted themselves into their assigned battle stations, *Olmis* changed from manned ship to an almost living thing. The crowded hunk breathed with an excitement that everyone could feel. Ishiwa knew they were ready. This is what they had been training for. This was the first true test of what *Olmis* could do in actual combat.

Minutes crawled by as the crew waited with anticipation.

On the command deck Ishiwa, Bon, and Kleber monitored the
subspace scanners with increasing interest. After half an hour
of intense watching, their interest changed to concern as the
Sondak blips slowly altered course.

"Do you think they've spotted us, sir?" Bon asked.

"No," Ishiwa answered, "but if they hold that new heading
we won't get much of a shot at them. Increase speed to M-
plus-three, Bon."

"But, Captain, the window will—"

"The window won't do us a damn bit of good if we aren't
close enough to use it."

"Speed M-plus-three," Bon ordered reluctantly.

"I count seven ships," Ishiwa said as he peered at the
screen. "Confirm, Lieutenant."

Bon leaned closer. "Maybe only six, sir. That trailing blip
looks like an erratic echo."

"Very well, Lieutenant, six it is." Ishiwa looked carefully at
his junior and decided to share the decision making. "Now,
Bon, suppose you were leading a Sondak convoy of six ships.
Where would you put the most important ones? In the
middle? Or in the rear?"

"In the rear, sir."

"In subspace, I think I would, too. Track your targets
starting from the rear, Bon. We'll only have time to fire three
missiles, at best, so we go for the last three ships, one missile
each."

"Isn't that a big risk?"

"It is, Bon. It is. But better to risk three on three, than to
concentrate on only one or two of those ships. If our missiles
are accurate, we get three at once. If they're not, we still might
get an additional shot at the last ship in line."

"By your orders, sir."

Ishiwa heard the implied disagreement in Bon's voice and
wanted to kick his junior in the tail. This was no time for
hidden feelings. "If you think I'm wrong, Lieutenant, enter
your objections in the log, now."

"No, sir. I mean, I don't think you are wrong, sir. As I said, I
just think you are taking a big chance."

"That's what we're here for—taking chances." Ishiwa turned
to his Fire Control Officer. "Chief Kleber, let us know when
you've locked on targets. When I give the order, I want three

missiles away as fast as your people can load and fire. Then I want a fourth ready in the tube in case we need it."

"Yes, sir," she said with the flash of a smile.

Ishiwa had argued for dual forward tubes when the fleet engineers had questioned him about design improvements for the new hunks. Now he cursed the shortage of materials and the stinginess of the designers. *Olmis* might be the fastest and longest-ranged hunk in the galaxy, but with only one firing tube forward and one aft, she, too, had limitations he would have to overcome to make her as effective a killer as a hunk should be.

The Sondak blips moved almost imperceptibly across and down the edge of the screen marking the slow passage of time. Bon had been right. The closer *Olmis* got, the more evident it became that there were only six sets of navigational signals, not seven. But six was a far greater number than Ishiwa could have hoped for in their first encounter.

Suddenly he was suspicious. Why would Sondak be sending a convoy in this direction? It was too far off course to be headed for Roberg or Matthews, so that could only mean—

"They're accelerating, sir!"

"Damn," Ishiwa whispered. "They must have spotted us. Chief? How soon before you can fire?"

"Ten minutes at the least, sir," she said without looking up from her scope. "Even then we'll be shooting through a one minute window at maximum range."

"Understood. Prepare to fire." Ishiwa did not want to lose this first opportunity. "Bon, lock onto the last ship."

"Aye-aye, sir."

There was no censorship in Bon's tone now, giving Ishiwa at least one small thing to be grateful for. As he watched the screen and waited for Chief Kleber to begin her countdown, he wondered what was happening on the command decks of those Sondak ships. Did they suspect what they were facing? Were they afraid? Were they preparing some defense he knew nothing about?

A change on the screen snapped him alert. The lead Sondak blip was separating from the others. "Look at this, Bon. I think one of them is coming after us."

"Shall I change targets, sir?" Bon asked with a quick glance at the screen.

"How much time, Chief?"

"Countdown in thirty seconds. Firing in one minute."

Ishiwa nodded. "Maintain original target, Bon. Lock on that new ship as your secondary target."

"Closing speed with secondary target point-zero-one to the minute," Bon said quietly.

"Chief, I want two missiles fired at the secondary target in record time. Then we're going to max speed and get out of here."

"Beginning countdown. Thirty seconds to firing."

"Secondary closing at point-zero-one-five."

"Twenty seconds to firing."

Ishiwa counted silently in unison with Chief Kleber.

"Ten seconds . . . nine . . . eight . . . Automatic control sequence initiated. Four, three, two . . . Missile away! Time to target twenty-seven minutes."

"Engage secondary target," Ishiwa ordered.

"Secondary closing at point-zero-one-nine, sir," Bon reported. "They're definitely accelerating, Captain."

"Fire when ready, Chief."

Olmis fired its second and third missile within seven minutes after firing the first, a full two minutes faster than the crew had ever fired during a drill.

"Full speed, Lieutenant." Ishiwa stared at the nav panel. "Course five-nine-three-fifty-one by six-zero-two-hundred."

Bon relayed the orders then looked at Ishiwa with admiration. "That will keep us in tracking range, won't it, sir?"

"Yes it will, Bon. I hate to fire and not know if we struck a hit."

Eleven minutes later the approaching Sondak blip disappeared from the screen. Ishiwa smiled with satisfaction. "Good shooting, Kleber."

"Thank you, sir," she said, returning his smile.

Eight minutes after that, the original target blip disappeared also. "Two out of two," Ishiwa said softly. It was almost too good to be true. When he finally spoke, his voice trembled. "Lieutenant, inform the crew that *Olmis* has made her first two kills."

Cheering rang through the ship when the announcement was made. Men and women hugged each other in joyous celebration, each sensing in some intrinsic way the importance of this moment for them and *Olmis*.

Ishiwa sensed it, too. No matter how glorious a record *Olmis* would go on to compile, this first strike against Sondak would always be remembered as her baptism in glory.

"Course, sir?"

Bon's question broke the spell. When Ishiwa looked at his junior he suddenly realized that Bon was not fully sharing in their joy, as though he failed to understand the emotional importance of this moment for the whole crew. That saddened Ishiwa and puzzled him, but he attributed Bon's apparent lack of feeling to his kyosei training.

"Return to our original course of opportunity," Ishiwa ordered. "Then go get some rest, Lieutenant. You've put in a full watch."

After the crew returned to normal running status, Ishiwa signalled their success to Yakusan. Then for several hours he sat almost alone on the command deck savoring the victory and anticipating the continuing havoc they would wreak on Sondak in the coming months.

* * *

"I still don't understand what took them so long," Lucky said quietly. "If she knew they were going to grant us the methane exporting rights, why didn't she just say so?"

"Proctor Leri works with her people," Morning Song said as he strapped himself into the couch beside Lucky. "She explained to me the necessity of letting them reach an understanding on their own. Only then was she free to make the final decision."

Lucky accepted Morning Song's explanation with a shrug and turned to prepare *Graycloud* for launch. So long as the matter was settled, he didn't really care how it had been done. All he wanted to do was leave Cloise and never come back.

Proctor Leri and the rest of her kind gave him chills and nightmares like no other aliens he had ever met. Even the crab-like Castorians hadn't bothered him. But Leri-the-snake? Lucky shivered. "Are you ready to launch?" he asked.

"Ready, Captain Teeman."

"Then let's get out of here and back to Oina."

"Have you forgotten, Captain? My father wishes us to go to Patros to pick up some cargo and a passenger for delivery—"

"Maybe," Lucky said as he initiated the launch sequence. "That depends on some cousin of his coming across with the credits, doesn't it?"

"Indeed it does. However, as soon as we are in a position to communicate with Oina, I recommend that we request his pleasure in this matter."

"His pleasure right now is making a baby."

"Do not be sarcastic, Captain. Mating is a very serious matter for us, more serious than you can hope to understand."

"I can see why. Takes a lot of thinking to copulate without ceasing for a whole year."

Graycloud's engines fired and lifted them quickly into Cloise's thick atmosphere. Morning Song sat quietly in his chair until they broke into open space and the acceleration compensators dampened the g-forces on them.

"We do not copulate for a year," he said finally, the anger clear in his voice.

"I know. I know." Lucky didn't want to hear this lecture again. "Your people copulate once and grow the baby together for a year. But you're still hooked together, and it looks like—"

"Enough, Captain Teeman. We do not ridicule the insensitive way humans reproduce without mutual support of the parents. Do not ridicule our way. No biological system is perfect, but if it ensures the continuation of the species, why do you humans consider it a subject of derision? Because it is different from your own biology?"

Lucky knew he had been rude, and he didn't really mean to offend Morning Song. "I'm sorry," he said sincerely. "I guess I just haven't been as tolerant as I should have been—about anything." When Morning Song didn't reply, he continued. "Blame it on this stupid war. I do. Ever since it started, the only time I've been happy was when I was addicted to the gorlet."

"An unfortunate occurrence," Morning Song said.

"Damned right it was. But not a bad one. It gave me a week's peace. . . . Anyway, I really am sorry about what I said."

"You could not help yourself, Captain. Humans rarely can. It is one of those strange phenomenon of nature that most members of your species seem incapable of ruling their tongues—or their lives—with the very intelligence which has made them so powerful. Do you not agree?"

Lucky laughed. "Who wouldn't? I mean it wasn't exactly our intelligence that started this war, was it? The Ukes are looking for some kind of emotional revenge for what Sondak did to them in the last war. And that war was based on emotion more than anything else. Sondak attacked the Ukes because they were afraid the Ukes were getting too powerful and adventurous."

"And greedy," Morning Song added, "if I remember my history correctly."

"Oh, that's always a factor," Lucky said, "but it's not limited to humans. Greed took us to Cloise, didn't it?"

"Not greed, Captain. Business."

"Sure, a chance to make some credits, a chance for your father and me to get a little richer. That's greed, my friend."

"That is business, Captain, and I hardly know you well enough to consider you my friend."

"Well, excuse me."

For more than an hour neither of them spoke as *Graycloud* accelerated out of Cloise's system. Morning Song's comment had hurt Lucky's feelings in a way he could barely admit to himself. Yet the problem had risen like a shadow over his life, a shadow that would not, could not be dispelled. Lucky had no friends.

Marsha had been his friend as well as his partner and lover. But Marsha was gone. Delightful Childe was his new business partner, but Morning Song's words made him wonder if Delightful Childe considered him a friend. Probably not, he thought.

It had been a long time since Lucky had felt so lonely, so long ago that remembering it was like looking through a narrow port hole into his past. His father had died first, then his mother, but he hadn't missed the father who had rarely been there. His mother . . . his mother had been far more than that. She had been his friend and advisor, the person to whom he could tell everything. When she had died, he had been truly alone, and felt the same sense of isolation he felt now.

"Perhaps it is my turn to apologize," Morning Song said, interrupting Lucky's thoughts. "My father told me he considers you a friend. Thus, I should at least attempt to do the same. However, I must admit to you again that it is extremely difficult for me to understand you, much less to make this offer."

"Don't bother," Lucky said from the depths of his self-pity. "The strain might be too much for you."

"That is exactly the kind of statement that makes it so difficult for me. Why can you not accept my apology and acknowledge the sincerity of my intentions?"

"Because I'm an emotional, suspicious human being whose feelings are easily injured and slowly healed."

Morning Song gave a long fluttering sigh through his wrinkled proboscis. "I shall try harder," he said finally.

"You do that," Lucky said, still unwilling to pull himself back to civility. "In the meantime let's try to contact Oina. We should be far enough away from the interference of Cloise's sun by now to hit that long-band relay station of yours off of Satterfield."

7

Throughout dinner Mica had listened with rapt attention to the conversation between her father and Henley Stanmorton. Much to her surprise they were soon calling each other by their given names as though they were old friends.

In a way they were, she realized, for they had a base of similar experiences from the last war that bound them together in an elemental way. If she hadn't been with her father during the battle for Matthews, she would never have understood the camaraderie they shared.

"The general population is eager for more real news from the fighting," Henley said as he finished his dinner. "They just don't believe the official Efcorps news releases from the Service, so I'd like to give them as much as I can, Josiah."

"You think the Service is lying to them?" Mica asked.

"No, just holding back a lot of facts, and feeding Efcorps information that is pretty old."

"Come," Gilbert said, "Let's adjourn this discussion to softer chairs and wine." As he led them into the family room, he

asked, "How soon do you expect to get out there?" For the first
time in months he felt free to relax a little and he did not want
to rush this discussion.

"Depends on the goldsleeves, Josiah. You couldn't give
them a little nudge, could you? All those deskbound officers
seem to think I'd be safer sitting around Service Press Center
than out where the action is, and I can't convince them
otherwise."

"That's my doing, I'm afraid," Gilbert said. "I advised the
Joint Chiefs to restrict civilian coverage of the war until we
could organize a more efficient Information Office."

"That's not fair, Josiah. Not fair at all. I know the service has
its own tellers there, but I—"

Gilbert held up his hand with a laugh. "All right. You don't
have to convince me. If anything, our discussion before dinner
made up my mind for me." He wasn't being quite truthful, but
he wanted Henley to suggest the direction of the conversation.
"How soon do you want to go out, and where do you want to
go?"

"Sutton. Immediately."

"That's crazy," Mica said. "The Ukes control Sutton."

"Only parts of it." Henley turned to her with a twinkle in his
eyes, "And I understand that we have some troops there
putting up pretty good resistance."

"I still think it's crazy." There's something else going on here,
she thought. But what?

"So do I," Gilbert added, "but I also understand why you
want to go." He leaned intently forward, cupping his wine
glass in both hands. "I can get you there, Henley. At least I can
give you a ninety-five percent chance of getting there. We're
sneaking supplies in almost every week. But I can't guarantee
getting you off planet when you're ready to leave."

"I understand that. That's part of the business," he said
calmly, but the thought of being stranded on Sutton did bother
him. It was easier to be near the action when he knew he could
escape if he had to.

"Fair enough. Mica, you arrange transport for Henley, the
best and fastest we have going."

"You're both crazy. You know that, don't you?" Mica
suspected her father wasn't finished playing with this idea, and
could not figure out where he was headed with it.

"Don't be insubordinate," Gilbert said with a smile, "or I'll send you as Henley's guide." There, he thought, let's see what she does with that.

"Oh, I'd be a great help. Sure I would. One Service communications officer with no dirtside experience leading a crotchety old teller across the wilds of Sutton."

"You mean one smiling, prime-of-life reporter," Henley said, "led by his charming and fearless guide to witness the retaking of Sutton."

They all laughed, but only briefly. "It will be a long time before we can even think about retaking Sutton," Gilbert said quietly. "We don't have the men, the equipment, or the ships to do much more than defend the systems we now hold. And most of those systems are vulnerable."

"Like the rest of polar systems?" Henley offered.

"Yes. And those are only the beginning of the problem. The reinforcements we send there will surely be needed elsewhere."

"Could I go there first? I mean to Yaffee or Satterfield, or wherever it is you expect the Ukes to hit next?"

Gilbert smiled. This was the request he had been hoping for. "You can and you may. But getting you from there to Sutton will be more difficult than getting you straight to Sutton."

"But why? I mean aren't they in the same—"

"Because officially we're not shipping anything from the other polar systems to Sutton. And for obvious security reasons, wherever you go you won't be allowed to tell anyone exactly where you are. Unless we make special arrangements, of course. No sense in giving that information away."

For a moment Henley felt a chill at the thought of what he was getting himself into. But it was an old familiar chill, and he had never let it stop him before. "I'm willing to take my chances on whatever situations I encounter just so long as I can report what I see."

"You can report it all, Henley, subject to the usual military restrictions."

"Pardon me," Mica said, "but I have to ask Mr. Stanmorton why he wants to take these risks?"

"It's my job. It's what I do—report on important events, I

mean." He saw the quizzical look still on her face. "Is that so strange to you, Captain?"

"Yes, it is. However, I suppose it is none of my business if you want to risk your life doing something as absurd—"

"You're right. It is none of your business." Why, Henley wondered, did she still have such a strange opinion of him?

Gilbert didn't want them to change the direction of the conversation. "You know," he said slowly, "I've been thinking about sending someone to Satterfield who would report personally to me. How would you like to be that someone, Henley? We could give you a reserve warrant—"

"Now wait a minute, Admiral. You want me to rejoin the Service? Why?"

"Look at it this way, Henley. As special liaison from my office, you would have freedom of movement that no civilian is going to have, and, you would have access to sources otherwise closed to you. That isn't such a bad offer, is it? Might even send Mica as your aide," he added, throwing the rest of his idea into her lap.

"Father!"

"Hush, Mica. You already told me you wanted to go out there. Haven't changed your mind, have you?"

"Make me an officer? With an aide?" Henley asked with a grin. He realized that Gilbert had to be joking now. "I don't know. Is she a good aide?"

"The best."

Mica couldn't believe what she was hearing. "Father," she said quickly, "I think we should discuss this in private."

"I don't. Not only could you serve as Henley's aide, you could also be of assistance to Commander Rochmon." Gilbert's smile grew. "He's been complaining that he needs to send more experienced people out there."

"I'm totally confused," Mica said with a shake of her head. "How could I serve as Mr. Stanmorton's aide and also contribute to Cryptography's efforts?"

"I'm confused, too," Henley admitted. Admiral Gilbert obviously was not joking, yet his proposal was sounding wilder by the minute. Him an officer? With Mica Gilbert as his aide? "You're serious, aren't you? What do you really want?"

Gilbert looked at them happily. "I want two people I can trust to send me direct information on what is happening out there, information that doesn't have to go through channels. I want some honest evaluations of morale and readiness from you, Henley—and from you, Mica, I want military evaluations of POLFLEET's officers and leadership."

Suddenly Mica understood. POLFLEET was still the command of his heart, and he wanted to know how it was doing without him. If he hadn't been her father, she might have felt insulted by the suggestion that she spend her time spying for him.

"But why as an officer?" Henley asked. "I still don't see what real advantages that would give me. And I certainly see some distinct disadvantages."

"As Chief Warrant Officer Henley, Tellers Corps, you don't think you would have some advantages over a civilian reporter?"

Now Henley understood. CWO's in the Tellers Corps were almost autonomous. "Putting it that way does make a difference. I would have access to reports from all the combat tellers in the sector, wouldn't I?"

"Exactly. And, Mica," he said, turning to her, "Henley wouldn't actually outrank you, if that is part of your concern."

"It wasn't. Or maybe it was. I don't know. But I do know that this is the strangest idea I've ever heard from you."

"Perhaps it is, but this isn't the first time I've thought about it."

"I suspected that," Henley said with a smile. "Who did you have in mind before I came along?"

Gilbert returned his smile. "That was the problem, Henley. Before you wandered into my office last week, this was nothing more than a notion I had of something I ought to do. After you left I dug out some of your stories—"

"Those old *Flag Report* you sent me for!"

"Yes, Mica. Read seven or eight of them, Henley, and they were even better than I remembered them. That's when I decided to delay our meeting. I wanted to be sure I could make this offer before I got your reaction."

"I should have known," Mica said suddenly. Then she turned to Henley. "This morning he told me he wished we had someone like you on Satterfield. We were so busy, I didn't have a chance to think about it."

Henley shook his head. "Who'd have guessed it? I mean, I

thought you were joking at first, Josiah. I really did. Then when I realized you were serious, I didn't know what to say. I still don't. But I'm certainly not closed to the idea."

"And you, Mica?" Gilbert asked.

She looked at both of them with a quiet grin. "You two beat anything I've heard lately," she said, "but it looks like I'll have to agree with Mr. Stanmorton—"

"Henley," he said.

"All right. I'll agree with Henley. I'm not closed to the idea either. However, I don't want to go out there without some very specific sense of what you want. Unlike Henley, I can't just go wandering around looking for stories."

"Good," Gilbert said as he rose to refill their glasses. "Now there's just one more element you need to know before we discuss the details of what I want you to do. Tomorrow Polar Fleet, Border Fleet, and Central Fleet will be combined under one command—mine."

* * *

Civil protests and demonstrations were nothing new to the planets of the United Central Systems, but they had been rare occurrences on the governing planet of Gensha—until now.

Protest meetings involving thousands of citizens in a few scattered cities had evolved into demonstrations involving millions in almost every major city and town. Gensha's people were angry—angry about rationing, and angry about conscription of their young people into the military, and most surprisingly, angry about the defeat at Matthews system. Bridgeforce had declared all information about the Matthews battle classified and restricted, but the people had seemed to have learned about it almost immediately after it had happened.

No one was sure how the general population had gotten that information, but many members of the military suspected that Marshall Judoff and her rising kyosei faction were responsible. She had withdrawn her forces from support of the war as was her right under the U.C.S. Charter of Confederation, but to most military officers, including Frye Charltos, she was considered a traitor to their cause.

Even more to Frye Charltos's dismay, Bridgeforce was allowing itself to be distracted by the riotous mood of the people. Admiral Tuuneo, Supreme Director of Bridgeforce, had even gone so far as to suggest a delay in implementing Frye's plan for the further invasion of Sondak's polar systems.

Such a suggestion had to be protested in person and Frye had immediately requested a meeting with Tuuneo. The admiral had granted his request, but after an hour of trying to make his case, Frye was becoming more and more frustrated. It appeared that Tuuneo was not going to relent. Yet Frye had no choice except to persist.

"Sir," Frye said slowly, "delay will only give Sondak more time to reinforce their defenses. Because of Vice-Marshall Yozel's reluctance to commit the full weight of his forces, we have lost precious time fighting for control of Sutton. If Ely hadn't been killed, this wouldn't have happened."

"As I have told you, Commander, Bridgeforce is well aware of your feelings about Vice-Marshall Yozel's tactics. And we will all miss Commander Ely's valuable services. However, that does not alter my suggestion."

Frye refused to be put off. "Surely, sir, we cannot afford further delay. With Yozel's ships added to the invasion fleet I propose, we can sweep through Sondak's defenses in a matter of months. If we wait, it may take us years. Or, worse, we might never—"

"That is quite enough, Commander," Tuuneo said sternly. "Do not forget that it is I who supported you, and continue to support you and your plans. However, I alone am not Bridgeforce, nor can I demand that we follow your schedule. Be patient."

"Patience could cost us victory, sir," Frye said. He did not want to anger Tuuneo, but he knew they had to begin the polar operation immediately. Hesitancy would be disastrous to all the hopes he had of striking a decisive counterblow to Sondak. The losses could be extremely high in such an operation, but the final defeat of Sondak would be worth any price in blood.

"The hunks will buy us time, Commander. Already Captain Ishiwa has struck his first blow against Sondak. Five more ships have now completed training and are following his lead. We are accelerating production and training to send the maximum number of hunks to destroy Sondak shipping in the polar sector."

Frye sighed with weariness. Tuuneo spoke with certainty about what the hunks could accomplish, yet Frye knew that nothing was certain. The strength of Sondak's forces was already on the rise again, and time was something the U.C.S. did not have to waste. "With all due respect, Admiral, it will take more than twenty hunks, or even two hundred, to buy us the time we need."

8

Generals Mari and Porras sat huddled under a stretchlon shelter by the base of the cliff listening to Warrant Officer Caffey. A steady, soaking rain beat on their canopy making it hard for them to hear Caffey's words.

Beyond them in the center of the broad canyon sat Caffey's aging, lightspeed freighter. Its flat, space-scarred hull looked almost natural against the rocky cliff on the other side of the canyon as troops unloaded much needed supplies from its holds.

"And you intercepted their transmission?" Porras asked.

"Yes, sir," Caffey said. "It was broadcast in the clear about an hour after *Taylor* got hit. The Ukes claimed to have destroyed two of our ships, but they didn't hang around to check or they would have known that *Barterer* only suffered minor damage. Whatever they hit her with knocked out her navigation gear, but Captain Arden got his secondary navs working pretty quick after that."

"What happened to the *Taylor*?" Mari asked.

"She was running straight for the Ukes when she caught it. Lost her whole command section. Twenty-seven good men and women dead and gone," Caffey said with a shake of her head. "Took us two days to get back and find her, but we rescued the rest of the crew and put them aboard the *Lipscomb*. They dropped in over on Elias about an hour before we landed here."

Mari liked this young warrant officer with her matter-of-fact way of giving her report. He knew enough about the problems of space navigation to know their rescue effort had been anything but as simple as she made it sound. Ships traveling at lightspeed weren't like boats on a lake. One didn't just stop, turn around, and head back.

"Some of them were hurt pretty bad, so *Lipscomb* might be leaving you some casualties."

"How did you get through the Ukes here?" Mari asked, looking up at the rolling thunderheads.

"The Ukes are funny about that, sir. They're pretty thin up there, except for a cluster of ships over the north pole. Don't know why they're not patrolling more, but I'm not going to complain about it, either. After we located their ships, I just kind of skimmed in on the equatorial plane like I did last trip then cut the atmosphere real slow so there wasn't much burn for them to see. Pretty simple, really."

"Your last trip?" Mari asked. "You mean to tell me you've made this run before?"

"Twice." Caffey's grin made her pale eyes sparkle. "First time we came in was the day after the invasion. That was pretty darned scary, I don't mind telling you, sir. Had to hunt for almost half a day to find Colonel Archer's beacon that time—"

"Colonel Archer?"

"Commander of the Ninth Militia Legion over on Elias," Porras said, "the one I told you about. A damned good man."

Mari had to think a second before he could sort Archer's name from all those Porras had given him. "Right," he said. "Go ahead, Caffey."

"Anyway," Caffey continued, "I found his beacon and set us down right next to a damned volcano."

"Mount Fashondua," Porras said. "It's the only active volcano on Elias."

"Archer was there to meet us, so we dumped our load of ammunition as fast as we could and blasted out of there. Burned engines getting back to Satterfield. That was the first run, and the hardest. Made the second run three weeks later—mostly heavy weapons on that one. Which reminds me. Admiral Pajandcan gave me a message to be passed on to the highest commander."

"General Mari is Planetary Commander," Porras said.

"Looks like I came to the right place," Caffey said with a look of delight that suddenly made her look ten years younger.

"When did Pajandcan take over POLFLEET?" Mari asked.

"Right before I left, sir."

"I'll take the message," he said, holding out his hand.

"It's verbal, General. Old Pancan didn't want to take any chances." Caffey smiled, then quickly raised a hand to cover it. "Guess I shouldn't call her that in front of you, should I? But that's what everyone used to call her when I served under her a couple of years ago."

Caffey took a breath, as though waiting for a response. When none came, she went on. "Anyway, the admiral wants you to know 'unofficially' that she will continue to send you whatever supplies you need that she can spare. Officially, she is supposed to use all equipment and supplies at her disposal for the defense of Satterfield and Bakke."

General Porras gave a low whistle. "Sounds like we're the holding action for a while."

Mari nodded. "It certainly does. And it makes good sense. The more Ukes we tie up here, the fewer there will be to use against the other systems." He rubbed his face, then looked up. "But that's none of your worry, Caffey. Thanks for the information. I have some official reports for Admiral Pajandcan to send back with you, but I—"

"Can't do it, General. Sorry, but those are the admiral's orders. Nothing but verbal reports. Too risky."

"Damn," Mari cursed. "How are we— Oh, never mind. Give Admiral Pajandcan this message. Tell her we need light weapons more than heavy ones, transport more than anything else—squad skimmers if she can dig some up—and as many battle rations as she can possibly spare. Tell her we have plenty of ammunition for the time being. Then tell her we'll hold out here until the Ukes cut off our last trigger finger. Got that?"

"You bet, sir." Caffey glanced out into the canyon, then up at the sky. "Looks like this storm front's about to pass, sir, and I'd like to use it for take-off cover if I can. If you don't have anything else for me, I'll get back to my ship."

"Just one more thing," Mari said. "Tell Old Pancan I said you deserve a promotion."

"Thanks, General, but I can't go any higher. I'm already a

Chief Warrant Four. The Service would have to create a new rank just for me, and I don't think—"

"Or commission you," Mari said.

"Not me, General. Begging your pardon, sir, but most commissioned officers I've had to deal with are a pain in the flaming tail section. I'd just as soon stay a warrant."

Mari laughed and admired her honesty. "All right, Caffey. But tell the admiral what I said anyway."

"Will do, sir." Caffey stood as high as the stretchlon would let her and pulled on her poncho. "General Mari. General Porras," she said with a casual salute for each of them. "Give 'em hell." Without waiting for a reply she ran out into the rain toward her ship.

"What the service wouldn't give for a thousand like her," Porras said quietly.

"How soon before we leave?" Mari asked, his thoughts already jumping ahead. Something Caffey had said had given him an idea.

Porras looked out at the troops loading the skimmers. "Looks like they're almost finished. I'd say we can get back to headquarters any time."

"Good. I want full reports on all supplies and equipment received today by all units so we can plan redistribution. Then I want you to get me over to see Colonel Archer."

"That's pretty dangerous, sir. You're talking about zig-zagging through fifteen hundred kilometers of territory the Ukes pretty much control, then another eight hundred kilometers across the Sea of Sabrina. I'd advise against it."

"Dammit, Porras, if I remember correctly, you told me that Archer was irreplaceable—some kind of hero among his troops. Am I right?"

"Yes, sir. He's an extremely charismatic leader."

"Then that means we can't risk losing him just to bring him here. And I can't risk sending you, because you're holding this whole show together. That leaves me."

"But I could go!" Porras exclaimed.

Mari sighed harshly. "Look, Porras, you were doing quite well before you rescued me, because this is your planet. You know the units and commanders planetwide. That's why—"

"As you were, sir," Porras said hotly. "I didn't send men into Esqueleada to die rescuing you just so you could run off and get yourself killed. I need your experience and assistance. This planet needs you."

"And the only way I can put that experience to work and be of real value to you," Mari said, "is to evaluate first hand every situation I can. Get me transportation to Elias."

The gentle roar of Caffey's ship taking off made it impossible for Porras to answer. When the noise finally subsided, it was Mari who spoke. "I understand your concern, Porras, and I appreciate it. But as of this moment, you are the Planetary Commander. I am now your senior services observer, number one liaison, technical advisor, and general morale booster. Until such time as I choose to relieve you of command, you are the ultimate Sondak military authority on Sutton responsible for all things except me."

Porras looked at him for a long moment and finally a thin smile split his pale face. "All right, General. Pack your kit and we'll see if we can't find you a ride to Archer's piece of the action."

*　*　*

Proctor Leri Gish Geril had underestimated her people. They fully supported the idea of selling methane to the Oinaise rather than to the humans from Sondak just as she expected them to.

But much to her surprise, almost immediately after the Oinaise and his human companion left Cloise, a delegation of ten directors urgently requested a meeting with her to propose new measures for Cloise's defense. To fully honor their unusual initiative, she received them in her private audience chamber.

"Peace to you, Proctor," Ranas said after the directors had entered and settled around the walls of the chamber.

"And to you all," Leri said. She still felt tense in Ranas's presence. It was no longer a secret that the young historian, Weecs, was her lover, and many suspected that the last guplings she had borne were his. The fact that Ranas, her first and only legal mate, seemed to accept that relationship with equanimity only served to make her more uncomfortable.

"We have come for advice, Proctor," Ranas said, observing the formalities.

"My life belongs to Cloise," she answered the ritual. "My advice is the people's."

"Then let us be frank, Proctor," Ranas said with a suddeness that startled her. "After much discussion and consultation with the Isthians, we have reached a difficult decision. We wish to suggest that it would be highly appropriate for us to request armed defense vessels from the Oinaise as partial payment for our methane."

Ranas said it so simply that it took a second or two for Leri to believe what they were suggesting. "Buy alien arms for the defense of Cloise?" she asked finally. "Buy the weapons of war from the soulless Oinaise? What obscenity is this?"

"No obscenity, Proctor. We fired the surface to help rescue you from Exeter the Castorian and to drive off Sondak's pirates. Why should other defenses be an obscenity?"

"The question remains valid, Ranas. However, we will set it aside for the purpose of discussion." She paused and wondered what the Confidantes would think of such a proposal. They would surely disapprove, and they were the final authority on all questions of ethos.

"If Cloise were to propose such a bargain to the Oinaise," she continued, "and if they were to agree, how would we utilize such vessels? Except for a few Isthian scientists and half-a-hundred historians, I know of no one willing to leave the surface, much less serve time in space."

"We propose that the Oinaise employ suitable crews to serve us in this capacity. The Isthians believe there are humans who would do this for recompense."

"Disgusting!" Leri was revolted by the idea. "Humans will sell themselves to anyone for anything," she said. "However, why should we sully ourselves by becoming party to such a despicable transaction?" She could almost guess what their answer would be, and in an odd way she was proud of them for being able to deal with a concept so basically antithetical to everything the Elett had taught them and her people believed.

"That is why we came to you, Proctor. We all agree that it is far better to sell our methane to the Oinaise. However, we recognize that Sondak might not accept our decision and seek to take the methane by force. If such should occur, we would need protection—protection of a kind we are not equipped to provide for ourselves."

Leri knew they had come to a wise decision, but the

necessities that had driven them to make it sent a madness through her brain. Once she had dreamed of leading her people in peace. Now she would agree to bring the instruments of war right to the entrances of their tunnels. All because of those soulless creatures who call themselves humans.

9

When mapping the belly of Caveness Galaxy someone with an odd sense of humor had looked at the long string of stars that formed its internal arm and named it the Great Sperm. Eight thousand parsecs behind the head of the Great Sperm lay Biery, the first settled star system. In the middle of its tail lay Nordeen, the capital planet of Sondak. At the very end of its tail, lay the Coulter star circled by the planet appropriately named, Summer.

Now as Scientific-Security Inspector Thel Janette watched Summer grow like a pink ball in the viewport, she wondered what had ever led the first pioneers to this remote tail of the Sperm.

Summer's greatest assets were a stable orbit, a warm, but relatively pleasant climate, and an overwhelming abundance of mineral resources. Iron, nickel, platinum, tin, gold, copper, zinc, bauxite, and silver were just a few of its plentiful minerals. Around the planet, lakes of sweet crude oil bubbled out of the ground, and rich seams of coal cropped up as naturally as the almost daily rain showers—all attesting to Summer's once lush climate and vegetation.

Janette dozed for the next few hours, and awoke only when the crew announced they were entering Summer's atmosphere. As the ship finally made its way through a bank of heavy pink clouds, Janette watched Summer's unremarkable terrain slip by.

Its surface was dotted with hundreds of thousands of tiny

lakes and ponds that sparkled with reflected sunlight. Yet Janette knew that most of those lakes were so saturated with dissolved minerals as to make them useless. Fresh water was scarce and difficult to find, and was recognized by even the earliest pioneers as the most valuable commodity on the planet.

With no seas, no spectacular mountains or thrilling vistas, Summer looked very uninteresting from the air. Most of the vegetation covering its monotonously rolling hills and broad flat plains consisted of low-lying shrubs, grasses, and thorny succulents in endless varieties of grey-green growth. Millions of square kilometers of its surface had been mapped in great detail, but by order of Summer's owner, had never been explored or touched by humanity.

Drautzlab Corporation totally owned and governed Summer. Because of that, Sondak's government had limited influence there. Yet in addition to the minerals, Summer contained other vital keys to Sondak's future. Only seventeen million humans and aliens lived there. A million of those were miners and drillers, working for Drautzlab's exporting division. They lived where the minerals were. Most of the remaining sixteen million lived on the low plain around Lake Roxie, the only freshwater lake of any size on the planet.

The place they lived was called Drautzlab, not because of any egotism on the part of its founder, Karl Drautz, but through common usage. When anyone from Summer was visiting other parts of the galaxy and was asked where he lived, 'Drautzlab' said it all. Many an immigrant arriving to work there had been surprised to discover that the planet actually had a name of its own, and the long city around Lake Roxie did, also. The city was officially named Lena after Karl's wife who proudly outlived him and ran the corporation until she died at a board meeting a month past her one hundred sixty-seventh birthday.

Drautzlab was actually five hundred semi-autonomous laboratories each with complete housing, maintenance, medical, and in some cases, even recreational facilities for its staff members and their families. There the employees of Dr. Caugust Drautz—oldest surviving child of Karl and Lena, and now controlling stockholder—worked on major weapons projects for Sondak's Combined Armed Services.

Drautzlab developed ideas, cultivated research into new technology, and built prototypes of weapons and weapon systems. Those weapons and systems which proved successful and useful to the military were later manufactured by the thousands of independent contractors whose planets surrounded Lake Roxie, or by factories on thirty other plants that eagerly bid for the privilege of building Drautzlab designs.

Caugust Drautz also prided himself in developing individuals as well as ideas. He had been explicit about that when Janette first met him, and now she was bringing him news not designed to please him. Ayne Wallen, a scientist Dr. Drautz had personally recruited, had disappeared.

As far as Sci-Sec could determine, Wallen was on his way to the U.C.S. They had managed to follow him as far as Patros, but by the time Janette and her team had traced his movement to the Oinaise broker known as Xindella, Wallen was gone. In his head were the essential equations he had discovered at Drautzlab for the development of Sondak's Ultimate Weapon.

Hours later as she waited in Drautz's office with Dr. Sjean Birkie, Janette wondered how Drautz would take the news.

"Ah, here she is," Caugust said as he entered the room.

Sjean smiled to herself as Inspector Janette rose to greet Caugust, and again marveled that Janette, as small and almost dainty as she was, could have such a commanding presence.

"I bring you bad news," Janette said simply. "Wallen has eluded Sci-Sec and appears to be headed for the U.C.S."

"As we suspected," Caugust said gruffly, taking a seat in front of his desk and allowing her to sit behind it. "However, as Dr. Birkie can tell you, he may not be quite the threat we first suspected."

"Why is that, Doctor? Have you discovered a flaw in his equations?"

Sjean almost laughed. "No," she said, catching herself. She didn't want Inspector Janette thinking she took this too lightly. "I think Caugust is referring to the fact that so far we have only managed to destroy a great deal of equipment in trying to make them practical, but we're not sure—"

"Our tests are inclusive," Caugust interrupted. "Dr. Birkie has proven that the effects Ayne predicted can be demonstrated on a small scale. However, to make a reciprocal action weapon that will function outside the lab may not be possible."

"Why?" Janette sensed some evasion here and wanted none of it. She knew enough theoretical physics to understand that reciprocal action at a distance was a bizzare concept, but she also knew that Drautzlab believed in it. "If you have proven his equations valid, what is the problem with building the weapon?"

"I thought you didn't want to know too much," Sjean said.

"Correct. However, if I understand the difficulties you are encountering, I can better understand what Wallen will be facing. That might help Sci-Sec narrow its search for him."

"But you said he'd escaped to the U.C.S."

"Correct again, Dr. Birkie. However, Sci-Sec is not totally powerless in Uke systems."

Sjean wasn't surprised. Sci-Sec seemed to know more than any bureaucracy had a right to.

Caugust cleared his throat and looked at Sjean before speaking to Janette. Sjean had seen that look enough times in staff meetings to know he wanted her to keep quiet.

"The main problem Dr. Birkie and her team face is a matter of scale, Inspector. Theoretically we could build a device which when fired into a star would destroy that star and almost simultaneously destroy a reciprocally seeded star somewhere along the same spacetime curve. Theoretically." He took a deep breath and Janette spoke before he could continue.

"How large a device would that take?" she asked.

"Medium cruiser size," Caugust said, "but that's not the problem. We now think we know how to *build* the device, but we do not know how to *aim* it over any distance."

The look in his eyes told Sjean it was her turn. "We could destroy neighboring stars, even ones up to one hundred parsecs apart if we had a clear line of sight. At least, I believe we could. Anything beyond that is too speculative even for us."

Janette was puzzled. This is not what she expected. "What would you need to test this?" she asked.

"We'd damned well have to test it outside of the galaxy," Caugust said quickly.

Suddenly Janette understood. "Because you cannot predict exactly what will happen? Is that the problem?"

"Exactly."

Caugust had obviously taken control again, so Sjean let

herself relax a little and watch Inspector Janette whose skintight black suit seemed to make her look even smaller as she hunched over in thought. For almost a full minute no one said anything.

"Outside the galaxy," Janette whispered, "with enough ships and equipment . . . All right," she said looking up at them with a smile. "I believe this will help us." After another pause, her smile disappeared. "But what about you? Where will you test your device?"

"In the first place, we don't yet have a working device for that kind of test," Caugust said. "In the second place, we are not sure we are going to test at all."

"But you have to!" Janette exclaimed.

"We do not, Inspector."

"If the Ukes develop such a weapon and we don't . . ."

"I don't think they will," Caugust said slowly. "They will be faced with the same problems, and will come to the same conclusions. Testing a star-buster may just be too dangerous."

Janette reigned in her anger with the control born of long experience. If she told the right people in the right places, even the autonomous Drautzlab could be forced to do things it did not want to do. This was not the place to argue with Dr. Drautz about it. "We can discuss that later," she said firmly. "However, I suspect that someone will test this weapon on a suitable pair of stars."

Sjean blinked and shivered. Inspector Janette's implication was all too clear. She meant to force Drautzlab to test.

"And if someone refuses?" Caugust asked.

"Someone else will agree," Janette said with a cold smile. "In either case, Sondak will determine the efficacy of this weapon before the Ukes do. I promise you that."

Sjean shivered again, and for the first time she regretted devoting her life to science. "We called it the Ultimate Weapon," she said quietly, "because we thought it would finally put an end to destruction. Now we're beginning to believe that it might lead to destruction on a scale we cannot control. And you, you are telling us . . ." Her sentence died in a wave of emotion that filled her throat.

"I am telling you both that this is too important to be left alone. You must proceed with your research and tests."

"What the hell," Caugust said with a mock grin on his ruddy

face, "if we blow up this galaxy, there are always others out there for someone to live in."

* * *

Olmis came to a stop one parsec away from Satterfield. For the last fifty hours Captain Ruto Ishiwa had been decelerating in normal space while monitoring Sondak navigation signals on the approach to Satterfield. In a few more hours he would be ready to strike.

"Why are we waiting?" Lieutenant Bon asked.

Ishiwa shook his head. "It is customary," he said slowly, "to verify one's targets. We could not do that in subspace, Lieutenant, but we can here, and that is what I intend to do. However, I do not understand your impatience. Perhaps you would be so good as to explain it to me?"

"We have verified eleven Sondak ships, and two possible Castorian ships in transit to or from the system, sir," Bon said defiantly. "What more verification—"

"Outbound ship approaching, Captain," the deck piper said excitedly from his console.

"Signals, bearing, and range?" Ishiwa asked automatically.

"Hard to tell, sir," the piper said after a moment's pause. "Their signal is Sondak-type all right, but it is still fuzzy."

"Warship, Bon."

"Shall I prepare to get under way, sir?"

"Negative. We sit tight and see what happens. Range, and bearing, Piper?"

"One hundred thousand kilometers and closing, sir. Bearing zero-zero-zero-one-four. Collision course, sir. Estimate their speed at eighty thousand kilometers per hour, relative, sir."

"We must get under way, Captain."

"No. That ship is outbound, Bon." Ishiwa moved past his junior to the piper's screen. Already the adrenalin was pumping through his system. "Chief Kleber, prepare to fire on that ship as soon as possible."

"Aye-aye, sir," she said quickly before relaying his orders to her firing crew.

"Lock on target, Lieutenant."

"Yes, sir," Bon said as he took the short step to his console, "But shouldn't we—"

"Target's accelerating, Bon. They don't know we're here."

"Then why are they going so slowly this far out? I don't like it, sir."

"I do, Lieutenant." Ishiwa thought Bon meant well, but he was annoyed by his constant questioning of command decisions.

"Ready for firing sequence," Kleber said.

"Locked on target," Bon said reluctantly.

"Fire when ready," Ishiwa commanded.

Forty-three seconds later the giant missile left *Olmis's* firing tube with a jolt felt throughout the ship. Ishiwa watched their missile blip and the Sondak blip drawing together on the screen. Suddenly a third blip appeared at the edge of the screen, then a fourth across from the first, then a fifth. All were moving directly toward *Olmis*.

"Start engines," he ordered without hesitation. "Prepare fore and aft tubes, Chief." Somehow Sondak had ships waiting for them out here. But how? "All crew to battle stations," he said over the ship's loudspeaker.

As they had so many times before the crew members not already on duty dropped what they had been doing and rushed to strap themselves to their battle stations. In less than a minute the ready board lit green, signifying that they were all in their places.

"Full stations," Bon announced.

"Target is turning, sir," the piper said.

Ishiwa glanced quickly back at the screen. They were surrounded and the enemy was closing fast. *Olmis* jolted again with the initial surge of her engines.

"Under way, sir," Bon said unnecessarily. "Course?"

"All Ought!" Ishiwa said.

"All Ought," Bon repeated.

It was a dangerous decision, but Ishiwa was praying that *Olmis* could follow her missile and escape past the initial target. To choose any other direction while still accelerating would only lead them closer to the other ships.

"Enemy missiles, sir. . . . Probably spikes."

Ishiwa let his breath go. *Olmis's* triple hull had been built specifically with spikes in mind, but he was in no mood to test her strength against those swift little missiles. "All screens up and evasive action," he ordered.

Olmis twisted and turned through space as she accelerated.

Everyone not as tightly strapped to something as they should have been soon regretted their carelessness.

The Sondak target blip dulled to a faint pulse on the screen. "A hit, Captain." Seconds later they were racing away from the blip toward clear space.

Olmis shook violently, once, twice, then a third time. Ishiwa prayed quickly as he waited for a fourth hit. It never came. The attacking Sondak ships and the rest of their spikes slowly drifted back off the edge of the screen.

"Damage control reports," he said finally.

One by one the stations reported in. No serious damage. Ishiwa smiled quietly. *Olmis* had survived her second engagement and managed to damage another of Sondak's ships. His missile should have destroyed that Sondak ship, but given the circumstances, he felt satisfied.

"A short warp to the other side of Satterfield, Lieutenant," he ordered. "Maybe it isn't as crowded over there." He hoped that was true, but again he wondered how the Sondak ships had found *Olmis*. However they had done it, Ishiwa knew that he and his crew would have to be more cautious from now on.

10

"An attack?" Admiral Pajandcan asked. She felt the tension in Dawson's headquarters ship tighten with her question.

"No, ma'am," the young tech answered. "At least there's no sign of one. Looks like they only found a lone raider."

"A damned fast one," Admiral Dawson said.

"Like one of the new Uke hunks the rumors have been talking about." Pajandcan hoped she was wrong, but could tell that Dawson suspected the same thing.

"Must be, Admiral. The *Veda* bounced three spikes off its hull and never fazed it."

"So now what will you do?"

Acting Quarter Admiral Dawson scratched his rough chin

and stared up at the overhead. "Well, Admiral, I'd say we have a problem. *Veda* tried to follow the Uke, but it warped faster than anything we've got, and disappeared. Seems to me we'll just have to keep our monitors out and hope it comes back."

"What did I miss?" Admiral Dimitri asked from the doorway.

"Just about everything, Dit," Pajandcan said with a grin. "Had a Uke raider encircled, but he got a missile into the cruiser *Zephyr* and escaped."

"Balls in space! How'd he do that?"

Pajandcan laughed and the crew in the Battle Center laughed with her. Tension melted away with the laughter. "We're still trying to find out. While the techs work on that, I think the three of us need to put our heads together."

Dawson led the way down to his office with Dimitri and Pajandcan following. As soon as Pajandcan shut the bulkhead door behind her, she sighed heavily. "Gentlemen," she said as she took a seat at a small table bolted to the deck, "I didn't want to say anything in front of the crew, but it looks to me like we've got a new problem on our hands."

"One raider?" Dimitri asked.

"One very fast Uke raider impervious to spikes," Dawson said as he sat a steaming pot of gentea on the table with three mugs.

Heavy creases folded along Dimitri's face as he frowned. "That's jumping to conclusions, isn't it, Mister?"

"Dit!" Pajandcan said sharply. "I warned you not to—"

"Apologies," Dimitri said, holding up his hand. "I meant no offense to Admiral Dawson. I call everyone mister."

Dawson poured them each a mug of tea before he sat down. "No apologies necessary. In fact, I'm far more used to being called mister than admiral. But to answer your question, I don't think we're jumping to conclusions. Rochmon and his Cryptography people have been warning us since I got here that the Ukes were about to send out a new model hunk—one faster and tougher than anything either side ever had before."

"What's the latest update on it?" Pajandcan asked.

"Not much beyond what we heard before, except that they now estimate it can go from a dead stop to subspace velocities in just short of three hours."

Dimitri whistled softly. "That's twicet as fast as anything we have can do it. How in bent space do they manage that?"

"We'll probably have to capture one to find that out, Dit," Pajandcan said, "but you can bet your whistle that their dampers are more than 'twicet' as big as ours, too."

"As small as *Zephyr* reported the Uke to be, they must have turned the whole ship into part of the damping mechanism."

Pajandcan took a long sip of her tea. "You could be right, Dawson. Might send that thought back to Nordeen with your report. In the meantime, I think we need to alert all commanders about this type ship and—" Suddenly she realized she had completely overlooked something.

"What is it, Admiral?"

Rubbing her mug with both hands Pajandcan wasn't quite sure. "Dawson, didn't you say that when *Zephyr* spotted the Uke it was sitting dead in space?"

"Not exactly. *Zephyr* first picked it up as it decelerated, but by the time *Zephyr* and the other cruisers began their approach it was sitting still. Why?"

"Because," Dimitri said before Pajandcan could answer, "that's a tactic we've never seen before."

"Right on the credits, Dit!" Pajandcan shook her head. "How do you like that?"

"Surely you don't think that the Ukes—"

"Oh, but I do, Dawson. Like a flipper in space, I believe in the unexpected. I think the Ukes have decided to sit these new hunks of theirs on the edges of our shipping lanes and use us for a shooting gallery."

Dimitri whistled again. Dawson's face slowly twisted into a dark grimace.

"Makes sense, doesn't it?" Pajandcan asked.

"With a hunk that fast, sure it does," Dimitri said, "but suppose it stopped for some other reason?"

"I think Admiral Pajandcan is right—so damned right it scares me, Dimitri." Dawson drank his still steaming gentea in three quick swallows, then reached for the pot. "And I think we don't have enough ships to do anything about it."

"We never have enough ships," Dimitri said, "and we probably never will. So what's new? We plan for new Uke hunks and keep going like we always do."

Pajandcan smiled grimly. "All right. Dimitri, put your staff to work on a plan that will give us maximum possibility of dealing with these hunks. Then coordinate that plan with Admiral Dawson. Tell your people I want detailed proposals in sixty hours and not a minute later."

"Can do," Dimitri said with a brief smile.

"What about the freighters?" Dawson asked.

"That brings us to another problem," Pajandcan said. "Not only do we have to worry about our incoming freighters, but we also have to devise a way to continue unofficially shipping supplies to Sutton."

"You got General Mari's message then?"

"I did. And we're going to do our best to give him what he needs. But with this new problem—"

"Pardon me, Admiral, but what message? And where is General Mari? We were told he was dead."

"No, Dit. Mari's anything but dead. His Planetary Troops and assorted militia are skinning the Ukes one by one on Sutton. Got a message out to us on the last freight run telling us what he needs, and I aim to see that he gets it."

"Should have gotten himself out," Dimitri said. "Member of the Joint Chiefs has no business being in the middle—"

"He volunteered for that job—at least that's what Admiral Gilbert told me. I suspect they'll have to carry him out in a utility sling before he'll come out on his own."

They both smiled, but Pajandcan couldn't join them. The thought of what Mari was up against robbed her of even a little grim humor at that moment. "So," she said slowly, "in addition to everything else, we have to come up with some realistic solutions for supplying Mari. But don't forget that the Joint Chiefs have written Sutton off as an eventual loss, so we still have to keep our actions unofficial. Any suggestions?"

"Don't look at me," Dimitri said. "I may have some people on my staff who can come up with some ideas for you, but what I know about logistics you could paint on your eyeball without ruining your vision."

Dawson looked at both of them. "I don't know, Admiral. We've been using small lightspeed freighters and they've gotten in all right, but none of them can haul much in one trip."

"And you don't think it would be wise to use anything larger than those?"

"Don't have them to spare. But even if we did, I'd say it would be a lot more difficult sneaking them in."

"What about that report from Warrant Officer Caffey? Didn't she say the Ukes kept most of their ships near Sutton's north pole? Suppose we used a south polar—"

"Suppose we attack their ships," Dimitri said suddenly.

"That's insane," Dawson said. "We barely have—"

"With what?" Pajandcan was immediately intrigued with the idea of an offensive operation. The victory at Matthews had been good, but Sondak needed more. "A launchship?"

"Why not, Admiral? If the Ukes are so sure of themselves to bunch their ships, they can't be expecting us to counterattack. With the *Sherrell* and two hundred of the Messerole-class long-range fighters we could—"

"That's more than half the Messeroles we have left, Dit."

"No balls, no glory, Admiral." Suddenly Dimitri looked at her and flushed. "Sorry about that."

Pajandcan laughed. "Don't be. I think this void-brained scheme of yours just might have some merit. Wow. Wouldn't that give the Ukes a shock?"

"We'd be stripping our defenses, Admiral. Our orders are—"

"I'm fully aware of our orders, Dawson. But I'm also aware that Nordeen is halfway across the galaxy from here and Sutton's damned near right next door. And they need our help. Besides, if we can burn the Ukes there, we just might delay any attack they have planned for Satterfield and Bakke." She leaned back and smiled. "So you could say that this was just a part of our extended defense perimeter."

"I'd like to see you convince the Joint Chiefs of that one," Dimitri said. "They'd skin you alive."

"They might," Pajandcan said quickly, "But Gilbert wouldn't. He'd understand. Now that the Combined Fleets are under his command, he might even be willing to lend us some help."

Dawson shook his head. "I hate to say this, Admiral, but since I got forced into this position, more or less, I don't have anything to lose. You take POLFLEET's biggest launchship and most of her long-range fighters to attack Sutton, and I quit."

Pajandcan grinned. "You can't, Dawson. It's too late. The

new promotion list is out. I have been promoted to Fleet
Admiral, and you and Dit have both been promoted to Post
Admiral. No one is going to let a Post Admiral quit—especially
when he's no longer an 'acting' admiral."

"Dammit, that's not fair," Dawson said. "I don't have to
accept that."

"Ain't war a pain?" Dimitri grinned.

"It's a long walk back to the Gyle Coalition," Pajandcan said,
looking at Dawson and knowing he wouldn't quit. "Might as
well stay here and have some fun." She held up her mug. "To
the new admirals," she said.

Dimitri immediately raised his mug with hers. "To the new
admirals."

Dawson stared at them both, then finally shook his head
with a rueful smile. "To the new admirals," he said, "and to the
attack on the Ukes at Sutton."

*   *   *

Marsha dared not guess how her father would react if he
ever found out what she had done. The house was quiet as she
sat in his private communications room knowing this was
probably the greatest risk she had ever taken. But if her plan
succeeded, she would fill the hollowness inside her. That
reward would justify the risk.

She had to make contact with Lucky and find a way for them
to meet somewhere. Her promises to stay—promises she had
made to herself and her father—no longer mattered. There
wasn't enough father left in Commander Frye Charltos for it to
matter.

It had taken a great deal of soul-searching for her to admit
that coming back to the U.C.S. had ultimately been wrong.
The depth of her love for Lucky might never have been so
clear to her if she hadn't come back to her father. But now all
she wanted to do was get away from him, and the U.C.S., and
the war, and back to the one person in the galaxy who loved
her as much as she loved him.

With a quick flick of her wrist she sent the message on its
way to Oina accompanied by a silent prayer. Leaning back in
her chair in the dimly lit room, she was afraid to think beyond
finding Lucky again. She was afraid to think that he might not
be on Oina, and more afraid to think he might not answer her
message or want her back.

"Transmission complete," the transceiver said in its quiet mechanical voice.

"What transmission?"

Marsha spun around and saw her father standing in the darkened doorway. Panic hit her in the solar plexus and made her gasp. The worst had happened. There wasn't time to erase the transceiver's memory.

"I asked you a question," Frye said calmly. The look on her face told him more than he wanted to know. "What unauthorized transmission did you just complete?"

"I, uh . . . I can explain."

Frye took the few short steps to her and stared down at his daughter. "You can show me the message." He tried to keep the anger out of his voice.

Sliding her chair away from him, Marsha stood up. There was nothing she could do to protect what she had done, but she wasn't going to show him. "Get it yourself," she said.

Frye was startled by the emotion in her voice. Part fear, part defiance, she seemed to be challenging him. "All right," he said, turning away from her and bending down to reach for the recall button. Before he touched it, something made him stop, and he looked up at her face less than a meter away. Her expression showed an anguish he didn't understand, but perhaps this was another chance for them.

Marsha trembled as her father turned back to the transceiver, and with quick, practiced motions entered the control sequence. Then he stood up and stared at her with the faintest of smiles on his face.

"Memory clear," the transceiver said moments later.

Frye fought the smile. "There," he said simply.

Marsha's jaw dropped open. She couldn't believe her ears. He erased it, she thought. But why? Slowly she pulled her mouth closed. "Why?" she asked finally.

"Because it was none of my business," Frye lied, "and you obviously did not want me to know about it. Now I have made it impossible for me to know."

"Unless I tell you," Marsha said slowly.

Again she surprised him. "Why should you do that?"

"I shouldn't. It would only . . . only make you angry." Even as she spoke she wanted to tell him and couldn't understand the impulse. It was crazy. It would serve no purpose.

Frye turned away and walked back to the doorway. He had a good idea of whom she had sent her message to—that Sondak trader she claimed to love. "I trust you, Marsha," he said over his shoulder. "You do not have to tell me anything you do not want to." Before she could respond, he closed the door and left her alone in the room.

Marsha wrapped her arms around herself in confusion. The more she had tried to understand her father, the more difficult it had become. Why had he erased the message? Did he really trust her? Or had he guessed who she sent it to?

That must be it, she thought. Who else would I be sending a message to? With a sigh she left the communications room and headed back to her own, thoughts of her father replaced by thoughts of Lucky.

Frye waited patiently until he was sure Marsha was in her room and asleep. Then he went back to the communications room and began seeking information. It only took a minute to retrieve the transceiver's backup copy of Marsha's message. What he read did not surprise him, but it did hurt. If Marsha had given up on their relationship, why did he feel so compelled to keep working on it?

For Vinita, a voice in the back of his brain said. Frye nodded automatically. For the memory of Vinita he would throw all of the U.C.S. forces against Sondak. For the memory of Vinita he would pay whatever it cost to win this war. For the memory of Vinita he wanted Marsha by his side when victory came, and he would do anything within reason to keep her there—but only within reason. He could not let his problems with her distract him from the critical tasks that lay ahead.

11

Henley struggled to free his restraining straps as the gravity aboard the *Lifeline* fell off to zero. This was the part of space travel he hated most. In a few minutes he would be floating in his tiny cabin with a bag over his face to catch the contents of his stomach. It never failed. Every time he traveled, the first thing he did when they hit zero-g was vomit.

With awkward motions born of just enough practice to make him overconfident, he released the bag and got his face into it. Several seconds later his stomach started to empty itself. Much to his dismay as he braced against the second wave of spasms, someone knocked on his door.

"Henley? May I come in?"

The sound he made was not a civil answer to Mica Gilbert's request. His body bounced softly against the bulkhead and he let himself do a slow spin toward the mattress. If she would wait a minute or two, he would be all right.

She didn't wait. The door slid back and there she floated, upside down and backward. His stomach rolled over one more time, spraying one last charge of detrius into his sickness bag.

"Can I help you?" Mica asked as she floated to his side. She was surprised by his space sickness, and felt suddenly concerned about him.

Henley shook his head and turned away from her. Pulling the absorbent flaps of the bag tightly against his face, he managed to wipe most of the mess off. "Go away," he said weakly.

"Didn't you take your pill?"

"Go away," he repeated. He could still feel wet bits and pieces sticking to his face.

Mica ignored his order and opened the tiny space toilet under his bunk. With the greatest of care she dampened a cloth and held it in front of his face. "Give me the bag, and use this. It will make you feel better."

Reluctantly he did as he was told. If she was willing to cope with the bag, he was ready to give it up. The very smell of it made him want to vomit again.

"Now," she said after he wiped his face, "Let me strap you back in again."

"No!" Henley clutched a handhold and pulled his back against the bulkhead so he could look directly at her. "I am sorry, Captain, but the best thing for me now is to move around. Believe me. I've had a lot of practice at this."

"You mean . . ." Mica let the sentence trail off. You poor man, she thought.

"I mean it happens every time," he said wiping his face again. "I've never gotten used to the first feelings of zero-g. If you will just move out of my way—"

"Please, Henley, if you have to move around as you say, then let me assist you."

Henley was in no mood to argue with her, and besides, he thought with a sad, inward chuckle, it's been a long time since an attractive woman wanted to take care of me. "As you wish, Captain, but first let me finish cleaning up."

"Certainly. I'll wait outside." Mica did a quick turn and hit the door closed as she exited his cabin. There was something about seeing him sick that touched her. That's a problem she thought, as she drifted lazily in the companionway with one hand holding her in place. This old man's creeping up on me and I don't like it. She knew that was a stupid thought, but it wouldn't go away. Henley Stanmorton isn't doing anything to me. I'm doing it to myself. But what am I doing? What is it about him that makes me feel so necessary and competent? His door slid silently open before she could come up with an answer for herself.

"If you are still willing, Captain, I'm ready to go," Henley said as he pulled himself into the companionway. "But, please, let me set the pace. I'll be a little shaky for a few minutes, but if we go slowly at first, I'll do just fine."

Suddenly Mica laughed.

"What's so funny?"

"Me, Henley," she said with the smile still brightening her

face. "I offered to help you, but now I'm not quite sure of what to do."

"Hold this," he said, holding out a new sickness bag. "If I need it, you'll know exactly what to do." He paused as she took the bag and was disconcerted by the look in her eyes. It wasn't pity or sympathy he saw there, yet he didn't know what it was. "Does this crate have a lounge of some sort?"

Mica saw the quizzical look on his face, but suspected it had nothing to do with the lounge. "This 'crate' has an officers wardroom, Mr. Stanmorton, but I think they'll let you in."

It was Henley's turn to laugh. "I'd forgotten for a moment," he said. "How does my uniform look?"

She eyed him carefully, as though conducting an inspection. "Not as sharp as it could, but not bad for a new Chief Warrant Officer." Actually, for a man who had just been sick to his stomach, he looked very good. There was even a little color in his cheeks that she approved of.

"To the wardroom, Captain," he said with a grin. "Let's see if I can pass myself off as a chief."

"You take the lead, and I'll give directions. The wardroom is that way and up two decks," she said, pointing left.

Henley made his way from handhold to handhold waiting with each movement for his stomach to rebel. When it didn't, he began to move a little faster and skip every other handhold, enjoying the flying sensation as his body accepted weightlessness.

"Up the next ladder," Mica said from behind him.

He swooped up the ladder three rungs at a time to the second deck above his, then swung off the ladder to a handhold on the bulkhead.

Mica swung around beside him a few seconds later. "Doesn't take you long to recover, does it?" she asked with admiration.

"If I recover," Henley said, "it never seems to take very long. I've made a few trips where I never recovered. Which way from here?"

"Should be the first door over there." As Mica followed Henley across the companionway and into the wardroom, she felt an illogical pride in the way he rebounded from spacesickness.

Henley drifted to a low railing inside the wardroom door.

He was surprised by the number of officers present as he brought himself to a stop.

"Chief on the deck!" a cute watchmate with blond curls boiling from under her cap announced. "Captain on the deck," she said quickly as Mica joined Henley at the rail.

"We're hardly on the deck, Mate," Henley said, looking at all the bodies drifting around the room. "Who's the ranking officer here?"

"Commander Schwartz, sir. She's with that group by the sipper, sir."

Henley looked at the people floating between him and the commander's group and wondered how he could ever get over to her without bumping into all of them. "Does protocol demand that we introduce ourselves?" he asked Mica.

She was surprised that she knew what was bothering him. "It does. Go for the overhead," she said with a smile, "and use the handholds there. Less traffic."

With a quick blow of air he launched himself gently toward the overhead, managed to reach a handhold without hitting anyone, and pulled himself across the room to a clear space on the opposite bulkhead where he caught himself with bent knees.

"Ah, Chief Stanmorton," a voice said.

Henley twisted to see who was speaking to him, lost his grip, and did a slow flailing spiral toward the deck. Mica caught his arm, kicked his legs, and flicked on his magnetic boots in three quick motions. Suddenly he was 'standing' in front of a commander who had to be Schwartz.

"Nice moves, Captain," the commander said.

"Thank you."

"Admiral Gilbert told me she was the best aide in the Service," Henley said with a smile. Then he drew himself to swaying attention and saluted carefully so as not to throw himself off balance. "Chief Warrant Stanmorton, ma'am."

"Welcome aboard, Chief. You, too, Captain Gilbert," she said with a casual return salute for both of them. "Did I hear you say that Captain Gilbert is your aide, Chief?"

"Indeed she is, ma'am."

"That's the strangest hookup this board's ever seen," Commander Schwartz said with a smile splitting her dark, thin face. "How'd you manage that?"

"It was Admiral Gilbert's idea, ma'am," Henley said. "My father thought—"

"Admiral on the deck!" the watchmate said.

Henley looked toward the door in time to see a tiny, fat woman in a skintight uniform sail into the room with her body tucked together like a blue ball. He ducked involuntarily as she flew past his head and hit the bulkhead. She came off it with a back flip and landed beside him with a sharp click as her boots grabbed the deck. Henley was too startled to speak.

"I am Admiral Devonshire," she announced. "Who are you?"

She looked so sternly at him that he felt silly and stupid. "Uh, uh, Chief Warrant Officer Stanmorton."

"Welcome aboard, Chief."

"Captain Mica Gilbert, ma'am," Mica said with a sharp salute and a delighted smile. She had met Devonshire before.

"You are Josiah's brat, are you not?"

"Yes, ma'am."

"Good, the two of you follow me." She launched herself through an opening in the crowd and headed straight for a side doorway in the wardroom.

Henley looked at Mica questioningly, then released his boots and followed slowly and carefully. As he floated through the doorway, a voice announced, "Fifteen seconds to gravity." He barely managed to get his boots back on the deck before he felt his weight returning.

"Sit down, you two," Admiral Devonshire said from a corner of the room. "How about a sipper?" Without waiting for an answer she brought each of them a long tube from a small sipper.

Henley wasn't sure his stomach was ready for anything yet, but he accepted the sipper anyway. He didn't know what to make of Admiral Devonshire, but he wanted to be polite.

"Thank you," Mica said as she accepted her own sipper.

"Let us get one thing straight," Devonshire said. "I will not have you two snooping around my ship."

"Pardon, Admiral?" Mica asked before Henley could respond.

"Do not play coy with me, Captain daughter-of-the-admiral Gilbert. You are snoops, both of you."

"And you are offensive, Admiral," Henley said without thinking. Then he remembered he was back in uniform.

Devonshire chuckled. "Yes, I am, Mister Stanmorton. How would you like to be busted to spacer?"

"No chance, Admiral," Henley said as he regained his composure. "You'd have to go through Admiral Gilbert and the Joint Chiefs to do that, so why don't you just drop the intimidation role and tell us what's itching your butt."

Mica was shocked, and from the look on her face, so was Admiral Devonshire.

"That is quite enough from you, Mister. On my ship—"

"Stick it in your waste chute," Henley said, dropping the sipper and standing. He had let his anger with his space sickness pass on to this obnoxious admiral, but something about her attitude kept him from backing off. "Or I'll do a sweet profile of you for the *Flag Report.*"

Mica put a hand on his arm, but he brushed it off.

Suddenly Admiral Devonshire leaned back in her chair and laughed so hard that her face turned red. "You did," she finally gasped. "You already did."

Henley searched frantically through his memory. "Fleet Lieutenant Devonshire? The scourge of Marine Supply?"

"That was me," Devonshire said, still chuckling. "That story you wrote almost ruined my career. But as you can see, it did not, so I will make you a proposition. Do a follow up story, you know, 'Rotten Lieutenant Becomes Grand Admiral' or something like that."

"Are you serious?" Henley asked.

"Most certainly," she said as she stood up.

He shook his head. Officers never failed to amaze him. "Sure, Admiral, I'd be glad to."

"Good," Devonshire said. "I will call for you." With that she turned and left the room.

"What do you make of her?" Henley asked.

Mica smiled at him. "I don't know what to make of either of you. You could have gotten yourself thrown in the brig."

"But I didn't, Captain. I never let an officer walk suitshod over me before, and I'm not about to start."

"Then I'll tell you something, Henley." Mica hesitated, then decided to go ahead. "For some strange reason I don't understand, I'm proud of you."

"Me, too," he said, offering her his hand. "Shall we go see if the rest of *Lifeline's* officers are as friendly as their superior?"

"I'd be delighted."

Even as she took his hand, Henley knew that something inexplicable had passed between them. He accepted the unknown as something positive and thought it might make their relationship a little easier for both of them. That gain just might make up for having to cope with Admiral Devonshire.

* * *

"This is impossible!" Marshall Judoff screamed.

Ayne Wallen cowered in his chair. She had asked what he needed and he had told her. Why was it impossible?

"There is no way we can assemble this much equipment for you, much less find the kind of scientists you want." She paused and stared at him. "You are supposed to build us a weapon," she said slowly, "not set yourself up as the head of some grand scientific institute."

"Cannot build weapon alone," he said meekly. "Must have proper equipment, qualified physicists, necessary—"

"I can read, damn you. I can read all too well. I'll tell you what, Citizen Wallen. You take this list and reduce it to the absolute minimum you need, and I promise to—"

"Is minimum. Need everything there."

"You reduce this list," she said as though he hadn't interrupted her, "and I promise not to take your gorlet from you. I believe that is reasonable enough."

"Then take gorlet," Ayne said with much more bravado than he felt. If she took away his gorlet, he knew he would suffer and die. "List is bare minimum unless you have facilities—"

"Do not tempt me, citizen," Judoff said coldly. "There are no facilities of the kind you say you need. At least not within my power . . . to make available . . ."

Ayne watched her closely as she pondered whatever idea had caught her attention. He had worked for twenty-five days on those lists, and he knew there was nothing left on them that he would not need to begin this project. "Pardon, Marshall, but already Drautzlab is far ahead of—"

"Sit silent," she commanded.

Again he cowered. Part of the problem with gorlet was that it made him live in fear. Sometimes he wished he was back at

Drautzlab working for Sjean Birkie again, admiring her luscious body, seducing her moment by—

"Texnor," Judoff said suddenly. She smiled when he started in his chair. "We'll send you to Texnor, Citizen Wallen. Do you know what Texnor is?"

"Do not know."

"Ah, Texnor is a very special place, a place where dissidents finish out their lives. There you will find the labor and the facilities you need, and what you don't find there, you can make there." She tilted her head with a cruel smile. "Do you understand what I am telling you?"

"No," Ayne said with a shake of his head, "do not understand. Is this Texnor a science institute?"

"It's a prison, you idiot."

Ayne was confused. "But Marshall, how can we be expected to do valuable work in prison?"

"This is a special prison, Citizen Wallen. I told you that. There are many scientists there, scientists who thought they should be allowed to emigrate to Sondak. You will join them."

Ayne did understand now, and wished with all his heart that he was wrong. "But Marshall—"

"Do not worry," she said. "You will not be kept in the prison itself. Oh, no. Not at all. But you will have all those scientists to assist you, and prison labor to build the things you need. However, for the time being we will send you to Yakusan for safekeeping with Kuskuvyet."

A sense of quiet resignation filled his mind. These Ukes were too stupid to understand him, and Marshall Judoff was the most stupid of all. He would go to this Texnor. He would do what he could with whatever they gave him. But there would be no Ultimate Weapon for the Ukes. They did not want it enough.

"Leave me now," Judoff said. "And leave the list with me. I have much to do."

As Ayne wandered back to his apartment he wished he had something to do, something with meaning. He absently chewed on a piece of gorlet. What he wished he were doing was seducing Sjean Birkie. That would be something with meaning.

12

General Mari's trip from Porras's headquarters on Jasper to the continent of Elias to find Colonel Archer took fifteen days. It culminated in an eleven-hour run across the Sea of Sabrina in a rust-stained old hydrofoil that constantly squealed and groaned in protest as its raised bow smacked through the high waves.

Twice in the late afternoon the crew had spotted Uke aircraft in the distance, but the captain had ignored them, and much to Mari's relief, the Ukes had ignored the foil. Apparently it wasn't big enough or unusual enough to interest them. Or perhaps the Ukes just hadn't seen its narrow wake in the rough seas and fading light. Whatever the reason, Mari felt fortunate to escape their attention.

As the foil finally slipped through the darkness into the calmer waters of Todak, Mari climbed from the cabin to the open cockpit. Cold wet wind bit into his face, but he was so numbed by fatigue that he barely noticed it. His body, still not fully recovered from his months of imprisonment, was running on willpower more than anything else.

Dull aches and pains were his constant companions. The medics had reduced his cast to a hard plastic sleeve, but his arm still throbbed occasionally to remind him that it was healing. The skin on his hands and face had toughened and cracked. Difficult bowel movements had begun to seem natural. Discomfort had become routine. But it pleasured him greatly to arrive on the shores of Elias.

On this, his first extended trip across Sutton, he had begun to appreciate what his forces were up against. He had ridden in nine skimmers and one heavily overloaded transport plane carrying ammunition and rations to a militia brigade. For a whole terrifying night he had bounced along narrow mountain roads in a three-wheeled piece of mechanical insanity called a grossencycle. He and a pikean courier had crossed the sandy Bwayne Desert in four days on a sled pulled by thirty-one tiny beckynoids, red-furred bipeds weighing less than twenty kilograms each, but possessed of enormous energy and endurance. They had to stop the sled eight times and cover themselves with sand to avoid being sighted by Uke aircraft and once by an Uke patrol crossing their route in heavily armored attack skimmers.

Mari had slept when and where he could, eaten whatever strange food was put before him, and marveled at the high spirits of the Suttonese soldiers and civilians who took him on his torturous journey. The Ukes seemed to have troops everywhere. But the Suttonese had not only talked confidently about beating the Ukes, they had talked about doing it regardless of how long it might take or what it might cost them. He was especially impressed with the attitude shown by the civilians he talked to. Young and old they seemed fiercely determined to accept nothing short of victory over the Ukes.

Now as the foil slowed to a stop and dropped its anchor he wondered how much further he would have to travel to find Colonel Archer. He prayed that it wouldn't be far. Even in the darkness he could make out mountains rising behind the harbor against the heavy clouds, and he had no desire to cross another mountain range if he didn't have to.

"Launch-launch coming, sir," the foil's captain said in thickly accented gentongue as he sat down next to Mari behind the low windscreen. "Be aside soon. Your gear is ready?"

Mari patted the small damp duffle beside him. "This is it." He could barely make out the captain's face in the faint lights of the instrument panel behind him. "Where will you go from here, auroolcian?" he asked, using the same honorific with which the three-member crew addressed him.

The captain smiled faintly, his broad teeth a bluish gleam in the dark. "Soon as we side you over, have to make down coast for pickup of soldiers for come back here. After? No can say. Hope for back to Coxlane or Bachman."

Bachman was the beautiful village on the shores of Jasper, a tiny oasis of fresh water and lush vegetation wedged between the desert and the sea. It had been their embarkation point. "Good luck to you."

"To you, sir, too, sir," the captain said. He stood up and stared beyond the windscreen. "Be here now."

Mari picked up his duffle and stood beside the captain. As soon as his head rose above the windscreen he could hear the muted whine of a turbine engine under the cold wind. He stared in the direction of the sound, but it was minutes before he saw the dim amber lights of the launch. By then it was almost abreast of the foil.

"You have passenger?" a voice from the launch asked.

"Bryant," Mari called back. It was the code name General Porras had picked for him.

"Board then, Bryant," the voice said.

Even in the calm swells of the harbor, stepping from the foil into the rolling launch was a tricky feat, but Mari managed to get himself into the other boat without falling down. As soon as he did, the foil crew released the launch's lines and it pulled away with a whine accompanied by the deep mutter of its exhaust. Mari half-sat, half-fell back onto a padded bench. The pilot was the only person in the boat, and he studiously ignored Mari as he made a straight run through the harbor.

After a ride that seemed to take far too long, the pilot slowed the engine, swerved the boat, and let it drift until it bumped gently against a low, stone dock. Shadowy figures grabbed the lines and pulled the boat snug, then one of them jumped in.

"Bryant?" a woman's voice asked flatly.

"I'm Bryant," Mari said as he carefully stood up in front of the large woman in her heavy coat.

"Who is Newman's father?"

"The boy who walked without shoes." Mari thought this exchange of code phrases could have waited until they left the rocking boat, but he understood their precaution.

"And who was his mother?"

"The girl who made him shoes."

"Follow me, Bryant," the woman replied. Without further comment she climbed out of the boat.

Mari followed, duffle slung over his shoulder. As soon as he was on the dock the woman marched off into the darkness. He had to hurry to keep up with her as she walked quickly down the dock then up a twisting street between dark, low buildings. The other shadowy figures walked behind him, but no one spoke.

As he trudged along, Mari tried to keep his bearings, but after half-a-set of turns he knew he probably couldn't find his way back to the harbor. For a moment he felt very vulnerable. What if these people were working with the Ukes? As quickly as he could, he pushed that idea aside. It didn't matter. He was totally in their hands, and he had to trust them.

The street got steeper and Mari began to breathe heavily. Suddenly a gruff voice said, "Take your bag, Bryant." Before he could protest, the bag was gone.

For a long time they followed twists and turns up through the town. Mari's legs screamed in silent protest. Up, always up. When they finally stopped, he was panting heavily.

"Wait," the woman said, putting her hand on his chest. Moments later she stepped through a green-lit doorway, then she and the light were gone.

Mari bent over, hands on his knees, and tried to catch his breath. His chest ached in the cold air, and his nose dripped and burned. All he wanted to do was sit and rest, but he forced himself to remain erect. When the green light appeared again, he stood up and stepped toward it. A hand grabbed his arm and held him back.

"Bring Bryant," the woman's voice said from the doorway.

The hand on his arm urged him forward. With a deep sigh he entered the building followed closely by the others. The door closed quickly and for the first time he faced the woman who had led him here. To his relief there was a broad smile on her deeply pockmarked face.

"Colonel will be here soon. Get yourself warm. Come."

She led him through a large room crowded with unmarked boxes and crates to a smaller room where two people sat at a polished wooden table. They rose immediately when he entered, stared at him with less than approval, then left the room with the men who had accompanied him from the dock through a doorway covered with heavy cloth.

"Be not of a mind to heed them-them," the woman said, offering him a seat on the polished bench next to a small military stove. "They worry always about strangers since the times started. You understand that as you can?"

"I understand," Mari said, "but I don't understand—"

"Good." She filled a large stoneware goblet from a pitcher

on the stove and held it out to him. "Drink this. Will grow the warmth inside you."

Mari accepted it and took a deep whiff of its sharp aroma. Somewhere beneath what he assumed was the smell of spices he suspected there was alcohol. One tentative sip told him he was correct. "Good," he said looking directly at the woman as she hung her heavy coat on a hook on the wall. "Very good."

"It will cure your pains and swell your brains," a man said as he stepped through the curtained doorway. "Drink it slowly, General Mari."

Setting the goblet carefully on the bench beside him, Mari stood up. "Colonel Archer?" he asked as his experienced eyes evaluated the man's trim form. Even without a uniform he had the look of military precision about him—and something else Mari couldn't put his finger on.

"Correct, sir. I'm glad you made it to us," Archer said as he accepted a goblet from the woman. "Thank you, Denise."

Mari detected no enthusiasm from Archer, but Porras had warned him not to expect any. "I'm pretty damned glad myself, Colonel. Porras told me it could be a rough trip, but he wasn't as, ah, explicit as he could have been."

Archer smiled slightly. "Please, sir, sit down."

Mari sat back on the bench and picked up his goblet. Archer sat opposite him on a high stool. Denise sat on a similar stool beside him. For a long moment there was silence between them.

"I've come over to evaluate your situation, Colonel, mainly so I can make the best possible disposition of troops, supplies, and ammunition in the future."

Archer pulled a fat brown envelope out of his vest pocket. "It's all in there, sir. We can have you on your way back to Jasper in six hours. You can read it on the way."

With a quick shake of his head Mari stayed the words that crowded his tongue. He couldn't understand why he would try to shake him off so quickly. Was he hiding something? Ignoring the envelope in Archer's outstretched hand, he took a long drink from his goblet. "What's in that?" he asked as the alcohol immediately warmed his stomach.

"Everything," Archer said, tossing the envelope onto the table. "Everything you need to know."

"Look, Colonel," Mari said calmly, "I didn't travel forty-three hundred kilometers just to pick up an envelope. It's obvious that you don't need me here. Porras made that clear. But I don't understand why you think you can get rid of me so quickly. Or why you want to. You have something against help?"

"Help I can always use. You I don't need," Archer said with a darkening of his eyes. "We don't have time to give some goldsleeve a tour, and even if we did, we wouldn't. I had enough of your type in the last war, and I certainly don't—"

"Enough," Mari said in his best command voice. As he expected him to, Archer shut up. "I'll make it simple for you, Colonel. Either I stay for as long as I want, and you show me everything I want to see . . . or"—Mari drew out the pause for emphasis—"or I stop all supplies to your units until they can find a leader who is willing to obey orders."

Archer laughed so hard he sloshed some of the brew from his goblet onto his trousers. As he brushed it off, he looked at Mari with a deep twinkle in his dark eyes. "You would threaten me? Here? You have to be crazy."

"No threat," Mari said, pausing to take a long drink from his goblet. "General Porras has orders not to send you any more supplies until I approve of them."

"Suppose I tell Porras you never arrived?"

Archer's smile quivered downward at the corners, and Mari sensed the colonel was bluffing for a way to put him off. He also felt sure that Archer didn't really mean him any harm. "Suppose we quit playing games, Colonel?"

"What is to keep us from locking you up and forgetting the combination?" Archer asked, looking straight at him.

It was Mari's turn to laugh. "Your intelligence," he said. "That and your need for supplies, and your famous decency."

Denise joined his laughter. "Told you this was foolish," she said. "Dealing with general, not scrubsniper."

With a sigh Archer looked from Mari to her and back to Mari. "I just don't have time for you," he said finally.

"I want to watch you, Archer, not get in your way. Make time. In case you've lost the overall picture, there's a war going on out there with the Ukes, and you're an important part of that war. If you're going to—"

"Don't lecture me!" Archer stared at him for an angry second then emptied his goblet.

"Then stop acting so stupid."

Archer slid off the stool and stepped across the room. Mari sat still, wondering for a second if this idiot would be foolish enough to hit him.

Instead, Archer refilled his goblet from a pitcher on the stove and stood staring down at Mari. "Porras said you spent some time in the Esqueleada Prison."

"That's right."

"And they didn't crack you?"

"No. Came close, though," Mari admitted. "Don't know how much longer I could have held out if Porras hadn't sent in his troops and pulled my ass out of there."

"You'll do, General," Archer said with a grin. "I hate to admit it, but you'll do. Denise, bring in the others."

"Does this mean you'll cooperate?" Mari asked as he stood and refilled his own goblet.

Archer's grin grew wider. "Want to see us in action, General?" He pulled a small chronometer out of his pocket and popped open its cover. "In three hours we're going to destroy a Uke outpost up on the mountain. Want to come?"

Mari was suddenly aware of how tired and sleepy he was. His body ached and his mind was beginning to buzz from the alcohol. He didn't want to go anywhere without some rest, but he knew he had no choice. "That's partly why I'm here."

"Then button your clothes and wipe your nose, General, 'cause we'll be leaving in thirty minutes."

As Archer spoke five rough-looking men all carrying heavy weapons entered the room. They leaned their weapons against the wall, pulled goblets off a high shelf and made for the stove, none of them speaking or acknowledging Mari's presence in the slightest way. He knew it was going to be an interesting night.

* * *

"This is my ship," Lucky said as calmly as he could, "and I'll go where I spacing well please." He was tired of arguing.

Morning Song stroked his long proboscis with both seven-fingered hands, making rude, snorting sounds with each stroke. "You forget, Captain Teeman, you are in partnership with my father. As his representative I do not believe that decision is entirely yours. Until we receive an answer to our message—"

"Wrong, blownose." Why is Morning Song so eager to wait? he wondered. "You said your father had an important message for me that he couldn't transmit in the clear. Since you don't have the codes—since he didn't trust you with the codes—we have to return to—"

"But Captain Teeman—"

"Did you tell me everything he said? Did you?"

"Of course I did."

"Well, did he say anything about waiting to go to Patros and pick up a passenger?" Lucky's anger was already out of control. The only person who would have sent him a message on Oina was Marsha. He didn't know what that meant, but he intended to find out as quickly as possible.

"No, Father said nothing about Patros, but—"

"Then I'm taking us back to Oina."

Part snort, part squeal, the noise Morning Song made with his proboscis forced Lucky to clamp his hands over his ears. The sound prickled the skin on the back of his neck and sent a violent shiver through his spine. "Stop it!" he screamed.

Morning Song's pale grey eyes widened as he immediately stopped making the noise. "Are you sick, Captain Teeman?"

"Sick and spacing tired of you," Lucky said finally. The ringing in his ears was like a distant siren. "Why in the galaxy did you do that?"

"Do what?"

Lucky frowned and shook his ringing head. "Never mind."

"I do not understand you, Captain."

"No one asked you to. Just get ready to head home. I'm plotting our course for Oina."

"But why, Captain? What harm can it do to wait for a response from my father?"

"It's a personal matter you wouldn't understand."

Morning Star gave the Oinaise approximation of a smile, baring his blunt, yellow teeth on either side of his proboscis. "Why did you not say so before? Personal matters must always be attended to."

"Right," Lucky said absently. He punched the final coordinates into *Graycloud's* nav-computer and stared at it impatiently waiting for the results. He was sure the message was from Marsha. It couldn't be anyone else. But what did she want? What did it say? Had she changed her mind? Had her father? Did she want to join him again?

The questions poured through his mind, questions he would have to wait weeks to have answered. Yet behind the questions lay an intimate swell of peaceful emotions. He still believed in Marsha and the love they had shared, and that belief would have to give him comfort on the way back to Oina.

13

"This ship is beginning to smell, Bon," Ishiwa said as the lieutenant entered his small cabin. He wrinkled his nose. "I mean really smell."

Bon stood at attention. "All sanitation systems are functioning properly, sir."

"Stand at ease, Bon. I know that those systems are your responsibility and that they are functioning flawlessly. However, when I walk anywhere on the ship I smell a disgusting odor—even here in my cabin. Can't you smell it?"

"Yes, sir." Bon looked truly perplexed. "But I do not understand why? If the sanitation systems are functioning properly, we should not have this problem. The *Leopold* never smelled like this."

Ishiwa smiled slightly. "This isn't a launchship, Bon. If you had served on hunks before, you would understand. When you pack sixty people into a confined hull over an extended period of time, odor begins to become a serious problem. On the old hunks we had no choice but to endure it."

Bon relaxed visibly. "Then am I to take it you have a suggestion, sir?"

"I do, Lieutenant. As of today I am ordering everyone to bathe after every fifteenth watch. That way—"

"Begging your pardon, sir, but such an order will place a serious overload on our water recycling equipment."

Ishiwa stared solemnly at his junior. He was tired of Bon's

continuing need to interrupt him. "Tell me, Lieutenant, is there anything I could order or suggest that you would not object to?"

"Sir! I resent the implication—"

"Resent away, Lieutenant. But answer my question. Why must you constantly interrupt with your objections after I have made my decisions?"

Bon stood with his hands clasped behind him looking down at the deck. "I am sorry, sir," he said in a low, firm voice. "I am only trying to carry out my duties to the very best of my abilities."

Ishiwa frowned. "Your duties, Bon—since apparently it is necessary for me to remind you of them—are from this moment forth, to act as my second-in-command, to follow and implement my orders, and to give advice if, and only if, it is requested." Ishiwa paused, the frown still hanging on his brow. "Didn't they teach you anything in command school?"

Bon hesitated, as though weighing an important decision. "May I confide in the Captain, sir?"

Ishiwa was immediately suspicious. What in the length of a hull could Bon wish to confide in him about? "Of course you may," he said. "What is the nature of this confidence?"

"Orders, sir." Bon looked squarely at Ishiwa with his eyes focused directly on the captain's. "I have sworn an oath, sir."

"As we all have," Ishiwa said.

"A kyosei oath."

So that's the engine driving this problem, Ishiwa thought, the kyosei and their damned allegiances. "Do you wish to tell me about it? Please, Lieutenant, maybe you should sit down and make yourself comfortable." He wanted his junior to tell him everything, and being gracious was a cheap way to ease Bon along in that direction.

Bon lowered his eyes and sat, almost reluctantly, opposite from Ishiwa at the tiny, dropdown, bulkhead table. "You must please understand, sir, that what I tell you is . . . is very difficult. To do so is to violate a trust placed in me."

"No one asks you to violate a trust, Lieutenant. However, if this kyosei oath of yours has bearing on the operation of my ship, then you are under a higher oath sworn to the service to tell me what it is." Ishiwa wanted to make it as easy as he could for Bon, but most of all he wanted this friction removed from between them.

"It is difficult to know where to begin, sir."

"Begin with the oath."

"As you wish," Bon said slowly. "I swore an oath, to the kyosei, a sacred oath that whenever possible I would use my position—"

The bridgecaller pinged beside him and made both of them jump to their feet.

"Let's go, Bon," Ishiwa said without hesitation. "We will finish this discussion later."

In twenty seconds they stood on the command deck listening to an excited deck piper. "There must be at least fifteen ships, sir. Maybe more. It's hard to tell. There are so many that their signals are mushing together."

"Battle stations," Ishiwa ordered immediately. "Looks like we moved to the right spot, Lieutenant."

"Aye, sir." Bon looked over the piper's shoulder for a moment then moved to his target scope. "If those fuzzy signals are true indicators, there appear to be at least five warships in that group, sir. I estimate twenty-five to thirty ships, total."

"What do we have, sir?" Chief Kleber asked as she jumped through the command deck door.

Ishiwa smiled. "Looks like an opportunity for some heavy hunting, Chief." He turned from her for a second and said, "Rig for scanless attack, Bon. Chief, have your crews prepare both tubes. We'll fire all six missiles, then try to duck around them and to fire some more. That will give you time to rerack for a second series of six."

"Aye-aye, sir," Kleber said as she reached for the microphone that would link her to the firing chambers.

In the forward and aft missile chambers the crews responded to Chief Kleber's orders and loaded a missile in each of their tubes. The forward crew then released the storage clamps on the rack containing the next three missiles they would fire. As soon as they had fired their fourth missile, they would unseal the bulkhead hatch and begin the arduous process of pulling four more missiles from the midship storage magazine to fill their rack again. The aft crew did the same for the one missile on its ready-rack.

In some ways restocking the ready-racks was more difficult

on the *Olmis* than it had been on the *Pavion*. On the old Zhou-class hunks like the *Pavion*, the missile storage magazines had been located directly behind each firing chamber, separated from them only by a thin bulkhead. After studying the records of accidents and premature explosions on some of *Pavion's* sister hunks, *Olmis's* designers had moved the magazines to midship for a higher margin of safety.

They had also designed *Olmis's* forward and aft firing chambers to be partially self-sustaining and completely detachable from the main hull of the ship. When the crews prepared to fire, the thick, spacetight bulkheads were automatically sealed shut. If an accident did occur, the designers' theory had been that the firing chamber would blow itself away from the body of the ship.

However, such a design necessitated that the missiles be winched from the magazines to the ready-racks when the gravity field was on. Since the gravity field was on most of the time, replenishing the racks was an arduous, time-consuming operation. Unfortunately for the missile crews, centuries of practical experience had shown that battle crews operated faster and more efficiently with the gravity field activated than without it.

The missile crews were told that if the ship itself was damaged, the firing chambers would serve them as temporary lifecraft. There was little evidence that the missile crews accepted that explanation. They knew that even if they did manage to survive a lethal attack on the ship, there was little likelihood that their automatic short-range disaster signal would attract rescuers before their life-support systems ran out of oxygen and power.

In the hot, sweaty confines of their firing chambers, the seven members of each missile crew were all too aware that they were expendable. That was a fact they accepted in exchange for the higher pay and prestige of their jobs.

"Range, leading ship, two-point-nine tachymeters," Bon said. "Bearing two-zero-three-three-seven by five-one-six-zero-niner. Vector thirty-four degrees. Closing at point-two-eight per hour, steady. Minimum crossing range, one thousand two hundred kilometers."

Ishiwa absorbed each new datum with a growing sense of anticipation. Here was a Sondak convoy headed directly across their bow presenting a passing gallery of targets for their missiles. What better hunting could *Olmis* ask for? "Lock on the leading warships, Lieutenant."

"Aye-aye, sir."

"Time to firing range, forty-seven minutes," Chief Kleber said quietly.

"Chief, target your last four missiles on the strongest nav-signals in the convoy. As soon as we fire the last . . ." Ishiwa paused as he stared at the convoy's movement reflected on the plotting screen. "Do you see that, Bon?"

Bon, too, stared at the screen. "It isn't possible, sir."

"Martyrs," Ishiwa whispered.

"Two ships breaking off from the convoy," Bon said flatly. "Maybe it is just a routine maneuver, sir."

"Convoy's slowing, sir," the deck piper added.

"I think they've spotted us, Bon. Damn." Ishiwa double-checked *Olmis*'s instruments to ensure that all her external scanners were off. They were. *Olmis* was sending no signals to give her presence away. Yet somehow Sondak's warships had managed to locate them again. But how? How? "What's their current range and closing ratio, Bon?"

Bon shifted back to the target scope. "Thirteen-fifty and accelerating, Captain. Closing at point-three-six per hour."

"Time to maximum firing range?"

Chief Kleber huddled with Bon over the scope. "Forty-one minutes, sir." They both looked up at Ishiwa expectantly.

"What now, sir?" Bon asked.

"No suggestions, Lieutenant?" He hadn't meant for his question to sound sarcastic, but it did.

"Accelerated attack, sir?"

Ishiwa wished Bon's suggestion had been stated more positively, but he paused only for a second. "Excellent, Bon. Start engines and prepare to initiate a direct accelerated attack. Alert all hands."

New commands rang through the ship. The crew quickly strapped themselves to their battle stations. The memory of *Olmis*'s last engagement was as fresh in their minds as the bruises they had suffered were on their bodies.

As he strapped himself in his command chair, Ruto Ishiwa wondered again how Sondak's warships had detected them. He made a mental note to reevaluate all systems in an attempt to discover what had given them away. Now there were far more important things to worry about.

"Course, all ought, sir?" Bon asked.

"Affirmative. All ought, maximum acceleration. Change to all ought minus five at three hundred kilometers. Time to range and firing window, Chief?"

"Thirty-two minutes to maximum range with five minute window, sir. A maximum two missile shot."

"Very well, Chief. Bon, target missiles three and four for the heart of the convoy. Chief, can we fire five and six after we pass the main body?"

Chief Kleber looked over at him with a frown. "Number five, is no problem, sir," she said, "but at full acceleration I doubt we'll be able to get number six away in time to hit anything."

Ishiwa cursed silently. This was not the attack role anyone had expected *Olmis* to play. Instead of head-on confrontations with warships, she should be sitting on the convoy's flanks picking off Sondak freighters one by one.

"Convoy's accelerating again, Captain," the deck piper said. "Targets one and two still closing at point-three-six."

With sudden inspiration, Ishiwa looked closely at the plotting screen. "Release target locks! New course . . . four-five-hundred by all ought! Speed, match plus point-four."

Bon quickly shifted his gaze to the plotting screen. "Is that an interception course, sir?"

Ishiwa smiled slightly. "It is, Bon. Let's see if we can't shake them up a little and do some hunting at the same time."

Olmis swung in a slow arc to her new heading. Before she reached it, the deck piper said, "Targets altering to follow."

"What about the convoy?"

"Steady as before, sir."

"Good," Ishiwa said. "Lock on for two aft shots. And make them count, Chief. I want to even the odds a little."

* * *

Commander Rochmon handed Admirals Stonefield and Gilbert each a sealed folder marked *Maximum Secret*. Admiral Gilbert immediately broke the seal on his and removed the contents, but Admiral Stonefield just sat there staring at the ceiling and tapping the folder with an idle finger. Rochmon had seen Stony like this before and waited with the patience of practice.

"So," Stonefield said finally, "just what 'do' we know about these Wu-class hunks the Ukes have sent after us, Commander?"

"Only what you have before you, sir. They can accelerate to lightspeed almost twice as fast as anything—"

"Then the rumors are true?"

"Yes, sir. Their acceleration rate is twice as fast as anything we have except the experimental XA-16 attack ships. They are certainly—"

"How do you know about the XA-16?" Anger burned in Stonefield's eyes. "That is a highly classified weapons system."

Rochmon shook his head. "Not any more, Admiral. What I'm telling you is what we've filtered out of a series of coded Uke transmissions—and 'they' certainly know about the XA-16." He paused for a moment trying to read Stonefield's expression.

"That's one leak you can't blame on Bock," Rochmon said quietly, "'cause none of us knew about it until the Ukes started telling each other." He knew he probably shouldn't have brought up Bock's name, but he missed her services in cryptography and hated the fact that she was considered guilty of spying until proven innocent.

Admiral Stonefield nodded with a sigh. "Very well, Commander. I'll remember that your Bock may not be guilty of that particular piece of treason. Please continue."

"As I was saying, these Wu-class hunks are very heavily armored. The one *Veda* attacked took at least three direct hits from our spikes and never paused. We also know they carry long-range missiles that allow—"

"How long range? How far away can they shoot at us?" Gilbert asked. The last thing the Combined Fleets needed was a threat like this one.

"Don't know, sir. Our best estimates from the two reports we've received are that they can fire from an effective range of at least one thousand kilometers."

"Damn," Gilbert cursed. How were his ships supposed to fight weapons like that?

"That's what we said, sir," Rochmon continued, looking at his old mentor, and thinking of Mica on her way to Satterfield within range of this new Uke threat. "But we do have some good information for you."

"Well?"

"Two things, Admiral. Maybe three. First, for some reason these new hunks of theirs are extremely easy to spot. Post Commander Jennings of the *Veda* said the one they attacked lit up their nav-screen with triple the normal luminosity. Our guess is that it has something to do with their new armament."

"That's something, anyway. What else?" Deep worry lines streaked across Stonefield's face into the depths of his thin white hair.

"The second thing is that we're pretty sure from the two attacks they've made so far, that like their old Zhou-class hunks, these new Wu-class hunks still only have one missile tube forward and one aft."

"Surely the Ukes weren't stupid enough to repeat that design mistake," Gilbert said. "That cost them a lot of ships because they couldn't reload and fire fast enough."

"May be, Admiral, but apparently they thought they could compensate for that with speed and improved armor. Anyway, their pattern of attack indicates they kept their old one-and-one design." Rochmon paused, looking from Stonefield to Gilbert and back again, and wondering how either of them had enough time to deal personally with this.

"The final bit of information is that the Ukes have had some production problems with this new hunk," Rochmon said with a smile, "and we estimate have only been able to put seven of them in service so far."

"All operating in polar region," Gilbert said without humor. He was thinking about Mica and Henley Stanmorton. "With how many more to follow?"

"Don't know the answer to that one, Admiral. We have a lot of sources in the U.C.S., but so far none of them can give us that kind of information. Our guess is that they—"

"Guess! Guess! I'm tired of guesses," Stonefield said. "Don't guess, Commander. Find out. That's your job."

Rochmon didn't need to be reminded of what his job was, but he held his tongue and let Stonefield continue.

"It's one thing for our ships to have to cope with half-a-set of these new hunks, and quite another if they're going to be spacing hundreds or even thousands of them out there."

After a long pause Gilbert said, "Tell us your guess anyway, Hew. I'll settle for that until you can come up with something more definitive."

"Of course," Stonefield added, as though trying to make up for his outburst of anger.

"Hundreds rather than thousands, sir," Rochmon said, keeping his smile. Stony had a right to want more information, but Rochmon was proud of what his Cryptography had already gathered.

"Probably the low hundreds. Part of their production problems seem to have been caused by certain material shortages. Consequently, we don't expect them to begin mass producing them any time in the near future. We also have some evidence that it is taking the Ukes six to eight Standard months to train their new crews before sending them out."

"Thank you, Commander," Stonefield said after a long silence. "And please understand that we appreciate this information. If I was short with you, it was because all this," he said with a wave of his hand at the file, "raises as many questions as it answers."

"I understand, sir," Rochmon said as he rose to his feet. "We'll keep you informed of anything new we learn."

"Yes. Thank you." Stonefield said absently.

Rochmon gave them both a quick salute and left the office with his thoughts going back to Mica Gilbert. He prayed that she was safe and mentally kicked himself for not spending more time with her before she left.

Josiah Gilbert watched him go and unknowingly shared the same thoughts.

"You'll alert all commands immediately, Josiah?"

"Of course, sir."

"Good. I'd like to see you back here this evening with any ideas you have about how we can counter these new hunks."

"Will do, sir," Gilbert said. But as he left Stonefield's office he knew the best place to go for those ideas was to the officers of POLFLEET, and he hoped he could get through to them.

As he walked out of the building he was startled to hear chanting protestors outside the gate.

"Attack the Ukes! Attack the Ukes! Attack the Ukes!" they shouted.

Gilbert smiled and wished it were that easy. He wished they

had the forces to attack the Ukes without holding back, and a small part of him wanted to be with the chanting crowd, adding his voice in the hopes that the Joint Chiefs—and especially Stonefield—might hear them.

Neither the legislative Tri-Cameral nor the Combined Administrative Committees had the power to force the Joint Chiefs to act, but nothing the J.C.s did could silence their persistent demands for the Services to take a more aggressive role in the war. Already a score of ranking members from both those branches of government had called on Gilbert to express their concerns. Like the crowd outside, the civilians in government didn't want to hear about defense. They wanted to hear about battles won and Ukes beaten back to the surface of their planets.

With another quiet smile he headed for his quarters. The civilians had given him at least part of the answer he would pass on to Stonefield. If the fleets were going to beat the Uke hunks, they would have to take the offensive and attack the hunks whenever possible.

14

"With all due respect to you and to the members of Bridgeforce," Frye said slowly, "I do not understand how we can embark on plans to build ships of this size. We cannot even find adequate materials to produce sufficient hunks and new launchships. How will we build bombships of such gigantic proportions?"

"It has been decided," Admiral Tuuneo said softly, "and there is nothing you or I can do about it."

"Can't you reform Bridgeforce, sir?"

Tuuneo shook his head. "Six months ago I could have. Six months ago the kyosei were still a weak faction. Now I find their perverted isolationism everywhere. If I tried to reform Bridgeforce, I would have a kyosei rebellion on my hands.

How they have gained such support so quickly, I do not know. But I am too much of a realist to try to fight them openly."

Frye suddenly felt sympathy for the old man and realized that he was making a great admission. If Bridgeforce was forcing these bombships on the U.C.S. against Tuuneo's advice, then Frye knew his arguments would carry little weight.

"Please, Commander, you do not eat. Is the food too warm?"

"Not at all, sir," Frye said absently. He forced himself to take a bite of the pickled rodiert. It was delicious, almost as good as Vinita's. But his mind was not on the food.

"I apologize for displeasing you," Tuuneo said.

That snapped Frye alert. He had been rude. "The apology should be mine, Admiral. I let my mind wander."

"Listen to me, Frye. Listen carefully."

Frye's breath caught for a second. Tuuneo's use of his first name was an unexpected breach of decorum. The intimacy of first names was reserved for the closest of family and friends.

"I have an illness," Tuuneo said, looking down at his food, "an illness from which I may not recover."

Those same words had foretold the death of the only woman Frye had ever totally loved. Now he was hearing those hated words from the one military leader in the U.C.S. for whom he had unqualified respect. Only politeness made him finish chewing the now tasteless food in his mouth.

"I tell you this," Tuuneo continued, "not to elicit your sympathy, for I know that you, above all others, will understand what is happening to me and my family." He lifted his eyes and looked directly at Frye. "Bridgeforce has suffered since the defection of Marshall Judoff's forces, and it will suffer more when I am gone. There will be a true power struggle. Judoff might even be foolish enough to return and participate in it."

Frye slowly nodded, not knowing what to say, or where Admiral Tuuneo was heading. Deep under his heart he felt a terrible ache that refused to subside.

"However," Tuuneo said with a slight smile, "I have made provisions for that contingency, and many others that Bridge-force will have to face in my absence."

"Please, sir. Do not speak with such certainty of your absence," Frye said softly.

"I hear the pain in your voice, but I must speak the truth, Frye Charltos, and you must face it."

Another echo from Vinita's death stabbed through him. 'Face the truth,' she had told him before she died.

"I invited you here to eat with me this evening for a very special reason. In order to maintain some balance on Bridgeforce and retain the point of view you and I share, you have been promoted to Vice-Admiral. Tomorrow you will be installed as a permanent member of Bridgeforce. You were the price I exacted for their stupid bombships."

Frye was stunned again. His emotions swirled with grief, honor, and disbelief before he could control them. "I, uh, I don't know what to say, sir. It is a great honor."

"And a great danger, Frye Charltos. Never forget the danger. Bridgeforce was born in treachery, and in treachery it will die one day."

Such a stark admission of the hidden truth about Bridgeforce was almost more than Frye could bear. It seemed that Tuuneo intended the impossible. "Is there more you wish to tell me, sir?" he asked hesitantly. Not since Vinita's death had he felt so emotionally adrift.

"Only the obvious," Tuuneo said with another slight smile. "If I live long enough, I will do everything within my power to ensure that you become Chairman of Bridgeforce."

"I can't take your place, sir," Frye finally managed to say.

"Then do not try. You must make your own place on Bridgeforce—but you must make it quickly. Already those with kyosei sympathies are prepared to pick over my bones."

Frye hung his head and fought the conflicting desires in his heart. He had no ambition to become a member of Bridgeforce yet, but he did have an overwhelming desire to shape its policies. If that meant becoming more involved in their squabbles and fighting the growing influence of the kyosei, then so be it. Against that was his overwhelming desire to concentrate all his attention on the war against Sondak and leave the politics to others.

He knew he could not have both without great compromises. It would mean delegating much of his direct responsibility for the daily conduct of the war, and he would need help to do that properly. He immediately thought of Melliman and wondered if his old AOCO would willingly serve him again after what he had done to her. If nothing else, maybe she would just be pleased to get away from Sutton and the lecherous Marshall Yozel.

"Forgive my intrusion on your thoughts," Tuuneo said, "but you will have time for them later. From this moment forward, you and I must waste no time on private emotions. We have much to accomplish for the good of the U.C.S."

"Of course, sir," Frye said, taking a deep breath as he tried to clear his mind. "Forgive my indulgence."

"There is nothing to forgive." Tuuneo paused and took a long sip of his ice water. "Now listen carefully, for I have much to tell you, beginning with the names of those who supported your Bridgeforce membership and why I believe they did so. Meister Hadasaki was the first to agree to my compromise. I believe he wants the bombships as much as anyone, but he also wants to maintain Bridgeforce's balance against the kyosei. He is also the only other one who knows I am dying."

Frye frowned without thinking. It pained him to hear Tuuneo speak of his death.

"Do not let yourself be distracted, Frye. There will be sufficient time for you to concern yourself with other matters after you join Bridgeforce tomorrow. Until then you must pay strict attention."

"Of course, sir. Forgive me."

"The most surprising supporter you have in Bridgeforce is Vice-Admiral Lotonoto. She, I would have expected much opposition from, but her support came on the heels of Hadasaki's probably because she, despite her kyosei sympathies, fears unbalance more than any threat you might pose. As for the others, the analysis is more difficult. However . . ."

For the next three hours Frye listened like an obedient schoolboy as Tuuneo gave him a brief primer on the intricacies of Bridgeforce's politics and factions. He forced himself to concentrate on everything Tuuneo said, and asked questions only when it was absolutely necessary. Then for another hour Tuuneo questioned him to ensure that he understood what he had been told. Finally satisfied, Tuuneo sent Frye home to rest.

But there was no rest at home. Marsha heard him come in and followed to his small study.

"You look tired," she said solicitously. For all their differences, she still felt great sympathy for him, and she knew he was working much harder than it was healthy to do.

"I am," he said as he sat behind his desk without looking at her. "A great deal happened today."

"Shall I fix you something to drink?"

"Yes," he said, still not looking at her. "Fix one for yourself, too. There is something I have to tell you." He watched her go with mixed emotions, but he had already decided on his course of action toward her.

Marsha had no idea what he wanted to talk about, but she could tell by his tone that it was something he considered very serious. As she fixed them each a drink in the next room, she wondered for the hundredth time if he had found out about her message to Lucky. She doubted it. If he had, he would have confronted her by now. And if he was going to confront her, he wouldn't have suggested that they drink together. In his old-fashioned way, he still reserved sharing drinks for very special occasions. No, this had to be something else.

"Thank you," Frye said when she brought him a tall glass full of the amber-flavored alcohol that was his favorite. "Thank you for remembering. Please, sit down."

She sat and waited. At first he seemed absorbed by the task of organizing the memo cards he took out of his pocket, but then she realized that he was working up to something. She sipped her drink in silence.

"There are going to be some significant changes in our command structure," he said without warning. "Since you no longer desire to remain with me, I am going to have you transferred to Yakusan as soon as it is convenient." Finally he looked at her and thought again of what an enigma she had turned out to be. "That is as close to Oina as I dare send you."

Marsha was shocked. He had discovered her message to Lucky!

"However," he said, before she had time to respond, "until I can recall my former AOCO from duty off Sutton, I will require your absolute and total obedience to duty. Will you give me that?" Frye had decided on the way home to recall Melliman to his side. Despite the emotions she expressed for him—or maybe because of them, he didn't know—Melliman was the best AOCO he had ever had.

"How did you find out?" Marsha asked finally.

"It doesn't matter. Answer my question."

"Of course. I mean, yes, I will continue to serve until my replacement arrives. But, Father . . ." She hesitated. During the battle for Matthews system he had spared Lucky's *Graycloud* when he could just as easily have ordered it blown from space. Now he was giving her a chance to be with Lucky again. Why? "It makes a difference to me how you found the message, and why you are doing this."

"There was a backup copy in the transceiver," he said after taking a quick sip of his drink. "As for why, my reasons are purely selfish," he said. Every day he knew what it was like to live without someone he loved. He could no longer deny her the opportunity to be with the man she loved.

"I don't believe you."

He ignored her protest and took another sip of his drink. The liquor was beginning to warm his stomach. He was too tired and preoccupied to get involved in another of their fruitless personal discussions.

"What you believe doesn't matter," he said firmly. "Now put that out of your mind and pay attention. We're going to be busy most of the night."

* * *

Inspector Thel Janette waited patiently in Xindella's empty outer office. Since Patros was an independent planet, technically she had no authority there. However, Sondak managed to exert far more than technical influence on Patros, and Scientific Security used many of the colony-states on the planet for its own purposes. Some of those states were unabashed supporters of the U.C.S. Others expressed strong sympathy for Sondak. Most proclaimed neutrality. All were centers of intrigue and corruption of one kind or another.

Here in Elliscity, neutral corruption reigned through the power of various "brokers" who controlled the trading in commodities ranging from raw ore, to information, to lives. If the price was right, they would arrange trades in anything and take what they considered to be a reasonable commission. Xindella was the richest and most powerful of all those brokers.

"Inspector Janette, please enter," a voice said from a hidden speaker. Simultaneously a panel in the wall slid back to reveal a doorway.

Janette drew herself up to her full one hundred and fifteen centimeters and walked confidently through the doorway. The panel closed behind her immediately after she entered the room.

"A slight precaution, Inspector. Do not be alarmed," said the huge Oinaise lounging on the opposite side of the room.

She looked at his flabby body with its wrinkled yellow skin lapping over the folds of bright red cloth he had wrapped around himself and almost laughed. "I am hardly alarmed, Xindella."

"Ah, so you know me. I am flattered, Inspector."

"I know all the major scoundrels on Patros," Janette said. "May I sit down?"

"Such quaint terms you humans use." Xindella snorted mildly through his wrinkled proboscis and displayed a full set of dull, yellow teeth. "Please," he said with a wave of his seven-fingered hand, "sit anywhere that pleases you."

"Thank you," she said, choosing a tall stool that placed her closer to Xindella's eye level.

"You were quite frank in requesting this meeting, Inspector, so I suspect you are one of those humans who does not care for undue ceremony. However, it is my obligation to offer you food and refreshment—even gorlet if you wish it."

Janette laughed. "Perhaps if we come to a suitable agreement," she said, "I will partake of your hospitality. For the time being, however, all I ask from you is information."

"Yes, of course." Xindella stroked his wrinkled proboscis thoughtfully. "That seems to be the commodity you humans most value. However, I do not know what information I could give you that your efficient Sci-Sec does not already know."

"Where did you sell Ayne Wallen?" she asked bluntly.

"Inspector! I do not trade in people's lives, even in lives as worthless as Ayne Wallen's."

Janette knew he was lying. "We tracked him here," she said simply. "He never left your complex."

"Ah, but he did, Inspector. He did. I recommended that he deal with the Castorian Beliss'hatot. After that?" Xindella held his hands open in an almost human gesture. "After that, who knows what the foolish human did?"

With a laugh Janette pulled a small notebook from a pouch on her belt. "Lies, Xindella. Lies badly told. Shall I tell you exactly what happened after Ayne Wallen came to you?" Without waiting for his reply she began reading. "On the ninth of your local month Menet, Ayne Wallen left your office in the company of two human technicians and was taken directly to your repair facility at Strickland Starport from which he never left until your ship departed—"

"Ah," Xindella said, holding up one hand, "I believe now that Sci-Sec has eyes and ears everywhere. But tell me. What does this Ayne Wallen matter to you?"

"Where did you take him, Xindella?" Janette was not about to let him lead her off on tangents.

Xindella snorted again. "I like you, Inspector. I do not know why, yet. Humans are not normally very likable. However, if we can arrange some just recompense for my troubles, I will tell you not only where Ayne Wallen was taken, but also where he is going."

Janette's eyes twinkled. "Sci-Sec does not pay what you call 'just recompense' for information, Xindella. It only ensures that those who refuse to cooperate are incapable of receiving information in the future."

"Is that a threat, Inspector?"

"Of course it is, Xindella." Janette let a smile creep to her lips. "Surely you understand threats."

"But I must have recompense!" he said with an angry wave of his hand. "The Ukas cheated me out of ten thousand credits. Surely you can understand that I have a right to receive something for all my efforts."

"You have the right to stay in business, Xindella. Nothing more. I'm sure it would be a terrible blow to your business if some of your ships got caught up in this war and disappeared or were destroyed." It was a neat bluff because he had no way of calling her on it without taking a great risk.

"Inspector! Such harsh measures are totally unnecessary. All I ask is some token of—"

"You want a bribe, Xindella. I cannot give you one. However, I can make you a business proposition."

Xindella looked at her with his large eyes half-hooded by folds of yellow skin. "Something better than merely allowing me to stay in business, I hope."

"Most certainly," Janette said with a smile. Now it was time to bluff some more. "If you give us sufficient information to find

Ayne Wallen and return him to Sondak, Drautzlab will pay you a, uh, 'commission' of fifty thousand credits."

"Such an extravagant amount," Xindella said with a sigh, "for such a puny human being. No wonder the Ukas wanted him so much. Very well, Inspector. As soon as half the fifty thousand is deposited in my account here in Elliscity, I will give you the information you seek."

Janette checked a large chronometer on her wrist. "If you do not tell me very soon," she said, "there is a very good chance the depository here in Elliscity will be robbed and you will have no account."

Xindella snorted. "All right, Inspector. I can see that this is all worth far more to Sci-Sec than it is to me. I delivered Ayne Wallen to the Ukas' outpost on Juene. However, since they refused to pay me all that was agreed upon, I took measures to keep track of his whereabouts. Several weeks ago I received information that he had been sent to Texnor."

"I'll need precise coordinates for both places."

With a sigh Xindella shook his large head. "Surely Sci-Sec has coordinates for Juene," he said, "but I will give them to you anyway. As for Texnor, I cannot help you. That is a system I know only by its dreaded name."

"Why was he sent there?" Janette asked.

"I do not know, Inspector. Nor do I care to know. Texnor is a system used by the Ukas as some kind of prison. Now if there is nothing else, I am suddenly tired. Forgive me for not offering you refreshments again."

"There is one more thing." Janette paused. "In return for your fifty thousand credits, you must take me to Texnor."

Xindella snorted so hard that it hurt her ears.

"Impossible!" he said. "I just told you that I don't know where this Texnor system is."

"Then find out," she said quietly.

"But this was not part of our agreement!"

"It is now."

"Why, Inspector?" he pleaded. "Why do you insist that I take you?"

Janette smiled and stretched. "Because, you Oinaise scoundrel, you can come and go as you please through the U.C.S."

"No," he said firmly.

"Yes," she said, checking her chronometer again.

"Of course," he whispered finally, "but I do not know what good you can do even if we should find this place."

"Leave that to me, Xindella," Janette said with far more assurance than she felt. She had played the whole scene with Xindella only partially by ear, basing key parts of her strategy on the deciphered trading reports provided by the woman, Bock. That Service Cryptography had dismissed Bock without evidence after accusing her of spying, was Sci-Sec's good fortune. Sci-Sec had quickly recruited her, and her information about Xindella had been priceless. That Xindella had given in to Janette's bluffs even easier than Bock had predicted, had compelled Janette to plunge past her suspicions of Xindella, and past all the information that she knew for certain was valid.

"I will return in five hundred Standard hours," she said quietly. "Be ready to leave by then."

Xindella merely waved at her with a long, bony hand and opened the panel in the wall.

As she left his offices, Janette knew she would have to do some quick planning and some quick talking with her superiors and with Drautzlab to get permission and to raise the fifty thousand credits. She wasn't sure she could get either, but she couldn't let Xindella suspect that. In her determination to retrieve Ayne Wallen, she had committed them both.

15

"We dumped our gear in our cabins and got here as soon as we could, Admiral Pajandcan," Henley said, bringing himself to attention and giving her a quick salute.

"Sounds like you two had an exciting trip."

"Too damned exciting for me, Admiral. Captain Gilbert might be used to space battles, but I think that I'd like to spend my old age in more sedate circumstances."

"Chief Stanmorton did quite well, actually," Mica said with a smile for Henley. "He stayed in the Battle Center during the whole engagement and—"

"Because I was too frightened to leave," Henley said with an exaggerated grimace.

"I don't have Devonshire's battle report yet, so give me your versions of what happened, starting with you, Captain Gilbert." Pajandcan handed them each a mug of strong tea. "I think we'd better let the Chief calm down for a little."

"I'm calm," Henley said. "As calm as I can get after almost having met my maker in the voids of space."

Mica smiled at him again. "Militarily it was a rather strange engagement. The *Mitchell* picked up the Uke ship about two hours before we were scheduled to leave subspace and start our deceleration. Admiral Devonshire was showing us the Battle Center when the report came in. She immediately ordered *Mitchell* and *Hughes* to intercept. They broke from the convoy—"

"And the Uke started from a dead stop and began its attack," Pajandcan said with a sad smile.

"Exactly, Admiral. Was that in Admiral Devonshire's preliminary report?"

"No, Captain, it wasn't. But that's what we received from an earlier hunk attack on another convoy."

"Hunks? Those little subspace hunter-killers? I thought the Ukes had given up on those things?"

"Apparently not, Chief. Please, Captain, continue."

"Well, it was a running fight for about thirty minutes. The Uke fired two or three missiles at *Mitchell* and *Hughes*, but only one of them actually did any damage. Admiral Devonshire pulled the other two line ships into a defense formation and sent the convoy to the emergency escape point here. I'd guess that we fired fifty or sixty spikes at the Uke while it fired four missiles at us. We must have hit it eight or ten times, but it never seemed affected. Meanwhile—"

"Meanwhile the *Lifeline* caught a missile in the stern that damned near sent us all to eternity," Henley said. He thought of how exciting the story would be when he wrote it up.

"Not quite," Pajandcan said. "Devonshire's preliminary report indicates the loss of one outboard engine and extensive hull perforations, but nothing extremely serious. You were still a long way from eternity, Chief."

Henley slurped the scalding tea. "It was serious enough when it hit us, Admiral. And I'll tell you what. I hope I'm never in any place more serious than that. I'm too much of a coward to want to live through—"

Mica's laugh cut him off. "He's so much of a coward, Admiral, that he volunteered to help the damage control parties with their emergency repairs."

"Bravado," Henley said with a smile. "Sheer bravado."

"Your father warned me he was a character," Pajandcan said, "but he didn't tell me the man was crazy."

"I'm not crazy. I was just afraid that all our air was going to leak out and I wanted to make sure it didn't."

Suddenly they all laughed together.

"Anyway," Mica continued, "after firing its missiles at us, the Uke slipped by at a fantastic rate of acceleration. Admiral Devonshire sent *Hughes* after it, but there was no way it could catch up. You know the rest, I think."

Pajandcan sighed. "I do. Unfortunately, I do. Admirals Dimitri and Dawson have worked out a defensive plan to counter this new hunk—that's classified information, Chief," she added quickly, "but they haven't had much data to go on. I only wish we could take the offensive against them."

"What's classified? The Plan? Or the fact that the Ukes have a new hunk?" Henley asked. He liked this Pajandcan, and he wanted to be sure he stayed on her good side. He also had to know what he could put in his story.

"Both." Pajandcan smiled grimly. It was time to confront them. "Look, Chief, I know all about your background, and I also have a pretty good idea of why Josiah sent you out here."

"I asked to come."

"Right. But not as a chief warrant officer. What I don't understand," she said, looking at Mica with a sudden wrinkling of her brow, "is why you're here."

"As the Chief's aide," Mica said, "and to assist the Cryptography staff."

"What else?"

"That's all."

"Lie to someone else, Captain, but tell me the truth. Right now," Pajandcan said with an even darker look. "If you are playing watchbird for your father, you'd better tell me. I have no intention of—"

"Tell her," Henley said quickly, sensing trouble. "Your father said she could be trusted."

Mica looked from one of them to the other with mixed emotions. As much as she had come to like and respect Henley on their trip together, she wasn't sure his snap decision was the correct one. On the other hand, her father had said—

"Well, Captain?"

The simmering anger was so evident on Admiral Pajandcan's face that Mica knew that Henley was right. "Call it whatever you like, Admiral," she said, meeting Pajandcan's stare. "Father asked me to send him unofficial reports on anything I saw that I thought would interest him. He's especially concerned about the morale of the fleet."

Henley watched the two of them closely and could tell that this confrontation was not going to be pleasant. He wanted to help Mica, but would have to wait for the right chance to do so.

Pajandcan's anger held steady. "All right," she said slowly, "I have no objections to that. It wouldn't be the first time your father has put an observer in someone's command."

"What do you mean?" Mica asked.

"I mean what I said. Years ago I did some dirty work for him myself," Pajandcan said with a tight, humorless smile. And learned to hate him as much as I loved him, she thought. "But I want to see copies of anything you send him."

Mica frowned. "I don't think I can do—"

"That's right, Captain. You don't think. You just give me copies of anything you send to your father." Pajandcan's anger was growing again. "I don't care if I get them before or after you send them. I'm not trying to censor you. But I damned well better get to see them. Is that understood?"

"Yes, ma'am," Mica said with a sarcastic salute. She had no intention of actually following that order.

"Chief, wait outside!" Pajandcan snapped.

"As you wish, Admiral," he said. It looked like he wouldn't get the opportunity to help Mica after all. As quickly as he could, he left her office and planted himself in the companionway to wait for Mica. He knew she could handle herself, but that didn't stop him from worrying about her.

Pajandcan waited for the door to slide closed before she spoke again. "You're a spacer's brat, Mica Gilbert, and there's nothing that can be done about that. But there's something you might as well know right here and now."

Mica thought Pajandcan's anger was out of proportion to the situation, but she decided it would be better to hear her out and tell her father about it as soon as possible.

"You know I served with your father—served with him for a long time at close quarters, if you know what I mean." Pajandcan waited until she saw the look of understanding on Mica's face. "That's right . . . close quarters. If he and I both hadn't been so ambitious," she said, hesitating for a long, purposeful second, "I could have been your mother." She leaned back with a smile of satisfaction.

"I don't know what to say, Admiral." What could anyone have said to something so bizarre? Pajandcan was telling Mica the most improbable thing she had ever heard. Or was it? Could her father and Pajandcan really have—

"There's more, brat." Pajandcan leaned forward with a quivering intensity. "Ever since that time your father has managed to keep eyes on me. After a while, in every command I served in there would always be someone who tried too hard to be my friend, or poked too deeply into my kit, and slowly I—"

"Surely you don't think—"

"Hush, brat, and let me finish." It felt good to tell this to someone after all these years, especially to someone as symbolic as Mica. Pajandcan wasn't about to be interrupted. "Slowly I began to pile it up, to realize that all those people were reporting back to your father. And you know what? Even after he married your mother it kept happening, and I was flattered—flattered that he still cared that much about me and what I was doing."

The words poured into Mica's brain like a shock wave. Her father? Pajandcan? Did he still—

"But burn it in space, brat! I'll not be spied upon by the woman who could have been my daughter—not without knowing everything she says about me!"

Mica rejected every rebuttal that popped into her mind. None of it seemed to make any sense. She stared at her hands feeling isolated and confused, holding back a flood of emotions she couldn't even recognize.

"Look at me, Mica," Pajandcan said softly.

Mica did as she was told.

"I don't mean to hurt you by telling you this. In fact, if Josiah hadn't put you in this position, you probably would never have known. But you have to understand my position. What he asked you to do doesn't have anything to do with the Service. Think about that. Then we'll talk some more. All right?"

With a numb nod Mica stood. "I think I need some rest."

"Certainly. We'll talk again later." Pajandcan watched her leave with mixed feelings of sadness and triumph. She had gotten rid of an old burden, but she might have done so unfairly. With a slow sigh she turned back to the endless paperwork that awaited her attention, but her mind kept drifting to the past.

Somehow Mica had remembered to salute before she left. As soon as the door closed behind her Henley took her arm.

"What did she say? What's wrong?" he asked. It was obvious that she was very upset about something. Maybe he should have resisted Pajandcan's order.

"Take me to my cabin, please," she said softly, the flood surging back and forth inside her.

It took an effort from both of them to find their way back to her cabin, and all the while Mica felt a need she didn't understand rising above her internal confusion. As he opened the door to her cabin, she looked up at Henley and knew what it was. Admiral Pajandcan had stripped some of the dignity from Mica's life by casting a large shadow over her image of her father. What she needed most was the support and comfort of someone she could trust. "Please come in for a minute."

Her words were barely audible. "Of course," he said. Henley followed her in and closed the door. When he turned around she was standing in front of him with tears rolling slowly down her face.

"Hold me," she whispered. "Just hold me."

He took her into his arms with fatherly affection and was startled by the fierceness with which she clung to him. Not knowing what else to do, he stroked her hair and whispered, "Shhh, shhh, it's all right."

Mica cried without understanding why she was crying or whom she was crying for. Slowly, ever so slowly, the gentle spasms subsided. Henley's arm was strong and sure around her. His hand was gentle in her hair. His voice was full of tender comfort. When she looked up at him finally, she saw the concern for her on his face, and on impulse she kissed him.

Henley accepted her kiss with passive disbelief. Before he could recover, Mica pressed herself against him and her mouth covered his with a second, more demanding kiss. Instinctively he responded with a swell of passion that startled him. Suddenly he wasn't so sure everything was going to be all right after all.

* * *

"You and Morning Song did very well, Captain Teeman," Delightful Childe said with a pleasant, rolling snort and a baring of his blunt teeth.

Lucky could only see Delightful Childe's head above the oddly patterned screen, and assumed that it was impolite for him to see any more than that. Obviously, Delightful Childe was still linked to his mate—or together they were linked to their child. He wasn't quite sure exactly how it worked. "Thank you, partner," he said calmly, "but I really would like to see that message now."

"What? The checkdroids failed to give it to you? My apologies, Captain. My sincerest apologies. You should have received it as soon as you landed. Here," he said, ducking his head, "this should bring them." How frustrating it was to be incapacitated like this. As physically pleasurable as mating and rearing were, Delightful Childe would have enjoyed them more if they took less time.

Lucky heard a rapid series of beeps before Delightful Childe's head reappeared. Moments later a side door slid open and an orange checkdroid, its naked, wrinkled body a miniature version of Delightful Childe's, ambled into the room carrying a flat plastic box.

"Messages for Captain Teeman," the droid said, as though the messages had just arrived.

"Messages?" Lucky asked. "I thought there was only one."

"Two messages for Captain Teeman," the droid said, handing him the box. Without another word it left the room.

Lucky looked at the box for a long moment before opening it. Suppose it didn't contain what he hoped it did? What would he do then? Unable to stand the suspense, he flipped open the lid and took out two thin sheets of plastic.

A quick examination told him why Delightful Childe hadn't

sent them in the clear. They were both from Marsha, and they were both in the ideos markings of his trader's code. Slowly he sat down on an overstuffed basee.

"Good news, Captain Teeman?" Delightful Childe asked.

"I don't know. I'll have to decode them," Lucky said slowly. But even as he spoke he was reading the code as easily as though it were written in pure gentongue.

The first message was brief. She wanted to escape from the U.C.S. and meet him somewhere, anywhere that they could be together. His heart swelled with anticipated happiness.

The second message was longer. It said she would soon be going to Yakusan, and that she would contact him as soon as she arrived. Her father was sending her there, but she didn't say why. The happiness subsided. "Where's Yakusan system?" he asked suddenly.

"I have no idea," Delightful Childe said. "Is it important?"

"Of course it's important!" Lucky looked up and immediately regretted his tone. "I'm sorry, Delightful Childe. I shouldn't have shouted at you. It's just that this message says that Marsha's father is sending her to Yakusan system, and I want to know where it is."

Delightful Childe stroked his proboscis. "Yes, of course. I understand that you are concerned. I will have the check-droids locate it for you. In the—"

Lucky heard another voice behind the screen speaking in rapid Vardequerqueglot.

"Perhaps you should come back tomorrow," Delightful Childe said finally. "My mate Nindoah reminds me that it is time to pulse our offspring."

"Sure. Anything you say." Lucky rose to leave as a check-droid came through the door.

"Message for Delightful Childe from his cousin Xindella," the droid announced in gentongue.

"Stay a minute, Captain," Delightful Childe said, putting an arm over the screen and accepting the box. "This message could concern both of us."

Lucky sat down without thinking about what Delightful Childe had said. His mind was on Marsha.

"Captain? Captain Teeman?"

"What?" Lucky was startled out of his thoughts.

"Now I have a mystery place for you. Does the name Texnor mean anything to you?"

It didn't take Lucky long to remember Texnor. "Yeah. It's a Uke prison planet over in the Steagn Cluster. Nasty place."

"My cousin Xindella has business for us there."

"Not interested." The last thing Lucky wanted to do was run off on some errand when he had a chance of finding Marsha again.

Delightful Childe looked at the message again and did a quick mental calculation. "For fifteen thousand credits would you be interested?"

"Nope. Not for fifty thousand. The Ukes on Texnor had to be the unfriendliest people I ever met. By the time I finished unloading, I almost didn't care if I got paid or not. All I wanted to do was get away from that place."

"A pity, Captain," Delightful Childe said. Nindoah was whispering to him again and he knew he would have to resume his parental duties. "However, for the sake of our partnership I would ask you to at least give the idea some consideration? After all, we will not profit from our methane venture for some time yet, and such a commission—"

"What's so damned important on Texnor?"

Delightful Childe had to hurry. Nindoah was starting the pulsing without him and that made his gonads extremely uncomfortable. "He wants to smuggle someone into Texnor and then bring two people out. It sounds simple—" Delightful Childe groaned. "Come again tomorrow."

Lucky almost smiled. "Whatever you say, partner." As he left the room he let the crazy idea of smuggling people in and out of Texnor slip from his mind. All he could think about was Marsha and what it would be like to be with her again.

16

General Mari was pleased by how quickly his body had recovered from the effects of his imprisonment. He still had his aches and pains, and he still suffered from a shortness of breath that he attributed to a thinner atmosphere than he was accustomed to. But some of his aches and pains were new ones. Colonel Archer rarely slackened the pace he set for his troops just to accomodate Mari.

In the preceding seven weeks Mari had accompanied Archer and three of his units on four separate raids against distant Uke outposts. All those raids were really training missions for the assault they were now preparing to mount. In those seven weeks he had learned a great deal about guerrilla warfare and what a determined force could do against a less determined enemy.

Now Mari felt he was ready to return to Jasper and put his knowledge to use. Instead he was putting on his combat gear to accompany Archer and the troops on this new assault. In a way, this would be the proof of Archer's thinking that the Ukes were far more vulnerable than anyone would have believed. More than that, it made Mari feel good to be back in the field again.

"Ready, General?" Denise called through the door.

Mari put the twelve millimeter pistol in his holster and snapped the safety strap. "Be out in a minute," he said. There was just one more thing he had to do. He held the small kit he was leaving behind up to the dim light and dug through it until he found what he wanted. Then he left the small room and joined the others in the kitchen.

"Better eat some of this," Archer said, looking up from a bowl of steaming stew. "It'll be battle rations for the next day or two if we're lucky, and nothing if we're not."

"First things, first," Mari said. He looked around the room

with a smile for the men and women who had done so much to earn his respect during his stay with them. "Since this may be your last hot meal for a while, maybe you ought to eat it as a brigadier." With a slight flourish he held out his hand to Archer. In it lay two spaceblack, metal stars.

Archer smiled. "Do I throw them at the Ukes, or wear them, General?" he asked as he stood up and accepted the stars.

Everyone laughed.

"Wear them," Mari said, "in good health and good luck. Those are my original brigadier's stars. I've been carrying them with me for the better part of fifteen years. Now it's time to pass them on to someone totally worthy of wearing them."

"Don't really know what to say about this—"

"Say thanks, fool," Denise said as she took one of the stars from his hand and started pinning it on his collar.

"Thanks it is, then, General. But I suspect that there's something behind this promotion."

Mari's smile widened. "That there is, Brigadier Archer. First of all, you should understand that your troops are at least partially responsible for this. Second, when I sent my messages to General Porras this morning, I told him that as of today you are his Deputy Planetary Commander, responsible for all of Elias and the Outward Islands."

Archer frowned.

A tall, bucktoothed woman in the corner whistled softly. "Old Bagbones won't like that," she said.

"I'll deal with Colonel Bagabond, if I have to," Mari said, "but I suspect that he'll fall into line."

"Don't worry about him," Archer said firmly. "I didn't ask for this, but since you gave it to me, I'll make sure that we do the best we can for you. And that includes Bagabond."

Denise finished pinning the second star on Archer's other collar and much to everyone's surprise said, "Attention!"

Everyone but Mari was slow to react. He thumped his heels together and saluted. The others quickly followed suit.

Archer snapped a return salute and suddenly they were all around him, slapping him on the back and congratulating him. He quickly put an end to it by saying, "The food's getting cold."

Mari laughed. "Then give me some now. I'd hate to follow a

brigadier who was grumpy because his breakfast had gotten cold."

Several hours before dawn as they hiked through the dense forest up the mountain to where their battle skimmers were hidden, Archer fell into step with Mari. "What are you going to do next, General?"

"Well, first thing I'm going to do," he said between breaths, "is ask you for five or six of your people to go back to Jasper with me and help train Porras's troops."

"I'd hate to give any of them up, but I know you'll make good use of them. What then?"

Mari concentrated on following the pale light clipped to the back of the woman in front of him. Then I'm going to try to sneak off Sutton on one of those freighters, and see if I can't stir up the Joint Chiefs into a counterattack."

Archer grunted. "Don't count your bullets, General. Porras and I both begged for a counterattack the first few weeks after the Ukes hit. The Joint Chiefs and everyone else pretty well ignored us."

After several deep breaths, Mari said, "I know that. But I've been here, and they haven't. They're building up the other polar systems for a defense, when they should be planning an offensive here. Porras tried to tell me that, but you convinced me." He panted heavily before continuing. "The Ukes are a lot weaker than anyone outside will believe. I have to convince them, if I can, that they're wrong. We can win the polar battle, here on Sutton."

"I'm glad you have that much confidence in us, but we're going to need more than just token help. Today's raid is going to be the biggest thing we've tried—and pretty close to the biggest we're capable of."

"If I can talk them into it, Archer, you can bet everything you have . . . that it will be more than a token—"

The faint whine of a skimmer interrupted him. He looked ahead, but it was still too dark to see. "Sounds like we're almost there."

Archer hurried up the trail and Mari contented himself with putting one foot in front of the other until someone told him to stop. By then there were eight or ten skimmers warming their engines in the cool, damp air, and the quiet murmurings of seventy voices provided a reassuring background to them.

"Your skimmer's this way," a young man said, taking his arm and leading him between the whining machines.

Mari climbed into the partially covered cab next to the driver. Moments later eight fully armed troopers climbed into the squad bay behind him.

"Watch your head," Denise said as she swung the twenty-one millimeter automatic rifle onto its mount over the cab.

After a few more minutes of quiet orders and questions passing through the dark woods, they were suddenly moving. Mari put on his radio headset and relaxed in the heavily padded seat, knowing that it would take at least an hour to reach the strike point. From then on there would be no relaxing.

Archer's plan called for forty-seven skimmers carrying almost four hundred troops to slide down three separate routes on the other side of the mountain and hit the Uke-controlled port of Spurgis. At the same time, saboteurs inside Spurgis were scheduled to detonate a series of explosions that should destroy the Uke fuel depot, the main approaches to the waterfront, and most importantly, the Port Authority Building.

Archer and his key staff members had been over and over the plan working out every detail. It had been a difficult decision for them to destroy the historic Port Authority Building, but that was where the Ukes had made their headquarters, and that was where they had to be hit the hardest. The one piece of information that no one had was how quickly the Ukes could call in reinforcements. By demolishing the Port Authority Building, Archer hoped to prevent them from calling in any reinforcements all together.

Mari had made little contribution to the plans, content to watch Archer and his people in action. His one suggestion had been made when he realized that Archer was considering a warning to Spurgis's population. Mari's alternative was to have the civilian leaders convince the Uke commander that a dusk-to-dawn curfew be established. Archer had reluctantly accepted that, and the day before yesterday they had received word that the Ukes had cooperated.

As he settled deeper into the seat, Mari prayed that the civilians would have sense enough to stay in their homes when the shooting started. Then his thoughts drifted to all that had happened to him since the war started, and he was surprised when a quiet voice in his ear said, "Wake up, General, or you're going to miss all the fun."

When he opened his eyes he realized they were sitting silently at the strike point. The first grey line of dawn was just dividing the black sea from the sky. It was time.

One by one the eleven skimmers in his group reported in over his headset. He knew without turning around that Denise and the other troops behind him were ready. "Green Leader, ready," he said quietly into his throat-microphone.

Red and Blue Leaders echoed him. Archer's voice said, "Go," in the headset. Three lines of skimmers started snaking down the mountain, gathering speed as they went.

By agreement, Mari's was the last of the eleven skimmers in Green Group. His would not be in the forefront of the attack, but Denise on the twenty-one-mike-mike would provide covering fire over the point skimmers.

They were still a thousand meters from the outskirts of Spurgis when the first explosions ripped open a premature dawn with bright orange flashes followed by a triple booming roar. Almost immediately Blue Group on their right flank started firing, first with their light weapons, then with the repeated thunder of the twenty-ones.

Adrenalin pumped through Mari's system as his skimmer sped down the hill. The battle was on.

Red Group opened fire seconds later. Another series of explosions spouted a pillar of fire from the center of Spurgis.

"Port Authority!" Denise yelled.

Mari strained for a view through his observation port as the lead elements of Green Group raced straight into the outskirts of Spurgis. They still hadn't fired a shot. As Mari's skimmer passed the first low building, a sudden clattering whine rocked his skimmer.

"Roof!" someone shouted. "Up there!"

The skimmer slowed slightly, its nose rising on the cushion of air. The twenty-one fired two bursts of fire at a rooftop silhouetted by flames from the burning fuel dump. Explosions raked the night above them.

Mari's ears rang with pain. The driver slammed the skimmer forward again and twisted through the falling debris as though it were alive under his hands. A large chunk of stone slammed off the cab. Bullets spanged against its side. The twenty-one fired again and again.

"Left," Denise yelled.

The driver swerved left. The skimmer slid around an abandoned lorry and scraped along a wall. Rifle fire rang over Mari's head, but his deafened ears could barely hear them.

"Right! Right!"

The skimmer accelerated, spun, and suddenly hovered. The chatter of fire swelled to a buzzing roar. Mari was surprised to realize that he had his pistol in his hand. He was just as surprised to hear the voice shouting in his ear.

"Blue Group has the docks! Blue Group has the Docks! Where are you Green Leader? Come in, Green Leader. Where are you?"

Mari looked around. A Uke soldier in his bright green uniform jumped from the shadows. Mari stuck his pistol through the observation port and fired. Once. Twice. A third time. The Uke was gone.

"Killing Ukes," he finally remembered to say into the throat-microphone. His voice was a fuzzy noise in the back of his head.

"Clear!" Denise shouted. "Good shooting, sir!"

The skimmer moved slowly forward again. Ukes seemed to be coming out of every side street and alley. The twenty-one belched death. Mari fired his pistol until it was empty, reloaded, and fired again.

"Green Leader! Green Leader! Rendezvous, Green Leader!" Archer's voice shouted in his ear.

"Head for the docks," Mari shouted to the driver.

The skimmer turned quickly, ducked down a narrow street, and minutes later slid to a stop between two other skimmers on the broad stone dock overlooking the bay. On the horizon a pale red sun was rising slowly out of the ocean. Behind them Mari could hear intermittent firing that seemed to be moving away.

He checked his chronometer. It had been slightly less than thirty minutes since they left the strike point.

"Glad to see you," Archer's voice said in his ear. "Your assembly point is five hundred meters straight ahead of you."

Mari signaled the driver forward. "We're on our way."

It took almost six hours to capture or kill the remaining Ukes in Spurgis. By then some of the civilians were furious at the damage and death and had to be restrained by the troops. Others had eagerly joined in the hunt. They brought the last stragglers in at the point of old single-shot rifles and captured Uke weapons. The strangest sight was a small girl and an old man who dragged in a Uke with a thin wire wrapped around his neck with each of them holding an end of it tied tightly to a stick. The blood on his neck testified to his resistance. The meek way he followed their orders testified to the effectiveness of their improvised weapon.

"I've got a surprise for you, General," Archer said later as he and Mari rested with a group of his troops outside a small building across from the demolished Port Authority. "See that hydrofoil entering the bay? It has your kit aboard. Denise, Ruby, Gretchen, Minor, Suzia, and Ben are ready to go with you."

"No sense in wasting time, I guess," Mari said, wiping the perspiration from his brow, "but I think I'm going to miss you."

"You know, I think we might miss you too, General. I wouldn't have believed that when you first got here. Anyway, we'll see each other again." Archer stood up. "Have a good trip, sir."

"Keep 'em ducking, Brigadier." Mari returned Archer's salute and began walking down toward the docks more determined than ever to convince the Joint Chiefs to aid Sutton.

* * *

Proctor Leri Gish Geril stared into the darkness overhead where the humans in their ships now guarded Cloise. The haunting vision had returned with a frightening new twist. Instead of showing her a way to lead her people to a better life, the vision now showed her leading them into fires of death.

It couldn't be right. It just couldn't. There was only one place to turn at a time like this. Weecs, whose brilliant body smelled of lust for her every time she touched him, would be of no help. Ranas, her patient mate, had never understood the visions. He could not help her, either.

Without hesitation she slid past the door to her burrow and slithered quickly to the brink of the Truth Cliff. It took her several impatient minutes before she located the right path in the dark, but finally she made her way cautiously over the edge and began the slow, twisting journey down to the grotto of her favorite Confidante.

When she arrived at the grotto, Leri paused only a second before slithering into the blackness. Immediately a pale light spread through the grotto and revealed the Confidante at its depth. The Confidante's grey, wrinkled bulk towered above her like the walls of the grotto itself, and Leri felt suddenly comforted just to be in its presence.

"Are you troubled, Proctor Leri?" the Confidante asked.

"Most troubled by visions, Confidante."

"When was your last exchange?"

"Too long ago," Leri answered. She waited patiently for the Confidante's next question. Much to her surprise, moments later she heard the familiar scrambling of an Isthian and felt it climb onto her back. With no word or pause it began fondling the nipple on her neck with its lips. Leri accepted its unusual presence in this place as a blessing from the Confidante.

"Can you relax now?" the Confidante asked.

"Yes," Leri answered as the Isthian began suckling, drawing nourishment from her blood while replacing her vital anti-bodies. "Yes," she repeated, "I can relax now."

"Will you speak the vision?"

Leri was surprised again. "In front of the Isthian?"

"This one can hear only me," the Confidante said. "Speak your vision with freedom."

Leri was startled. Only one other time had her Confidante made a statement instead of asking a question. Yet the Isthian's vigorous suckling eased her tensions and her mind, letting the words flow. The vision returned to her with painful clarity.

"I am leading the people down a broad path when suddenly I come to a division of the ways, one up and one down. The way up is crowded with aliens, hated Castorians scuttling along in their crab-like shells, and soulless humans in their artificial skins. The way down is empty and dark, and I feel compelled away from the aliens. I lead the people down, down the twisting dark way until fires spring up all around us. A fury of death roars up and cries, 'Pain! Pain!' And there we are all consumed."

"Does this frighten you?" the Confidante asked.

Leri's thoughts drifted around the question. The Isthian slurped enthusiastically on her nipple, sending sensuous ripples along her spine. "Yes," she finally managed to say. "It frightens me."

"Why? Have you not already chosen the way up?"

The way up? Leri thought dreamily. "Oh, Confidante, I am confused. Can this vision mean I have chosen the proper path?"

"Can it mean anything else?"

It was becoming more and more difficult for Leri to concentrate. Her shivers of delight seemed to spur the Isthian to stronger and stronger suckling. "I don't know. I don't know," she barely managed to say as she trembled with spasms of joy. Then she felt herself sliding toward deep contentment.

The Isthian slowly released her nipple and slid off her back with tender caresses. "May your blessings triple, tender one," she said softly.

"By the Grace of the Elett," the Confidante answered for it. Then the Isthian scuttled off into the darkness.

"Are you still troubled?" the Confidante asked.

"No," Leri mumbled. She felt weak and tired, but very, very happy. "I am no longer troubled."

"Will you sleep here?"

Leri didn't answer. She was already asleep. Deep in the grotto of the Confidante the vision returned, but this time she led her people up the high way. The path was treacherous and difficult, but the aliens helped her up, and up, and up, until she came again to the grotto of the Confidante where she slept without dreams.

17

The longer Chief Kleber served with Ishiwa, the more he admired her. Now her face showed a kind of excitement that almost made her look beautiful. "It might work, Chief," Ishiwa said. "It just might work. What do you think, Lieutenant?"

"It would place us in great danger," Bon said slowly, "to wait in ambush so close to one of their systems. However, I recommend that we should at least try it, sir."

Chief Kleber's smile grew even bigger, and Ishiwa thought he saw some silent signal pass between her and Bon.

"Thank you, Lieutenant," she said.

Suddenly Ishiwa was sure the two of them had discussed this before coming to him. Yet it still pleased him to hear Bon's recommendation. After his junior's admission of the oath he had sworn, Ishiwa had retained his doubts about Bon.

In some totally inexplicable perversion of patriotism, the kyosei had convinced Bon to swear that he must always act first for the safety of the ship, and only second for the accomplishment of their mission. After hearing that, Ishiwa had worried that he might have to relieve Bon of duty as his executive officer. Now it appeared as though their continuing discussions about the duties of an officer had begun to have the effect on him Ishiwa wanted.

"Then we shall indeed try it, Chief Kleber," Ishiwa said with the slightest of smiles. "Bon, have Enseeoh Nunn begin calculating the logical subspace exit points from all major routes approaching both Bakke and Wallbank from the main Sondak systems. Then put us on a course to Wallbank."

"Aye-aye, sir."

"Chief, when you set up these new targeting procedures, be sure we can compensate for the deceleration factors. We'll have to hit those Sondak ships as accurately as we possibly can."

"There is one other thing, sir," Kleber said, "that might give us some targeting assistance. If we could orient *Olmis* on an acute angle to the targets moving toward a hypothetical convergence point, I think we would improve our chances."

Ishiwa looked at her for a long moment as he thought about what she wanted. Yes, she was definitely getting prettier by the day. Maybe if this idea of hers worked he would invite her to his cabin for a private celebration. "That approach would mean heading into the system instead of across its plane," he said quietly. "That really would be dangerous for us."

"True, sir. But it would also make it easier to compensate for their deceleration. I know this new computer of ours is supposed to be an improvement over the old HighScan-Two.

But it still seems to handle closing with a target much better than it does heading away from one."

"Very well, Chief. Once Nunn and Bon have the exit points plotted for us, we'll plan our own exit based on your acute angle approach. Anything else?"

"No, sir," she said with a quick salute.

"Then get to work—both of you."

After they left his cabin, Ishiwa sat down on his bunk with a grim smile of satisfaction. Somehow Sondak's ships had found a way to spot *Olmis* when she tried to ambush them in subspace. But he very seriously doubted if the Saks would have the same luck in normal space. With the Sondak ships decelerating, their dampers would occlude any long-range scanning. If *Olmis* could hit them, change to a position near a new exit point, and hit them again, Sondak might never be able to mount an effective defense against the hunks.

Nine of *Olmis's* sister ships had already joined her in service, but several of them had also reported being spotted before they could fire on the Saks. Chief Kleber might just have discovered a tactic they could all use. Stick it to the Saks before they knew they were vulnerable.

Yes, he thought as he lay back on his bunk and absently scratched his crotch, if this idea of hers worked, he would definitely have to give her a private celebration.

Eight set watches later *Olmis* exited subspace well away from Wallbank and decelerated under full power. Her dampers absorbed the strain almost without protest, bringing her to the optimum course Bon, Kleber, and Ishiwa had calculated. Now all they had to do was wait for Sondak to provide them with targets.

They didn't have to wait long.

"Ship exiting subspace," the deck piper said twenty minutes later. "Range, three hundred thousand kilometers, bearing one-niner-niner-seven-two by . . ."

Ishiwa ordered battle stations, and the crew leapt to their places even as the piper finished calling the data. Ishiwa watched the plotting board, looking for additional targets to appear. "Looks like a loner, Lieutenant," he said finally.

"It must be loaded to start its decel this far out," Bon said. "Locked on target."

"One missile or two, Chief?"

"One should do it Captain. Target should be in firing range in eleven minutes."

"Fire when ready, Chief." He looked again at the plotting board. Suddenly he realized that for the first time they might actually be able to see what they were shooting at. "Piper, give me extended visuals."

The small screen over his head flicked to life. He switched on the plotting overlay, found Wallbank's star, and looked hopefully for a sign of the Sondak ship. Behind him Kleber was beginning her countdown.

Everyone on the command deck felt the tension as Kleber marked the passing minutes. Finally she said, "Firing, sir. One missile away. Time to target, seventeen point-two-two minutes. Beginning reload."

Ishiwa waited patiently as the second countdown began. He moved his eyes back and forth from the plotting board to the viewscreen, hoping to actually see the missile strike home. Kleber moved beside him and looked up at the screen with assurance written all over her face. He was startled by how sharply distinctive her odor was—and how stimulating.

"Any time now, sir."

She had hardly finished speaking when a tiny flash erupted on the viewscreen. A split second later the blip on the plotting board broke into tiny fragments that gradually disappeared like flakes of snow against the glacier of space.

"Wow," Kleber whispered.

"Target's gone, sir," the deck piper reported.

"Well done, Chief," Ishiwa said, giving her a broad smile and patting her arm. He let his hand linger there a moment longer than was necessary.

Her face was flushed. "Thank you, sir."

"Bon? How much longer can we hold this course before we have to circle back?"

"Approximately ten hours, sir."

"Steady as she goes, Lieutenant."

Three hours later they picked up a group of three ships exiting subspace. Kleber's missiles destroyed two ships, but the forward crew had a minor delay in loading the third missile. By the time she was ready to fire, the third Sondak ship had accelerated out of range. Ishiwa decided to let it go.

"Circle to primary alternate course, Lieutenant. I suspect

the Saks will be looking for us out here in a little while. The ship is yours."

"Aye-aye, sir." There was delight in Bon's voice.

"Chief, report to my cabin as soon as your crew has secured the forward tube."

"Will do, sir."

A warm sense of elation filled Ishiwa as he slid down to the work deck and went to his cabin. Three ships with three missiles. Three visually confirmed hits. Now *Olmis* would truly come into her own as a force to be reckoned with. Kleber's new technique was absolutely excellent, and damned near foolproof.

He smoothed an imaginary wrinkle on his bunk, then unlatched a small chest from under it. Opening the chest he withdrew a vacuum bottle of his favorite Yotoyo liquor and two polished steel ceremonial cups. Setting the bottle and cups on the small table, he took a quick glance around the cabin just as Kleber knocked on his door.

"Chief Kleber reporting as ordered, sir," she said happily as the door slid open.

Again Ishiwa was aware of her distinctive odor. In a ship now permeated with the stale smell of human bodies, it struck him as odd that her scent should stand out so. Very odd indeed. "Come in, Kleber. Come in," he said, closing the door behind her. "Have a seat."

"Thank you, sir."

"I think the successful proof of your idea calls for a celebration drink." He handed her a small steel cup and noticed the delicate way she fingered its fine engraving as he filled it with the fire-red liquor. "To the *Olmis* and her future," he said after filling his own cup. With one quick motion he emptied it. The liquor burned a path to his stomach in a satisfying way.

Following his example, she drank the whole cupful without stopping. Ishiwa could see her eyes watering, and laughed. "That's it, Kleber. Let it warm you up. We'll drink the second one more slowly."

"Good, sir," she said hoarsely. She let out a long sigh. "That stuff has a big bite."

Ishiwa was now fully aware of his intentions toward her and suddenly embarrassed. There was no formal regulation against what he wanted to do, but there were strict social prohibitions against any personal actions that might adversely affect the running of the ship. The strictest of those were on the captain. It also occurred to him that the look that had passed between her and Bon might have meant more than he thought.

"Is something wrong, Captain?"

"Please," he said, looking at her as directly as he could, "call me Ruto." He hoped the intimacy of sharing his given name with her would help her understand what he was feeling.

"Captain, I, uh . . . oh, brackets!"

Her exclamation startled him. He looked down into his cup as his embarrassment turned into shame. "I apologize," he said softly. "I meant no—"

"Please, Ruto, it is I who should apologize." Kleber reached across the table and touched his cheek lightly with her finger tips. Then she stood up without warning, stepped across the cabin, and dimmed the lights.

Ishiwa looked up at her in amazement and confusion.

"Take me," she said as she zipped open the front of her tunic. "Take me quickly the first time."

Like a man in a dream out of control Ishiwa moved across the room to her, pulling his clothes off as he went. Even in the dim light he could see the hard lines of her body marked by scars he didn't understand. When she pressed herself against him, there was no room for scars or prohibitions or understanding.

Flesh to flesh they slid down onto his bunk. Her mouth devoured his with eager kisses. Her hands pulled at him insistently, demanding only one thing. Her scent went straight to the center of his loins and drove him with a sensuous madness.

There were no slow, gentle caresses as they explored each other. There were no lingering kisses to be savored. Their bodies pounded against each other in a blind, panting fury of lust that bruised their flesh with exquisite agony.

Her hips found a stacatto rhythm of their own, bouncing under him with unstoppable desperation. Suddenly she arched her back in a series of hard, trembling spasms. She bit sharply into his shoulder. Ishiwa clenched his teeth to keep from screaming as his body was paralyzed in the moment of release.

"Missiles, missiles, missiles," a faint voice whispered beyond his shuddering moan.

For a long minute or two neither of them moved, their bodies stuck together in momentary exhaustion. Then Kleber turned her head slightly and kissed the hollow where his neck joined his shoulder. A quiet joy pushed against the lethargy in his muscles as he buried his face in her hair and sucked in the delicious smell of her.

Ishiwa didn't want to leave her. He rocked gently on his elbows and knees, fighting the drowsiness that threatened him, enjoying the slick feel of her. Kleber's fingers traced the muscles of his back and the ridges of his spine with slow, delicate movements. Gradually her hips responded to his rocking with a motion of their own.

He raised his head and kissed her softly, gently—her mouth, her nose, her cheeks, and her mouth again. She returned his kisses and teased his lips with a flicking tongue. When his body paused, her hips moved insistently until they rocked together, synchronized by a need only partly sated.

Slowly, but relentlessly they moved toward a second peak until Ishiwa thought he would die at the moment it came. All his energy focused on that one overwhelming sensation as she pulled him over the crest of the peak and down into the deaf and blind oblivion of relief.

Finally he collapsed beside her, his breathing and hers shaping a ragged melody that seemed to fill his cabin. As his mind drifted quickly toward sleep his fingers traced the scars along her ribs, and he wondered faintly how she had gotten them.

She gently stilled his hand and pulled herself against him. "You may call me Andria," she whispered.

* * *

"We're agreed on that, then," Pajandcan said, with a smile. "The next item of business is the command structure. I have chosen Admiral Dimitri to command the main attack group and Admiral Devonshire to command the reserves." She looked around the crowded conference room and said a quick silent prayer that she would get to see all these faces again.

"Are you sure we can't muster another legion of Planetary Troops, Admiral?" General Schopper asked.

Pajandcan appreciated and respected his concern, but they had already covered that problem and she was ready to move forward. Still, it wouldn't hurt to reinforce what she had already told them. "No, we can't, General. The Joint Chiefs have authorized us to undertake whatever defensive operations we think are necessary. Admiral Gilbert is the only one who knows how far reaching our defensive planning actually is, but there are a limited number of ships and troops he can afford to divert to us. Besides, when we—"

"Pardon, me, Admiral," a brevet sergeant said, entering the room without ceremony, "but this just came off the code from Wallbank, and I thought you'd better see it immediately."

As she read the brief message a dry lump formed in Pajandcan's throat. "Damn," she whispered. With a quick shake of her head she passed the message to Dimitri. "Read it aloud."

Dimitri quickly scanned the message, then stood up. His voice was filled with cold anger as he read. "Be advised that the light cruisers, *Devera* and *Entios*, and the troopship *Skidmore* carrying two legions of reserve Planetary Troops, were all attacked and destroyed by parties unknown within thirty thousand kilometers of Wallbank. All hands were lost. Suspect U.C.S. hunk or hunks operating on the fringes of this system."

The room was filled with grave silence broken only by the hoarse clearing of throats and a few ragged sighs.

Admiral Dawson was the first one to speak. "Hunks," he said softly. "We've got to stop those damned hunks."

"You and I can worry about that later," Pajandcan said finally. War meant losses, and they had to be accepted as they came. Yet no matter how much she understood the rational logic of that thought, Pajandcan had never learned how to take the losses in stride. Every one hurt.

"I was counting on those reserves to free the Hundred and Second Legion for the landing on Sutton," General Schopper said.

"We know that, General. We can still use the Hundred and Second."

"But, Admiral! That will cut Wallbank down to—"

"Dammit! I know as well as you do what that means to Wallbank. And it's all the more reason not to flinch from the Sutton operation. We have to hit the Ukes where it hurts, General, or they're going to hit us even harder."

"I'm sorry, Admiral, but I don't see how I can commit the Hundred and Second now."

"Are you saying you won't, General?"

"I would be within my rights, ma'am," Schopper said. "There's no way you can force me to commit troops I don't have. And I no longer have a legion to spare for this operation."

Pajandcan held her temper. She knew if she pushed Schopper hard enough, he'd go straight to the Joint Chiefs. That was within his rights also. Then the whole Sutton operation would be blown off the planning boards. But there was a lever she could use against him. "Suppose we consult with General Mari on this? I understand his next communication is due in a day or so."

"Of course," Schopper said quickly. "Technically he is still my commanding officer."

"There's nothing technical about it, Schopper. In the meantime I want the Hundred and Second ready to ship off Wallbank on one day's notice."

"Can't do it, Admiral."

Pajandcan put her palms flat on the table, stood up, and leaned forward. If Schopper couldn't orbit on his own, she'd kick his engines out in space. "Let me put it to you this way, General. Either you have the Hundred and Second ready to ship within a day's notice, or when we talk to General Mari, I'm going to demand that you be replaced."

"I still can't—"

"Dammit!" she said, interrupting him with a vengeance, "You'll do what I tell you. Otherwise, I'll write such a scathing report for your service file that you'll be lucky to hold on to the two stars you have."

Schopper rose slowly to his feet, his face swollen with anger. "You can't do that," he said with a defiant shake of his head. "You don't have the authority."

Pajandcan gave him a tight, bitter smile. "Try me, General. Just try me. But I'm warning you right now that you'll regret testing my authority."

Everyone in the conference room hung poised in the tension until Schopper slowly lowered himself into his chair. Any support he might have found among his fellow officers went down with him into glowering silence.

"Now," Pajandcan said without emotion, "if there are no further comments about our troop dispositions, we'll move onto the next item on our agenda," Pajandcan said slowly.

There were no further comments.

18

With a sigh Frye rolled over and looked at the clock. Zero-three-hundred hours. Too early to get up, and too late to go to sleep. Or had he slept? It was getting hard to tell anymore.

These days he worked as long as he had to, went to bed with details swimming through his mind, and got up with them still there. Sometimes the clock indicated that he had slept, but he got up feeling exhausted. Sometimes he knew he had lain awake all night planning strategy, but he got up in the morning feeling totally refreshed.

At this very moment he wasn't sure what had happened since he had climbed into bed three hours earlier. Frye tried to clear his mind. He took slow measured breaths and focused on his body, waiting for the insensitive heaviness that signaled the brink of sleep. Through the haze of his relaxation he saw an image of Melliman that triggered immediate thoughts about her.

For some reason he hadn't been surprised by the delayed response from Personnel to his inquiry about Melliman. She was on her way back to Gensha for permanent reassignment. The officer who had given him the information told Frye she was listed on a roster of "unnecessary" personnel sent back by Marshall Yozel.

Frye had almost laughed when he heard that. Any commander who failed to appreciate Melliman's skills and knowledge and got rid of her as "unnecessary", had to be mentally incompetent. Or . . . The alternative made him frown. He had gotten rid of Melliman once, and he had certainly appreciated her talents.

Could Marshall Yozel have . . . No. He rejected that thought immediately. He knew Melliman well enough to be sure she hadn't gotten personally involved with Yozel. Yozel wasn't the type of man who interested her. No, Frye knew only too well what kind of man Melliman wanted. Him.

He rolled over on his back and stared at the ceiling by the dim light from the clock. He could remember that night he had spent with Melliman as clearly as he wanted to. Now, for reasons he refused to explore, he chose to remember.

Vinita's ashes had hardly had time to settle on the slopes of her beloved Mount Cosio before Frye had turned to Melliman and smothered himself in her arms.

With an angry grunt he threw an arm over his eyes. That wasn't quite true. Vinita had been dead for almost one hundred days by then.

But following his wanton use of Melliman, he had been overcome by guilt and shame. Despite all of her assurances that she loved him, Frye knew he had used her that night—used her without thinking, as a substitute for Vinita. Now he was planning to use her as a substitute for Marsha.

With still another sigh he rolled over onto his side. That wasn't true either. He had tried to use Marsha as a substitute for Melliman, and that experiment had failed miserably. Now he was taking Melliman back as his AOCO because she was the best one he ever expected to have. And because . . .

Frye twisted under the blankets and sat up angrily. The clock read zero-three-ten. Better to get up now than to torture himself like this. But better to get rest of some kind than to take his exhaustion to the Bridgeforce meeting later. With grim determination he straightened the blankets and lay back down.

Once more he let his body relax and tried to clear his mind. Bridgeforce meeting . . . I'm ready, he thought. Have to be absolutely sure . . . attack Satterfield proceeding . . . reinforce Ca-Ryn garrison . . . Melliman . . . father . . .

". . . Father? You said to get you up at six."

Frye tried to dismiss the disembodied voice.

"Father? Are you all right?" Marsha asked as she crossed the room to his bed. When she put a hand on his shoulder he started.

"What?"

"It's six," she said. "You told me to—"

"Fine. I'm fine. Thank you."

She left his room with a small pang of concern. He was working too hard without rest. Even if she hadn't just had trouble waking him, the dark circles under his eyes would have told her that. It's his problem, not mine, part of her mind said as she went to make sure breakfast would be ready when he was.

Frye struggled out of bed and into the bathspa. Shouldn't have slept, he thought groggily as he turned on all the water jets and let the steaming spray slowly massage the fatigue from his muscles. Dreams? he thought. No. Melliman. Thinking again about Melliman.

"Frye," he said aloud as the water stabbed him from every side, "you might as well accept how you feel about her. She's not Vinita . . . never will be. But if she still cares about you, there's no sense in torturing yourself like this. No sense in it at all. Why don't you meet her ship when it lands this evening and start this off right?"

He had no answer for himself, but he was awake enough now to realize that meeting Melliman when she arrived was probably a good idea. There was no sense in waiting any longer than necessary to find out what their relationship was going to be.

It wasn't until the middle of the day during a break in the Bridgeforce meeting that Frye thought of Melliman again. Quickly he called his office.

"Marsha, find out when that troopship is arriving from Sutton, and arrange for ground transportation to get me to the port in time to meet it."

"Your AOCO?" she asked.

"Just make sure I'm there."

"Yes, sir," Marsha said. As the line went dead she wondered why in the world he wanted to meet Vice-Captain Melliman himself? He could more easily send someone . . . unless there was something more to it than . . . It's not fair to Mother, Marsha thought suddenly. Or me, either.

Frye returned to the Bridgeforce meeting feeling much better. That feeling was shattered when he saw Marshall Judoff sitting alone at the table.

"What's this?" she asked with a vicious smile. "A new Vice-Admiral to contend with?"

"Greetings, Judoff," Frye said quietly. "How does it feel to return to the scene of your treachery?"

"Listen, you—that will cost you, Charltos."

"Not from you. You don't outrank me anymore, Judoff, and I'll say what I damned well please to you. Traitor."

Judoff jumped to her feet with a snarl.

"Make that *animal*," Frye said with a smile.

"Enough," Admiral Tuuneo said from behind him. "The two of you either make your peace or shut up. We do not have time for your petty quarrels."

"Petty quarrels, sir! How can you call this a petty quarrel? Her treachery probably cost us the Matthews system."

"I heard the Saks caught you with your legs spread," Judoff said. "Careless of you, *Admiral*."

Frye stared at her for a long second. "Is your mother still bearing Castorian bastards?" he asked. "Or are the crabs all in your bed now?"

A low growl issued from Judoff's throat as she started moving around the table.

Meister Hadasaki laughed as he grabbed Judoff and held her by the arms. She was no match for his nine hundred kilograms.

"Let go of me, you idiot!"

"Enough!" Tuuneo shouted. Pain shot across his face.

"Be calm, Marshall," Hadasaki said as he pulled her arms farther back, "or I will gladly break you."

"This is insane," Tuuneo said. "I want you—" His voice broke into a gurgling gasp as he clutched his chest and fell across the table.

Frye jumped to his side. "Call the medics," he shouted. "It's his heart." Even as he eased Tuuneo onto his back and pulled his legs up to the table, Frye knew the worst was happening. Tuuneo had warned him that it might happen at any time, but he still wasn't ready to face the old man's death.

"Let me help," Hadasaki said as he loosened Tuuneo's tunic with nimble fingers.

"Pulse," Frye said. "Check his pulse."

"I can barely feel it," Hadasaki said. "Put something under his feet. Hurry!"

Frye grabbed a stack of folders and slid them under Tuuneo's feet. Don't die, he thought. In Decie's name, don't die.

The first medic arrived moments later and pushed Frye aside as she jumped onto the table beside Tuuneo. After quickly checking his pulse, she balled her fists together and hit the old man in the solar plexus. "Breathe for him," she ordered as she started pumping his chest with locked hands.

Without hesitation Frye tilted Tuuneo's head back. He remembered to hold Tuuneo's tongue down with his thumb as he opened his mouth. Taking a deep breath he put his mouth over Tuuneo's and exhaled. Then again. And again, until a second medic rushed into the room pulling a cart and told him to stop.

They put an airway down Tuuneo's throat, hooked it to a mechanical respirator, and with the help of several arriving medics hauled Tuuneo out of the conference room and headed for the hospital.

Frye looked around the now crowded room and knew he needed to be alone. In a corner he saw Judoff leaning against a wall with a faint smile on her lips. How he hated her. Oh, how he hated her. How he wanted to make her pay for her treachery. But that would have to wait. Quickly he stalked out of the room.

Two hours later as he sat in the solitude of his office, word came that Tuuneo had died of massive heart failure.

Frye spent the rest of the afternoon alone. Other than one call on his private line to the Transient Officers Quarters, he spoke with no one. There was a numbness in his mind that slowly dissolved under his anger and revealed a core of determination even harder than it had been before. He would win this war at whatever cost, for Tuuneo now as well as for Vinita.

Marsha kept everyone out of his office and told all callers they would have to talk to him in a day or two. When the guard station called and announced that his transportation had arrived, she was hesitant to tell him, but she decided that for the moment she was the only person who could bring him back to the present.

"Father," she said as she knocked on the door, "your transportation to the starport is here." Much to her surprise, the door opened immediately.

"Don't wait up for me," he said, brushing past her. As he reached the door to the outer office he paused. Without turning around, he said, "Thank you, Marsha. Don't wait up for me. I'll be very late again tonight."

She watched him leave with an ache under her heart. What he needed was someone to hug him, but there was no one around who could do it.

Frye was startled when his driver said, "We're here, sir."

He looked at the driver, then out at the vast expanse of the starport studded with hundreds of ships. He had made the whole trip without seeing a thing. "Thank you," he said as he got out of the skimmer. "Wait here."

As quickly as he could, Frye made his way through the crowds of spacers, technicians, and travelers in the terminal to the operations room where he located the duty officer. From the joking and laughing going on, he guessed that they didn't know about Tuuneo yet.

The duty officer listened politely to his request, then suggested that he wait in her office while she went to check with the processing center. She was back in less than five minutes with Melliman following close behind her carrying a bulging shoulder bag.

"Perfect timing, sir," the duty officer said. "Captain Melliman had just finished processing in."

"Thank you, Lieutenant," Frye said absently. His attention was totally focused on Melliman.

"Congratulations, sir," she said, saluting him with a broad smile. "When Lieutenant Knox told me an admiral wanted to see me, I didn't expect to see you."

"Yes, well, a great deal has happened," Frye said as he returned her salute. She looked pale, but beautiful. Without taking his eyes from Melliman he asked, "Lieutenant Knox, may we use your office for a few more minutes?"

"For as long as you need it, sir," the Lieutenant said with a quick salute.

Frye realized that he was staring at Melliman when she suddenly dropped her eyes and blushed. There was no time to contend with the sudden awkwardness he felt, so he pushed it aside. "Listen, Melliman," he said quickly, "I know I hurt you and there is a lot you and I have to talk about, so I reserved a suite at the Transient Officer's Quarters. We can have some privacy there, and I can fill you in on the current situation."

"Situation, sir?"

He saw the ghost of a frown shadow her face, and hesitated. "I know this is all unexpected," he said, "and I don't mean to pressure you. But if those arrangements are acceptable to you, I'll explain everything when we get to the TOQ."

"Of course, sir." Her frown melted into a smile. "I have all my essential gear," she said, patting her bag.

As they headed away from the starport in the skimmer, Melliman began giving him a status report on Sutton, including, as always, her incisive analysis of what had happened there since the invasion, and why.

Frye was content to listen to her. It gave him an opportunity to evaluate her attitude, and the time to prepare himself for everything he wanted to tell her later. Yet as they rode through the fading twilight, he found it more and more difficult to concentrate on anything except her presence.

* * *

"I wonder what people would think of this thing?"

"According to our immigrant scientists, Caugust, the people of Sondak would probably approve. According to their reports, people on every planet are eager to win this war at any price."

He ignored the sarcasm in her voice and looked at the assembled equipment with a cocked eyebrow. "This is much smaller than I thought it was going to be."

"That's because it's incomplete," Sjean said quietly. "The detonator is half-again as big as all this together."

"So, show me the detonator."

Without a word Sjean touched a button on the remote controller in her hand. Two blast doors on the side of the room slid back to reveal the detonator sitting alone in a darkened chamber. "I recommend that we transport it separately—in a totally different ship," she said.

"It frightens you that much?"

"Not just the detonator, Caugust. This whole project frightens me." For a brief instant she wondered if her sister, Vanse, had been frightened before she died over Sutton.

"Very well. We will use separate ships to transport the equipment. However, won't that give us an assembly problem?"

"What if we can't control the reciprocal reaction?" she asked, refusing to answer his question yet.

Caugust shook his massive head. "I don't know the answer to that. What I do know is that the future of Drautzlab depends on this experiment."

"But, Caugust! There's no guarantee that it will work. Surely you didn't tell—"

"We've been through all this, Sjean. I told the Inspector Admiral's office what they wanted to hear, that we would conduct the test. That's all."

"Did they insist on picking the test stars, too?" she asked sarcastically. As much as she respected Caugust, she sometimes felt that his principles were too tightly linked to Drautzlab business. "Or do we get to pick the starting point for the end of the galaxy?"

"We do," he said without blinking. "Now what about the assembly problem?"

Sjean pushed the button to close the blast doors. "It doesn't have to be assembled. The detonator can be tethered to the Wallen with a simple cable."

"The what?"

"The Wallen. That's what I've been calling it." Sjean gave him a bitter smile. "Seemed as good a name as any."

"I don't like it."

"Then name it yourself!" she said angrily. "Call it the Asshole of Doom, or the thing-with-no-name, or anything else you want! There won't be anyone around to know what either of us—"

"This outburst is unnecessary, Sjean."

"Unnecessary? Unnecessary? Here we are standing next to a device that could destroy our whole galaxy, and you think my anger is unnecessary? Don't you care what happens to us?"

Caugust turned away from her and stared at the thing-with-no-name. "We shall call it the D.U.D.," he said finally.

"Dud? What does that mean?"

"Daringly Undestructive Device." He turned back to her with a smile on his face. "How long will it take your people to assemble another of these?"

"Why? I don't understand what you want, Caugust, and until you explain it to me, I'm not doing another damned thing."

"Then pay attention, Doctor. What will happen if we take this Wallen of yours out to a star in the March Cluster and send it on its way without the detonator?"

"Nothing, of course."

Caugust's smile widened. "Exactly. But we would have run the test the I.A. wants, and could then tell them we have to do more experiments."

It was finally beginning to dawn on Sjean what he was suggesting. "Fraud? If Sci-Sec found out about that, they would really kick the bottom out of Drautzlab, Caugust."

"Then we have to make sure they don't find out." Caugust grunted. "Sci-Sec already has enough to worry about going after the real Wallen."

"I have another idea," she said excitedly. "Suppose we take the Wallen and the detonator, load them with telemetry equipment, and ship out with them to the star of our choice."

"And suffer an extensive equipment failure?"

"Yes. Then we'll have megabytes of data to sift through for anyone trying to rush us into another test."

"Sjean, that's an excellent idea—especially if you and I are the only ones who know this isn't a real test. Can you arrange that?"

"Absolutely."

"Good. Make whatever 'adjustments' are necessary to get the Wallen ready as quickly as you can. We'll load and launch as soon as you say we're ready."

Four Absolute Standard Weeks later the Wallen and its tagalong detonator suddenly stopped sending telemetry data as it fell toward the star GA-72-6694 in the March Cluster. To the dismay of the I.A. observers, Sjean and Caugust declared the experiment a failure and headed their ship back toward Summer.

Unbeknownst to anyone, a huge solar flare on GA-72-6694

tickled the Wallen's electronic systems for nineteen minutes causing its small guidance rockets to fire. As the Wallen whipped through perihelion, the cable between it and the detonator snapped. The detonator fell into the star's gravity well. The Wallen swung into a long elliptical orbit around GA-72-6694 with its telemetry equipment again sending out signals, but to now empty space.

19

"How long can we transmit?" Mari asked.

"Even at full scramble it only takes the Ukes about ten minutes to home in on our signal, sir," the pikean co-sergeant said, "so, General Porras has ordered us to limit all of our transmissions to a maximum of seven minutes."

"Damn!" Mari shook his head and rubbed his tired eyes. "Not much time to get a whole lot said, is it? But I agree with General Porras." There was no sense in giving their position away. "All right, Sergeant. If you're sure Admiral Pajandcan is going to be on the other end, I want the full seven minutes."

"That's what they told us, General."

"Then that's what we'll plan for. When do you expect the call to come in from Satterfield?"

"Sometime within the next couple of hours. It's been pretty tough for us to coordinate with them, so we just sit open and wait most of the time."

"Then I'll wait here." He looked around the damp cave with a little shudder. "You have anything hot to drink?"

The co-sergeant smiled. "There's some instant tea in the pot, and some battle coffee back in the rear of the cave."

"Ugh," Mari said with a frown. "Never could stand battle coffee. Burns my stomach and gives me gas. I'll take some of your tea." He poured himself a mug of the tea, sweetened it with the thick, sweet syrup the pikeans always seemed to have for that purpose, and sank into one of the inflatable chairs just outside the communications area.

As soon as the channel opened to Satterfield, his first priority was to tell Pajandcan that he would be leaving on the next freighter. Then he could give her the gist of his invasion idea. It would be easier if Porras were there to answer any questions Pajandcan might have, but Mari knew how critically important Porras's attack on the Gresham starport was. If he and his pikean regulars destroyed the Uke ships as they planned, Sutton would be an even softer invasion target.

It had taken Mari twenty-three days to get from Spurgis to Porras's new headquarters in the Halsey Mountains. One of the most important things he noted on the return trip had been that the Uke forces seemed thinner, both in the air, and on the ground than they had been on his trip over to Elias.

He and Porras hadn't had much time to talk about that before Porras left, but they agreed that the Ukes appeared to be reverting to a defensive posture around all the major cities, leaving the smaller towns and the countryside alone except for irregular security patrols.

That new deployment pleased them both. It meant easier troop movement for them, and most critically, an opportunity to attack the Gresham starport near the north pole. Porras was convinced that the Ukes least expected an attack there, but he had been concerned about massing sufficient troops for such an attack without being observed.

As the withdrawal of the Ukes to an enclave defense had become more and more apparent, Porras had decided the risks were worthwhile, and had made his plans accordingly. Mari had returned only one day before Porras left, and after reviewing the plans, agreed with Porras and wished him well.

Now as he waited for the call from Pajandcan, he wondered what Porras was going through at that moment. If he and his troop were on schedule, they should be less than ten hours away from the start of their attack.

Mari finished the mug of tea and leaned back in the chair. His eyes were heavy for want of sleep, but he dared not close them, even for a minute. Otherwise he might . . .

An hour and a half later a trooper shook him roughly. "Your call's coming through, General."

Forcing himself to his feet, Mari shook off the lethargy of

sleep, but he couldn't stop the burning in his eyes as he walked slowly to the communications area.

"Some tea, sir," the trooper said, thrusting a hot mug into his hands. "I fixed it extra strong."

"Hmm," Mari said, taking the mug and forcing himself to try a sip. Its bittersweet flavor burned his tongue slightly, but it tasted good, and he took another sip as he sat on the padded bench next to the co-sergeant. The screen in front of them was filled by a ragged test pattern.

"I won't respond until you're ready, sir," the co-sergeant said. "Don't want to waste any time."

"'Course." Mari fought to clear his head. After a few more sips of the tea he said, "Ready."

The co-sergeant pushed a button on the console and the test pattern was replaced by a rapidly moving series of symbols. Moments later the symbols dissolved and the shadowy image of Admiral Pajandcan's face appeared.

"Mari, here," he said automatically.

"Good to see you, Fortuno." Her voice was scratched by static.

"Not much time, Admiral. We're fully scrambled, but the Ukes still don't take long to trace our signal." Mari took one more sip of tea to relieve the dryness in his mouth, then set the mug down. "I'll be leaving here on the next available transport," he said quickly. "Will notify you of my arrival as soon as possible. In the meantime I want General Schopper to prepare a preliminary invasion plan for objective Delta-One. It is imperative that this plan utilize the maximum number—"

"Excellent, General," Pajandcan's image said. "We've already begun planning on that."

Mari was startled. "Good. The Joint Chiefs have surprised me again. How soon can you be ready to—"

"No Joint Chief approval necessary." Pajandcan's face cracked in a static filled smile. "This is part of our extended defense plan. We would request that you choose a coordinator on Delta-One as quickly as possible to facilitate—"

"Do you have enough reserve without Joint Chiefs' approval?" Mari asked. He was suddenly worried about Pajandcan's judgement.

"Yes, sir. But you'd better tell Schopper yourself."

Schopper's face replaced Pajandcan's on the screen.

"You heard what I told Admiral Pajandcan. I want the maximum number of troops you have available, Henry."

There was a long pause in the transmission before Schopper answered. "Not enough to do that, sir."

"Find enough, Henry, or I'll relieve you and find them myself. Is that understood?"

Again there was a pause. "Understood," Schopper said reluctantly, "but that will strip Delta-Nine below a safe minimum. If the Joint Chiefs find out about this—"

"You let me worry about minimums. And Henry, don't forget that I'm still a member of the Joint Chiefs. Now listen to what I'm about to tell the admiral. I want those preliminary plans ready by the time I return."

"Yes, sir."

"Thanks, Fortuno," Pajandcan said as her face returned to the screen.

Mari glanced at the clock. He had slightly more than five minutes to tell Pajandcan what he wanted her to know. "I'll give you the current setup," he said, "and the best general approach we could come up with. The details I'll send in a series of burst messages as soon as it is safe."

Giving her first the general disposition of the Ukes forces, and then his assessment of their weak points, Mari quickly used all but the last few seconds of his allotted time.

"The rest to follow," he said quickly. "Mari, out."

The co-sergeant cut whatever response Pajandcan made with a sharp flick of the shut-down switch. "Cut it close, there, General, but I don't think the Ukes—"

A distant rumble made them both look up as drops of water splattered the plasheet covering over the communications area.

"Antenna's down," a tech in the back of the area said. "No response on the line."

"Ukes are getting better, General. Maybe you'd better—"

A series of rumbling explosions overhead shook the whole cave. Pebbles and small rocks joined the water showering down on them from its roof. Instinctively Mari crouched beside the bench and checked his pistol.

His greatest fear was that the cave would collapse on top of him. The sudden claustrophobia made him want to run, but his self-discipline kept him still. In the distance he could hear officers yelling orders, and beyond that the sharp barks of a twenty-one millimeter automatic rifle.

Mari forced himself to stop the building panic and control his rapid breathing. As he debated what to do next, the twenty-one stopped firing, and the yells became less frantic. He stood up in time to greet a breathless, young, pikean gun-sergeant, her face flushed from running. "All clear, sir," she panted.

"What was it, Sergeant?"

"Two Uke flyers. We shot 'em down. Lieutenant Morris is calling for salvage parties now to check wreckage."

"Who's in charge out there?"

"Post-Captain Pena, sir."

"Tell him I want to see him," Mari said. While he waited he poured himself another mug of tea and calmed his nerves. The communications crew was methodically checking their equipment, their voices counterpointed by water and pebbles still trickling from the cave's roof onto the plasheet. Mari shivered. The last place he wanted to die was in a cave.

Pena reported a few minutes later.

"Captain, what is the damage to our antennas?"

"Can no say yet, Heneral," Captain Pena said in a thick pikean accent. "We did send parties up the top, but will be several hours before we have report down. All communications lines broken."

"We don't have several hours, Captain. If the Ukes hit the antennas, that means that's how they found us. So if they're damaged, we have to get them down and get out of here. I want a report in thirty minutes."

"Heneral, we can do no faster than—"

"Thirty minutes, Captain," Mari said, "or I'll relieve you of your diamonds and give them to someone who knows what to do with them. Git!"

Captain Dias appeared as quickly as Post-Captain Pena disappeared from in front of him.

"We should have to move to alternate site, sir," Dias said with a quick salute. "There was third flyer that escaped."

"Very well, Captain. Prepare the move. Where is this alternate site?"

"Rattail Cavern, sir. About four kilometers up valley."

Mari frowned. "You think that's far enough away?"

"General Porras thought it was, sir. Rattail is much less easy to find."

"How long will it take to set up there? I want to let Porras know we've moved as soon as possible."

"Five hours. Maybe six. Be dark soon and we can go faster to move the equipment."

"Give the orders, Captain. As soon as it's dark, we'll move all the communications equipment and—"

"Signal coming through!" a voice shouted from the communications area. "Ice Cat is operational."

"Change one," Mari said immediately. Ice Cat was the code name for Porras's attack on Gresham. For some reason it had started ahead of schedule and Mari was loath to break their connection with Porras for any reason, now, if he could hold onto it and still make the move safely.

"The radio section will remain here until you can set up a new receiver in Rattail." Mari didn't know how Captain Pena had managed to reconnect the antenna, but he was going to hang onto that link as long as he could. As Captain Dias left to get the move started, Mari's thoughts were with Operation Ice Cat.

* * *

Inspector Thel Janette smiled with satisfaction as Xindella's lightspeed freighter settled onto its pad on Oina. It had taken much longer than she wanted to get the approval from Sci-Sec for this mission, and even longer to pressure Drautzlab into guaranteeing the fifty thousand credits. Yet this stop at Oina was the first real step toward finding Ayne Wallen.

Only the knowledge that Drautzlab's first star-size experiment had failed darkened her mood. She was sure that failure was not all the report had indicated, but for the moment she had other things to worry about, not the least of which was dealing with this new Oinaise.

Xindella had insisted that he could not accomplish this task she had set for him without the assistance of some powerful cousin of his, and Janette had sense enough to accept that reasoning for the time being. However, she was totally unprepared for the human who greeted them when they finally left Xindella's ship.

"I'm Captain Teeman," Lucky said. He was as startled by

the imposing beauty of Inspector Janette as she was by his presence.

"Pleased, Captain," Janette said, ignoring his outstretched hand, "but I thought we were to meet—"

"Delightful Childe is mating," Xindella said as he shuffled past both of them. "I told you that."

Before Janette could say anything, Xindella had shuffled around a corner and disappeared.

Lucky laughed. "He certainly doesn't have Delightful Childe's manners, but he's headed in the right direction. Shall we go, Inspector?" Janette grabbed his arm before he could move and stared at him with cold blue eyes. Her grip was as strong as she was beautiful, but she had immediately lost some of her attraction by grabbing him.

"Not yet, Captain, uh, Teeman, is it?"

Lucky slowly removed her hand from his arm. "It is, Inspector. Where'd you learn your manners? From Xindella?"

Janette frowned. "Why are you here?"

She was making it easier and easier for him to dislike her and Lucky knew that she wasn't likely to impress Delightful Childe much with her attitude. "Because Delightful Childe couldn't be here. And because I'm his partner. And because he has some totally bizzare notion that I'm going to help you and Xindella rescue some idiot from Texnor. Any more questions, Inspector?"

"Yes. What do you know about this 'idiot' we want to rescue from Texnor?"

"Not a damned thing, Inspector." Something about her, a certain coldness in her voice, finally pushed him over the edge of anger. Without a word he turned and started walking away from her. Much to his surprise she ran up beside him and slipped her arm gently through his.

"My apologies, Captain Teeman. I am afraid I was so surprised to be greeted by a human that I quite forgot myself."

"Things are strange all over," Lucky said, looking down at her with a forced smile. Even her arm felt cold on his.

"Indeed they are. Shall I tell you about the man I want to rescue, or shall I save that until we meet Delightful Childe?"

"Might as well save it, 'cause I have no intention of helping you, Inspector."

"And why is that?"

Lucky thought she sounded genuinely dismayed. "Because Texnor is one of the nastiest places in the galaxy for one thing. For another, there's only one thing I want from the U.C.S. and you can't get it for me. There aren't enough credits in your pockets or anyone elses to lure me back into the U.C.S. except for my own reasons."

"You sound bitter, Captain."

"You're damned right I'm bitter," he said, pulling his arm away from hers. "Aren't you? Or hasn't this war affected the cold hands of Scientific-Security?"

"What is it you want from the U.C.S.?" she asked, ignoring his question.

"None of your business." Lucky was ready to be shed of her. The rest of the way to Delightful Childe's he kept his mouth shut and let her ask questions of the thin air. Finally she got the hint and quit asking.

Janette was amused and annoyed by Captain Teeman, but she knew that there was more to him than he was willing to show her. Because she understood that she had approached him wrong, she made a mental note to try a softer note with him later. Might even offer to teach him some zero-g exercises.

Hours later Lucky's opinion of Inspector Janette had changed considerably. Not only had she seemingly convinced Delightful Childe that there was more than a matter of credits involved with 'rescuing' Ayne Wallen, she had almost convinced Lucky. But rescue had turned out to be the wrong word. Kidnapping was a more appropriate term. She had given them absolutely no indication that this Ayne Wallen wanted to leave Texnor.

"All right," Lucky said during a brief lull in the conversation, "I'm convinced that you're a super snoop and that this Wallen character is a real threat to peace. I even believe that you and Sci-Sec have a respectable plan for getting us safely dirtside on Texnor. But how in a blazing nova are we going to find Wallen? And then, how are we going to get him out of there? Especially if he doesn't want to come?"

"As I told you, Captain, we have connections on Texnor." Janette was beginning to wish that Xindella had attended this meeting. At least she could bluff him.

"That is insufficient and vague," Delightful Childe said with a sharp snort. "You ask us to risk a ship and Captain Teeman's life on this venture, while revealing far too little about your plan. I fear we must decline our assistance."

Lucky was surprised and pleased by Delightful Childe, but kept his mouth shut and watched Inspector Janette to see how she would respond to that.

"Then Xindella and I will proceed alone," she said with much more confidence than she felt.

"That would be difficult," Delightful Childe said, holding his head higher above the screen and showing his teeth. "Cousin Xindella sends his apologies, but claims it is necessary for him to return to Patros."

"He cannot!" Janette said. "He promised to—"

"He is leaving now," Delightful Childe said calmly. "I believe you are—what is the gentongue word?—ah, yes. I believe you are stranded here, Inspector."

Janette was furious, but she quickly brought her anger under control enough to sputter, "Stop him. Stop him."

"Stop him? I cannot do that. Xindella is free to come and go as he chooses. There will be other ships to take you to Patros, Inspector." Delightful Childe did not like her very much, but he, too, felt anger toward Xindella for placing this unwanted burden on him. "Perhaps we could arrange for Captain Teeman to take you there."

Lucky laughed. "Sorry, Inspector, but it looks like you're stuck with us for a while, because I'm not about to take you to Patros for less than ten thousand credits."

Janette had a sudden idea that tempered her anger. "On one condition," she said slowly. "I'll pay you the ten thousand credits to take me back to Patros, but there is a star in the March Cluster I want to visit on the way."

"The March Cluster is neither on the way to Patros, nor inhabited," Delightful Childe said. "Why should you wish to visit it?"

"For ten thousand credits, I'll visit where I please," Janette said.

"Outside the U.C.S.," Lucky added.

Janette knew there was little hope now of getting to Texnor, but perhaps there was another approach she could use to get her hands on Ayne Wallen. "Very well," she said slowly, "outside the U.C.S. But I want to go as soon as possible."

Lucky shrugged his shoulders. Marsha wasn't due to reach

Yakusan for another month or so according to her last message, and until then he had nothing better to do. And ten thousand credits was more than he could earn doing anything else during that time. "If this transaction pleases my partner, and you pay the credits in advance," he said with a nod toward Delightful Childe, "I'll do it." The rapid babble of Vardequer-queglot from behind the screen told him Delightful Childe's mate was nagging him again.

"Nothing pleases me," Delightful Childe said, ducking his head below the screen to silence Nindoah. "Do as you will," he called finally when Nindoah refused to stop talking. Delightful Childe swore in violent gentongue never to mate again.

Lucky laughed again and Janette allowed herself a smile. Perhaps this trip would not be in vain after all.

20

Olmis had moved from Wallbank to Yaffee and destroyed seven more Sondak ships with eleven missiles during a Standard month of hunting. After conferring with Bon and Kleber, Ishiwa had signaled for a resupply rendezvous with the hunk-tender off the third star in the Ivy Chain. *Olmis* was down to two missiles for her forward tube, and one aft, and Ishiwa decided it was time to rearm the ship, and give the crew a much deserved rest.

Ruto Ishiwa needed a break from their patrol even more than the crew did. In addition to all the battle duties that interrupted his rest periods, he and Andria Kleber had spent every moment they could making love in his cabin. He had begun to think she was trying to set new records for sexual endurance. Andria Kleber was almost insatiable.

At first her extravagant sexual appetite had been delightfully exciting for him. Ishiwa had reveled in the new joys and desires she had aroused, and the levels of response she had brought him to. However, the more often they made love, the less eager he was to do it again right away. The intensity of her demands had worn away his excitement until his weary body cried for rest.

Kleber never seemed to need relief from their excesses the way he did. She seemed more than content to hold him when he slept and drain him again when he awoke. When Ishiwa refused to respond to her sexual advances, he felt guilty about leaving her unsatisfied. When he gave in, fatigue later tore at his reserve of strength during his hours on duty. Neither choice satisfied him, yet he was reluctant to put her off any more than he did. Her unlimited desire for him was still enough compensation for his fatigue—but only barely enough.

"You are tired, Ruto," she whispered in his ear. "I can feel the trembling in your muscles when you hold me."

"Yes, I am tired. The rest will be good for all of us."

"Are you angry with me?"

"No, Andria. Of course I am not angry with you," he whispered, dreading where this would lead. "How could I be angry with one so lovely as you?"

"Because I tax your strength. My mother warned me that I wanted more than one man could give. I did not believe her."

"Nor should you," Ishiwa lied, pulling her closer. With a slow, soft movement she pulled one of his thighs between her legs and rocked gently against him. He had hoped that just this once she would be willing merely to go to sleep. After a moment's indecision, Ishiwa chose to respond, and turned his face to hers.

She reacted without hesitation, and it didn't take them long to couple. Andria quickly got on top and pressed down on him with deliberate slowness. Ishiwa's response changed from decision to instinct as he shifted under her sensuous weight.

They were both panting heavily in their gallop toward fulfillment when the bridgecaller began pinging insistently over their heads.

Suddenly Kleber giggled. It was all so silly that Ishiwa giggled with her. As he twisted to reach for the bridgecaller, his giggles combined with shudders of pleasure. His body jerked involuntarily as the spasms controlled him. The bridge-caller provided an odd counterpoint to their unrelenting giggles and his delightful collapse into release.

When he got to the command deck five minutes later, Ishiwa

was still weak in the knees, but he was smiling. "What do you have, Bon?"

"I think we're being followed, sir."

Ishiwa thought there was a leer in Bon's return smile, but he ignored it. By now the whole crew knew that Kleber was sleeping with him, and Ishiwa no longer cared. "Range?"

"Hard to say, sir. About twenty tachymeters behind us, I'd guess, but steady on our course."

"That's quite a distance to guess, Bon. What makes you think they're following us?"

"I've made several course adjustments by a few degrees each time. Both times the ship behind us adjusted accordingly. From its nav-signals, I think it's Castorian, sir."

"Castorian? Why in the galaxy would a Castorian ship be following us?" Ishiwa scratched his chin and was consciously aware of Kleber's strong odor still clinging to him. He had to fight to suppress another smile. He was too tired and feeling just a little too crazy to make decisions. "You have some suggestions, Bon?"

"We could exit subspace. That would cause them to—"

"I know what it would do, Bon," he said, the humor leaving him for the moment. "I also know it would delay our arrival at the rendezvous, and might cause us to miss the tender." Ishiwa had not meant to cut Bon off, but the sweet ache in his body seemed to have spread to the center of his bones. "Any other ideas?"

"We could continue to monitor and proceed as scheduled."

"And if it closes with us?"

Bon shook his head ever so slightly while pressing his lips together. "I don't know, sir."

Ishiwa covered a loud yawn with one hand and wondered why he didn't feel more concerned about what Bon was saying. "I don't know either. What else?"

"If it doesn't close with us, sir, we could proceed as scheduled and deal with it when we exit subspace."

"All right. Do that."

"Very well, sir."

Again Ishiwa thought there was a hint of a leer in Bon's smile, but as long as they agreed on a temporary solution to this problem, Bon's opinion of his private affairs was irrelevant. Something tickled the back of his mind, something he thought

might be important. As quickly as it came, it was lost, and all
Ishiwa wanted to do was get some sleep. "Just one more thing,
Bon. Don't wake me again unless something serious happens.
Understood?"

"Understood, Captain."

Ishiwa made his way slowly back to his cabin and after
closing the door, he took off his clothes in the dark, a slight
smile teasing the corners of his mouth. As he slipped in beside
Kleber, she murmured quietly in her sleep, turned over, and
made room for him. A little to his surprise and much to his
relief, that was all she did.

Fatigue seeped from his muscles like a warm bath that
weighted his limbs and numbed his senses. Details of the day
drifted through his thoughts in lazy spirals as he sank toward
the heavy darkness of sleep. He was almost gone when a
fragment of memory floated to the surface of his mind and
demanded his attention.

Somewhere in one of his briefing books he had read that the
Saks were using Castorians as emissaries to the other aliens. If
his memory was correct, then a Castorian ship following them
could mean that not only was Sondak using the Castorians as
emissaries, but also as spies.

For a long time he lay there in the dark, trying to keep his
eyes closed, trying to let himself be absorbed by the warmth of
Kleber's body, trying once again to find the path to rest, but the
thought of Castorian spies refused to go away. With a long,
quiet sigh he finally admitted to himself that he would never
get any sleep until he got up and consulted with Bon. Maybe
they should send a burst message to the tender and drop out of
subspace like Bon had suggested.

Slowly and gently Ishiwa extracted himself from the tangle
of Kleber's body and got out of bed. If we act quickly enough,
he thought as he wearily pulled his clothes on, we could
ambush the Castorian ship before it knows what we have done.
But what if we are wrong? We cannot attack a neutral alien
ship without some justification—can we?

When he finally left his cabin for the bridge, his worries
about what they should do wiped out any residual good humor
he had felt and marked his face with an ugly scowl.

* * *

Henley had written and filed seven stories, including one fluff piece that detailed Devonshire's rise from marine lieutenant to admiral. But the more he wrote for the *Flag Report*, the more he chafed under the restrictions the military placed on him. He was a reporter, not a military hack, and all he wanted to do was to report the war as it was happening. Instead of letting him report the attack on the convoy, they had him writing personality profiles of egotistical officers, and meaningless stories for the "Life in the Fleet" column. It didn't take him long to regret accepting the warrant, or to realize that at heart he really was a civilian.

The only thing that made the mounting military excrementia bearable was the almost constant presence of Mica Gilbert by his side. Not only was she with him most of the days, she had become the focus of his private thoughts. But after several long talks during which she had cried repeatedly in his arms, Mica had convinced him that their relationship was better kept a friendship than a love affair.

He understood that. In his head he even accepted it, but not in his heart. Henley had found no suitable way to cope with the emotional shock he had been through with her. What he felt for her was not simple friendship. It was part love, part concern, and part a twisted kind of paternal desire.

Henley despised himself for what he felt, yet no matter how much he cursed himself or swore to purge his emotions, he could not wipe the feelings from his heart. He wanted Mica Gilbert in a way that he could never justify, but wasn't sure he could escape. She was like a drug to his aging body.

Or more truthfully, Mica was like a reincarnation of the daughter his first wife had stolen from him—the daughter he would never know. But his feelings for this daughter were totally unforgivable.

Henley had dreamed about his missing daughter for twenty years. Now in his dreams, his new daughter, in the form of Mica, had miraculously taken him into her arms and into her body, not once, not twice, but three precious times, just as she had in reality. Henley had awakened after each dream elated and shameful, with tears of joy and sorrow running down his face.

It had been too much to bear.

With skills learned through years of persuading people to

help him, Henley had talked his way aboard a shuttle going down to Satterfield. Once dirtside, he had talked his way aboard a lightspeed freighter bound for Sutton, convincing the pilot that he really was authorized to do a story there. He had come out to the polar systems first and foremost to see the war and those who actually fought it. This was the only way he could do that—and the only way he was going to escape his damning fascination with Mica.

"We're about to exit subspace, Henley," the pilot's voice said over his tinny earphones. "After that, it can get pretty interesting around Sutton. Want to join me?"

Henley climbed out of his space hammock and started crawling through the narrow tunnel toward the cockpit. He'd come to appreciate Warrant Officer Caffey during their relatively brief trip together, and he especially admired her courage. This was her fifth run from Satterfield to Sutton.

"I'm ready for something interesting," he said as he wormed his way into the empty couch.

Caffey laughed. "'F'sall right with you, I'd just as soon we skipped anything 'too' interesting. Last time the Ukes damn near caught me as I came in. Had to make a powered equatorial run through the stratosphere to lose them. Almost lost the ship on that one."

"A picturesque tour of the planet followed by a gentle landing will be quite interesting enough, Caffey." Already Henley could feel his palms sweating.

"Comin-n-n-g-g, out!" Caffey said as they exited subspace. "Damn, that's fun. I love it every time."

Henley nodded as his stomach turned over. Caffey began braking the ship with full dampers. The ship responded by vibrating violently and screaming in protest. Just when Henley was sure the ship would break up at any second, the vibrations got worse. As he clutched his armrests in panic, he managed to look over at Caffey. She seemed totally absorbed in flying the ship. "Aren't we slowing just a little too hard?" he shouted above the noise.

"See that grey-green light?" Caffey asked, pointing to a corner of the viewport. "That's Sutton. If we don't slow this fast, we'll whiz right by it. But if we exited any farther out, the Ukes would spot us for sure. Don't you worry, Henley, I'm going to set you down all in one piece."

"What? Me worry?" Henley clung so tightly to the couch he felt like he was braking the ship with his body.

Caffey laughed, then stopped abruptly. "Ukes," she said loudly, pointing to a heads-up display on the viewport.

Henley saw a cluster of amber blips superimposed on the corner of the viewport above the now growing ball of Sutton. "What now?"

"Nothing. They're not heading this way, and we're not heading theirs. As long as it stays like that, we're all right."

"And if it doesn't?"

"Then you really get to see me fly this crate. Hang on."

Much to Henley's dismay, the ship vibrated even harder after Caffey adjusted the controls. Obviously its dampers weren't absorbing the g-forces because Henley was pressed deeper into the heavy padding of the couch. After almost an hour of interminable shaking, he wanted to ask Caffey how much longer this was going to last, but he couldn't form the words.

The viewport was growing fuzzy. His eyes and head ached. When he tried to turn toward Caffey, he couldn't move. Then he realized the fuzziness in the viewport was Sutton reaching out to grab them. They were going to crash right into it. There was no way for Caffey to slow the ship in time.

This is it, he thought. This is how I'm going to die.

Miraculously, the shuddering slowed, then stopped as Caffey brought the ship into a high orbit around Sutton's equator. Miraculously, Henley felt his body relax. Miraculously, they didn't die. "My God," he whispered finally.

"Scary, isn't it?" Caffey asked with a grin.

"You could have warned me."

"What? And spoil the fun? Damn, Henley, I did this four times all by myself. It's kind of a kick to give someone else a trickride like that. Aren't many pilots could do what we just did and hold a ship together, you know."

Henley was too busy swallowing the lumps in his throat to answer her. He felt suddenly very sick, but he wasn't about to—

"Here," Caffey said, handing him a bag.

With great relief he emptied his stomach in three giant heaves. For the first time he wasn't embarrassed about being

spacesick. In fact, he was surprised his body had held out as
long as it did. "Whew," he sighed after wiping his mouth.

"Don't worry. The rest is easy."

Much to Henley's surprise, it was.

Caffey made three tighter and tighter equatorial orbits as
she eased them through the atmosphere. Then she set the ship
on a curving course across a small ocean coming in lower and
slower until they crossed a coastline.

"Ah, there's the beacon," she said. "Right on schedule and
not a Uke in sight." After following a chain of mountains for ten
minutes homing on the beacon, Caffey gently brought the ship
down into a deep valley to a hastily marked landing area not
much larger than the ship itself.

"Welcome to Sutton," she said with a smile as she shut down
the engines.

"Thanks, Caffey. You're a damn fine pilot."

"I know that, Henley. And you're an all right passenger. Be
glad to take you back with me if I didn't already have a return
passenger."

"Passenger?"

"Don't ask. Top secret stuff."

"Well, can't say that I didn't enjoy your company, but I'll be
glad to stay dirtside for a while," Henley said as he climbed out
of the couch. Through the viewport he could see troops in
planetary uniforms closing in on them with small transport
skimmers. "Looks like your unloading party."

As he followed Caffey out of the ship, Henley was surprised
to find himself facing a full general. This could only be General
Mari.

"Who the hell are you?" Mari asked.

"Chief Warrant Stanmorton, sir," he said with a slow salute.
It only took him a second to realize that his good luck had
probably just run out.

"Who sent you out here? Pajandcan?" The combat tellers
insignia on Stanmorton's collar already told Mari more than he
wanted to know, but he couldn't understand why—

"No, sir. I came on my own."

"You can just climb back aboard, Mister. The last thing we
need around here is a teller."

"Only room for one of you," Caffey said with a quiet grin.
"You send him back with me, and you'll have to stay, sir."

"Stuff him in your freight bay, or something. I just want him off this planet," Mari said. After years of reading and listening to their lies and distortions about himself and his friends, Mari had no use for tellers. As far as he was concerned they were the scum of the galaxy—worse than pikeans and aliens.

Henley kept silent and watched the troops as they began to unload the ship. If Mari wanted to leave, let him. Henley fully intended to stay.

"No life support back there, General, but if you want to wait for the next ship, I'll be glad to take him." She flashed Henley a smile. "He's pretty good company."

Before Mari could answer, a low siren blared down the valley. "Ukes! Get away from the ship!" he shouted.

Henley followed Mari at a dead run up the hillside. The transport skimmers, most of them still empty, scattered in every direction. Overhead he heard the roar of aircraft.

He looked up, then dove for a shallow stream bed. The first explosion landed less than fifty meters behind him. The second and third sounded even closer.

Caffey rolled down the bank and landed on top of him. "My ship! The bastards are bombing my ship!"

Henley pulled her flat as dirt and debris showered down on top of them. In the distance he could hear weapons firing as the aircraft moved up the valley.

There was another brief explosion much farther away, followed quickly by a tremendous roar that flooded the valley. When it died away only stillness and dust filled the air.

Slowly Henley and Caffey stood up and climbed up the soft dirt bank of the stream bed. When she got to the top, Caffey gasped. "My ship!" she screamed. Immediately she started running down the hill.

Henley stared after her for a full second before he realized that her ship was on fire. "Stop!" he yelled.

When she didn't stop, he ran after her. Someone tackled him from behind and he fell hard into the dirt, knocking the air from his lungs with a loud grunt.

"They'll get her," a deep voice said.

Coughing on a mouth full of dust and gasping for air, Henley managed to get to his knees just in time to see Caffey's ship explode. He immediately fell flat again as the blast wave rolled over him. Where was Caffey?

Someone was crying. Voices were shouting commands. Henley trembled as he climbed to his feet and surveyed the scene.

Caffey's ship was barely visible under a boiling column of flames and smoke. High across the valley a second column of smoke rose from behind an outcrop. The Uke aircraft, he thought. Returning his gaze to the valley floor he saw several skimmers full of troops speeding south away from the wreck.

A moment of panic seized him until he saw General Mari standing with Caffey thirty meters off to his right. She was staring at the wreck with a look of disbelief. As he walked over to them on still shaky legs, he could see silent tears running down her face.

"I'm sorry," he said, touching her arm.

"Bastards," she whispered without looking at him.

"Looks like neither of us will be leaving Sutton for the time being, Mister," Mari said quietly, "but it's time to get out of *here*." For the moment he was glad to be alive, but already he was thinking ahead. The next freighter was scheduled to land in two days, over a thousand kilometers away. If he couldn't get to that one in time, Mari wasn't sure how he was going to get off of Sutton.

The three of them climbed aboard Mari's skimmer, and with another skimmer full of troops acting as their escort, they headed rapidly toward the north end of the valley on a twisting course between low trees and high rocks.

Caffey held onto her seat support with one hand and Henley's arm with the other as they bounced along. He wanted to offer her some kind of comfort, to say something to ease her grief, but he didn't know how. The last time . . .

He let the thought slip with a grim smile and wondered what Mica would think if she could see him now—dirty, frightened, and running away from a disaster.

What she thought didn't matter. Henley was where he intended to be, although a bit closer to the action than he would have liked. But it was hard to tell what was really going on in a war without getting close to the fighting. The fear he had felt had been replaced by a growing sense of elation.

Let someone else report the big picture. This was where everything important really happened—even to generals, he thought as he smiled at the back of Mari's head.

21

Frye stood before Bridgeforce and chose his final words carefully. A series of clandestine political maneuvers had put him, at least temporarily, in the position Tuuneo had wanted for him. He had been forced to agree to a continuation of the bombship project, and the promotion of tens of officers he knew openly expressed kyosei isolationist sentiments, but in the end all of Tuuneo's groundwork had paid off. Now as acting chairman, it was incumbent on Frye to convince Bridgeforce to act now.

"It is extremely important that we initiate this attack as quickly as possible," Frye said slowly. "We've finally chased Sondak out of the Michel Cluster and our hunks are beginning to decimate their shipping in the polar regions. A devastating blow against Satterfield now, followed swiftly by the secondary attacks I've outlined against Bakke, Yaffee, and Wallbank will cripple Sondak's already depleted fleets."

He paused and glanced quickly at Melliman, then gave Bridgeforce what he hoped would be the ultimate inducement for accepting his plan. "If we take Satterfield and do sufficient damage to the other polar systems I mentioned, I believe we could convince Sondak to sue for peace before they suffer anymore—peace on our terms."

"I agree," Marshall Judoff said with no trace of emotion.

Frye was startled, but held his tongue when it was obvious that she had more to say.

"Not only do I believe Admiral Charltos is correct in his assessment of the situation, but I will recommit my forces to this historic effort."

"Under Admiral Charltos's command, of course," Meister Hadasaki said.

Judoff gave him a tight smile. "Of course. How could it be otherwise?"

Hadasaki stared at her. "I guess your use of the term 'historical' made me remember unpleasant events of the past—events I would not like to see repeated in the future."

"You have no cause to concern yourself in that way, Meister Hadasaki. I have given my word."

"Excellent, Marshall. I am sure all of Bridgeforce appreciates the value of that." When she scowled, he smiled. "However, there are several other considerations to be dealt with. Would we not be better served if our first two bombships were completed before we undertook such far-flung operations?"

"We cannot wait that long," Frye said grimly. "Already the bombships project has cost us valuable time and materials needed elsewhere. It will proceed on schedule, but we cannot wait for the bombships—regardless of how valuable they may prove to be in the future. If we delay this action, we risk losing the initiative in this war."

"Again I agree with Admiral Charltos," Judoff said, "both about the value of the bombships, and the necessity to avoid delay. Shall I call for a vote approving the plan, Meister Hadasaki, or will you?"

"I do not believe we have given this sufficient discussion for a vote yet, Marshall Judoff." It was beyond Frye's comprehension why Judoff was supporting him like this, but he suspected only the most self-serving motives from her. "Are there any additional comments?"

There were.

Bridgeforce haggled late into the night before Marshall Judoff again demanded that they vote. With reluctant unanimity the members of Bridgeforce voted to begin immediate preparations for attacking Satterfield, and for follow-up attacks using hunks and auxiliary launchships against Bakke, Yaffee, and Wallbank. As soon as the vote was settled, Frye called for a fifteen hour adjournment, then began putting his papers back in their folders. Almost at once he was aware of Judoff staring at him.

"I surprised you, didn't I, Charltos?"

"Yes, Marshall Judoff, I must admit that you did. But it was a very pleasant surprise."

"Of course," she said, turning her back on him and heading for the door. "All my surprises are pleasant—for someone."

"Beware, Admiral, or she'll bite you again," Hadasaki said before following her out the door.

"Judoff's gotten even worse," Melliman said when only the two of them were left in the meeting room, "and Hadasaki is a mystery to me."

"Hadasaki has his own concerns, but he is at least consistent in his position." He paused and gave Melliman a warm smile. "You're only too right about Judoff, though, my dear Clarest, but without her ships, we would have to take most of Yozel's away from Sutton to use against Satterfield. Given your report on Admiral Yozel, he can barely handle what's happening on Sutton with what he has."

"But you are going to take some of his launchships?"

"Yes. Yozel obviously isn't using them, and we will certainly need everything we can muster over Satterfield."

"Don't sound so negative, sir. This is an excellent plan you've given Bridgeforce, and I know it will lead to a resounding victory."

Frye smiled at her again and marveled again at how swiftly things could change in one's life. First Vinita, then Marsha, then Tuuneo, and now Melliman. With Marsha on her way to Yakusan, there was no reason— "Clarest, let's go to my house and talk about it," he said quietly. "We'll toast Bridgeforce's acceptance, and ponder Judoff's latest enigma."

"Anything you say, sir," she said, returning his smile.

* * *

Admiral Pajandcan took a deep breath, closed her eyes, and massaged her temples. The medics wanted to run another series of tests on her to determine if there was some physical cause for these severe headaches, or if she was merely suffering from the strain and tension of overwork.

Pajandcan didn't have time for more tests. The attack group was scheduled to leave in ten days to hit the Ukes at Sutton. She was still trying to make sure that the striking force was strong enough while leaving sufficient personnel and ships behind to protect the rest of the polar systems—and all that with a limited methane supply. Dealing with those problems gave her headaches enough. Her physical headaches would have to wait.

At least Schopper was cooperating now. After receiving his instructions from Mari, Schopper's whole attitude had changed, and he was providing more help to her than anyone else. Given the dangers Schopper's troops would be facing, Pajandcan knew that his was also the most difficult part of the task.

Hours later when Schopper and Dimitri entered her office, she was pleased that Mica Gilbert was with them.

Dimitri smiled at her as he sat in one of the hard chairs and made himself comfortable. "I asked Captain Gilbert to attend this meeting because I want her on my staff for the attack," Dimitri said.

"That's totally up to Captain Gilbert. She is not under my direct authority." Pajandcan gave Mica a look of approval and hoped that by publicly acknowledging her status, the tension might ease between them. Pajandcan rather liked Josiah's daughter.

"Wouldn't mind having her on my staff, either," Schopper said easily.

"Admiral. General," Mica said with a slight blush. "I am pleased by your offers, but perhaps I can serve you both and POLFLEET at the same time." She looked directly at Pajandcan when she spoke, wanting this woman who had loved her father to approve of her.

"In what way?" Pajandcan asked.

"I could serve as your liaison to the attack force," Mica answered. "With my access to Cryptography's communications network, I could keep you updated on the mission without having to burden the normal channels."

Dimitri laughed. "Cryptography handling battle reports? Rocky would have a fit if he knew about that."

"On the contrary, sir. I've already cleared this with Commander Rochmon. He heartily approves."

"What? You told Rochmon our plans?" Pajandcan was suddenly angry and her headache pushed itself forward. "This was supposed to be a secret operation."

"He already knew, Admiral. My father told him. Father also told him to render whatever assistance he could."

It was Pajandcan's turn to laugh, but she couldn't. The pounding in her head was too strong. No matter where she turned in her career Josiah Gilbert was always there—in the shadows, but always there. Why couldn't he . . . She dropped that thought. He was doing what he thought best for the Service and Sondak, not for her.

"Very well," she said slowly, "I think that is an excellent idea, but I suspect there is more to it than what you told us."

"Just what we talked about before," Mica said, unsure of what she could say in front of Dimitri and Schopper.

"Reports directly to your father?" Pajandcan wasn't about to keep that a secret from her top leaders.

"Yes, ma'am."

"What kind of reports?" Schopper asked.

"Confidential ones, General."

Admiral Dimitri frowned. "Spying for the old man, huh? Doesn't surprise me. Doesn't change my mind, either. What about you, Chop? You mind her spying on you?"

"It isn't spying. Father only wants—"

"Spy all you want, Captain," Schopper said with a wave of his hand. "But once this operation starts, you'll do as you're told, stay out of the way, and when it comes time to send your secret reports, tell your father the truth. I respect him, so I'll trust you."

"Thank you, sir."

"Good," Pajandcan said quickly. "Now that we've settled that, I want to review this attack schedule staff has worked up for us. It seems to me . . ."

Mica stood, assuming that her part in this meeting was over.

"Don't leave, br—Captain," Pajandcan said, allowing herself a faint smile. She had almost called Mica 'brat' in front of the others. "You'd better know what's going to happen when, so you can inform me of changes as the attack takes place."

"Then may I ask a question, Admiral?"

"Certainly."

"Is there any way we can attack sooner? The reports from Cryptography you received yesterday indicate that the Ukes are building up another attack fleet and—"

"What?" Pajandcan realized that she hadn't read yesterday's Cryptography reports. She had been so busy—

"Another attack fleet, Admiral." The look on Pajandcan's face told Mica this was new information. "Their target still isn't clear, but we do know they have pulled in the militia fleet under Marshall Judoff and are consolidating their positions. The sooner we can strike them at Sutton, the better."

Pajandcan rubbed her temples in a futile attempt to ease

the pain. "What about that, you two? Can we begin any sooner?"

"If we have to, we have to," Dimitri said. "But the best we can probably do is cut it to eight days."

"And that will be tighter than a prowhore," Schopper added.

After thinking for a moment, Pajandcan said, "I have another duty for you, Captain. From this moment forward, you are responsible for briefing me orally on any and all Cryptography reports you consider significant to this mission."

"Yes, ma'am."

"Then here we go." Pajandcan looked at each of them in turn. "One way or another we are going to launch the attack force in eight days. Agreed?"

"Agreed," Dimitri and Schopper answered simultaneously.

Mica only nodded, and hoped they wouldn't have to pay a severe penalty for rushing their plans.

Pajandcan took another of the pain killers from her desk and downed it quickly. It was going to be a long eight days.

* * *

"And what did he say?" Janette asked.

"He repeated what he said before," Lucky answered slowly, trying to calm his reaction to her anger, "that help was on the way, and that we would have to be patient."

"So how long do we have to wait?"

"Until help arrives. Now if you don't mind, Inspector, I'm going to fix something to eat and get some sleep."

"Aren't you going to keep working on the Gouldrive?"

"Inspector," Lucky said with impatience vibrating his voice, "I told you before and I'll tell you again. I've done everything I know how to do. The Gouldrive is running well enough to keep us in communication with Oina, and that's all it can do for us until someone gets here who knows more than I do. Why can't you accept that? You think that just because you are pretty and a Sci-Sec Inspector that you can always get what you want?"

"You have no cause to speak to me—"

"Lady, I've got all the cause I need. You're on my ship as a passenger, yet you refuse to accept my authority or my evaluation of our situation. If you want something to eat, you can follow me to the galley."

Much to his surprise she did just that. She even helped him fix their rations and tried to carry on a normal conversation with him as they ate. For some reason Lucky found that almost as annoying as her continuous questions.

Later as he lay in his bunk staring at the overhead, he wondered what made Janette's electrons jump. Power? Prestige? He had no idea. For all that he knew about her she might be motivated by the thrill of the chase, or by pure altruism, or any one of a set of other things. She was as foreign to him as she was beautiful.

In fact, her beauty was her only trait that he could admire, and obviously she hadn't had much to do with that. But living with her for a month in close proximity aboard *Graycloud* had led him to the opinion that her beauty was almost flawless. It was with thoughts of that beauty that he fell asleep.

Lucky dreamed of Marsha, a dream that swept him through a complex of emotions into a scene of misty eroticism, a dream so real and exciting that he awoke in the middle of his orgasm to find himself lying under Janette.

Even as he fought the gasping spasms, anger tore at his brain. As he caught his breath and tried to speak, she placed a small finger on his lips.

"Shhh," she said, "I just wanted to apologize. I thought maybe you would—"

"You thought wrong," Lucky said fiercely, pushing her off of him and climbing from the bed. "If I had done that to you, you would have called it rape." Without waiting for a reply he went into the head and slid the door shut behind him.

Standing there in the dim light he felt dirty and used and ashamed. As quickly as he could he turned on the jet sprays and climbed into the cleanser, letting the sharp needles of water tear away her odor and slime. Yet in the hot, steamy air her odor seemed to cling to everything, and with an angry twist he turned the sprays up as hard as they would go.

He knew he was wasting water, but he didn't care. If *Graycloud* couldn't recycle it fast enough, Janette would just have to do without cleansing herself. Be interesting to see if she could keep her beauty looking so fresh without water for her cleanser.

Why? Why had she done that? What right did she think she had to use his body? Lucky didn't know and he didn't care what she thought she was doing or why. It didn't matter anymore. She had violated and disgusted him, and he wanted nothing further to do with her.

As soon as the Gouldrive was repaired, he was going to take her back to Oina and let her try to get to wherever she was going from there. He wasn't about to spend any more time than necessary with a woman who had no scruples about using another human being for her own pleasure.

Finally he turned off the water jets and turned on the blowers. He still didn't feel clean, but he knew it would be a long time before he would ever feel clean again. What did she think he was? One of those sexual ephemera like the ones they sold on Nordeen—a device to be used and thrown away?

Lucky shuddered in the warm air and wrapped his arms around his chest. He wanted to cover himself and hide. The dirt was gone—the physical dirt at least—but his shame remained, a shame as illogical as it was damning.

How could he have let this happen? How could he not have guessed that she might do something like that? He didn't know. He must have done something very, very wrong. As the blowers dried the last of the water from his body, tears ran slowly down his face, and Lucky cried without knowing why.

22

Henley stood in the little cul-de-sac facing General Mari and tried to control his anger. Yet when he spoke, he knew it was a losing battle. "What in the Corps have I done to you, General? All I want to do is observe and report the war from Sutton? What's so wrong with that?"

"Look, Mister, I've got no use for tellers—whether their in the Service or not—and I don't want you here. Pajandcan says you left without authorization, so as soon as that transportation gets here, you're hopping off this planet with me."

"Fine. Just fine, General." Every time Henley thought he

had made points with Mari, the general turned around and read him the same story about how he would have to leave. He had thought his story about the downing of the Uke aircraft might have pleased Mari. It hadn't.

Now Henley was just tired of the arguing with Mari and tired of losing every argument. "I'll be sure to put all this in my story for the *Flag Report*, and since Admiral Gilbert authorized me to come here, I'll put your actions in my personal reports to him. I'm sure he'll appreciate the cooperation you've given me and want to commend you to the rest of the Joint Chiefs."

Mari stared at the little stalactite over Stanmorton's head before shifting his eyes back to the persistent teller. "As a member of the Joint Chiefs, I seriously doubt that I will have to concern myself with that." He secretly admired Stanmorton's grit and determination to stay on Sutton, but he had made up his mind, and no converted civy was going to change it.

"However," he said after a long pause, "if you're going to write me up in the *Flag Report*, be sure to spell my name right. That's Fortuno, F-O-R-T-U-N-O, Mari, as in Marie with no 'e' on the end. You got that?"

"You bet," Henley said. He was sick and tired of fighting the general's unjustified stubborness. It was time to push as hard as he dared. "Let's see, that's Mari, 'M' as in mud, 'A' as in ass, 'R' as in rude—"

"That'll do, Mister!" Mari was startled by Stanmorton's continuing effrontery and fast losing any patience he had left. The teller's admirable persistence was one thing, but his insults were quite another. "One more crack like that from you and I lock your ass up for the duration."

Henley sighed and rubbed his forehead. "Look, General, can I say one more thing?"

"Build your own cell," Mari said sharply. "I'll watch you."

"Then listen to me for once. I've tried to be reasonable. I've tried to understand your point of view. I've tried everything I know how to stay out of your way and off your mind, but you just won't let go of it." Henley heard the fatigue and resentment in his voice and changed his tone.

"I respect your abilities as a soldier, sir. I truly do. And I have no doubt that you have the power to lock me up somewhere till the end of the war. But I also know that one of the few guaranteed liberties left to a citizen of Sondak is the freedom of speech."

Mari snorted. "Go on."

"So you can lock me up, General. You can throw me off this planet. You can do whatever it is you feel you have to do because of some irrational paranoia you have about tellers." Henley meant to pace his words, but they rushed out of his mouth. "But I'll tell you this. If you do any of those things, I swear to you that I'll make your paranoia come true. I'll dig up every bit of dirt you ever stepped in, and I'll spend the rest of my life making sure the public knows *everything* there is to know about General Fortuno Mari."

"How dare you?" Mari asked as the blood flushed his face. "How dare you threaten me like that?"

Henley took a deep breath and let it out slowly. "I'm not threatening you, sir. I'm almost as old as you are, and I know better than to threaten a general. I'm just making a promise to Fortuno Mari, the man—the one with pacifist tendencies who beats his pikean mistress."

Mari clenched his fists and his jaw, and strained to keep his anger from erupting into violence. Every instinct in his body wanted him to lash out at Stanmorton. Yet even through the red mist of his fury, Mari knew that short of killing Stanmorton, there was nothing he could really do to stop him from carrying out his threat. Mari also knew there was more than enough information in his past to make him vulnerable to a scandal that could ruin his career.

Henley could almost smell Mari's hatred for him, but the look on Mari's face told him he had made his point. He might still have to leave Sutton, and he might still find himself locked away somewhere, but at least Mari understood that he would have to pay for doing that—and pay dearly.

"You don't quit, do you Mister?" Mari asked through clenched teeth.

"No, sir, I don't. Especially when I think I'm right."

"Then let me tell you something, Mister. I don't think you are right. Not one damned bit. I don't think you belong here, and I don't want you here." Mari paused and slowly unclenched his fists, forcing his anger back under control. He had far more important things to worry about than Stanmorton.

"But I don't think you're worth all this trouble, either," he said with his voice well under control. "So I'll tell you what I'm going to do. You want to report on this war? You want to be with the people doing the real fighting?"

Henley knew the question was rhetorical, but he nodded anyway, as though by agreeing with Mari he could defuse the general's anger.

"Fine. I'm going to send you over to Elias and you can spend your time with General Archer and his troops. Report the war from there, and if you survive this war, don't ever let me see your face again."

Before Henley could answer, Mari turned and left the cul-de-sac, all too aware that he had lost this fight. Yet as he headed for the command section, he felt a grudging admiration for Stanmorton that refused to be dismissed.

For a long moment Henley listened to Mari's retreating footsteps and the distant sound of water dripping from the roof of the cave. He wondered more than ever if the torture Mari had suffered had left him stable enough to remain a member of the Joint Chiefs, much less to be leading troops.

With a quick decision Henley, too, left the cul-de-sac and went to look for the captain in charge of transportation. He wanted to leave before Mari changed his mind. With General Porras now back from the victory at Gresham and all the shifting of troops taking place and the movement of the crudely effective civilian support groups, he just might be able to start on his way to Elias without delay.

* * *

Leri had brooded over the decision and turned it in her mind until she knew it could no longer be avoided. Her vision had shown the Castorians helping her people, and the Confidante had confirmed the vision. It was time to contact the Castorians.

Yet even as she had Weecs make the arrangements for the transmission, her thoughts went back to Exeter. The memory of that horrid Castorian made her shiver. She had trusted him. She had believed that he was worthy of fairer dealing than the inferior humans. But he, he had drugged her and taken her up to his ship and had been prepared to *eat* her. Leri shivered again and almost told Weecs to cancel her request for a transmission.

Then she had an idea, a thought that held her in its grip with a special kind of attraction. Maybe there was an answer for her in Exeter's rude actions, an answer for the revenge she dearly wanted against him.

It took three seasons before a transmission window opened to Castor. Leri spent most of those thirty hours thinking and rethinking her plan until she was sure of exactly what she wanted from the Castorians and what she was prepared to pay for it.

Once communications were established, Weecs spent several hours negotiating with several Castorian diplomats before he called Leri to the communications station the humans had built for Cloise. There she found herself facing the picture of a Castorian on the small screen.

"Proctor Leri?" the scratchy voice of the Castorian asked. "We are most honored by your communications."

"Do not rush to judgment," she said. "I do not expect you to be pleased with me or my people after you have heard my requests. To whom am I speaking?"

She waited several seconds, expecting a response.

"There is some natural delay," Weecs whispered. "The name he gave me was Solliccet."

"Then I shall wait to hear your requests," the Castorian said finally.

"I want the one who was here as an agent for Sondak, the one the humans called Exeter. Do you know the one I refer to, Solliccet?" She waited patiently this time.

"I believe I do, Proctor Leri, but I fear he is unavailable to come to Cloise at the moment."

"Make him available," Leri said quickly. "I want to kill him. He is the price of our bargain."

"What bargain, Proctor? Castor has no bargain with Cloise."

"You do now. Either way you do. If you send Exeter here so that we may exact our revenge for his treachery, you have the bargain that we will not broadcast the location of Castor to every power in the galaxy interested in methane. If you refuse to send Exeter here, you have our promise that your true location will become common knowledge to every methane pirate living."

"This is a strange bargain you propose," Solliccet said after a long delay. "You promise to keep the secret of our location or reveal it in exchange for a Castorian life? Half the galaxy already knows our location."

This was not going at all like she had planned it, but Leri was too caught up in the idea of revenge to stop now. She had to let the Castorians know how deeply Exeter had offended her and Cloise by his despicable actions.

"I'm talking about the location of Castor—the true Castor—not the one you let aliens visit. I'm talking about the planet Castor located on the Standard grid at"—Weecs handed her the coordinates—"polar sector B-four-seven-one-six-six-point-nine-zero-etcetera, equatorial sector A-one-three—but perhaps I shouldn't continue with this quite yet." Leri barely had time to shift her weight before his reply started coming in.

"Stop! Stop! We believe you. For the sake of our souls, stop this Proctor. . . . Ah, thank you. Yes, we would indeed be interested in your bargain." Solliccet paused and clacked something to someone out of view. "However, Exeter may be something of a problem. You see, we currently have him imprisoned for the crime of eating his offspring."

Leri almost laughed when she heard that. "That does not surprise me," she said quickly, "but should that not make you happy to get rid of him?"

Again there was a longer than normal pause before Solliccet answered. "That is a question I am not at liberty to answer, Proctor. We are concerned that you would so willingly threaten our whole planet just for the life of one worthless individual. Such an attitude must naturally give us pause to consider any request you make of us."

"Then consider this, Solliccet. In exchange for the life of Exeter we also offer you a neutral alliance against the humans—Sondak and the U.C.S. both. Let them fight their wars, but let us protect each other." Desperation was creeping through Leri's brain. She had meant to start with this proposal and work her way to claiming revenge on Exeter. What is wrong with me? she wondered. What made me change from the plan? Whatever it was, she would have to do something quickly to make amends or her whole proposal would be lost.

"Now you make us a different offer? Are all of your race as inconsistent as you, Proctor Leri? Or have you yet another of your 'bargains' waiting behind this one?"

"My apologies, Solliccet. My desire for revenge against Exeter has blinded me to the greater purpose we should be considering. Please think on what I have said with that in mind and forgive my impatience."

"Perhaps if you told us what offense Exeter committed against you we would be better prepared to consider your suggestions. Otherwise, I fear that these proposals are far too outrageous to merit serious consideration."

"He tried to eat me," Leri said. "He drugged me, took me from my home, and tried to eat me."

Solliccet's reply was preceded by an outburst of clacking. "Understandable," Solliccet said after the clacking faded into the background, "but hardly acceptable actions for one acting in a diplomatic capacity. You see, Proctor Leri, on Castor you would most certainly be regarded as a delicacy—"

"You, too?" Leri asked in dismay.

He continued speaking, quite unaware because of the delay, that she had interrupted him. "—worthy of the finest meal. However, now that we understand what he did, we will most gladly give your 'bargain' the most intense consideration."

"That is all we ask," Leri said with a sigh. "But we need your answer at your earliest possible convenience, of course."

"Of course, Proctor Leri. Of course."

The screen went blank and Leri felt a great weariness as she and Weecs made their way back to her chambers. Neither of them spoke, and Leri was grateful. She had almost ruined a great and necessary opportunity for Cloise because of her personal need for revenge, and did not want to discuss that with anyone. Soon enough she would know if her visions could still become reality.

* * *

Marsha sat in her room at the LoSazo Transient Officers Quarters on Yakusan and fought back the tears. Never in her life had she felt so isolated and alone. Never had she felt so desperate for something she did not know how to obtain. She was still a hundred light years from Oina, with no guarantee that even if she could find some way to get there that Lucky would be waiting for her.

A knock on her door helped her maintain her composure. When the door slid back, she was so shocked that she couldn't speak. In front of her stood a huge Oinaise.

"A thousand pardons for intruding on your privacy, Captain Yednoshpfa," the alien said, "but I had need to speak to you in private. May I enter?"

Marsha stood back with a nervous wave of her hand and quickly slid the door closed after he entered the room. "Are you from . . . I mean, did Lucky send you for—"

"Patience, Captain. My name is Xindella, and in a moment I will try to explain what I can." He slowly settled his bulk on the floor against an empty space along the wall.

Marsha stood waiting impatiently, afraid to hope and afraid not to. Xindella seemed more concerned with getting comfortable than talking to her. "Please, uh, but if you would just—"

"Yes," he said, stroking his long, wrinkled proboscis, "I have come at the behest of my cousin, Delightful Childe, whom I believe you know."

"Of course I do. Where is Lucky? Is he with you?"

"Hardly, Captain. At the moment I believe he is stranded somewhere in the March Cluster with a rather unfriendly official from Sondak."

Confusion swirled through Marsha's mind. "Stranded in the March Cluster? Why? What . . . I don't understand."

"Neither do I, Captain. However, my cousin assures me that he is quite well, and I have obtained the services of a qualified technician to repair his Gouldrive. All that remains is for us to go to the March Cluster and find him."

"But I can't just leave here." Marsha caught herself. Why not? Why couldn't she just leave? "You have a ship?"

"Of course."

"Then if I can get aboard, we can—"

"I have arranged for that," Xindella said, "but we must be careful. There are those who do not approve of what we are about to do."

"My father?"

"I do not know your father, Captain Yednoshpfa, and I would rather not reveal the names of those who are so agitated about my presence. Suffice it to say that they are powerful and I have something they desperately want."

"I, uh—"

"Come to my ship after dark," Xindella said rising to his feet. "Enter the launch area through Gate A-Seven, and you will see it immediately. As soon as you are aboard we will leave."

"Please, don't go yet," Marsha said, putting her hand on his arm. His skin felt like soft leather. "Why are you doing this? What makes you think they will let me into the launch area? I don't understand any of this."

"Just trust me, Captain. If you follow my instructions, I will be able to take you to Captain Teeman."

Reluctantly Marsha stood back and let him leave. After the door closed, her confusion overcame her and tears rolled freely down her face. Yet even as she cried she began repacking the few clothes and possessions she had taken from her bags.

She didn't know how any of this had happened, or why, but she wasn't about to pass up the opportunity Xindella offered her. If he could get her to Lucky, that was all that mattered.

23

Olmis's readyboard lit green. The crew was at battle stations. "Ready to exit subspace, sir," the boater said.

"Our Castorian still will us, Bon?"

"Yes, sir."

"Watch him. Boater, by the count from ten, Exit," Ishiwa commanded. His voice was calm, but inside he felt a tremor of anticipation.

The boater counted down from ten to zero as the seconds ticked off and *Olmis* slid back into normal space. Silent tension gripped the bridge.

Somewhere a braking-day ahead of them lay the hunk tender *Osoto.* Somewhere behind them was the Castorian ship. If it was going to follow them into normal space, it would have to exit subspace within thirty or forty seconds after *Olmis* did. Even that timing might be too slow unless the Castorian had a terrific set of inertial dampers.

"It's veering off," Bon said finally.

"Range?"

"Fifteen-point-four-plus tachymeters and moving away at eleven degrees," Kleber said.

"Any chance for a shot, Kleber?"

"Negative, sir."

"Very well then. Secure from battle stations. It looks like that ship isn't as interested in us as we thought."

Ishiwa felt a quiet flash of disappointment as Bon repeated his order. After all the tension caused by the Castorian, it would have been a relief to have taken a shot at it. "Full braking, Bon."

"In effect, sir."

"Good. Prepare to alert *Osoto* to our presence and request instructions for—"

"—knowledge *Misbarret*," a scratchy voice from the overhead speaker said. "Acknowledge."

Ishiwa quickly grabbed the microphone for the lightspeed transmitter. "Hunk One-Zero-One, *Misbarret*, acknowledging."

"We copy, *Misbarret*. This is tender *Osoto*. You are directed to proceed to us at maximum safe speed for rearming, refueling, and new orders. Please give your estimated time of arrival at our station."

Bon glanced at the instruments. "Twenty-one Standard."

"Twenty-one Standard hours," Ishiwa repeated into the microphone. "Request use of rest and recreation facilities for all crew members as—"

"Sorry, sir. No R-and-R. We will send your preliminary orders as soon as possible. Confirm E.T.A. twenty-one Standard hours. *Osoto*, out."

"*Misbarret*, out," Ishiwa said dully. No R-and-R? But why? The crew desperately needed a rest. And so did he.

"I don't like it, sir."

"Neither do I, Bon. But before we second-guess headquarters and make any judgments, let's wait and see what our new orders say. Will you take the first watch?"

"Of course, sir."

"Thank you. I shall be in my cabin. As soon as the orders come in, please bring them to me."

"Aye, sir."

Ishiwa returned Bon's salute feeling more tired than ever. As he went to his cabin to complete the final entry in *Olmis's* first hunting report, he suddenly wondered if they were going to be sent back to Yakusan for R-and-R? He doubted it. Headquarters wouldn't do that unless they also had some new weapons or equipment to add to *Olmis*. Unless . . .

As he entered his cabin it occurred to him that headquarters might call *Olmis* back if they planned to present decorations to him and the crew for the success of their first mission. As great a waste as that would be of time and energy, he knew it was the kind of thing Admiral Entungee might think was good for morale.

With a shake of his head he pulled out the hunting report and folded down the little desk. He was doing exactly what he had told Bon not to do—second-guessing the orders. That was always what happened. It was the rare commander who could sit and wait for orders without speculating about what they might contain, and he wasn't one of them. The regular spacers were even worse about it. Bets about where their new orders would send them were probably already being made and covered throughout the ship. With a quiet grin he set about finishing his report.

It was less than an hour later when Bon knocked on his open door. "Orders, sir."

"Come in."

Bon entered with Kleber at his heels. They both seemed to be in a better mood than he when he had left them. Bon handed Ishiwa the code disc, then he and Kleber pulled down the other two seats from the bulkhead.

"Want to bet on what they are?" Kleber asked.

Ishiwa laughed. "No. But I will bet that a lot of credits change hands when we announce this to the crew." He put the code disc in the slot under his viewscreen, and responded to the disc's requests for identification. As the first page of the orders came up on the screen, he read them aloud.

"Refuel and rearm with all good speed and report to—" As he read the coordinates he had a good idea of where they were going—back to Sondak's polar systems. "You will command a five-hunk timino, a team consisting of *Misbarret*, *Holody*, *Rader*, *Porcefs*, and *Koshina*."

"Group attacks? We've never even considered that, sir, much less practiced it," Bon said.

"Then we shall have to think about it, Bon—and practice it if we possibly can. Please, let me continue."

"My apologies, sir."

Once they knew they were going back to the polar systems and would be leading a hunk timino, the rest of the orders came as little surprise—except that Commander Kuskuvyet would be in overall command of all the hunks. That pleased Bon, but not Ishiwa. Kuskuvyet was another kyosei political hack whose military reputation was not highly regarded by anyone Ishiwa knew. Kuskuvyet had risen through the ranks in Marshall Judoff's wake of influence, but as far as Ishiwa knew, Kuskuvyet had little respectable military experience.

But what worried Ishiwa even more than the remote presence of Kuskuvyet, was the prospect of going into the attack against Satterfield with a tired crew while trying to direct four other tired crews to act as a team. Their physical and mental condition and everyone's inexperience at this kind of attack would be a much greater handicap than Kuskuvyet.

"Do you think the Saks will expect us, sir?" Kleber asked after Ishiwa finished reading the orders.

"I do not know, nor do I care," Ishiwa said firmly. "Our orders are clear, and we must do our best to execute them." As he spoke, Ishiwa heard the slight hint of uncertainty in his voice and paused to chide himself.

When he continued, the uncertainty was gone from his voice, if not from his mind. "Bon, I want this crew to get as much rest as possible between now and when we join the fleet. We will obtain whatever extra rations we can from the *Osóto*, and make them available to the crew during all watches. If this attack is as important as I believe it will be, I want them in the best possible condition."

He paused and looked thoughtfully at Bon. "You and Kleber and I, however, will not get much rest. We have to decide how to mold five independent hunks into an effective fighting unit."

* * *

"You have secured it well?" Xindella asked.

"Yes," Ayne said sullenly. "The woman is checking my work."

Xindella fondled his proboscis. "But you still do not wish to speculate what it is?"

"Can only guess. As we told you, looks like directed energy device of some kind, typical Drautzlab design." Ayne suspected much more than that, but he no longer knew where to turn or who to trust. Since Xindella had drugged him and dragged him from the rooms on Yakusan where Kuskuvyet had left him, Ayne's head had whirled with confusion. As long as he had his steady supply of gorlet, Ayne wasn't about to tell Xindella anything he didn't have to.

"What is that thing?" Marsha asked as she entered the cabin. She could feel the increasing tension between them, but she had more serious worries on her mind.

"Our scientific friend here thinks it is a weapon, but—"

"Did not say weapon."

"But," Xindella continued, "I believe he suspects more than he is presently willing to tell us."

"What are you going to do with it?" Marsha asked. She was ready to put this delay behind them and get on with the business of finding *Graycloud* and Lucky, yet there was something going on here that intrigued her.

"I will attempt to find a buyer for it, of course," Xindella said with a shrug of his huge shoulders. "If I cannot find someone who wants it whole, I shall have it disassembled and sell the parts. Everything is valuable to someone."

Ayne stifled a brief gasp and tried to cover it with an exaggerated coughing fit. As he covered his mouth and turned away from them, he knew he couldn't let Xindella dismantle the device. It was too valuable.

Marsha smiled slightly. She still had no idea who Ayne Wallen really was, but it was increasingly obvious to her that he was more than a little strange and very much in fear of Xindella. "It's a weird-looking thing, whatever it is," she said. "But now that we've picked it up, isn't it about time to resume the search for *Graycloud*?"

"I've already found it, Captain Yednoshpfa."

"Where? How soon can we get to them?" Marsha's heart jumped with excitement.

"There," Xindella said, tapping the navigation screen with the longest of his seven fingers, "on the other side of the sun.

We should be in communications with them in ten Standard hours or so, and reach them in forty."

"Why? And if we can't communicate with them, how do you know *Graycloud's* there?"

"Please, Captain, do not bombard me so."

"I wish you'd quit calling me 'Captain.'"

Ayne listened to them with growing agitation. As he popped a piece of gorlet into his mouth, his thoughts drifted back to the cargo hold and what they had secured there.

"Very well, Citizen Yednoshpfa. I understand your discomfiture at the military appelation, and respect—"

"Can't you ever cut through all the tensheiss and get to the point?" Marsha asked. "How do you know Lucky's ship is on the other side of the sun?"

"Because," Xindella said slowly, "I located it before I put the sun between us."

"You mean . . . you mean you knew all along that we had picked up signals from a piece of space junk . . . that it wasn't *Graycloud* at all?" Marsha wanted to say more, but what he had done was so outrageous that words refused to form in her brain.

"Do not rile yourself, Citizen. *Graycloud* is in no immediate danger. Fifty hours more or less will not make any difference."

"Damn you," Marsha said quietly. "Damn you to the void and back. You're nothing but a rotten mercenary, you know that?"

"Mercenary is hardly an appropriate word, Citizen. I am what you humans call an opportunist, and a good opportunist never passes up the chance to make a profit. As a former lightspeed freighter, you should understand that."

"The only thing I understand is that Delightful Childe would never have done what you just did. Nor will he approve, I think, when he finds out."

"My affairs are no concern of his. Nor is his approval a concern of mine."

Ayne cared nothing about their argument and quietly slipped out of the cabin. He wanted another look at the Drautzlab device they had found.

Despite some peculiarities of design whose purposes baffled him, he was sure it was a prototype for the Ultimate Weapon. Worse, its design suggested that Drautzlab had found and understood his equations. But what was it doing in the March Cluster? And why had it been abandoned? Those were questions that no examination of the device could answer, but for the moment they were less important than the thing itself.

If it was a prototype for the Ultimate Weapon, and if, as he feared, it had been built on the basis of his equations, that would mean that his whole life had changed once again.

* * *

"That is the last one," Frye said with a sigh of relief. He had been dictating orders, directives, and memos all day and he was feeling close to exhaustion.

"When should I send them, sir?" Melliman asked.

"Immediately, AOCO. You and I will be leaving in the morning to join the fleet near Alexvieux."

"Isn't that where your daughter—"

"Yes," Frye said quickly, cutting her off. He tried not to think about Marsha any more than necessary. Only that morning he had received a report from Personnel that said she had failed to report for duty and was missing from Yakusan. He only hoped she was heading in the right direction. "I'm sorry, Clarest. I didn't mean to snap at you."

"No apology necessary, sir. I understand."

"Thank you." He looked quietly at her and felt again a reserve of strength in her that enhanced her appeal. She could never take Vinita's place in his heart, but he was glad she was back by his side. "Tell me, what do you really think of this plan of ours to attack Satterfield?"

"I think it is an excellent decision, sir. However, I still worry about stripping Yozel's fleet over Sutton."

"I know. I do, too. But those ships are no good to us just hanging there in space. Yozel has resisted every order to become more aggressive on Sutton, and it is costing him. This strike against Satterfield will cut Sondak's supply line to Sutton and relieve the pressure on Yozel."

"Maybe you should relieve Yozel himself, sir."

"You've suggested that before, AOCO, but I can't do that without support from Bridgeforce, and right now I don't think I could get it. I'm only beginning to understand the pressures the kyosei were putting on Tuuneo, but I fully understand the pressures they're putting on me. Until I find a way to turn that pressure around, Yozel stays."

He stood and stretched. "And now, you'd better send those orders. As soon as you have done so, we'll go home and pack."

Hours later as they sat in Frye's skimmer, the driver turned and said, "Sorry, sir, but it looks like we're caught in this traffic jam. The peacetraps have blocked all the roads again."

Frye leaned back with a sigh and unconsciously took Melliman's hand in his. These demonstrations had become routine around every military installation on Gensha. They were never large, but they were always well organized and effective. He didn't understand why these people felt the way they did, or how they thought that blocking traffic would help accomplish their goals. In fact, he wasn't even sure what their goals were.

"Why did he call them peacetraps," Melliman asked.

"I don't know. It is a slang term that suddenly seemed to be on everyone's lips when the demonstrations . . ." Frye let the words trail off into a little chuckle. "It really is an ironic name, isn't it? Peacetraps? Trap us in peace? I think I detect some anti-kyosei influence at work there."

When they finally got to the house, Frye went into the kitchen and just stood there. He couldn't seem to find the energy to think about what they might eat. Melliman came up beside him and slipped an arm around his waist.

"Shall I cook tonight?" she asked.

"No," Frye said as he turned and pulled her into his arms. "We'll send for something. All I want to do for the moment is hold you. Then we have to pack. The orderly can bring us a couple of hotplates from—" The end of his sentence was smothered by her kiss.

"I'll cook," she said after pulling away from him slightly. "I don't want anyone else near us tonight."

"But you're such a rotten cook," Frye said affectionately. That was a joke between them. Actually Melliman was a fairly good cook, but her meals could not compare with his. He had had too much practice cooking for Vinita during the last years of her illness.

"But better than you," she said in response. With a quick kiss on his cheek she pulled out of his arms. "You start packing and I'll put some food on."

He was too tired to resist. "All right. But keep it simple and light. I'm just not in the mood for anything else."

As he left the kitchen and walked down the hall, he automatically went into his private office. The bell on his microspooler was turned off, but its light was flashing insistently. Frye almost turned away, willing to put off whatever the message was until after he had a chance to eat something and relax. Habit and routine discipline led him to the desk and switched the microspooler's message onto the screen.

When Melliman called to tell him their dinner was ready, he was still sorting through the messages. Most of it was routine and could be diverted to headquarters. "I'll be there in a minute," he said as he scanned the remaining messages. One caught his eye and he quickly froze its contents on the screen. What he read gave him serious reason to worry.

A hunk reported that Sondak was massing warships off Satterfield. Did the Saks know his fleet was coming? Or had they just guessed that Satterfield would be his next point of attack?

Frye cursed quietly as he turned off the microspooler. He refused to accept a repetition of the defeat at Matthews. This time he had the new hunks working for him and he would send them in to discover the exact location of Sondak's forces. If Sondak could prepare for him, he could prepare for them, and strike from a position of knowledge.

"No more defeats," he said softly as he went to join Melliman. "No more defeats."

24

Mica Gilbert sat in her small cubicle off the *Walker's* command deck and watched her screens with a growing sense of excitement. Behind her she could hear Admiral Dimitri quietly giving the final exit orders.

In seven minutes the widely dispersed attack force led by the *Walker* would be exiting subspace, and shortly thereafter would begin its attack on the Ukes over Sutton's north pole.

Despite all the intense planning that had gone into this operation, Mica knew that the outcome of any battle was in doubt until it was over.

And this would be no simple space battle. While the fleet was attacking the Ukes, Schopper would be positioning his ships to land three legions of Planetary Troops dirtside.

Mica shivered. The Suttonese were supposed to begin their attacks on the ground as soon as the Ukes were hit in space. But it had been more than five days since a clear communication channel had been open to Sutton, and no one knew for sure if Mari and his strange assortment of local forces, militia, and Planetary troops were ready to act.

As she continued to stare at the screen, she wondered what Henley Stanmorton was doing and if she would ever see him again. Ever since he had left without saying goodbye, she had felt a little guilty about the way she had used him. She hadn't meant to use him, but she had. He had given her comfort—physical comfort as well as mental comfort—and she had returned his kindness by distancing herself from him.

Why? She liked him, probably more than she would admit to herself. He had been kind and gentle, demanding nothing of her and accepting whatever she gave him. Yet . . . yet there was something wrong between them, something wrong for her.

He grated on her in ways she still couldn't delineate very well. But the more time she had spent with him, the more his presence made her feel crowded and nervous. It was almost as though he cared about her too much, wanted her too much, needed her too much. How could she care so deeply about him and also be irritated by his company? It didn't make any sense.

No matter how she turned it over in her mind all she could see was a yawning gulf of need in him. And she knew instinctively that she couldn't fill it. It wasn't what he said, or what he did, so much as it was his attitude toward her. Yet even that attitude was confusing, because under his need for her she sensed his own feelings of guilt that he refused to confront or explain.

Suddenly she thought of Rochmon. He often left her with the same impression, that under his affection for her—an affection he showed only in the most circumspect ways—there was a layer of unexplained guilt.

Was she attracted for some reason to men who harbored deep internal guilt? Or was there something so wrong with her that she brought out feelings of guilt in men she cared about? What did she do that made them—

"Exiting subspace in thirty seconds," the speaker announced.

Mica immediately turned all her attention back to the screen, glad for the interruption. She didn't like the dark directions her thoughts had been taking, and besides, what did the problems of her life matter in the face of what was happening in her beloved Caveness galaxy?

The screen shifted from grey to blue as the *Walker* carried them back into normal space. Almost immediately the deck vibrated under the strain of the inertial dampers slowing them down. The screen was dotted with other ships of the attack force moving with them toward Sutton.

"Launch in eleven minutes," a voice behind her said.

Quickly Mica checked her communications coordinates and sent her first message to Admiral Pajandcan, the message that would tell her the fleet had arrived on schedule and was preparing to launch the first wave of their fighter attack. As she waited with the others, she watched her screen carefully for some sign that the Ukes had spotted them and were launching fighters of their own.

"Launch commencing," the voice behind her finally said.

Mica sent her second message without hesitation. From now on the messages would be far from routine. She would have to report whatever Dimitri told her to as the battle developed. Once the second message was dispatched, she left her cubicle and joined Admiral Dimitri on the command deck. "POLFLEET HQ has been notified, sir," she said with a quick salute.

"Good, Captain. Now comes the hard part—waiting."

* * *

Leri waited patiently for Ranas to speak after he had made his formal greeting. She was surprised to see him alone. They had not been alone together in hundreds of seasons, ever since Weecs had moved in with her. Now she felt uncomfortable in Ranas's presence, yet she also found him more attractive than he had been in a long, long time. However, this was no time for indulging her personal emotions.

"The Castorians have arrived, Proctor," Ranas said.

"Did they bring . . . him?"

"Yes, Proctor—at least they say they have him aboard one of their ships. But they insist on discussing the matter further."

"There is nothing to discuss," Leri said coldly. "I want him brought to me immediately."

"I told them as much, Proctor. They were unmoved and requested permission for a negotiator to land."

"And you gave them that permission, I suppose?"

"It seemed best. Surely after all this time a slight delay will matter little. Exeter will be yours. I promise."

Leri sighed and flicked her tongue to her shrunken teats. "Promises, as you and I know only too well, Ranas, are more easily made than kept. Why would you promise such a thing for these aliens?"

"Because I would please you, mate-of-my-nest."

His use of that term disturbed her, but she hid her reaction. "Very well. When will this negotiator arrive?"

"He awaits outside."

"Then send him in! I want this over with." As she waited, she wondered what Ranas hoped to gain from his terms of endearment? Or was he just trying to let her know how much he still cared for her?

Moments later the negotiator scuttled in with a translator device slung on the back of his dark brown carapace. "Greetings to you, Proctor Leri, from all of Castor. I am called Glights, and am here to assist in our alliance."

"I want the one called Exeter," Leri said simply.

"We know that, Proctor," Glights said with a clacking flourish of his claws, "but we feel that certain formalities must be observed before we can surrender him to you. After all, he is a citizen of Castor, and as such—"

Leri spat a fireball of disgust over Glight's head. "He tried to eat me. By doing that he gave up any—"

"Please, Proctor Leri. We understand your need to revenge yourself on the one you call Exeter, but the formalities must be observed. We cannot merely claw him over to you without an agreement between us about how he will be treated."

"He won't be treated!" Leri screamed. "He will be killed."

"Of course. Of course. That is understood," Glights said, bending his hind legs and lowering the end of his carapace to the floor. "But the manner of his killing must be acceptable to us. Otherwise, we cannot deliver him to your custody."

Growing anger caused Leri to tighten her coil, but at least she now understood what the problem was. The Castorians were squeamish. "How do you kill your own?" she asked sharply.

"We do not kill our own, Proctor. That is why we have this negotiating problem with—"

"You don't? How do you punish those who are evil? What do you do with those who have violated your sacred laws?—assuming you have sacred laws." She hoped her sarcasm would make it through the translator.

"We have laws and suitable punishment," Glights said slowly, "but we do not believe in killing one of our own race. Such a thought is abominable to us."

"Then what in the smell of burning methane do you do with them?" She sent another fireball over his head, but she did it more from frustration than anger. It was becoming all too clear to her that this was going to be much less simple than she hoped it would be. She reluctantly admitted to herself that the Castorians—soulless as they might be—could have laws and customs that she would have to respect if revenge on Exeter was to be achieved.

"Please, Proctor. Please try to understand. When one of our own is found guilty of violating the High Laws, we imprison that individual until a suitable place can be found to banish them from all communion with any Castorian community. The one you call Exeter was being held prior to just such a banishment."

"Then banish him here," she said quickly. "Your law will be satisfied and we will have our revenge on him."

"It is not that simple. The High Laws demand that such Denied Ones be banished to places where there is no known danger to them, and no possibility of—"

"No danger? What kind of punishment is that?"

"For us, the worst kind. If one faces no dangers, and has no community to share dangers with, one cannot be considered a true Castorian. Facing shared danger is an essential part of our cultural heritage. Surveys of the banished ones show that they soon lose the ability to survive. Their minds no longer function appropriately and they begin to—"

"You mean they go insane?"

Glights paused. "Yes. As I understand the translation, I believe that term describes their condition. They go insane and die, and just punishment is complete."

"We cannot wait for Exeter to go insane," Leri said, "although I must admit to a certain beauty to your form of punishment. However, from what you said in the beginning of this discussion, I assume that there are some forms of death your people would find acceptable for Exeter."

Glights dropped his gaze and crossed his claws. "Yes," he said softly, "I am ashamed to admit that there are certain kinds of death we would be willing to allow Exeter to suffer."

"Well?" she asked when he said no more. "Will you tell me? Or must I guess?"

"Unfortunately, Proctor, you must guess. We cannot in good conscience suggest ways in which you—an alien—should kill one of our own."

Despite her frustration, Leri could appreciate Glights's dilemma. She would certainly be reluctant to tell him how the Castorians could kill one of her people. Yet by telling him she wished to kill Exeter, she would be revealing how the sacred laws of the Elett dealt with such offenders. "One form of death," she said slowly, "would be to place him in a pit and roll rocks upon him."

"Unacceptable," Glights said quietly. He pulled his head back into his shell and covered the opening with his claws.

"We could poison him with oxygen."

"Unacceptable."

"We would dismember him."

"Unacceptable!"

"We could burn him alive," Leri said softly. She had saved that method until last, hoping with all her heart that it might be the one way Glights would accept.

There was a long pause before he answered. "You would not kill him by some other means and then burn him?" Glights asked.

"No. We would burn him alive."

"Then that is acceptable, Proctor. There is dignity in such a death. On your promise to kill him in such a manner, we will surrender to you our wretched brother Exeter. . . . On one other condition," he added after a slight pause.

"And that is?"

"This is difficult for me, Proctor, but we have a few others like Exeter whom we have not been able to find proper banishment places for."

Leri was startled. "You want us to kill them for you?"

There was a long pause before Glights answered. "We would not be offended if they died in the same fire that consumed Exeter."

Act as executioner for the Castorians? If it would get her Exeter and secure the agreement with them, Leri had no objections to killing them. After all, they were only soulless aliens. "How many others?" she asked.

"Forty-three," Glights said softly.

"We will do this thing. Go now and bring them to us."

Glights clacked his thanks in the same way that Exeter had done so many seasons before, and slowly backed from her chamber. As she watched him go, Leri felt no sense of triumph. The triumph would come only when Exeter and his fellow outcasts were consumed in flames.

* * *

"You knew about this, didn't you, Josiah?" Admiral Stonefield asked. "And you approved it."

There was no anger in Stonefield's voice, but Gilbert knew he was dealing with an angry man. "I approved an extension of Satterfield's defensive actions to include Sutton, yes. It was an opportunity both General Mari and Admiral Pajandcan thought we should take advantage of, and I agreed with them."

Sitting beside Admiral Gilbert, Rochmon wanted to smile, but he held his lips firmly pressed together. The old man had really put one over on the Joint Chiefs with this one. Now it was a matter of seeing how they would accept it.

"So Mari was in on this, too. I'm not surprised, but I want—no." Stonefield shook his head. "Josiah," he said finally, "I think this a foolish plan, but I can see that it is far too late to call the attack force back. I only hope for our sake—and for yours—that this works. Pajandcan has left the polar systems with the minimum level of defense, a level that has to cause me great concern."

Gilbert waited until he was sure Stonefield was finished

before he responded. He had prepared carefully for this situation, but did not want to irritate Stonefield any more than was absolutely necessary. "I think, sir," he said slowly, "that given the advantage of a surprise attack, we can deal a serious blow to the Ukes in the polar region."

"I understand your reasoning, Josiah. I just don't happen to agree with it."

"I appreciate that, sir."

"Then appreciate this. At best this action is barely within the scope of your command—even with Mari's complicity. The Joint Chiefs are going to scream for your head if this goes wrong, and I will be hard pressed to keep them from getting it."

"But if it succeeds, sir, this could be our first step toward putting the Ukes on the defensive. We can't afford to conduct this war as a defensive waiting game."

"Until now I would have violently disagreed with you. If this attack succeeds, I might be forced to adopt your point of view. But I still don't like it, Josiah. I don't like it one bit. And you," he said, turning his cold gaze on Rochmon, "you knew about this, too, didn't you?"

"He did, sir," Gilbert said before Rochmon could answer.

"But under your direction he kept it a secret? There could be charges brought—"

"Only against me, sir. I ordered Commander Rochmon to confine his knowledge of this plan to very specific people."

"No," Stonefield said quietly. "Regardless of your orders, Commander Rochmon had a duty to inform Bridgeforce of certain activities involved with this operation which affected all the fleets. His failure to—"

"Begging your pardon, sir," Rochmon said quickly, "but we were very careful to include all that information in our reports to Bridgeforce."

"Then why didn't I see—" Stonefield stopped in mid-sentence and gave Rochmon a grim smile. "You buried them."

"Not exactly, sir," Rochmon said, refusing to return the smile. He knew he was in a delicate position and didn't want to jeopardize it. "The information is all there in the daily 'Manifests and Movement Reports.' We just didn't point to it."

Suddenly Stonefield laughed, but it was a laugh without humor. "You're good, Commander. And so is your boss. But I'll repeat what I said before. If this attack doesn't succeed, the Joint Chiefs will demand a price—from both of you, I suspect. As much as I may admire how you pulled this off, I want you to know that I will join them in demanding that price."

Rochmon and Gilbert left Stonefield's office in a grim mood, their thoughts centered on what was happening halfway across the galaxy. Neither of them would have been surprised by what the other was thinking, and neither of them was willing to think beyond a battle that was totally out of their control.

* * *

As the second wave of fighters left the launchship *Walker* Mica Gilbert began to think that victory would come easier than anyone expected.

The Ukes had been caught totally off guard with their ships in a docking formation. The reports from the first fighters had been almost too good to believe—little or no resistance from the ships, only a handful of fighters coming out to meet them, and most incredible of all, no apparent attempt by the Ukes to disperse their formation. The only thing missing from those reports had been a sighting of a large Uke launchship.

"This is Schopper," a voice said over the loudspeaker. "We're going in."

"Shall I alert Pajandcan?" Mica asked.

"By all means, Captain. And be sure to tell her how far ahead of schedule we are and that we haven't found the mother-Uke launchship."

"Will do, sir." Mica hurried to her cubicle and began composing the message. No sooner had she sent it than she heard cries of alert from the command deck. She confirmed the transmission, then rushed back to Dimitri's side.

"Heavy resistance coming right at us. Ninety, maybe one hundred fighters. Still don't see any big launchship, Admiral, just the same little ones."

"We're picking up your visuals now, Selkit," Dimitri said. Mica followed his gaze to the overhead screen. "Doesn't look like they have as many ships as we thought they did."

"Unless they've moved them somewhere else," Dimitri said quickly. "Better pass that on to Pajandcan in a hurry."

"Suppose they're just lurking on the edge of the system, sir? Shouldn't we—"

"No sign of them. You pass on that message, Captain. If they pulled ships out of here, especially a mainline launchship, that could mean they're planning another major offensive. Pajandcan should know that."

Once again Mica went to her cubicle and composed a message. After she sent it, she wondered if this had been such a good idea after all. Sending messages to Pajandcan every two minutes was hardly an efficient use of her time. But if Dimitri's suspicions were anywhere near correct, then Pajandcan would need every scrap of evidence they could send her.

With a sigh she confirmed the transmission of this latest message and again headed out onto the command deck. As she listened to the reports coming in and watched scenes from the swirling battle high over Sutton, she thought about Schopper landing his troops.

There had still been no communications with Mari or General Porras, and she only hoped that they were too busy winning to talk. And for his sake, she hoped that Henley was getting all the stories he could handle.

25

The attack fleet was named Tuuneo in honor of the late Admiral. After taking on fuel, provisions, and a full load of missiles, *Olmis* had barely had time to make the rendezvous with it. There had been no time for Ishiwa to train his timino of hunks before they were dispatched by Kuskuvyet toward Satterfield.

He and Bon had managed to compose a brief plan of operations, and after consulting with the other hunk captains enroute, Ishiwa had adopted a very loosely coordinated system for them to follow. He knew it was terribly inadequate, but it would have to do.

Their primary mission had not been attack. It had been surveillance. *Olmis* and the fourteen other hunks assigned to this operation had been given the task of determining how many Sak ships there were around Satterfield—their type, their classes, and their disposition. Only after doing that and receiving clearance from Admiral Charltos himself, were they to be allowed to attack Sondak ships in or around the Satterfield system.

Ishiwa's timino had performed its surveillance mission very admirably. None of its hunks had been spotted by the Saks, and all of them had followed his orders explicitly. He had reported back to Tuuneo Fleet that there were fewer than one hundred ships of any significant size in orbit around Satterfield, and that completed the first part of their mission. Ishiwa had then requested permission to pull back and attack the crowded spacelanes leading into the system.

The longer he waited for permission to attack, the more he suspected that they would not be given that clearance until Tuuneo Fleet arrived. His suspicions were justified.

When *Olmis's* transceiver finally rang with the words, "Attack all orbiting targets," Ishiwa knew that Tuuneo Fleet had already exited subspace.

"Battle stations," he ordered. "Lieutenant, we will begin the attack as planned against those communications ships in equatorial orbit."

"Aye-aye, sir," Bon said enthusiastically.

Ishiwa had chosen the simplest tactic he could think of. With carefully controlled speed he eased *Olmis* into an equatorial orbit of its own a thousand kilometers beyond the outlying Sondak ships. Then he applied enough power to send *Olmis* in the opposite direction of Satterfield's spin. That would bring all the ships in stationary equatorial orbits one by one into *Olmis's* line of fire. Thus he could loose missiles upon them with either fore or aft tube as best suited the demands of targeting and reloading. It would be like practice shooting.

"Fighters approaching, sir! Coming in fast astern!"

Ishiwa accepted the boater's announcement with a soft curse. Somehow Sondak's detection equipment had managed to find them again. "Increase speed to one-third," he said. The last thing he wanted to do was waste missiles on fighters when it would be so easy to outrun them.

"First target coming up," Bon said, "light research carrier, Kesterson-class."

"Fighter's still closing."

"Targeting control is yours, Lieutenant." Ishiwa hated relinquishing targeting control, but in this case he had no choice. "I'll keep us steady on this course. Kleber, I want the stern tube independent. I may need it to put some flak between us and those fighters."

"Forty seconds to firing."

"Unidentified blip coming up from planetside, sir. Range thirty-one thousand kilometers and closing at point-seven-five."

"Thirty seconds to firing."

"Could be a freighter," Ishiwa said. "Steady on course and speed." He hoped it was just a freighter, because he dared not throw Bon's targeting off now.

"Twenty seconds to firing."

"Fighters still closing, sir. Accelerating fast."

"Kleber, set the stern missile for one kilometer proximity and we'll see if we can break those fighters up. But wait for my command."

"Aye, sir. Stern tube one-K prox," she said quietly into the microphone that connected her to the firing chambers.

"Eight, seven, six . . ."

Ishiwa followed Bon's count and enjoyed the thump when the forward missile fired. "Now the stern tube, Kleber."

The second thump followed his words like a period at the end of his sentence.

"New blip closing . . . missiles this way, sir!"

"Speed, point-eight. Bon, at this speed you'll have to target forward and fire aft. What's the closing speed on those missiles, boater?"

The boater hesitated. "Dropping, sir, as we accelerate." The relief was obvious in his voice. "Wait. I'm picking up ships at range—they're ours, Captain! Our fighters are entering the system!"

"Calm. Be calm," Ishiwa ordered. He felt the tension as much as anyone, but it wouldn't do for any of them to let it show. "Continue searching for targets," he said as he waited calmly for the next problem.

"First missile hit, sir," Bon announced.

"That was awfully fast, wasn't it?"

"But, sir—"

"Check it, Bon."

Bon quickly looked at his screen. When he looked back at Ishiwa there was pride on his face. "A hit, sir."

"Very well, Lieutenant. Now continue—"

"New missiles coming from forward, sir. Two of them! Range seventy kilometers and closing—"

"Hard course ought-ten-ten!" Ishiwa shouted. Even as he gave the order he knew it was too late. *Olmis* rocked under the explosion of a missile that found its mark.

* * *

The stone ledge was too inviting for Henley to resist. He sat on it, wiped the mud from his hands on the sleeves of his battle jacket, and tore open his ration packet.

"Better eat that on the move," General Archer said as he walked up beside him. "The Hundred and Second Planetary Legion just broke through the Uke defenses along the river about five kilometers north of Turner City, and we're going to try to link up with them before nightfall. But at least you won't have to leg it this time. I found a skimmer for you."

Henley groaned as he stood up, looking from Archer to the heavy grey sky. "I appreciate that," he said as he stretched his tired back. "But you know, I think maybe I'm getting too old for all this tromping around, General."

"I doubt it, Mr. Stanmorton. Besides, the excitement of a new battle will take the aches right out of you."

"I've seen enough fighting these two days for my excitement to be as tired as I am," Henley said before stuffing a handful of the moist, chewy rations into his mouth.

Archer laughed. "Sorry to hear that, because if you're still determined to stick with us, you're going to see a lot more. The Ukes aren't anywhere near being whipped."

"Oh, I'm determined to stick." Henley grinned. "But wouldn't you worry a little if I wasn't complaining?"

Archer ignored his question. "There's your skimmer," he said, pointing to a drab, battered little three-seater. "The driver knows her place in the formation, so all you have to do is enjoy the ride."

"Thanks, General." He almost saluted as Archer turned away, then remembered that saluting in the open field was frowned upon. It was a good way to point out the officers to enemy snipers, and sniping was one of the few things the Ukes had shown a high proficiency for these past two days.

With a weary sigh Henley trudged through the mud to the open skimmer and accepted the driver's nod. "I'm Henley," he said, offering his hand. "Don't call me Mister or Chief, just Henley."

"Squader Nellsson, sir," the dark-faced woman said, accepting his handshake with a firm grip and a smile that showed straight, even teeth. With her other hand she patted the skimmer's dialboard. "And this here's the *Lost Divot*."

Taking off his pack and putting it behind the thickly padded seat, he said, "That's an odd name, Nellsson—I mean *Lost Divot*, not yours."

"Don't know, sir. Comes from an old game called 'Fore' my father taught me."

"You don't have to call me sir, either. Henley will do fine. So what does the *Lost Divot* have to do with Fore?" he asked as he climbed into his seat and pulled the restraining straps over his shoulders.

Nellsson laughed. "'Fraid I'd have to teach you the whole game to explain that, sir—uh, Henley. But simply said it's a chunk of earth your club knocks out and you can't find to put back. Anyway, looks like we're about to get floatin'."

Henley looked up and saw the leading skimmers begin to rise. The damp air was quickly filled with the whining of tens of skimmers lifting from the ground. "So where are you from?" he asked as Nellsson throttled forward and *Lost Divot* slid slowly forward toward the middle of the convoy.

"Born and raised on Mungtinez," Nellsson shouted. She gave him a quick grin. "Service brat. Mother was a pilot in the Flight Corps."

"Your father?"

"A miner," she shouted without looking at him. "Died in an accident when I was eleven."

"Sorry." He looked at her closely and thought that under the light spattering of dirt on her face she was probably attractive in a plain sort of way. "You mated?"

"That a proposal, Henley?" she asked with another grin.

He laughed. "No, just curious. I'm a teller, you know."

"Saw your insignia. You gonna do a story on me?"

"I might, if you don't mind."

"Seems silly, but you can if you want to." She swerved behind a large transport skimmer and brought *Lost Divot* to a hovering halt. "To answer your question, no, I'm not mated. Don't plan to be, neither."

Henley took out his notebook and flipped to a blank page. "May I ask why?"

Nellsson adjusted the hover before looking at him. There was no grin on her face this time. "'Cause I never found a man I could trust, Henley. They all wanted somethin' different than I did—somethin' less. Enough said, okay?"

"How did you get to Sutton?" he asked, veering away from the subject of trustworthy men. He had no intention of prying into Nellsson's private life.

Her eyes narrowed. "Came in under General Mari with the first wave of reinforcements just as the Ukes hit us. I 'bout near bought the planet then, I'll tell you."

"How?" He knew the expression, and he immediately wondered what had happened to her.

"We were fighting for position on a low ridge the middle of the second day when I caught a hunk of Uke shrapnel in my back," she said, watching the transport in front of them and lifting *Lost Divot* to follow. "That's how come I'm drivin' this tub 'stead of leadin' a squad. Can't leg it too good, yet."

"You mean you'd rather be with the combat troops?"

"You're barrel straight I would, Henley. Even leadin' a squad of muck-eyed reservists would beat the crud out of bangin' around in this bucket." As though to emphasize her point, the skimmer bounced over a low hummuck. Nellsson's grimace of pain lingered even after the skimmer leveled out again.

"Still hurts you, doesn't it?"

"Most all of the time," she said simply. "No sense in complainin', though, 'cause old *Divot's* still better than that hospital bed." She paused. "Listen."

In the distance Henley heard the all too familiar sound like rolling thunder.

"Artillery. Somebody's raisin' the mud up ahead."

"You think it's ours?"

"Don't rightly know, Henley. But from the sound of it, I figure we'll find out soon enough. Can't be more than eight or ten kilometers away."

Henley stared at the sodden countryside with its grass covered hills and rain-swollen streams and its constant lines of civilian refugees tromping through the mud away from the fighting. His heart went out to those refugees struggling along with their blank faces and their meager possessions on their backs, and part of him prayed that the artillery was farther away than Nellsson thought. But washing over and around that prayer was a wave of anticipation that revealed his eagerness to be close to the battle again.

*   *   *

Satterfield had been prepared for a Uke attack, but nothing this massive. Cryptography had failed to warn them about this, and now with Dimitri's attack group fully engaging the Ukes at Sutton, there was little Admiral Pajandcan could do except follow Dawson's defense plan and pray it worked. Yet the more she watched and listened to the battles being fought around the planet and throughout the system, the more she doubted that defense plan would hold together.

"Damn," she said. "There are just too spacing many of them, Torgy." Her eyes darted from one of *Mishel's* screens to another. Each screen showed the Ukes swarming around her ships like gutbirds around a kill. Outside her command station all available fighters were doing their best to keep the Ukes from getting through, yet she knew at any moment their defenses might fail. "Get me Dawson."

It took Captain Torgeson less than a minute to make contact with Admiral Dawson.

"Looks like you're holding your own," Dawson said as soon as his face came on the viewscreen.

"Doesn't look that way to me."

"Maybe not, Admiral, but if the Ukes agree with you, they just might let their guard down. We're almost ready to loose the reserves on them."

Pajandcan wanted to smile at his bravado, but the grim set of her jaw kept the smile from forming. She feared that Dawson's reserves would do no more than slow the Ukes down for a little while. "Good. How soon before we see them?" she asked as calmly as she could.

"Less than an hour. I think the—"

"Slime it, Dawson! In an hour I may not have any ships for your precious reserves to rescue. Bring them out now."

Dawson turned away momentarily as he spoke to someone

out of view. "Can't, Admiral. Half of them are still moonside and—"

"Then send what you've got and the rest can follow. Freezing comet tails, man! Can't you see we're taking a beating out here?"

The sound of an explosion echoed through the corridors of the command station. Simultaneously the deck jerked sideways under Pajandcan's feet.

As she tried to catch her balance, the gravity system failed. She floated free and slammed upside down and backward into a communications panel. People and equipment were drifting out of control in the Battle Center. Pajandcan fought to catch her breath.

"Admiral? Admiral? What happened?" Dawson's voice shouted from the speaker.

"What do you think happened, you dirtsider? We got hit," Pajandcan yelled as she steadied herself on a handhold. "Launch those reserves!"

"But, Admiral, if you can just—"

"Now, Dawson," she said more calmly as she pulled herself back to the viewscreen. "I don't think we can hold out much longer without them."

"Very well, Admiral. But this isn't going to give us much of a chance to hit them like we planned."

"We may not have any chance if you don't get—" A second explosion interrupted her as it shook *Mishel*.

"We're on our way, Admiral," Dawson said before the screen went blank.

"Damage reports coming in," Torgeson said from behind her. "Light so far. They rattled us a little, but except for gravity all systems are up and functioning."

"For now," Pajandcan said sharply as she turned to *Mishel's* commander. "Dilbeck, time to move to our alternate position. Torgy, alert the fighters and the rest of our ships." Even as they were following her orders, Pajandcan was thinking ahead. The alternate position was less favorable for communications, but closer to Satterfield and its planetary defenses.

As much as she hated to do it, she clung to a stanchion and wrote out two short messages. The first one was for Admiral Gilbert on Nordeen giving him her most honest assessment of their situation. The second one was for Dimitri at Sutton telling him that they might not be able to hold out much longer.

"Code and send these as fast as you can, Torgy," she said as she floated over to her communications chief.

"Have to go by relay to Nordeen," he said as he glanced at the messages.

"They can't help us much anyway," she said with a frown. "Just get them there as soon as you can."

"Will do," Torgeson said as he hooked a leg around his seat and punched up the coder. "Bad news has a way of traveling faster than good. They should know in a few hours."

"That's soon enough."

"Commencing move, Admiral," Commander Dilbeck called from across the Battle Center. "All fighters in place."

Pajandcan watched the screens anxiously as *Mishel* began its move under Commander Dilbeck's expert guidance. The Ukes seemed to be hanging back, unsure of whether to attack the *Mishel* or continue harrassing her fighters.

With sudden acceleration *Mishel* and its fighter escort darted toward their alternate defense position. Much to Pajandcan's surprise, two-thirds of the Uke fighters broke contact and headed away from Satterfield. The remainder of the Ukes resumed their attack. It looked as though it was going to be a running battle all the way. There were still no signs of Dawson's reserves, but at least the odds were greatly improved by the Ukes' inexplicable withdrawal.

26

Admiral Frye Charltos stood on the command deck of the *Chaicong* and read the message with a growing anger that darkened his already tanned face. "You read this, Melliman. Can you believe it? Bridgeforce wants me to break off part of the fleet and go to Yozel's aid at Sutton."

Melliman nodded slowly. "Stripping Yozel's fleet was a risk we knew we were taking, sir. There is a message coming in now from Marshall Judoff."

"Probably volunteering to rescue Yozel and leave us short-shipped again." Frye shook his head slowly, fighting the bitterness he felt in his heart toward Judoff and Yozel and all the rest of the kyosei. No matter which direction he turned they seemed to be there to thwart him.

It was already obvious to Frye that Satterfield's defenses were under a killing strain trying to withstand the pressure Tuuneo Fleet was putting on them. Between the hunks, the fighters, and the long-range destroyers, Tuuneo Fleet was pounding half the Sondak ships in the system. Even the arrival of more Sak ships from behind the second moon wasn't going to cause his forces that much trouble. In a day or two he would have the Saks beaten into surrendering the system or running for their lives.

How could Bridgeforce expect him to give up such a sure victory in favor of trying to salvage Marshall Yozel's incompetent command? If they had built more conventional ships instead of wasting credits and valuable materials on their vaunted bombship project, this problem would never have occurred. What in the name of Heller's Fleet was wrong with them?

In a quiet corner of his mind he knew the answer to that question, but he refused to face it. There had once been a man named Frye Charltos whose heart and assistance would have immediately gone out to Yozel's fleet. That man would have wept at the unnecessary loss of life, and done everything he could to prevent it.

But that Frye Charltos had disappeared when the one woman he had loved in his whole life had suffered without mercy and died in his arms, by his hand. That Frye Charltos had died with Vinita and been buried with Tuuneo's ashes.

In his place, the new Frye Charltos lived for revenge against Sondak, and at the moment he felt only anger and frustration. Yozel was a proven incompetent and should be made to pay for his mistakes. That others suffered with him was regrettable; however, as far as Frye was concerned it was unavoidable.

But Bridgeforce—that collection of trembling fear-safes—

had decided to delay equipping the secondary fleets destined for the attacks on the rest of Sondak's polar systems. Now that same Bridgeforce wanted Frye to jeopardize his own success to rescue a political fathead. Such a request was inexcusable— totally inexcusable.

"You were right, sir,"Melliman said, tearing the message off the decoder. "Look."

Frye took the sheet from Melliman, and as he read Judoff's message, his anger grew. Judoff was regrouping her ships in preparation for a sortie to Sutton, and her choice of words left little doubt that she would go with or without his permission. "I want to talk to Marshall Judoff," he said. "Now."

"Now" took several minutes longer than he wanted it to, but the delay gave Frye the time to bring his anger under control. Somehow he had to convince Judoff to hold her ships here at Satterfield until the battle was won.

When Judoff's image finally appeared on the communications screen, Frye's face registered no emotion. "Greetings, Marshall Judoff. I have received your message, but I must tell you it has caused me great concern."

"And Marshall Yozel's plight has caused me great concern, as it should also concern you, Admiral Charltos." Her intense dislike of him dripped from her voice like acid from a leaking disposal vat.

"We are all understandably concerned about the developments at Sutton, Marshall Judoff." Frye measured his words and kept his tone as neutral as possible, refusing to respond outwardly to her censure. Attempting to persuade her would probably be a wasted effort, but persuasion was the only tool he had. If he ordered her to stay, he knew she would disobey and bring further turmoil to an already fractious command.

"However," he continued, "I must request that you to reconsider this plan of yours if at all possible. Given our current situation here, we need your ships to bring *this* operation to a successful conclusion before we can consider any attempt to assist Yozel's fleet."

"I cannot do that, Commander—I mean, Admiral."

The slip was intentional, and Frye knew it, but again he held back any emotional response. Let her have her petty spite if that was what she needed. He needed her ships.

"We have an obligation to assist Commander Yozel if we can," Judoff continued, "and with the ships under my command, we are quite capable of meeting that obligation. Therefore, in response to Bridgeforce's directive, I am withdrawing my ships and hastening to Sutton."

"It was not a directive," Frye said quickly. "It was a request. However, would you consider a twenty hour delay?" He knew that even in his anger he was coming very close to begging her, and he hated her all the more for that.

"Absolutely not, Charltos. My forces have beaten the Saks back. Yours can complete the task and give the U.C.S. the success it needs here."

Frye's anger broke. "By the saints, Marshall!" he shouted. "You vowed to support me on this! You said you would follow my orders, so now I'm giving you one. Your ships will resume their attack and stay with us until I—"

"Order refused," Judoff said with a dark smile. "Fight the Saks with what you have, Charltos."

Before Frye could answer, Judoff's image disappeared in a pattern of static.

"She broke the transmission, sir."

When Frye finally took his eyes from the screen, his jaw was set in a firm line. "I know, Melliman. I only hope she hasn't broken our surge to victory as well."

* * *

The sky was bright green. The walls of the freshly dug pit were mottled layers of red-and-brown clay. Forty-four yellow-shelled Castorians huddled in loudly clacking groups at the bottom of the pit, their claws waving, their sounds meaningless to all but themselves.

As her people chosen to perform this honorable duty lined the rim of the pit, Leri surveyed the Castorians. Somewhere down there was her enemy, Exeter. This was the first time she had ever seen so many Castorians at the same time, and they all looked alike to her. Leri was having a difficult time trying to pick Exeter out from the rest of them.

Yet she refused to start the execution until she saw Exeter and spoke to him. She wanted to spew her hatred onto his back along with the fire that would consume him. She was so intent on locating him that she did not hear the Castorian ambassador, Glights, scramble up beside her.

"Forgive me, Proctor," he said with a ritual clacking of his claws, "but I must take my leave now."

Leri detected a nervousness in him and in his voice, even through the translator, but Glights and his emotional qualms were not her concern. "Where is he?" she asked.

"Who, Proctor?"

"Exeter, of course, you shell-bound idiot."

Glights made a sound that in another atmosphere might have passed for a sigh of dismay. "There," he said, pointing the longer of his two claws to the smallest group in the middle of the pit.

Even with Glights's pointing it took a moment for Leri to finally recognize Exeter. What convinced her more than anything was the way he stared defiantly back at her. "Toss him your translator," she said.

After struggling with the straps that held the translator to his carapace, Glights finally got it off. "I shall return at your call," he said quickly before tossing the translator into the pit. Before it hit the bottom he was scrambling away through the emerald green light toward his ship.

"You can hear me now, Exeter," Leri shouted, "and understand me, as well. I want to hear your vain boasting now. I want you to tell me again what you planned to do with me."

The Castorians quieted. They encircled the translator laying in the dirt, but none of them touched it. Finally a weak voice answered her. "I hear you Proctor Leri, but I have no boasts. I have but one question. What uncivilized humiliation have you devised for me and my beleagured comrades?"

"Soon enough, Exeter," Leri said with grim satisfaction. "Soon enough you will learn your fate. But while you wait and wonder about that, do you have nothing you wish to say in your own defense?"

"Nothing, Proctor, for I have done nothing wrong. Neither have my comrades here."

"Nothing wrong? Nothing wrong?" Leri asked mockingly. "You have eaten your children, yet you say you have done nothing wrong? You attempted to eat me, yet you say you have done nothing wrong? Come now, Exeter. Surely you can see that I find that difficult to believe."

The translator crackled faintly with a sound like laughter.

"Believe what you will, Proctor, but beware of those who brought us here. They, too, might well find you irresistible. In the meantime, I will ask you again what you intend to do with us? Are we to be some exhibit for your people to stare at? Is that the shame these innocents are to suffer?"

There was no mistaking Leri's laughter. "Far from it, Exeter. You and your *innocent* friends will pray for such painless suffering before this season has passed."

The Castorians stirred and crowded closer to the translator. An unintelligible babble of voices rose from the pit in a wave of anger and indignation.

"Silence!" Leri shouted.

Slowly the mix of voices subsided until only one spoke through the translator. "There is suspicion among us, Proctor, that we have been delivered to you for punishment of some sort. Is this true?"

"Are you fools not to know your crimes? Do you think us fools to be deceived by your words? You know why you are here. You are standing in your grave."

There was a long pause before the first voice spoke. "Impossible. It is against the laws—" Again a babble of voices quickly drowned out understanding.

Leri was tired of this and suddenly all she wanted was to have it over with. She pulled the oxygen from the sacks behind her gills, mixed it with as much methane as she could suck in, and spat the largest fireball of her life. It roared to the bottom of the pit and consumed the translator. The Castorians scrambled over each other to get away from the fire. But it was too late.

Leri's action was the signal to begin. From all around the rim of the pit her people spat fireball after fireball down on the Castorians. Their screams of outrage and pain were muffled as they withdrew into their shells for protection.

When a slender black hose dropped into the pit, even the Castorians' shells were insufficient. Nothing could protect them now. The hose was an oxygen line, and the fire that roiled around its nozzle consumed everything in its path.

The stench of burning flesh mixed with a smell like sulphur that roared out of the pit in angry clouds, driving Leri's people back from the rim. Still the hose spewed its oxygen, feeding the-flames, giving them a life of their own. Leri clung to the rim, wanting to see the whole victory. The smoke stung her eyes. The heat scorched her snout, until even she was forced to retreat from the fiery brink.

Later, after the oxygen had been turned off and the fire had died out, she returned to the blackened rim of the pit. The charred corpses spilled like black tar from shells split open in the heat. The stench hung in the air like bloated needles that stung her gills and choked her at the same time.

She should have been sickened by the sight of so much death. She should have felt something that would justify the sight before her. But all Leri felt was a hollowness.

Revenge did not satisfy her. It only made her sad. Yet she knew it had been necessary—for her and for her people—and nothing else mattered. As she turned away from the pit and began the long slither toward her burrow, Exeter's words lingered in her thoughts.

Had some of those Castorians indeed been innocent? Were Glights and his companions subject to the same obscene temptations that Exeter had given in to? Would they, too, turn on her and her people to satisfy some lust for flesh?

Without answers, the questions wouldn't go away. But there were no simple answers for her anymore. The humans had seen to that. With their despicable quarrels they had destroyed the peace and harmony of her life and her world, and driven away all the simple answers.

Proctor Leri would trust the Castorians to keep their part of the bargain because she had no choice. Leri, the mother and mate, would never trust them.

* * *

Commander Hew Rochmon checked the message one more time before punching it into the coder. It was against regulations to send personal messages like this. Poor Bock, his brilliant Bock, had been dismissed with no evidence even this damning against her—judged guilty until proven innocent. He could suffer a far worse fate than she had. But he had worded the message very carefully so that Mica, and only Mica, would know what he was really saying.

Yet once the message was coded, he couldn't bring himself to release it for transmission. It was too much—too much for him to tell her, and too much to ask of her. He missed her more than a hundred messages could tell her. That's all he wanted her to know. He dared not reveal even to himself what made him miss her, for to reveal that would be to admit that inside those carefully constructed walls he had built around himself there lay an emotion he could not trust. It wasn't even an emotion he dared put a name to, but its strength and influence on his actions were growing almost uncontrollably.

As he sat in stasis fighting the conflicting urges to withdraw the message or to send it, there was a knock on his door. "Come in," he said quickly. With a jab of his finger he pushed the transmit button.

"I thought you'd better see this," Captain Londron said as he entered Rochmon's office waving a blue urgent-signal sheet. "The Ukes have hit Satterfield, and Admiral Pajandcan isn't sure how long she can hold out against them."

Rochmon took the signal and rushed out the door. "Call Admiral Gilbert and tell him I'm on my way," he called over his shoulder. "Then call Admiral Stonefield and tell him that Gilbert and I are bringing him some urgent imformation." He hurried through the door without waiting for Londron's reply.

Stonefield was going to be furious. This was exactly what he had feared might happen.

Ten endless minutes later Rochmon handed the signal to Admiral Gilbert. "Looks like the worst, sir."

Josiah Gilbert read the signal without expression, but his heart ached with a pain that had no cure. Those were his people dying out there because of a plan he had approved, and there was nothing he could do to help them. When he finally looked up at Rochmon, he felt as though he had aged ten years in the past one. "We'll have to show this to Admiral Stonefield and the Joint Chiefs immediately."

"My headquarters notified Stonefield's office that we're on our way."

"Very well," Gilbert said as he rose slowly from his chair. "I guess you know this means the end for me, Hew."

"Not necessarily, sir," Rochmon said. He had never seen Gilbert look so depressed. "After all, Pajandcan doesn't say that she's been defeated, only that the odds are against her."

"Doesn't matter. The Joint Chiefs will exact their price and

I'll be the one to pay it—whether Pajandcan manages to save Satterfield or not. All I can do is try to keep them from getting Pajandcan and Dimitri, and you, too."

Rochmon felt a sense of desperation. It wasn't important whether the Joint Chiefs went after him or not, but if Sondak wanted to win this war, it was important that the Joint Chiefs continue to make use of Gilbert's brilliance. "What about HOMFLEET, sir? Couldn't they send some ships from—"

Gilbert smiled weakly. "No chance, Hew."

Minutes later after reading the signal, Admiral Stonefield pushed the red button on his intercom. "Activate Operation Heartstopper," he said calmly. When the acknowledgement of his order came through, he looked up to face Gilbert and Rochmon. "That will dispatch the *Royal Oak* and the *Willard* with a suitable escort immediately. The Joint Chiefs were afraid this might happen, so after much heated discussion, we prepared a contingency plan."

"But, sir," Gilbert said, "How can HOMFLEET afford to send two launchships when . . ." He let his words trail off as Stonefield stared at him with an unreadable look in his eyes.

"We cannot afford to send them, Josiah. But we can less well afford the loss of Satterfield. The Joint Chiefs were finally convinced that however dangerous this plan of yours and Pajandcan's was, that it was the best of many poor options."

Gilbert started to speak, but Stonefield held up his hand.

"No, don't thank me for that. My feelings haven't changed. It was Hilldill and Lindshaw who argued in your favor—and Mari. His messages convinced the J.C. that retaking Sutton was worth the risks. And it was Lindshaw who volunteered the *Willard* and three wings of her Flight Corps to stand by in reserve."

After a long, uncomfortable pause, Rochmon asked, "How soon can they get there, sir?"

"Four days—three at best. You will signal Pajandcan to conserve her forces as much as possible, and to temporarily withdraw if necessary until the reinforcements arrive."

Gilbert shook his head sadly. "Perhaps I should offer my resignation now, sir."

"If I were you, I would," Stonefield said slowly, "but I'm not, and I will refuse to accept it—as will the Joint Chiefs." For the first time he smiled slightly. "Don't you understand, Josiah? Against my best arguments, your point of view and General Mari's, and Admiral Pajandcan's—all of you who have demanded an offensive war are winning. And for some totally perverse reason, I am glad."

For a long moment Gilbert pondered what Stonefield had said and finally rose with a sigh. "I wish I were, Stony. Come on, Commander. We have work to do."

27

Ishiwa carefully readjusted his position in the command chair. The bruise on his knee ached in throbbing counterpoint to the lump on his head. His eyes itched with a dry, gritty feeling. His stomach churned up waves of acid for every cup of tea he poured into it. His bowels were producing gas like a constipated creamcow. Fatigue made every movement an effort he had to think about. But his mind was wide awake.

The missile had hit the forward firing chamber, and only the reinforced bulkhead there had prevented the damage from being fatal to the whole ship. All the emergency damage control training he had put *Olmis's* crew through had paid dividends measured in lives. Some had sacrificed their own lives to save ship and comrades. Others had survived by freak luck. Still, the damage to *Olmis* and her crew had been bad enough, and Ishiwa knew from the expression on Bon's face that he would have to absorb more grim facts.

"The hull is sealed, Captain. All fires are out, but it will be several hours before we know if we can restore any of the communications systems."

"And the final casualty count?"

"Seventeen dead, sir, two officers and fifteen ratings," Bon said sadly. "Twenty-three injured in some way, including you and myself. Five of those are in serious condition—Enkenohuura, Tahooto, Nagasi, Demarest, and Tokayota."

"What about you, Bon? How's your arm?"

"I'll be fine, sir. It's a clean break. But I'm afraid *Olmis* has fought her last battle for a while. Chief Moino says the hull won't withstand the transition into subspace."

"Well at least the Saks have lost track of us, Bon. Now all we have to do is get to one of our launchships and see if they can take us aboard. Kleber—" Ishiwa wanted to bite his tongue off. Kleber had been slammed against the bulkhead by the force of the explosion and broken her neck. By the time Ishiwa had reached her side, she was already dead.

He was still too numb to cry for her, but he knew the tears would eventually come. She had filled a much larger place in his life than he had ever expected her too. Now her body filled a sealed spacesack waiting for decent disposal.

He looked over at Enseeoh Nunn who was monitoring the navscreens. "Nunn, what is our position relative to the main body of the fleet?"

"From the last fix we took, sir, it looks like they're about eight tachymeters on the other side of the sun."

"Plot the shortest course to the fleet that will keep us at least five hundred thousand kilometers away from Satterfield."

"Will do, sir. It will take a few minutes."

"That's all right, Nunn. There's no immediate hurry. You just take your time and get it right."

"Begging your pardon, sir," Bon said, "but perhaps you should get some rest—I mean as soon as Nunn plots our course. You've been up for over forty hours."

"Your concern is appreciated, Bon, but perhaps you should rest first. I will start us on our way to the fleet, and you can relieve me in ten hours."

Bon shook his head. "I'm not sure I could sleep, sir. As tired as I am, I feel like something's wound up inside me that won't let go."

"I understand," Ishiwa said with a quiet smile, "but try anyway. The medics can give you something."

Again Bon shook his head. "They already did, but it just seemed to make me more awake."

"Try, Bon. That's an order. I don't know how much longer I can keep going, so I'll need you rested and ready to replace me."

After Bon left Ishiwa waited patiently for Nunn to finish

plotting the course. He could have helped her, of course, but that would have done nothing for her morale. She needed to feel he had confidence in her, and he needed to be able to trust what she did.

So he waited as she plotted, and as tired as he was, he never once doubted that they would make it safely to the fleet and home. They had survived a blow that should have killed them. Now all they had to do was retreat with dignity.

* * *

Mari returned General Schopper's salute. "Porras can fill you in on all the details, but basically I can tell you that we've got the Ukes on the run all over the planet. They're still pretty well entrenched in Esqueleada and a few other cities, but General Archer and your Hundred and Second are mopping up over on Elias. The forces we caught in the open have been retreating since the attack started."

"What about our supplies?"

"That's our biggest problem right now, Thedd. Porras is working on it, and so is that colonel of yours, uh—"

"Blickle?"

"Right. Anyway, I don't think it's anything that can't be overcome. You and Porras may have to kick some tail, but I know we have the troops and equipment to keep everything moving."

"We'll do what we have to." Schopper frowned. "You know about Satterfield?"

"That's what I'm going up to talk to Dimitri about. If he has things as well under control up there as we do dirtside, we ought to be able to break part of his attack force away to go back and help Pajandcan."

"And strip our space cover?"

"Thedd," Mari said firmly, "you just worry about securing this planet. Dimitri and I will make sure you have more than enough space cover. I'll be back in a day or two at most." He returned Schopper's quick salute then climbed aboard the shuttle.

"Welcome aboard, sir."

Much to Mari's surprise it was Caffey who greeted him. "Thank you, Chief, but I thought you had—"

"Been carrying supplies down and casualties up. You hurt?"

"No."

"Good, then ride up with me. I could use the company."

Once the shuttle lifted, Caffey filled him in on a side of the war he hadn't seen. According to her, the biggest problem was getting the shuttles close enough to the troops. The Ukes still had a fierce number of operational aircraft and weren't reluctant to use them against the unarmed shuttles.

"Maybe you didn't notice how battered this crate is, General, but I do believe I'd rather be flying something with a little more armor," she said as they broke free of Sutton's atmosphere. "Would make it a bit more comfortable."

"Next war," Mari said with a smile.

"Hope there isn't a next one, sir. This one looks like it's going to go on long enough."

Mari nodded. "I'm afraid you're right. Mind if I nap until we get to the *Walker?*"

A look of disappointment flashed across Caffey's face, then she gave him a small smile. "You've got about an hour till we get there, sir. Make the best of it."

Two hours later General Mari was standing in the *Walker's* main conference room with Admiral Dimitri, Captain Gilbert, and most of Dimitri's staff. Mari motioned them all to their seats and immediately cut through the small talk. "What are your estimates, Dit? Can you afford a launchship and two destroyers?"

"I think so, General. The Uke ships still functioning are scattered all around the system, but they're spending more time running away from us than fighting."

"Seems like the same thing on the ground." Mari rubbed his chin thoughtfully. "You don't suppose they're expecting reinforcements, do you?"

"May I answer that one?" Mica asked.

Dimitri nodded.

"Sir, there has been heavy exchange of messages between the Ukes here and the direction of Satterfield. If they are expecting reinforcements, I believe they will come from the Uke fleet there, rather than from their home systems."

"From either direction we jeopardize what we've won here," Mari said, "but if they're coming from Satterfield, that could only mean one of two things. Either we're too late to help Pajandcan, or the Ukes are taking a chance, too."

"Could be something else, sir. Cryptography on Nordeen

has information that Marshall Judoff is leading an element of the Uke fleet. She could be coming here on her own initiative."

Mari waved his hand dismissively. "That's stupid. Surely the Ukes wouldn't allow something like that to happen."

"We know that she withdrew her element of the fleet before the battle for Matthews system. What would keep her from repeating her actions now?"

"If that's correct, Captain, we'd run right into them on our way back to Satterfield."

"Not exactly, sir," Dimitri said. "We would have to plot for interception. Otherwise we would probably be on a totally different space-time curve and never know we passed each other."

"All right. Suppose you plot for interception?"

"It would certainly take us longer to get to Satterfield, but if they are coming here, they certainly wouldn't expect us to be coming out to look for them."

Mari slapped his palm on the table. "Plot it. Give me the best time estimates you can on both courses. And you, Captain Gilbert, find out how Pajandcan's holding out. We'll make our decision in the next five hours."

* * *

Lucky sat at the galley table holding Marsha's hand. Since they had been so unexpectedly reunited, he couldn't seem to stop touching her. She was everything that Janette was not, and Lucky knew that sooner or later he would have to tell her what Janette had done to him. But it would have to wait until after they got back to Oina and he was rid of Janette forever. Even now Janette was causing new problems.

"In the name of Sondak, I order you to follow him," she said angrily.

"Order away, Inspector. You heard what Xindella told us. He said if we tried to follow him he'll blast us from space. Since *Graycloud* doesn't have any weapons to fight him with, I intend to take Xindella's advice and go back to Oina."

"But he has the secret weapon, I'm telling you, and the man who can make it work. Don't you care anything about—"

"It's a piece of space junk," Marsha said quickly. She didn't know who this Inspector Janette thought she was, but Marsha had managed to develop a severe dislike for her. It was obvious that Lucky didn't like her either.

"That's right," Lucky said. "He has a piece of space junk that you *think* is a weapon. And no, I don't care anything about it, or Wayne whatever his name is, or you, either. All I care about is that he fixed the Gouldrive. After we've waited as long as Xindella told us to, we're going—"

"Maybe 'this' weapon will persuade you," Janette said holding a small blaster pointed at them.

Marsha kicked under the table without thinking. The hard toe of her boot caught Janette's knee. She jumped to her feet as the inspector doubled over with a scream of pain. Lucky flopped across the table and snatched the blaster from her hand with a wide sweeping motion.

Janette grabbed for his arm. He brought it back as hard as he could and slammed the barrel of the blaster against her head. She fell off the chair with a loud grunt.

Lucky scrambled across the textured surface to hit her again, but Marsha already had Janette pinned to the floor.

"I think she's unconscious," Marsha said as Lucky climbed off the table and squatted beside them.

"Serves her right. Here," he said, handing Marsha the blaster, "you keep her still. I'll be back in a minute."

Marsha was surprised when he returned moments later with a thick blue band of metal. "What's that?"

"A security collar," he said. He knelt beside Janette's still form and slipped the collar in place with a loud click. With a smile of satisfaction he stood up and pulled Marsha up with him. Then he handed her a finger-sized device with a clip on it. "If she tries anything else, flip the top off that and press the button. The collar will strangle her."

Marsha was shocked. "Lucky! That's terrible."

"You think so? What do you suggest for a rapist who wants to steal *Graycloud*? A golidium chain and a slap on the wrist?" The words were out of his mouth before he could stop them.

"Rapist?" Marsha looked from the inspector to Lucky. "I don't understand? What happened? Why do you hate her so much?"

"You heard me," Lucky said. Tears pooled in the corners of his eyes. "She raped me. Thought I would like it." The shame and guilt were returning in waves that threatened to fill his throat. "Snuck into my cabin and . . ."

Marsha stepped over Janette and pulled Lucky sobbing into her arms. She didn't understand how Janette could have done what Lucky accused her of. She didn't understand how that tiny woman could have forced him to have sex with her. But she did understand that Janette had wounded him in some terrible way, and it took all of Marsha's restraint to keep from flipping the cap off the activator and killing Janette right then and there.

* * *

"Well, I believe Captain Teeman is going to follow my instructions," Xindella said as the *Profit* approached light-speed. "He is a wise man—much wiser than you, Citizen Wallen."

Ayne sat strapped in his own sweat in the oversized couch wanting nothing more than a piece of gorlet. He didn't understand why Xindella was punishing him. He had fixed the Gouldrive. He had been steadfastly obedient. Why? "Why?" he finally asked aloud. "Why will you not give my gorlet?"

"It is not yours, Citizen. It is mine. You must always remember that."

"But we be knowing that, Xindella. We be doing everything you told us to do. Even killed that guard when—"

"Yes, well, perhaps I've been a little harsh with you," Xindella said, pulling a small tray out of the console between them. He touched a small button and four pieces of gorlet rolled out onto the tray, barely within reach of Ayne's bound arms.

"Thank you," Ayne said as he managed to pull a piece into his fingers. By straining againt the straps he bent over enough to pop the gorlet into his mouth. Its creamy sweetness filled him with a sense of peace. After eating the second one he could feel the tension draining from his body. "Where be you taking us now?" he asked softly.

"To the bargaining table."

"Do not understand."

"Of course you don't, Citizen. And neither, apparently, did Marshall Judoff when she made the bargain she failed to keep. But now, you see, you are twice as valuable to me and to the Ukas, for now I have not only you to put on the table, but also

Drautzlab's little toy. And this time I will demand my credits up front."

Ayne's heart sank. He thought he had escaped the Ukes when Xindella rescued him, and never dreamed that Xindella might sell him back to the gruesome Marshall Judoff. As quickly as he could he bent over and scooped the other two pieces of gorlet into his mouth and leaned back staring at Xindella.

"Do not look so hurt, Citizen. Did you think I stole you away from Yakusan because I liked you? And did you also think that your stupid little lies could hide what we carry in *Profit's* hold? You must take me for a fool, just as Judoff did."

"You be wiser to sell me to Drautzlab," Ayne said hopefully.

Xindella snorted. "Perhaps we should hold a festbid. Do you know what a festbid is?"

"Do not know."

"It is when a piece of merchandise is placed on the market and interested parties offer increasing numbers of credits to obtain it until one party is willing to pay more than any other. What an intriguing idea, Citizen! You have been an inspiration to me." Xindella bared his blunt, yellow teeth.

For a reason he did not understand, Ayne felt brave. "What be happening if merchandise is spoiled?"

"Then I would have to dismantle it and sell it for scrap. I understand that the Castorians will pay excessive prices for certain human organs that they consider delicacies."

Ayne's bravery disappeared as quickly as it had come. The thought of his body being eaten by the gruesome Castorians sent chills up his spine. "Festbid is better," he said softly.

"Especially if all the merchandise is in working order," Xindella added. "Consequently, I am going to release you now and let you go back to the hold and determine what makes our precious cargo work. Will you do that?"

"Will do that." Ayne knew he had no choice. From the first piece of gorlet he had eaten in Xindella's office he had lost all control of his life. "Will do as best I can," he repeated, knowing that his best might very well cause destruction unlike anything the galaxy had ever seen.

28

Henley crawled the last ten meters up the hill to a small outcropping of rock at its peak. He could hear the scattered firing in the distance and he wasn't going to take a chance by standing up. There were snipers everywhere.

The breeze was filled with the smells of smoke and cordite and rotting flesh. The ground was strewn with broken bodies and equipment. The Ukes might be losing, but they were still fighting for every meter of land they gave up.

He peeked around the rock and a bullet twanged over his head sending a shower of splinters against his helmet. This is crazy, he thought as he pulled back and hugged the wet ground. What in the galaxy am I doing here?

With grim determination he crawled to the other end of the outcrop. Again he cautiously peeked around its damp, rough surface. The rocky ground spilled away from the top of the hill in a series of natural terraces. Near the bottom he could see a battle skimmer moving slowly across the flats followed by troops in a skirmish line. He couldn't see the Ukes, but he knew they were there, and he knew at least one of them was between him and the units below.

"Hey, troop!" a voice behind him called.

Henley pulled back behind the rock again and turned to see who was calling.

"You deaf, troop?" a soldier asked as he ran in a low crouch up to Henley's position. "What's your outfit? Where's your weapon? What are you doing here?"

"Easy, Sergeant," Henley said as he risked sitting up. "One question at a time."

"Aren't you . . . Oh, damn. Sorry, sir, but I didn't recognize you like that."

Henley looked at his mud-stained uniform. "Be hard to recognize myself. As for what I'm doing here, I don't know. I was sticking with the Forty-Ninth when I stopped to talk to some of the wounded. Been trying to catch up with them ever since, but there's a sniper popping this rock, and I don't want to give him another chance at me."

"I'm Sergeant Vessle, sir, and if you'll come with me, I think I can get you safely to the Forty-Ninth."

"Whatever you say, Sergeant. I'm too much of a coward to take risks I don't have to."

"Not what I heard, sir," Vessle said as he turned and started back down the hill in the same low running crouch.

Henley strained to keep up with Vessle while forcing himself to stay low. When he finally huffed to a stop at the base of the hill between two large coniferous trees, he knew the exhaustion he felt was temporary. It would soon sink into that bone-weary fatigue that had become a part of him.

"It's that teller," Vessle said to a young pikean captain. "A sniper had him pinned down."

"Good to see you, Chief Stanmorton," the captain said, holding out her hand.

"Thanks, Captain." He paused as he accepted her handshake and looked at the insignia on her collar. "Don't tell me you're with the Forty-Ninth?"

The captain looked puzzled and Vessle laughed. "Told you I'd get you there safely, sir."

"That you did, Sergeant. Request permission to attach myself to your unit, Captain."

"It's our honor, Chief. Your stories on the landings made you a lot of friends in this unit. But enough of that. You can ride in the skimmer with—" Her sentence ended in a gurgle of blood as she dropped dead at his feet.

The shot was still ringing over his head when Henley hit the ground beside her, cursing the damned Uke sniper and crying at the same time.

* * *

"Have you determined who they are and what they want?"

"Methane poachers," Glights said, "probably sent by Sondak to test you. They appear to be well armed."

This was not part of Leri's visions. But her precious visions had first gone astray, and then mutated into forms she no longer understood. Nothing was right anymore. "Send them away," she said sharply.

"We tried that," Ranas said softly. "They refused to leave. I fear we will now have to fight them, Proctor."

Leri's tongue flickered in and out in anger. The humans had sucked Cloise into their war, the same way they wanted to suck the methane from Cloise's atmosphere. Now Leri and her people were allied with the soulless Oinaise and the despicable Castorians. Weecs was somewhere high in space aboard a Castorian ship, and Cloise was at the mercy of elements out of Leri's control. "Ranas, will those humans we hired stay loyal to us?"

"Their loyalty is to the paymaster, but they will fight. None of them have any love for Sondak."

"Then attack the poachers! Drive them off!"

"By your orders, Proctor," Glights said as he backed from the chamber with a flourish of his claws.

To her surprise, Ranas stayed where he was. She could smell the disturbance in him. "You have something more?" she asked.

"No, I have nothing more for the proctor," he said slowly, "but I feel pain for the mate-of-my-nest. I know you did not pray for the souls of the Castorians that we so freely executed. That is not good, Leri. You should have—"

"How do you know so much? Are you spying on me?" Despite her tone, Leri was secretly pleased that Ranas still cared so much about her.

"It is easy to know such things when I know you."

"I smell censure in you."

"No." Ranas looked at her and sighed. "It is sadness you smell, not censure—sadness for all that has happened, and all that is yet to come—sadness for you, Leri."

"Pity, you mean. I do not need—"

"The pity is that you have to carry the burden of these events by yourself. The sadness is that you are letting the burdens of being proctor eat at your soul."

Leri was again startled that he understood so much. "Would you have me give less of myself? Did I not promise all of my energies to this duty?"

"Yes, you did promise, but that does not mean that you should compromise your faith."

"I have not," Leri said quickly, "and I will pray for the dead Castorians now as is my duty. Your duty is to go and follow our

fight against the poachers. When you return, I expect to hear
that they have been driven away or defeated."

"As you wish, Proctor," Ranas said before turning to slither
from her chamber.

After he was gone, Leri selected a symphony by Shetotem
as appropriate music for what she knew she must do. If the
Castorians truly had souls, she was obliged to pray for them.
Otherwise her own soul might end up serving those of the
Castorians in the eternal seas of the hereafter. In that—and all
too many other things—Ranas was right. She should have
prayed for them immediately after they died.

As the music started she curled herself into a tight coil and
began chanting the Litany of Peace. At first her mind resisted
its flow, but the repetitious verses eased her tension, and the
music soothed her thoughts, and soon she was totally involved
in the prayers for those alien souls.

Her mind was clear and fresh. Her thoughts were simple
and pure. Eternal love and eternal truth filled her with peace.
For the few brief hours those prayers would take, Leri Gish
Geril would live free from the battle being fought over her
planet, and the war being waged in her galaxy.

* * *

Ten minutes after Judoff's fleet exited subspace, alarms rang
through the *Woro*.

"Enemy fighters, Marshall," the range coordinator said
calmly. "A hundred, maybe a hundred and fifty of them. And a
couple of big blips, too. Could be destroyers."

"As I feared," Commander Qunoy said with a dark scowl.
"What are your orders, sha?"

"Prepare to launch a defensive screen—naggers only." Judoff
hadn't been prepared for this, because she had refused to heed
Commander Qunoy's warning. Even so, she wasn't about to let
a few Sak fighters stop her.

"Commander, I want to blow through those fighters and save
our main strike for Sutton. Let the Saks follow us if they can.
Tell the fleet that stragglers will be left behind. Understood?"

"Understood, sha, but braking will make it hard to launch
the naggers very efficiently."

"Just get us to Sutton!" Judoff watched and listened as her
commands were relayed to the other seventeen ships. Already

the Sak fighters were hitting the fringes of her fleet while the rest streaked toward *Woro*.

"Commencing nagger launch," a distant voice over the speaker announced. "First flight away."

"Incoming missiles!" the range coordinator shouted.

"Hard left ten degrees," Qunoy ordered.

Judoff braced herself, and raised her eyes to the visual screens. The Saks were already swirling around the *Behot* like leaves in a whirlwind.

Woro trembled as the first missile glanced off its stern. It shook violently when the second missile struck square in its midsection. Shouts and commands rang through the ship and over the speakers.

"More fighters approaching!"

Judoff cursed. Where were they coming from? How had they known she would be here? The situation was slipping through her hands, but she refused to let go of it even though Qunoy had far more space battle experience than she did. "What is our status, Commander?" she demanded.

"Too soon to tell, sha." He turned away from her without adding anything further.

"Dammit, Qunoy," she said, jumping from her chair and grabbing his arm. "I want an answer!"

"*Behot*'s lost an engine," the communications boater yelled above the noise. "Can't reach the *De Vries*."

Qunoy yanked Judoff's hand off his arm. "The answer, Marshall Judoff, is that this was a stupid idea," he said, glaring at her. "The answer is that we flew right into a trap. So if you want to save your ships, you'd damned well better get us out of here."

"*Allsdon* is heading for subspace, Commander!"

"How dare you presume to tell me what to do? Hold course to Sutton until I order otherwise."

"Yes, sha," he said with a quick salute. "And would you like your cremation with or without music?"

Qunoy's sarcasm coupled to the speed with which the Saks were crippling her fleet shook Judoff's confidence. Qunoy was her best officer. If he thought they were in that much trouble, then perhaps it was time to adjust her plans. "I'm sorry, Commander. By all means save the fleet."

"And Sutton?"

Judoff shook her head. "I'm afraid Marshall Yozel will have to survive on his own. Retrieve as many naggers as you can, and head us for home space."

She hated to concede the battle without a real fight, but she hated the thought of losing her fleet even more. The fleet was part of her power base, and without it she would have much less to bargain with in Bridgeforce. This war was still a long way from being over, and Judoff had every intention of coming out ahead. Victory—personal victory—was the only thing that mattered to her. If that meant cooperating with Charltos or retreating from a battle now in order to be the ultimate winner, that was acceptable strategy.

The victor would be the person with enough intelligence to conserve her strength and win the *final* battle.

* * *

"I don't know how they've held out this long, Clarest," Frye said softly. "This is the second time they have cost me more ships than I ever expected them to. You have to give the Saks credit for courage and tenacity, if nothing else."

Melliman snuggled closer to him. "I don't think we ever doubted their courage. But what surprises me most is that they didn't withdraw when they still had the chance. Now that we have them confined to close orbit, theirs is a lost cause."

"But we still haven't gotten through to the planet itself."

"If we destroy their ships here, what will it matter?"

"I want to destroy their starports as well. I want Satterfield out of commission—especially after the losses we've taken here. No thanks to Judoff for that," he added bitterly.

Melliman ran her fingers lightly over his chest. "Why do I suspect that you are working on some new plan?"

"Because, my dear AOCO," he said, slipping out from under her fingers and sitting up on the side of the bed, "that is exactly what I am doing."

"No rest for the wicked," she said as she climbed naked out of her side of the bed.

"Nor for you, either. Get dressed."

Twenty minutes later they stood in the planning room huddled over a holomap of Satterfield system. Shifting points of colored light marked the locations of all the known ships in the system.

"Look, Clarest," Frye said. "All but one of Satterfield's

starports are in its southern hemisphere, and the Sak commander has concentrated his forces above them. Suppose we were to launch missiles from low orbit above the northern hemisphere? We might just be able to—"

"Begging the Admiral's pardon, sir," a young piper said with a quick salute, "but we just received reports of a large Sondak fleet headed in this direction."

"Reinforcements," Frye said. "How far out?"

"A day at most, sir."

"All right. Get me Commander Belera." After Judoff's desertion and the damage Tuuneo Fleet had already suffered, Frye did not want to risk a set battle with a fresh Sondak fleet. But there was something he could do.

"Commander Belera reporting, sir."

"Ral, look at this map," Frye said after returning Belera's salute. "We have pretty accurate coordinates for each starport on Satterfield. They're the targets marked in orange. I want you to slip your missiles in from here," he said, jabbing a space above the northern hemisphere with his finger, "and here, and here, and hit as many of those starports as you can. You think you can manage that?"

"With enough protection I can, sir."

"I'll get you the protection. You get the coordinates programed into your missiles and be prepared to launch them in five hours."

"Will do, sir. And, sir?"

"What is it, Ral?"

"I just want you to know that I am honored by this opportunity, sir."

"Orders, AOCO," Frye said after Belera left. "I want to begin the gradual regrouping of the fleet. All damaged ships first with complete assessments of their conditions. All others to regroup immediately after Belera has completed his strikes. When Sondak's reinforcements get here, they won't find us, but they will find a smoking planet."

Fourteen hours later Tuuneo Fleet began its withdrawal from the Satterfield system. As Frye assessed the summary damage reports, he felt a mixture of sadness and elation. A third of his original number of ships had either been destroyed over Satterfield or had to be blown up because they were too heavily damaged to make the trip through subspace. Almost half his fighters had been lost or damaged. Six hunks were missing, including the *Misbarrett* commanded by the brilliant Captain Ruto Ishiwa.

But Satterfield was a planet dotted with radioactive clouds. The remnants of its defensive forces were stranded in space. Satterfield had paid for Frye's defeat at Matthews system.

29

"The fleet is withdrawing, sir," Nunn said. "I don't think we can catch up to them."

"Sir!" the nav-boater shouted. "I think I'm picking up Saks! Two of them."

Ishiwa shook his head and the pain rang in his ears. If Tuuneo Fleet was withdrawing, *Olmis* was truly on its own again. "Range and closing rate?" he asked automatically.

"Ninety thousand kilometers and closing at point-six-plus."

"Call Lieutenant Bon immediately. Nunn, ready the aft tube. All able hands to battle stations."

As his orders were relayed through the ship, Ishiwa climbed wearily out of his command chair and limped over to the targeting screen. The two Sak blips moved toward them from the edge of the screen like tiny cancerous spores eight degrees off their present course. His choices were all too few.

"Engines stop," he ordered without hesitation. "Reverse orientation, one hundred eighty degrees."

"What's happening, sir?" Bon asked breathlessly as he rushed onto the deck.

"Saks," Ishiwa said simply. *Olmis* was turning now so that her remaining firing tube would give them a shot at the two Sondak ships.

"Captain, we can't do this," Bon said when he realized what Ishiwa was doing. "We'll be completely vulnerable."

"We don't have any choice, Lieutenant. We can't run. We can't call for help. Honor requires that we fight."

"Aft tube ready, sir," Nunn announced.

"Targeting for the lead ship . . . locked. Prepare to fire at my command." Ishiwa almost held his breath as he stared at the targeting screen and watched the distance closed between *Olmis* and the Saks. "Fire, Nunn."

The normal firing thump was followed by several seconds of severe rattling that spoke for *Olmis*'s condition.

"Missile away, sir."

"Reload," Ishiwa ordered. "Locking on second target."

"I'm picking up a third one, sir. No! They're firing at us. It's a missile headed this way."

"I see it. Engines on. Take over targeting, Bon." Ishiwa's voice was much calmer than his emotions. For the first time he questioned whether or not they were going to survive.

"Aye, sir." There was look of resignation on Bon's face that matched the tone of his voice.

"Enemy missile closing at point-nine-six."

Beads of cold sweat rolled down Ishiwa's face. He couldn't reverse *Olmis*'s orientation until Bon fired the second missile, but if they didn't move quickly, the Sak missile would surely hit them. The scent of fear mixed with the crew's normal stench.

"Aft tube ready, sir."

"Fire!" Bon ordered.

"Reverse orientation one hundred fifty degrees. Course one-zero-one-zero by nine-thousand. Engines full ahead." Ishiwa clung to a stanchion and watched with horror as the blip of the Sak missile streaked toward the center of his screen.

Olmis turned with agonizing slowness. Just as her engines started their thrust, the Sak missile exploded against her damaged bow. The screams of tearing metal drowned out the screams of the crew. Ishiwa thought of Kleber and wept.

The torque forces on *Olmis* were more than her damaged hull could withstand. It twisted and split, then broke apart with agonizing slowness.

The first of the Wu-class hunks and its crew had ended their honorable service to the United Central Systems.

* * *

Henley walked slowly down the slope to where the three generals were sitting at a camp table under a spreading tree. His eyes darted to the rock-strewn hillside behind them, then to the stand of trees less than fifty meters away. As he presented himself to General Mari, he felt an itch on the back of his neck that wouldn't be cured by scratching.

"Well, Chief Stanmorton, I had heard that you survived." The only thing that surprised Mari was that he wasn't totally displeased to see the teller.

"General Archer let me tag along with some fine units, sir," Henley said giving Archer a nervous wink. "Even had my own skimmer for a while."

"Nothing too good for a teller, huh?"

It had been five days since the captain from the Forty-Ninth had been killed beside Henley, and he was all too aware that her blood was mixed with the grime on his uniform. He had been looking for a clean uniform, but now he was glad he hadn't found one before Mari saw him. "Not to worry, General, as you can see, I did my fair share of mucking around."

"Well, I'm not going to worry about you, Mister. I figure you earned your right to be here. Wouldn't you agree, Archer?"

"That I would, sir."

"Join us," Mari said waving at a folding chair beside the table. "The local wine is quite good, and the fresh air only adds to its excellence."

Henley looked quickly around before sitting in the chair. The place they were sitting was exposed on three sides, and despite the presence of hundreds of troops, Henley felt very vulnerable. "At the risk of angering you, General Mari, I really have to ask if you think it's safe to sit in the open like this?"

"Snipers, sir," Archer said quickly. "The Chief has seen more than his fair share of them."

Mari gave Henley a faint smile. "I understand, but I think it's worth the risk. It's good for the troops to see us this confident in them. Now that they're down to flushing out the isolated Ukes, they need something to replace the morale of battle."

"That's an odd term, isn't it, sir?"

"Not at all, Mister. Battle is ninety-five percent boredom and five-percent fear and exhilaration. Anticipation of the exhilaration keeps you going the rest of the time. That's battle morale. But once the battle is over, morale tends to sink. The troops aren't quite sure what they've accomplished or what they will have to do next. If they see their officers relaxed and in good spirits, you can bet that will rub off on them in a hurry. It's more effective than any speech we could make, because the troops will know instinctively that they've done well and the danger's behind them for a while."

"That's quite a theory, General, but I'm not sure—" Something slapped Henley hard on the right shoulder. He heard the shot before he felt the pain. Then he saw Mari with his hands over his chest and blood seeping through his fingers.

Mari watched Chief Stanmorton slump over the table, but he never lost consciousness. Everything seemed to be happening in slow motion. Voices shouted around him while he sat in the midst of stillness. Archer pulled him down to the ground. Other hands pulled his hands away from the wound and applied painful pressure to his chest. Then a needle jabbed into his arm. Mari closed his eyes and drifted, hearing the sounds, smelling the blood and antiseptic, but distant, uncaring.

Henley came slowly out of a fog of pain to find himself lying close beside General Mari. His shoulder throbbed dully, but Mari looked pale and awful. There were tubes running into both of the general's arms, and a thick bandage on his chest. The medic beside Mari caught Henley's eye and shook his head.

As Henley turned away from the sight, he saw several troopers dragging a bound Uke soldier toward them. Quickly he turned his head back to Mari. "Can you hear me, sir?"

Slowly Mari opened his eyes and turned to the voice. "I hear you," he said softly.

"I think they caught the sniper, sir."

"She surrendered," one of the troopers said. "Claims to know the general."

Mari tried to focus, but the edges of his vision were blurred. "Closer," he whispered.

"Bring her closer," Henley repeated.

For a brief instant Mari's vision cleared, and he stared into Giselda's sad, pale face.

"We are even now, Fortuno," she said.

Her words seemed to take forever to make sense. "Yes," he whispered finally. "Kill her."

A moment later Henley smelled the pungent fecal odor of death and knew that Mari was gone. The general's eyes stared blankly up at the trees with a look that only dead men have.

"What did he say?" one of the troops asked.

Looking up, Henley stared at the pikean woman, and suddenly he knew who she was. She was Mari's mistress, the one who had absorbed his legendary sadism for so many years. Any teller worth his byline would have recognized her from all the times she had appeared in public as Mari's bruised but smiling consort.

With a sigh Henley shifted his eyes back to the trooper. "General Mari said to take her away."

"All right, let's go, you pukin' Uke," the trooper said, jerking the woman out of Henley's sight.

The weight of fatigue and drugs pulled Henley's eyes closed again. Leaden thoughts dragged him down toward sleep and rest. He knew he would write the story of Fortuno Mari, hero of Sutton, but he also knew he would never be able to tell all of it.

* * *

Avitor Hilldill sat beside Pajandcan's bed in the *Royal Oak*'s sickbay. "Looks like you're going to make it, Admiral."

"Maybe," Pajandcan said softly, "but I'm one of the few."

"It's not as bad as you think. Your Admiral Dawson just told me that two of the starports will be operational again in a matter of weeks."

"But the fleet—and the people." Pajandcan shook her head slightly in the painful confines of the brace that held her rigid from the waist up. Her back was broken, and so was her spirit. "The Ukes beat the life out of us."

"Quit feeling sorry for yourself. A lot of survivors and salvageable ships are beginning to make their way back, and we're out looking for more. Dimitri's ships are pulling into the system now, and they'll be able to speed up the rescue operations. All in all, I think you can count this operation as a success."

Pajandcan closed her eyes for a few long seconds and fought the hot wave of pain surging through her body. Only part of the agony she felt was physical, and she knew it. When she finally looked at Hilldill again, part of the bitterness she felt spilled out on him.

"I don't want to hear that," she said. "POLFLEET lost almost thirty percent of its ships, and Satterfield's atmosphere is filled with radioactive dust, and a million people died unnecessarily because of my stupid plan. What kind of success do you call that, Hilldill? Answer me that."

"A wartime success," he said without flinching.

For the moment, that was an answer Pajandcan couldn't cope with. After the catastrophic damage Reckynop had suffered in Matthews system, and the terrible losses that were her responsibility here, she wasn't sure she could accept any more successes like those.

* * *

"This is incredible," Caugust said.

"It is our own fault. We shouldn't have left the Wallen out there." Sjean looked at him and waited for some response.

"But who would ever have thought that some damned Oinaise would find it and Ayne Wallen, too? Doesn't that strike you as incredible, Sjean? I mean, what are the odds against that?"

"Nothing strikes me as incredible anymore, sir—especially the odds for a random event. How much does this Xindella want for Wallen and the weapon?"

Caugust ran his fingers through his thick hair. "He wants to hold a festbid—an auction of some kind. He wants us to bid against other unnamed parties for possession of both of them."

"Against the Ukes, you mean."

"He doesn't say that, but you and I both know that's who he means. Now that the Ukes know about it, they're sure to be interested."

"Have you informed Sci-Sec, sir?"

"Hell, no, Sjean. I'd bet a full share in Drautzlab that Sci-Sec's own Inspector Janette is partially responsible for this 'Xindella' finding the weapon in the first place. I'm not about to let Sci-Sec bungle this, too."

"Then what are you going to do?" Sjean had a hard time believing that the competent Inspector Janette had bungled anything, but she understood why Caugust might feel that way.

"I don't know. I just don't know. Maybe we should just let the Ukes have Ayne and the weapon. Maybe we shouldn't worry about this at all. By the time he analyzes what we did— if he can analyze it—and what we didn't do . . . Who knows? This war could well be over by then."

Sjean wished she had his confidence about the war, but she

hadn't heard anything that made her believe Sondak was going to win. Despite all the Efcorps propaganda, it seemed fairly obvious to her that the Ukes still had the advantage and were making the most of it.

"I think that would be a mistake, Caugust. If we don't bid on getting Ayne and the weapon back, then I think you should notify Sci-Sec and let them handle it. The risks are just too great not to."

"And if I don't like either of those options? What then?"

"Then I'm afraid I would have to tell Sci-Sec myself," she said softly.

"You'd do that, too, wouldn't you?"

"Yes, sir, I'm afraid I wouldn't have any choice." Sjean looked up at him and wondered why he was finding this so hard to understand. "Don't you see, Caugust? It's at least partially our fault that this Oinaise found the weapon. It's totally our fault that the thing exists at all. Somewhere along the line we have to accept the responsibility for that."

Caugust sighed. "You sound like my conscience, and you're as right as it is. But whatever we do, however we handle it, we'll do this on our own. No Sci-Sec this time. We'll use our own security people and no one else. We've let enough things get out of our control already."

Sjean released a small sigh of her own and swore to herself that regardless of what happened, once this war was over, she was going to get out of the weapons business forever.

30

Admiral Josiah Gilbert stood before the Joint Chiefs and waited for their censure. Only a few hours earlier he had learned that the Ukes were attacking Bakke and Yaffee and he was sure Wallbank would be next. He had failed in his evaluation of the Uke's strategy and strength. All that remained was for the Joint Chiefs to do their duty and officially relieve him of his.

Stonefield, Lindshaw, and Erresser looked back at him without speaking. Hilldill was still at Satterfield, and no replacement had been named for Mari. These three had already determined his future.

The only expressions on Gilbert's face were fatigue and sadness. Even the news that Mica was uninjured had done little to bring him cheer. There were too many dead and dying, too many losses for there to be joy in his life. He fully expected to be stripped of his command and forced into retirement. At best they might assign him to some relatively meaningless office job—in which case he intended to resign. Even he had difficulty believing that what he had done was right.

"This has not been an easy decision for us, Josiah," Stonefield said, breaking the tension in the room. "Despite the optimistic reports from Avitor Hilldill about the condition of Satterfield, we believe your actions, and those of others that you approved, have caused the fleets to suffer appalling, and perhaps unnecessary, casualties and losses of ships, materiel and equipment."

"I am thoroughly aware of that, sir." Gilbert knew he had no right to speak, but a desperate voice inside of him wanted the Joint Chiefs to understand how greatly he felt the pain and responsibility for what had happened. Yet he fully respected their traditional right to drag him through the mire of his grievous errors.

"You will let me finish, Josiah," Stonefield said. "In considering what action, if any, should be taken against you, we chose to ignore the demands of the Combined Committees and the TriCameral. This is purely a military-executive matter and there were certain mitigating factors which we took into consideration which our civilian branches would not understand.

"Those factors were the intensive duties you assumed as the Combined Fleet Commander, the pressures upon you to take the offensive against the Ukes—partially from within the Services, but also from influential civilians inside and out of the government—and also the considerable influence exerted upon you by General Fortuno Vasquez-Yohansin Mari, late of this body."

Why couldn't he just get on with it? Gilbert wondered. Why did Stony have to drag it all out like this? Tradition and form notwithstanding, Gilbert was ready for their verdict.

"Furthermore, the Joint Chiefs must necessarily assume full responsibility for any military action—sanctioned or not—within the realm of its executive jurisdiction."

Gilbert saw a twitch in the corners of Stonefield's mouth when he paused, and knew the answer was finally coming.

"Consequently, after much thoughtful deliberation and, I might add, considerable heated argument, it is our judgment that you shall retain your command—not only to do what you can to defend the polar systems under these new attacks, but also to proceed with further offensive planning against the U.C.S."

Those words were so unexpected that Gilbert couldn't talk. He could barely think until he realized what he had to do. "I am sorry, sir, but I cannot accept that. I an unworthy of retaining my command and request that you accept my resignation from the Service as of this date."

The twitch in the corner of Stonefield's mouth turned into a very tight smile. "We anticipated that," he said slowly, "and agreed—unanimously I should say—that we would refuse to accept your resignation. The defeat at Satterfield was costly, Josiah, and the polar systems are now in grave danger because of all that has happened. No one argues that." His smile was gone. "But we were forced to the reluctant conclusion that your initiative which led to that defeat at Satterfield was the lesser of all evils. Neither Sondak nor the Service can afford the absence of your experience and abilities—especially now."

Voices of protest rose inside him, but Gilbert's sense of duty held those voices down. By accepting this continuing responsibility he could at least try to make up for the mistakes he had made. That was the deciding factor for him—the only deciding factor.

"Very well," Gilbert said with a great sense of resignation, "I will do as you wish." As he spoke an old co-sergeant entered the room and handed Stonefield a message.

Stonefield read it aloud. "Wallbank and Roberg both report initial skirmishes with light enemy attack fleets."

Gilbert's burden settled onto his shoulders and his conscience like a tangible weight that threatened to crush him.

* * *

"And just what am I supposed to do, now?" Janette asked.

"Whatever you void well please, just so long as we never see you again," Lucky said, throwing her space duffle at her feet. "Because if we do, you're as good as dead, Inspector." Without waiting for Janette's reply, he turned and walked quickly toward Marsha on the other side of the dock, full of an anger that he dared not release.

Janette watched him leave with the faint shadow of a smile flickering around her lips. Not if I see you first, Captain, she thought. No man treats me like you did and gets away with it.

With a flick of her lashes she dismissed Lucky Teeman from her thoughts for the time being. Her problem now was to find transportation to Patros and wring Xindella's fat neck— figuratively, of course. She would save Sci-Sec's ability to eliminate him and his corrupt enterprises until he had handed over the Drautzlab device. And Xindella would hand it over. She would leave him no choice.

An hour later when Marsha and Lucky walked through the door into Delightful Childe's presence, he spoke before either of them had a chance to greet him.

"Your absence left me with a great deal to do on my own, Captain Teeman," he said with the Oinaise version of a smile revealing his teeth on either side of his proboscis. "However, I am pleased to tell you that all has gone well and that our position with Cloise has been greatly reinforced."

Lucky grinned and squeezed Marsha's hand. "Can you tell it directly, or is there more fluff to this speech of yours?"

Delightful Childe snorted, then ducked his head quickly behind the screen and muttered soothingly in Vardequerque-glot. When his face reappeared, his smile was gone. "Nindoah resents your rudeness, Captain, and I must agree with her."

"Then I apologize."

"Very well. I accept. Now, as I was saying, Cloise has formed a protective alliance with the Castorians, and we have agreed to join with them in their coalition."

"It's about time. I told you this was your war as much as anyone's." Lucky was less pleased by the announcement when he saw the stunned look on Marsha's face.

"That means . . . what? Who are you—I mean, who is this alliance siding with?" Marsha was frightened by this news.

"No one," Delightful Childe said. "We will be serving notice to all combatants that we are neutral and expect free passage throughout the galaxy."

"But the Castorians are working with Sondak. That's hardly what I'd call neutrality."

"You have proof of this, Marsha?"

"No. But Castorian ships have been following ours—I mean the U.C.S. ships, all over the galaxy."

"That is no proof that the Castorians are—"

"Maybe not," Lucky interrupted, "but I think Marsha's right." Despite what had happened with her father, her loyalty to the U.C.S. was unquestionable, and Lucky's sympathies still ran toward the Ukes more than Sondak. "If the Castorians have been following Uke ships, their neutrality has to be questioned, doesn't it?"

"Are you making a statement, or asking a question, Captain?"

"I don't know . . . a question, I think."

"It is a statement," Marsha said quickly. "If they are following U.C.S. ships, then their neutrality is suspect."

"That is an unverified premise followed by a logical, but not necessarily valid statement. However," he said, fanning the seven fingers of one hand as though physically holding her protests back, "I shall look into the matter. In the meantime, you should know that our methane operation is almost ready."

"But who can we sell it to now?" Lucky asked.

"To whoever wants it, of course. Neutrality is not the same thing as isolationism, Captain Teeman."

"Maybe not, but it's not going to make either side very happy if we're selling methane to the other."

"Perhaps not, but we shall deal with that when the time comes. I know you are both tired, but before you leave, I have to ask what became of the rude Inspector Janette?"

Marsha frowned. "We dumped her on the dock when we landed and told her she was on her own."

Delightful Childe snorted softly. "I see. Am I to take it then that we will not receive a transportation fee from her?"

"That's right, partner."

"Ah, well. Go. Rest now, both of you. Take what leisure you can for the next few, uh, what you call weeks. Soon we will all have to be active again." Before they even left the room Delightful Childe had to duck behind the screen again to silence Nindoah. He would be greatly relieved when this child's umbilical was severed from both of them.

Parenting was a constant distraction from the more pressing matters in his life. With Oina aligned with the Castorians and Cloise, a power shift had taken place in the galaxy, one that would have implications no one could predict. That frightened Delightful Childe. He liked things to be predictable, and he did not like power struggles. Now he was part of an unpredictable power struggle that involved even more than the alliance of the non-human races.

He had not told Captain Teeman about the outrageous message from Xindella, but there would be time to discuss that later. It troubled Delightful Childe deeply that his cousin might suggest that Oina become involved in a festbid for such a terrible weapon. Hadn't it been enough that he had helped Xindella find the monstrosity?

Reluctantly Delightful Childe admitted to himself that in spite of all his objections there might be good reason to participate in the festbid, if only to prevent the humans from re-acquiring the weapon.

The problems of the weapon and the alliance would call for much prayer and thought before any new decisions could even be considered. Yet prayer and contemplative thought were difficult at best these days. With a growing sense of weariness Delightful Childe responded to Nindoah's chattering demands and turned his attention back to their offspring.

In their quarters Lucky and Marsha stepped into each other's arms and kissed passionately. This was the first time they had been truly alone since right before they parted on Alexvieux. They had done their talking aboard *Graycloud*, but because one of them had always been watching Janette, they had not made love. Now when they finally pulled apart, they both knew it was time.

Without a word they took off their clothes in a frenzy and scrambled into the bed. For a little while, at least, the only thing in the galaxy worthy of their attention was two happy people locked in a rollicking, sensual embrace.

* * *

"We were bruised. They were bloodied," Frye said to the assembled members of Bridgeforce. "Sondak cannot withstand much more punishment before its leaders must sue for peace."

"From your casualty and loss reports, it appears that Tuuneo Fleet was bruised rather badly, Admiral Charltos," Meister Hadasaki said quietly.

"Yes, our losses were heavy, but thanks to the diversionary action provided by Marshall Judoff's attempt to aid Yozel at Sutton, we managed to inflict far more casualties than we received." He hated treating Judoff's desertion as something positive, but Frye was reluctant to antagonize her further. By describing her actions as a contribution, perhaps she might at least remain neutral in this discussion.

"But we lost Sutton and did not gain Satterfield."

Frye had thought that Hadasaki was his ally. Now he wasn't so sure. "That is true, Meister. But we rendered Satterfield basically useless to Sondak, and destroyed much of their Polar Fleet in the combined operations. The first reports from the harrassing fleets attacking the remaining polar systems have been positive. Surely you can see that this amounts to a significant victory for us."

"I agree with Admiral Charltos," Judoff said. "In comparison to the devastation our joint forces caused, our losses, while regrettable, are certainly within acceptable limits. As soon as the new bombships are ready for action, we will take them back and deal the final blows not only to Sutton and Satterfield, but also to every Sondak system within reach."

"Politics and war make for strange alliances," Hadasaki said with a smile. "If you two agree, shall we officially declare this a victory?"

"A victory in honor of Admiral Tuuneo," Frye added with a catch in his voice that surprised him.

Vice-Admiral Lotonoto seconded that motion, and Bridgeforce declared the battle at Satterfield a victory dedicated to the memory of Admiral Tuuneo. Immediately thereafter they adjourned.

As he walked out with Melliman, Frye felt a rewarding sense of accomplishment. "I think we should celebrate—a special evening for a special occasion."

She touched his arm discreetly. "By all means, Admiral."

For one brief moment Frye saw Vinita's face instead of

Melliman's and he felt a distant pang of sorrow. With a quick mental shrug he pushed that emotion down and away. Vinita was gone. Marsha had deserted him. But Melliman was here and now. This was a time for happiness, not sorrow.

Yet as he led the way out of the headquarters building, he knew that this victory over Sondak was less meaningful than it would have been if Vinita were still alive.

* * *

"How much time do you have?" Henley asked as they strolled around the *Walker's* exercise deck. He still felt uncomfortable in Mica Gilbert's presence, but now that they were going to be parted again, he wanted whatever time he could have with her.

"Less than an hour. Dimitri wants to leave for Bakke as quickly as possible." Mica sensed the distance between them and blamed herself.

"So you are going to stay out here?"

"Yes. Rochmon wants me back on Nordeen"—and more than that, she thought—"and so does Father, but for the time being I'm going to stick with Dimitri."

"You like the action, don't you?"

"Some of it," Mica said after a slight pause.

Henley chuckled. "You thought I was crazy when you found out I was drawn to it."

"I thought a lot of things were crazy then. What about you? What are you going to do?"

"Oh, I'll stick with Schopper and his troops. I figure that they'll probably get involved quickly enough for me."

"Well, from the looks of things right now, I would agree with that." When she looked at him she suddenly hoped it would be a long time before he saw action again. "Henley, who do you think will win the war?"

"We will."

"You seem awfully sure of that. Don't you have any doubts?"

"Of course I do." Henley stopped walking; sat on one of the benches along the bulkhead, and adjusted the tension of his sling to relieve the ache in his wounded shoulder.

"Look, Mica," he continued when she sat beside him, "by all rights the Ukes should already have won. They took Fernandez and Cczwyck and the Ivy Chain and Ca-Ryn. But they didn't take Roberg when they had the chance. They lost the battle of Matthews system. They lost Sutton and they didn't take Satterfield. Despite these new attacks, I'd rate the current situation a stalemate—a stalemate where the Ukes have lost the important part of their initiative. Unless they get it back, we're going to win."

"And you don't think they're going to get it back?"

Henley told her what they wanted to believe, what he had to believe to keep going. "No, I don't think they can. We know their fighting a pacifist movement called the kyosei on half of their planets, and unless they find a quick victory, that movement will only get stronger. I think these new attacks of theirs are acts of desperation."

"I'm not sure I'm convinced," Mica said, "but I believe you are." There was a gleam of enthusiasm in his eyes that she was glad to see there. "Furthermore, I'm impressed by your analysis. You've given this a lot of thought, haven't you?"

"Since I got shot I've spent most of my time thinking about the war . . . or about you."

Mica looked away. She had wondered when they would get to this. Given the brief time she had left with him, it was just as well that it had come quickly. "I owe you an apology," she said.

"I was about to say the same thing," he said softly. "I feel like I used you, Mica, and I'm sorry."

"Then it looks like we used each other a little."

"Lovers who don't know each other very well do that sometimes." Henley wanted to take her hand, but didn't trust himself. She solved the problem by taking his and looking squarely into his eyes.

"I don't think 'lovers' is the right word but I won't argue terms with you. You are a very special man, Henley." Mica hesitated, then decided to say it all. "You've irritated me at times, but I've grown to like you a great deal. If you'll accept my friendship now . . . then later, when all this is over, maybe we can find some way to build from there."

He held his eyes on hers and stilled the tremor in his throat. He wanted more than friendship, but he was happy to accept what she had to offer. "Friends," he said, gently squeezing her hand, "and let the rest come when it may."

Mica sensed a stronger feeling in him that she was willing to match, but as she stood, she couldn't let go of him. "After the war," she said, looking down at their clasped hands.

"Yes, of course. After we win the war." Henley stood and released her hand. "Goodbye, Mica, and . . ."

"Goodbye, Henley," she said before he could add anything else. "I'll see you at the victory celebration." She gave him a brief smile, then quickly turned and walked away with a strange feeling under her heart.

If we win, he thought as he watched her leave. If we win.

—The End—

Mel White

ABOUT THE AUTHOR

WARREN NORWOOD began writing when he was nine and got hooked on science fiction when he was eleven reading Tom Swift and Tom Swift, Jr. books. At seventeen he made a serious commitment to become a writer. College, marriage, the Vietnam War, and eleven years in the selling end of the book business intervened before he saw the publication of *An Image of Voices*, the first book in his Windhover Tapes series. The other books in the series are *Flexing the Warp*, *Fize of the Gabriel Ratchets*, and *Planet of Flowers*. Warren was twice-nominated for the John W. Campbell Award as one of the best new writers of 1982-83, and also co-wrote *The Seren Cenacles* with his best friend, Ralph Mylius, author of the "M.A.C. Gate" stories.

Warren has taught poetry and fiction writing courses at Tarrant County Junior College in Ft. Worth, Texas, worked in retail and wholesale book sales for fourteen years, and spent three years in the army. He is an avid wildflower photographer and a self-proclaimed pseudo-botanist.

After living temporarily in Missouri, Warren again resides in Ft. Worth, Texas, where he is currently working on *Final Command*, the last book in his Double-Spiral War series.

WEST
of
EDEN

Harry Harrison

From a master of imaginative storytelling comes an epic tale of the world as it might have been, a world where the age of dinosaurs never ended, and their descendants clash with a clan of humans in a tragic war for survival. . . .

"An astonishing piece of work."　　—Joe Haldemann

"A big novel in every sense . . ."
　　　　　　　　—*Washington Post Book World*

"Brilliant."　　　　　　—Phillip Jose Farmer

"Epic science fantasy."　　　　　—*Playboy*

"The best Harrison ever—and that's going some."
　　　　　　　　　　—Jerry Pournelle

"I commend this rich and rewarding novel to those who know and love Heinlein, Asimov, Herbert and Clarke; they will find no less than what those masters provide here."　　　　　　—Barry N. Malzberg

"This is the way they used to write them, high adventure with lots of thought-provoking meat."
　　　　　　　　　　—Thomas N. Scortia

Don't miss Harry Harrison's WEST OF EDEN, available in paperback July 1, 1985, from Bantam Spectra Books.

Announcing a new publishing imprint of quality science fiction and fantasy:

BANTAM SPECTRA BOOKS

SPECTRA

Science fiction and fantasy have come of age—and there's a whole new generation of readers searching for fresh, exciting novels, fiction that will both entertain *and* enlighten. Now, from the house of Ray Bradbury, Samuel R. Delany, Ursula K. Le Guin, Anne McCaffrey, Frederik Pohl, and Robert Silverberg comes the first full-spectrum publishing imprint that delivers all the excitement and astonishment found only in imaginative fiction. Under the Bantam Spectra Books imprint you'll find the best of all possible worlds: from serious, speculative novels to the most lighthearted tales of enchantment, from hard-science thrillers and far-future epics to the most visionary realms of magic realism.

Look for Bantam Spectra Books—we've rediscovered the wonder in science fiction and fantasy.

SPECIAL MONEY SAVING OFFER

Now you can have an up-to-date listing of Bantam's hundreds of titles plus take advantage of our unique and exciting bonus book offer. A special offer which gives you the opportunity to purchase a Bantam book for only 50¢. Here's how!

By ordering any five books at the regular price per order, you can also choose any other single book listed (up to a $4.95 value) for just 50¢. Some restrictions do apply, but for further details why not send for Bantam's listing of titles today!

Just send us your name and address plus 50¢ to defray the postage and handling costs.

BANTAM BOOKS, INC.
Dept. FC, 414 East Golf Road, Des Plaines, Ill 60016

Mr./Mrs./Miss/Ms. _____
(please print)

Address _____

City_____ State_____ Zip_____

FC—3/84

OUT OF THIS WORLD!

That's the only way to describe Bantam's great series of science fiction classics. These space-age thrillers are filled with terror, fancy and adventure and written by America's most renowned writers of science fiction. Welcome to outer space and have a good trip!

☐	24709	**RETURN TO EDDARTA** by Garrette & Heydron	$2.75
☐	22647	**HOMEWORLD** by Harry Harrison	$2.50
☐	22759	**STAINLESS STEEL RAT FOR PRESIDENT** by Harry Harrison	$2.75
☐	22796	**STAINLESS STEEL RAT WANTS YOU** by Harry Harrison	$2.50
☐	20780	**STARWORLD** by Harry Harrison	$2.50
☐	20774	**WHEELWORLD** by Harry Harrison	$2.50
☐	24176	**THE ALIEN DEBT** by F. M. Busby	$2.75
☐	24710	**A STORM UPON ULSTER** by Kenneth C. Flint	$3.50
☐	24175	**THE RIDERS OF THE SIDHE** by Kenneth C. Flint	$2.95
☐	25215	**THE PRACTICE EFFECT** by David Brin	$2.95
☐	23589	**TOWER OF GLASS** by Robert Silverberg	$2.95
☐	23495	**STARTIDE RISING** by David Brin	$3.50
☐	24564	**SUNDIVER** by David Brin	$2.75
☐	23512	**THE COMPASS ROSE** by Ursula LeGuin	$2.95
☐	23541	**WIND'S 12 QUARTERS** by Ursula LeGuin	$2.95
☐	22855	**CINNABAR** by Edward Bryant	$2.50
☐	22938	**THE WINDHOVER TAPES: FLEXING THE WARP** by Warren Norwood	$2.75
☐	23351	**THE WINDHOVER TAPES: FIZE OF THE GABRIEL RATCHETS** by Warren Norwood	$2.95
☐	23394	**THE WINDHOVER TAPES: AN IMAGE OF VOICES** by Warren Norwood	$2.75
☐	22968	**THE MARTIAN CHRONICLES** by Ray Bradbury	$2.75
☐	24168	**PLANET OF JUDGMENT** by Joe Halderman	$2.95
☐	23756	**STAR TREK: THE NEW VOYAGES 2** by Culbreath & Marshak	$2.95

Prices and availability subject to change without notice.

Buy them at your local bookstore or use this handy coupon for ordering:

Bantam Books, Inc., Dept. SF, 414 East Golf Road, Des Plaines, Ill. 60016

Please send me the books I have checked above. I am enclosing $_____ (please add $1.25 to cover postage and handling). Send check or money order —no cash or C.O.D.'s please.

Mr/Mrs/Miss _____

Address_____

City_____ State/Zip_____

SF—4/85

Please allow four to six weeks for delivery. This offer expires 10/85.